THE ARTFUL BARGAIN

AUDREY LYNDEN

PENSKE
PUBLISHING

Cover Design: *Okay Creations* - Sarah Hansen
Editing: *All That Editing* - Lynne Pearson
Proofreading: *One Love Editing* - Sandra Dee
ISBN: 978-0-09973400-1-3 (paperback)
ISBN: 978-0-9973400-2-0 (ebook)

Published by Penske Publishing
audreylynden.com
triciaquinnies.com

Dedication

*For my husband Craig, thank you for proposing to me at your first exhibit.
Ever since…art, love, and family have prevailed.*

Chapter 1

Claire Beaumont squinted at Lake Michigan through the hippie mobile's windshield, nibbling on her thumb. The chalky taste of paint hit her tongue. "Yuck." She wiped off the smudge of blue onto her overalls. It looked better on her pants than on her canvas. This morning's attempt to layer a sky had been an exercise in futility.

She may have to invest in better brushes or search out her dad's old ones. Claire cringed. Either way, her first priority was to get her exhibit with Sinjin Reid's sculpture up and make sure the Lafferty Museum stayed open.

Orange-Mina's engine grumbled, so Claire released the brake and coasted down the steep gravel driveway lined with dense forest on both sides. She stopped a safe distance from Reid's front entrance and bailed out of the stifling van. She took in a quavering breath and considered the sprawling and intimidating estate owned by the famous sculptor. With the flat roof and the expanse of windows, it resembled a design by the architect Frank Lloyd Wright.

Her phone pinged. Another text from Larry. Ignoring her boss, she walked across the flagstone path on shaky legs, then hesitated. *Relax. Another day on the job.* As she gaped at the expansive Prairie-style doors, they swung open.

The wunderkind known for welding and tangling magnificent metals into works of art appeared as if he'd just woken up and rolled off a futon. Shocks of ginger hair protruded from his scalp as he rubbed the stubble on one of his cheeks.

"You're a bit early, aren't you?" He gave her a cockeyed smile then and gazed past her shoulder. "Bloody gorgeous, that antique auto." He sprang from the front porch steps and jogged to the vintage VW bus.

Thrown off by his nonchalance, her heart skipped in a double-dutch fashion. She jammed her fists into the back pockets of her overalls.

From what she'd read about Sinjin Reid—without assistance from social media since he had zero presence on it— Claire had expected to meet an eccentric British *artiste*. Not unlike the pompous Masterpiece types she'd grown accustomed to meeting: haughty professors, pedantic curators, and the blight of the art world—critics. This man seemed approachable. Or friendly, like a surfer who greeted everyone with, "Hey, dude."

"Mr. Reid... I..." She squelched the unprofessional thrill that bubbled up from nowhere. "I'm the curator. Here to pick up your donation for the museum exhibit."

"What are you talking about? I thought you were delivering my wine bar for tonight's opening." He caressed a chrome bumper. "This VW though...shouldn't be doing any heavy lifting. It belongs in a museum."

"Her name is Orange-Mina," she said defensively. "For its owner, Mina. And she would never allow it to be put out of commission." Claire corralled her stampeding thoughts. "I'm not certain what you're referring to, Mr. Reid. I'm Claire Beaumont, a curator from the Lafferty Museum."

He glared at her. The friendly vibe she'd caught earlier vanished.

"Not sure about any wine bar." She forged onward. "My exhibit, *Victorious Vectors*, is scheduled to open at the end of October. And since your wife donated—"

"My wife? You mean ex-wife. And I've had nothing to do with the Lafferty for several years."

Dammit.

In her head, Han Solo yelled, *I have a bad feeling about this.*

Claire caught sight of his ring finger, where a wedding band should have resided. Quickly, she stared down at her phone to regain composure and check the last text from Larry. Maybe it wasn't in her best interest to ignore her fastidious boss —the arrogant museum director.

Bring sculpture to me as soon as you get back to Milwaukee.

Larry must have been misinformed. Or had he misinformed Claire?

He had assured her that Sinjin Reid or his wife would be at the residence to hand her the sculpture—about the size of a french horn—made from tubes of semi-precious metals. A good example of the steampunk genre but more beautiful, rare, and, most importantly, famous. A piece that would have folks in the art world talking for the next decade and the kind of celebrity exposure she absolutely needed for the museum and her exhibit.

The last thing she wanted was to be in the middle of a pissing war between a well-known sculptor and his ex-wife. Her conscience had taken a beating the past few years, and she had the ultimate chance with this exhibit to make a posthumous apology to her dad.

"There must be a mix-up. I was told your sculpture *Coal or Steam* would be here for me to pick up. I apologize." She shoved her phone into her bib pocket. Her thoughts chugged along, picking up steam and heading for a tantrum.

They started to kick... *It's the keystone for* Vectors. *The livelihood of the museum. Art patrons from everywhere are coming to see it.*

And then they screamed... More Lace Please*! An original David Raffen. Proof for anyone who believed the critic who had buried Dad's reputation.*

"Are you all right, Ms. Beaumont? You've gone a bit pale."

His voice sounded miles away. She nodded stiffly. "Claire. Please. Let me explain. Larry was supposed to pick up the sculpture weeks ago but asked me to get it today. I'll give him a call to find out what's going on and get out of your hair."

"Larry? As in Lawrence Chambers?" His British accent suddenly sounded lethal.

"Yes?"

He scrutinized her face. "Claire, why don't you come inside and have something to drink? You can ring Larry from there."

"I don't want to take up any more of your time," she lied politely. "It's obvious, you had no idea your sculpture was donated to the Lafferty."

"No, but...I insist." His smile bordered on pity. "You can't turn around and drive from Lake Bluff without something to wet your whistle."

"Wet my whistle?" She laughed. Maybe a little too hard, but she wanted to learn more about this *bloke*, as her dad would say. Also, she had to see what was in the damn flat-roofed mansion.

"An icy cold mug of A&W root beer sound tasty?" He leaned back against the VW and crossed his arms.

Threads from the frayed hem of his stone-colored cargo shorts hung over his bronzed, muscular thighs. She batted the hot LA surfer image out of her brain. "I don't think I can say no to your kind invitation. Thank you."

He was right. The last thing she wanted was to get back

4

into the un-air-conditioned VW and drive back to Milwaukee. Where she'd have to restrain herself from wringing Larry's neck. So hot with anger she could melt paint off canvases.

Following him to the main entrance, she jogged to keep up with his lengthy strides. Passing the expansive front windows, she could have sworn Lake Michigan sparkled as if waving at her through the glass wall on his multimillion-dollar home. "Nice digs. Is it an original Frank Lloyd Wright?"

"Yes. And thanks. *Coal or Steam* paid for it."

"The sculpture's been sold?" She grasped onto his forearm to steady herself. "But it's the saving…"

He touched her hand. "Sorry, Claire."

His attempt to comfort her was a lost cause. She'd been sucker punched and had no clue who exactly had hit her.

Chapter 2

Sinjin contemplated at what point he'd become distrusting and too comfortable with falsehoods. Once Claire Beaumont let go of his arm, a bout of wretchedness rushed through him. Her unexpected arrival stirred up something forgotten. But since the divorce, and thanks to that prat Larry Chambers, his survival depended on autonomy.

His sneakers squeaked on the foyer floor, and like clockwork, the dogs rushed out from the kitchen, yapping and jumping around Claire's legs.

She crouched down and held out both her hands.

Her delicate fingers trembled as the dogs sniffed them. A wave of self-loathing nearly knocked him off his feet.

But he could not tell her the truth about the sculpture.

With acute clarity, Sinjin recalled the moment he'd resorted to telling tall tales. It started when he'd said *I do* to Meg. Her deception over his sculpture had turned his life into a nightmare, and they'd been married for less than a year. Lying had preserved his sanity through their brief and toxic relationship. When it came to *Coal or Steam*, he had to lie to keep it safe.

"Fred. Ginger. Get down." He brushed the paws of the two

long-haired dachshunds away from her knees. "Their barking is a nuisance but harmless. It's taken the past year for the three of us to learn to get along. Of all the flatmates I've had, I think Fred and Ginger are the least demanding."

"They're adorable. Did you adopt them?" Her voice sounded level, not too shaky, but she still seemed rattled about the sculpture.

"Not at all. They were an insidious going-away gift from my ex-wife. She left the dogs to see how long it would take before they chewed up the house and then me. Dachshunds can be quite vicious."

Meg's departure had diminished his scope of trust, forever altering and tattering his bond with loyalty. Sinjin had not one iota of guilt in throwing his ex-wife under the bus. She had slept with Larry Chambers and was most likely still in cahoots with him.

As the dogs obediently sat with long noses turned up, Claire scratched their minute heads. "They adore you," she said, standing. "I think if your ex pops around, they may snack on her ankles."

"They have lasted longer than my marriage, and they're fantastic guard dogs. They may not bite her, but their barking will let me know if she breaks the restraining order." He added, "And they're much more fun."

"Oh…I'm sorry." She clutched her hip, adding a full-on contrapposto stance. "I didn't mean to get so personal."

He made her nervous. His reclusiveness had marred his social skills. "Not at all. I shouldn't give away all my deep dark secrets. After all, we only became acquainted minutes ago." He chuffed. "Too much time alone. But tonight, I'll be back in the land of the living. At least, I think so. The guests are solid patrons of the arts and getting on in years but still alive and kicking."

A smudge of paint on her ear drew him a half-step closer

to her. It was similar to the shade of her eyes—blue with hints of violet. He blinked and pointed to the gallery. "Would you like to see the show?"

"I am curious about it." With fingers no longer trembling, she brushed wayward strands of jet-black hair off her cheek.

As he stepped into the gallery with her, a bit of a thrill budded, and he grew excited for tonight. "There are cabins next to the lake. This property housed a Girl Scout camp back in the day and was in complete shambles when I bought it. After more renovating, I'll be able to open them up next summer. I'm planning a retreat for student artists." He turned on the spotlights and let her stroll around the display of paintings hung on corrugated screens made of patina copper. "This is a selection of twenty-first-century portraits by Midwest painters. The proceeds from tonight's sales will cover travel and room and board costs for the kids coming in from Chicago. It's a small exhibit with big names. I'm quite proud of this…a wonderful pool of talent."

"It's an admirable presentation." She stopped to stare at one of the watercolor portraits by a Wisconsin artist. "Wow. The brushwork is so vigorous. And I love the bright palettes. They're juicy."

She was an artist. "A curator *and* a painter? What's your medium?"

"Gouache. I dabble. A little. Mainly landscapes," she said in a hush, then blurted out, "Can't wait for that root beer you talked about."

"Drinks. Right. Don't want your trip to Lake Bluff to turn into a total waste." His mum's good sense and British manners unexpectedly attacked him. "What is your exhibit about at the Lafferty? What did you call it? *Victorious Vectors*?"

He led her outside to the back balcony jutting out over the ravine. Immediately, she grasped the railing, stretched over it, and gazed out toward the lake. "It's a compilation of pieces within the steampunk genre. With an emphasis on women's issues. Examples of their momentum or *push* through contemporary times. Several pieces are two-dimensional and others three."

"Sounds lovely." *Absolutely brilliant.* He handed her a bottle of soda. "Any punk? I'm a huge fan of Sid and Nancy."

She laughed, and the color flowed back into her cheeks. "Some crossovers, except more aviator goggles than mohawks."

"My protective eyewear has become a new fad. Should have known."

"It's the first in the Midwest. The only other steampunk exhibit opened in LA last year. For mine, Larry let me have total control. I've handpicked paintings and sculptures to exemplify a mix of Victorian and gearhead styles. A few of the artists are going to dress up in costumes at the opening on Halloween."

To get rid of the sour taste in his mouth from the mention of Larry, he took a sip of soda and gave her a quick smile. "I recall hearing about the LA exhibit. Metal and mayhem from the Industrial Revolution. A gathering of gadget-loving artisans wearing leather and lace."

After guzzling down the entire bottle of root beer, she handed the empty to him. "Thanks for your time. I should get going."

Her statement—strangely—drained him.

"Don't you want to call your boss before you take off?" Not entirely understanding why, he wanted to get to the root of this woman's dismay. "Even though *Coal or Steam* isn't available for your show, I'd like to assist you somehow."

She pulled her phone from the bib pocket on her overalls and stared at it for a second too long, then tapped in the number. "He's usually giving tours to special benefactors and patrons on Saturdays. Not sure if he'll pick up."

The tremor in her voice didn't escape him. "A director giving tours? That's interesting."

Meandering over to the trio of birches, she hid the phone under a sweep of lovely black hair. Seconds later, she slipped the phone back into her pocket. "No luck."

Were Larry and Meg up to their old tricks? "Why don't you come to the opening tonight," he said. "Many of the guests are major donors to the arts. Your *Vectors* exhibit in Milwaukee could benefit."

"Oh, no. But thank you. I have to get back." She glanced down at her denim overalls and headed back into the gallery. "Besides, not exactly dressed for an artsy event."

He escorted her to the front door and held it open. His breathing hitched. To squash a spike of overeagerness, he made sure to keep his tone light. "You'll fit right in with the students and profs tonight. No worries about appearances."

Shaking her head, she jogged to the VW.

"If you change your mind, you know where I am." Scooping up the two unusually quiet dogs, he cradled one under each arm and watched her climb into the van. An unfamiliar feeling spread through him. Curiosity.

Chapter 3

In the rearview mirror, Claire stared at the man buoyed by two dogs barely bigger than squirrels. She made a U-ey, drove up to the front porch, reached across the passenger side, and rolled down the damn window. "Nice meeting you, Mr. Reid."

"Sinjin, please." He stuck his head in the open window. "It's lovely meeting you, too. Any chance you'll reconsider my invite?"

Fred and Ginger panted hard, sounding as hopeful as their person.

"I'm in a mood. Not sure what kind exactly, but driving home to Milwaukee may sink me into a state of artistic wallowing." Her insides were tossing about with too many disappointments in one day. "Hey, I have a good friend in town. I'll stop in and play catch-up with Lucy—"

"Lucy Maxwell?"

She gripped the steering wheel. "Oh? Do you know her?"

"Lucy and her mother are good mates. Julie designed the wine bar. Should be arriving soon."

"Right. The wine bar." She really had to get accustomed to living in Wisconsin again. People were always connected to one another somehow. It made perfect sense her college roommate from their Madison days would know this guy. In Chicago, she was blissfully anonymous along with the rest of the city's population. "Lucy and I, we go back. I'll let you know—maybe."

"Ta." He patted the edge of the open window, then waved.

One of the dogs licked and nudged his upper arm, exposing an ornate tattoo on a chiseled bicep. The image of a surfer, with the arms of a rock 'n' roll drummer, parked in her mind. Her cheeks grew warm.

"Hope to see you later," he said, stepping away.

"Ta," she mimicked, sounding like a tourist. Slinking down a smidge in the seat, Claire made another U-ey and drove away without daring to glance in the rearview mirror again. Once on the main road, she fiddled with the wooden knob on the dashboard and turned on the radio. With AM playing in the hunk of junk, she settled on the oldies station. Blasting Sonny and Cher, she sang loudly to "I Got You Babe."

As if. Without Sinjin's damn sculpture, *Victorious Vectors* would fail.

She pulled over to the side of the road next to a field of grazing cows and their fresh eye-watering smell woke her up. While deciding who to call, she stared at the bubbles floating on her phone's screen saver. Should she call Larry or her real boss?

Claire didn't want to bother Mina. The president of the Lafferty was her mentor and the only empowering female around her at this point. She couldn't disturb her again. Cancer took a toll, and even though Mina had made it safe and sound through the rigors of lifesaving poisons, she needed to give Mina a well-deserved break from the petty politics in her family's museum.

This time for real, she tapped his contact, and Larry answered right away.

"Why on earth did you have me pick up Sinjin Reid's sculpture? It's been sold."

"I don't know what you're talking about. There's paperwork to prove that he's still in possession of that sculpture." His voice, already on the high side, pitched up. The word *sculpture* sounded squeaky.

"And you neglected to tell me his wife is now his ex-wife. Better have the legal department reexamine the forms, or else the Lafferty will keep losing solid donors." She took a deep breath. The museum was floundering in loss, and she had to figure it out.

"He's lying."

"Why? And about what? The piece or his wife?" She shook her head, disgusted. In the time she'd been working at the Lafferty, Larry's machinations—at first annoying—had turned maddening.

"There is absolutely no record of his sculpture being sold," Larry said, excluding any mention of the ex-wife. Then he went into one of his blustery diatribes. "I'm *thee* director of the Lafferty Museum. You are a curator only because Mina Lafferty hired you. I answer to the museum's board, not *you*, Ms. Beaumont."

Because of Larry's ego—a masterpiece in itself—and her close relationship with Mina, Claire knew her curatorial authority was critical to the survival of the beleaguered museum. She'd grown used to his belittling nature and continually overrode it with healthy doses of kindness and a modicum of reserved respect. "Maybe you can meet with Mr. Reid here in Lake Bluff. Talk it out and clear up the confusion." She kept her tone even and professional.

"Are you telling me what to do?"

"No," she replied, becoming more certain that she may have to contact Mina before the end of the day. "Not at all."

Dead air.

"Did I lose you?"

"I don't have time to make a half-day jaunt to baby a narcissistic artist. The rightful home of Sinjin Reid's sculpture is in our permanent collection, and I'm certain it's still on his property."

The vitriol in his voice echoed in her ear. Claire had to figure out what the hell was going on. Not only for her show but also for Mina and her family's museum. "I'll figure something—"

He disconnected.

She stared at the phone. Expletives floated in and out of her brain. Larry was a sniveling, pretentious asshole and up to no good. Again, she would have loved to call him on the carpet and tell the truth about his deceptions, but up until now, she had no proof, and worse, it might aim the attention on her. She needed to avoid the spotlights until well after her exhibit opened and closed. For her sake and, above all, her father's.

When Arthur Silver questioned the authenticity of several of his works in a review, the article had torn David Raffen's career into tatters. The Earth shifted, and Claire had fallen on her ass.

Her dad's eyesight had diminished to blurs, so Claire painted along with him. She'd been his protégé since kinder-garten, and his brush style was as familiar to her hand as signing her own name. His signature, even though he could barely see, always landed in the precise spot on the canvas and included his trademark loops.

"Show off," she would say.

Her own talent would never live up to her father's. The work of David Raffen had been compared to the masters. She wasn't as gifted as her dad, but she was his beacon. The two of them were a family, and he was her North Star. Like many creatives, the business side of art wasn't his forte. Money was always tight. No ears had to be severed, but when his health diminished, Claire left grad school in Italy and supported her dad.

She shut her eyes and licked a bead of sweat off her upper lip. If she'd only known what a clusterfuck would come from her loyalty. Or was it pure stupidity?

Gravel spit out from the tires when she pulled back onto the highway and careened through a roundabout. Forgetting to yield, she triggered a chorus of angry horns. Ten minutes later, she safely drove into the sleepy town of Lake Bluff. In good time, because she had to pee.

Damn root beer...

WHEN THE THICK smoke trailing from the rear of the VW disappeared, Sinjin went back inside and set down the dogs. As they scampered into the kitchen, he followed to dole out their treats. Then he went into his office to google Claire Beaumont. He could've sworn he'd seen her before; if so, he definitely would have remembered. Her quirky energy and violet eyes were sexier than hell.

After clicking about, he'd only uprooted a vague LinkedIn profile confirming she was an employee at the Lafferty. Even the museum's website had no photos of her. No other social media at all? Frustrated, he gave up and shut his laptop. He tried to picture Claire and recall where he'd seen her or how they'd crossed paths. Without a glint of recognition, he rubbed his eyes and gave up. The gallery needed his attention. Guests would be showing up in a few hours.

Double-paned glass panels made up two walls in the gallery. Installing shades between the panes should have made his life easier, but it hadn't. He had to devote a considerable amount of time to lighting, and tonight, the sun would be setting at opening time. The shadows from Lake Michigan would reduce the brilliance of the faces displayed in the portraits.

Sinjin shook off his annoyance and retrieved the remotes. He closed the electric shades in the windows and maneuvered the halogen spotlights hoisted on the ceiling track. Many of the portraits were framed in pine and white birch branches that would bounce the illumination around.

He inspected each portrait to make sure a distinguishing feature of each person was highlighted. The last piece troubled him. It was of a young girl done in chalk pastels and oils. The face hinted of baby right before rosy cheeks and dimples dropped off in young adulthood.

The artist wasn't in the same school as the rest. Sinjin had fastidiously followed David Raffen's career. The man's brush-strokes and tremendous way of blending colors and oils had made him a hard-core fan of his work. Since his death a few years back, Sinjin continued to search for Raffen pieces. Even though there were already several paintings in his collection, he wanted to acquire more of Raffen's drawings because they were rare.

Using a remote, he tried to aim a light on the face in the portrait before him. It didn't move, so he retrieved a ladder and adjusted the canister light by hand. The thing kept squawking, and he just about gave up when the fixture angled into place and showered the girl's cherubic face with a halo of light. The intense violet color of the girl's eyes popped off the canvas. And the dimples. He stumbled off the step stool.

"Shite," he shouted into the empty gallery.

He jogged back to his office, nearly tripping over Fred and Ginger elatedly dancing around his feet. When he punched in Claire Raffen instead of Beaumont, the list of news articles streamed down the screen of his laptop. He didn't know which story to read first. He had learned long ago to ignore the multiple news outlets fixated on the diabolic art world.

It was no surprise to discover that the critics had damned David Raffen to eternal hell, torn the dead man's soul to pieces, and thrown his daughter into shark-infested waters as punishment.

Knowing about the brouhaha a few years ago, Sinjin still considered Raffen's work to be on par with John Singer Sargent or Edward Hopper. The man's lines were methodical and his brushstrokes sublime. He designed with a sense of color. Sinjin had never seen it on any other canvas. But when a critic from *Art & Form* magazine questioned Raffen's authenticity, his reputation was sullied.

The highest branches of art world aficionados shunned him. The Royal Society of Portrait Painters removed Raffen's masterpiece. His portrait of Princess Anne was taken off the wall and put into storage. Embarrassed collectors of his work whispered the name Raffen to only the closest of allies. Untouchable and buried, the artist couldn't defend himself.

Sinjin clicked on Google Images to see pictures of Claire. In the scant few photos, she was beside her father. Smiling. Admiring. And loving an undoubtedly good man.

God, he wanted to ask Claire so many questions about her father. About her. The temptation to ring Lucy or Julie took hold of him. Had Claire made it to Maxwell's yet? He needed to focus. Tonight's gathering required all of his attention. With any luck, Claire would show up. However, he still had to make one call. To confirm *Coal or Steam* was safe and sound.

Chapter 4

The shop doors up and down the two sides of Lake Bluff's Main Street were painted with bright primary colors. Matching striped awnings shaded each entrance. Claire parked in front of the black-and-white awning emblazoned with Maxwell's House and hopped out of the oven-on-wheels. Desperate to see a bathroom and Lucy Maxwell.

"Lucy, I'm home," she said, laughing as a beautiful blast of air-conditioning smacked her in the face. The greeting had been standard fare while they lived together in a decrepit flat on Madison's campus.

She swung her messenger bag over her shoulder. Catching a faint whiff of cinnamon or maybe apple, she poked around the vintage retail shop. Lucy's store, or more accurately, her mother's store, was eerily quiet for a Saturday afternoon.

Absorbing the chilly air and gathering the thoughts running amok inside her brain, she fixated on the hodgepodge of inventory surrounding her. The round clothing racks with zigzagged edges looked oddly familiar. *Damn*. These racks and wall displays were made of the same metal as those in Sinjin's gallery. A collection of velvet riding jackets hung off a corrugated metal panel displaying a palette of fall colors: copper, gold, auburn, and rust.

Side tables made of metal gears were arranged around caramel-colored leather furniture, and an oversized coffee table displayed a variety of mechanical pieces to hybridize high tech with a steampunk fashion. They all had the mechanical flare she'd grown to appreciate while creating *Vectors*.

She spotted the mannequin wearing a vintage Mondrian color-cubed dress. When it had been their roommate a decade ago, it wore a pair of red-and-white-striped overalls with Bucky Badger sprawled across the chest.

She admired the dummy's dress and arranged its hand to point to the galvanized steel counter. This shop had an incredibly high-art and low-tech vibe. Her Lafferty exhibit required a shot of *this* kind of steampunk. Maybe she needed to rethink this day trip to Lake Bluff. A longer stay might be beneficial to her creativity and energy. Taking advantage of the weekend and using her PTO seemed appropriate and necessary, especially given that her show was on a downward spiral because of Sinjin Reid.

"I'm...I'm here!" Lucy screamed, jogging from the back entrance and rushing up to her. "The smokin'-hot farmer from Kohler just delivered pumpkins and gourds for me. Sorry. But my first batch of pumpkin smoothies won't be ready anytime soon."

Wearing Frye boots, a black miniskirt, and a T-shirt silk-screened with Charlie Brown in the great pumpkin patch, Lucy wrapped her in a bear hug.

The hug melted away all of Claire's worry. Yep, she deserved some time away from the Lafferty and required more time with Lucy. She pointed above at a tin sign that read Jule's Juices as they walked down the hallway leading to the part of the store operated by Lucy. As a botanical expert, Lucy's turf was a juice bar, scent emporium, and candle workshop all in one. "Weren't you going to change the name from Jule's to Lulu's?"

"My mom actually listening to me? Ha! That will be a cold day in hell. But please, do me a favor. Call it Lulu's. The sign will change eventually."

Claire arranged her laptop and phone at the counter, then spread out her folders and files she'd brought along for *Vectors*. This eclectic store had shifted something in her plans, and since she had no idea what was going on with the star-sculpture-gone-missing, she needed to think outside the parameters of the museum. Her research for the exhibit was varied—handwritten notes about the donors and computer files on each artist. Still, the biggest chunk was a thick manilla file loaded with pictures and documents detailing the history of *Coal or Steam*. Claire needed to start at square one. And Sinjin *had* invited her to his opening tonight.

"Do you want a smoothie?" Lucy strode behind the counter, then barked out a laugh. "As if?" She dug around the lower cabinets and held out a bottle of Korbel brandy. "How about a nice classic old-fashioned?"

"You're my favorite mixologist," Claire said, "and I'm sure you have only the best cherries and oranges to muddle."

Lucy set about mixing up a couple of cocktails. "I'm also working on an old-fashioned scented candle."

Since their days as roommates in college, Lucy had been Claire's dearest friend and confidant. Besties, she thought but disliked the cuteness of the expression. They were soul sisters. And when it came down to it, Claire's trust in Lucy Maxwell was unbreakable. Bonded by a lot of shenanigans while studying and partying in Madison. Their trips to the House on the Rock, Forevertron Park, and the New Glarus breweries had welded their lifelong friendship. Lucy had a rare quality: integrity.

An old black rotary phone hanging on the wall next to a

blender started ringing. The sound jolted Claire. A plastic answering machine rigged with adapters answered the call.

"Guess who I just met?" Claire took a sip of her drink. "I'll give you ten guesses."

"I only need one. As soon as you texted that you were coming today, I knew you'd have to have some kind of artsy reason for being here. And there's one well-known artist in the area, if you don't count my mom." Lucy dropped extra cherries into both of their glasses.

"The incomparable Sinjin Reid. My mom's been a *cougar*, obsessed with the man all summer. She's around fifty years old and throwing herself at him like a teenage groupie. I'm embarrassed for her." Lucy shook her head, disgusted. "I don't get it. How can an incredibly creative and talented person be so childlike? I'll never get used to her behavior."

"I'm really sorry." Claire let out a lengthy sigh, knowing that Lucy's mom suffered from several toxic vices. A constant thread in her good friend's life was that Lucy had to parent her own mother. What a heartbreaking job.

Lucy pointed toward the shop. "Her coffee table is a piece of art built from monstrous parts. The copper band came from farm equipment she'd salvaged out of an abandoned barn. It took a lot of sweat and blood. She's a terrific artist."

Nodding, Claire asked, "Isn't she going to deliver a wine bar to Sinjin?"

"She's on her way there now. A wine bar? Is that irony or what? Julie can't stop drinking her chardonnay."

"When I met Sinjin, he was a complete gentleman. I can see why your mom is attracted to him. Maybe he's a positive influence?" Claire attempted to sound upbeat.

"She's desperate and sex-starved."

"But wasn't Sinjin married?"

"Uh-huh. Ugly divorce. He's been a free man since last winter. His ex-wife, Meg Fisher, came in here complaining about the cold house, so she bought up all our angora wool blankets. Not sure what he saw in her. There was a rumor, one of many in this small town, that he married her because she was pregnant, but then it turned out she wasn't really preggers. If it's true, she set back women's rights a hundred years with that stunt."

"Fake pregnancy?" Claire let the sweet brandy rest on her tongue before swallowing it down. "By chance, are you going to his gallery tonight?"

"I'll be the bartender. Making smoothies and cocktails. What did *you* really think of Sinjin? And don't go all googly-eyed over his James Bond accent. He's been in the States since he was a kid." Lucy lifted an auburn eyebrow.

"I'm on a professional mission for the Lafferty. It's best to stay neutral. But he did surprise me. I had expected a stuffy upper-crusty Brit, but he reminds me more of a Taylor Hawkins."

"Always and forever a Foo Fighters fan." Lucy laughed. "According to my mom, the *bloody bloke* is an artistic perfectionist. Did you talk to him about your dad?

"Not at all," Claire said. "Why?"

"He's a huge collector of David Raffen's."

━━━

SINJIN KEPT the conversation with his father short. Before the divorce papers were drawn up and signed, George Reid had bought the sculpture from him for a measly ten bucks. It was the deal of the century. A recent appraisal had set the value of *Coal or Steam* to over a hundred grand.

George had stuffed it into the trunk of his Cadillac, between mounds of angora and cashmere blankets. Another evil goodbye gift from Sinjin's ex since he was allergic to wool.

Only then was he sure that the curse of his existence couldn't get into Meg's or Larry's slimy paws.

A decade ago, Sinjin never considered the prospect of this piece becoming such a jinx. He had created it when he was young, practically a kid. When they'd moved to Wisconsin, he'd taken a welding class at the tech school. Because his dad was an engineer who came to the States as a new executive at Kohler Industries, Sinjin was fascinated by the interior parts and levers and metal gadgets of everyday items. After learning about precious metals, ideas came into his imagination in a rush. Designing with twists and turns of silver flooded his brain. His hands—melting the pieces together—could barely keep up.

Polly Easom, the Kohler company's matriarch, had loved the piece and contacted a gallery in NYC. And the rest became too many years of sheer madness. The piece, simply an homage to his father and Kohler, sold at an auction for an unprecedented amount and had made Sinjin a wunderkind. He worked hard to move past the over-the-top label and to obliterate any branding of being a one-hit wonder. Peaking during tech school had never been his dream.

Thanks to his supporters, he'd reclaimed the sculpture that had taken too much control. He thought there would be some peace. Then he met Meg Fisher. Who ended up making his life a living hell.

For the second time that day, Ginger and Fred broke into fits of barking and panting. His thoughts came to a full stop. Relief. Going back in time was not healthy, or so his shrink had advised.

He opened his door, hoping to see a vintage van; instead, a Penske cargo truck was parked out front. Behind it, a Jeep Wagoneer. Julie Maxwell hopped out and marched up to him, letting out a loud huff. The dogs hid behind his legs.

"Where are the caterers?" she shouted, meeting up with

the two men unloading the wine bar from the back of the truck. "Shouldn't they be setting up already? I told you not to hire those goofs from Kohler."

He shooed the dogs back into the house. Any barking would set Julie off on another rant. As much as he admired the woman's impressive talents, her artistic eccentricities were worse than his own. "The city of Kohler is home to a host of top-rated chefs. Maybe a trip to the American Club would do you some good. A full-day spa treatment."

"As if I could afford that." She stared at the two men unloading the wrought iron bar. "Careful," she barked. "This is a valuable piece of art."

The two workers had straps around their backs and divided the weight of the wine bar in half. Both could have been from the same gene pool as The Rock. Julie followed in their footsteps. Sinjin jogged to the side entrance of the house that led to the back balcony. Already, tables had been set up for the caterers.

He held the gate open for the movers. "Thanks, men. Set it on the far end of the deck. Beside the trio of birch trees."

"Lucy should be here." Julie sighed with dramatic exasperation while fixated on her phone. "She blocked me! Always thinking about herself. At least, if the caterers don't show, I'm sure you'll have smoothies and cocktails to placate your guests."

As they strode together onto the back deck, he did not offer Julie a drink. At the beginning of the summer when he'd first hired her as an apprentice, something his shrink had recommended to get beyond his pettiness and anger over the divorce, he'd learned the hard way that liquor, hell, even a glass of chardonnay, turned Julie into a raving madwoman.

He'd also discovered that the other source of Julie's talent was her daughter, Lucy, who rarely considered herself. If not for her, Julie would have succumbed to alcoholism like his own mum. Sinjin tried to be sensitive. Julie and Lucy Maxwell were two women in his life who had shown him what mattered—compassion and authenticity. Which sometimes escaped his gear-loving head. "Let me grab you a root beer," he said.

She gagged. "No, thanks. I hate that stuff."

With Julie, he knew exactly what to expect. She had never beaten around any bush; he only hoped she'd forget about her unrealistic crush on him. He had no intention of mixing business with pleasure; she wasn't his type. Besides, Meg had twisted him up and wrung him out. He didn't have the energy to develop any kind of intimate relationship with another woman. Except all day, thoughts about Claire had been tugging and yanking him around.

The movers pulled off reams of plastic wrapping, exposing not a random tavern bar but an ornate sculpture with an additional use: to house bottles and glasses. The top was made of an industrial-size strip of patinaed copper. Adhered to the four corners were gilded table legs, and on the front were steel cutouts of tulips painted in orange, purple, and pink. The piece epitomized an energy—quirky energy. Claire would love it. A twinge of hope stabbed him.

"By any chance, did you see Lucy today? Or her friend?" He tipped the movers as they left, then strolled around the bar, admiring it. "What's her name?"

Julie pulled a cloth out of her bag, a purse the size of a small suitcase. It had the look of an expensive designer and new, but he wasn't about to ask about it. Money complaints were her top conversation starters.

She knelt in front of the orange tulip on the face of the bar and began to dust it. "I have no clue who you're talking about. I've been at the barn all day. Getting this ready for you."

"I think her name is Claire Beaumont. A mate of Lucy's?"

Her hand stopped short, mid-polish. Sinjin could see the wheels turning under her head of floppy gold hair. After a second's hesitation, she blew at nonexistent dust on the tulip, her overplumped lips nearly kissing the sculpture. Julie was a master of metal but nowhere near to being a master of disguise.

"Claire. Sure, I've met her. Once or twice. She roomed with Lucy in college. Kind of snobby, if I remember. Probably because she's from Chicago." She stood and arched her back. "What do I know though? My daughter barely speaks to me. In town? I had no idea."

"She's a curator at the Lafferty," he said, leaning against the side of the bar and brushing the copper top with his fingers. The touch of the cool metal tingled. Why was she so dodgy? "This piece is beautiful. You've outdone yourself."

She stuffed the cloth back into her purse. "I've learned from the best. It's been an incredible summer working for you. Any chance you'll reconsider for fall?"

"At this point, I've taught you everything I've learned. You could be *my* mentor."

She tittered. One of her annoying habits he'd learned to accept while training her. He'd shown Julie all the tricks of his trade. Every welding move that made the magic of metal come alive. He'd done it for her and her daughter but also for himself. It was the best antidote for getting past the nightmare with Meg and her lover, Larry Chambers.

A Decline Like No Other?
Critique by Arthur Silver

At this year's Armory Show, while triumphant in every expectation, it was a sight for this reviewer's sore eyes to see Anita Finegold's gallery in attendance. After unknown challenges had kept her gallery out of the exhibition fair, she made a glorious re-entrance and celebrated her eminent client, portrait artist David Raffen.

Finding my way past Arusha, Pace, and Gagosian galleries, the Finegold Gallery booth was a tribute to Anita's century-old gallery on the Upper East Side. The brownstone she has lived in her entire life houses a stellar collection of American art. The dividers separating her booth from all the other galleries exhibiting in the Javits Center were constructed of faux brick walls to replicate her home and gallery.

David Raffen's portraits have been the darlings of the contemporary art scene since the seventies. During an era in America filled with discotheques, bad dancing, and even worse fashion, Mr. Raffen's sedate and glamorous portraits of illustrious patrons were a refreshing break from the trends. Although his rendition of Princess Anne wearing orange and yellow gave the tabloids fodder, Raffen was awarded a member of distinction in the Royal Society of Portrait Painters.

During my own minimal painting phase, Mr. Raffen's brushwork had been an example of true genius. His hand and eye work in tandem so closely, the tremendous effort creates layers of brilliance.

When entering the Finegold booth at this year's show, my breath was stolen away when I came upon Raffen's latest works, *Seasons*. Four portraits for each season of his deceased wife, Monique Beaumont. Monique kicks her way in *Golden* through a pile of gold, amber and honey-colored leaves. *Fever* is an homage to spring with a detailed face: blushing pink cheeks and earth-colored eyes. *Midnight* portrays a winter solstice as a woman traverses the ice-white landscape and onyx-blue sky. In *Sugar,* a pregnant woman relaxes poolside with happy expectations etched into her face.

Raffen's devotion to his minute brushstrokes is mind-boggling. It sustains the flawless appearance of his award-winning portraits. As a fan for twenty years, I was humbled to be in the presence of David Raffen whilst in the queue for champagne. However, imagine my confusion (and disappointment?) when he wasn't able to distinguish between a twenty, a fifty, and a hundred-dollar bill when paying the vendor.

Had David Raffen been quaffing too much of said champagne? Or was his slipup a hint of something far more distressing? The question must be asked. Could the artist's vision be failing?
@Art Silver

Chapter 5

Claire gulped down the rest of her old-fashioned. It seemed to make sense. But not really. Why had Sinjin, a sculptor, collected her dad's paintings? She understood why because her dad was brilliant and a fantastic painter. But Sinjin seemed, well, more… She had no idea how to finish the thought. More physical than brainy?

"Yep. I have all of the ingredients here," Lucy said, shuffling about bottles and jars on the counter.

"For what?" Claire asked.

"Sinjin's favorite smoothie." Lucy opened the fridge and scanned the contents, then pulled out a bottle of champagne, two pomegranates, and a tangerine. She set them with the other items in a metal milk crate. "This is for him. A thank you and an apology. For putting up with my wayward mother in a kind and generous manner."

A determined need to see more of Sinjin's big house spread through Claire's bones. She wondered about another studio or gallery space. Had he stored her dad's paintings in those cabins near the lake? No! The damp climate and moisture could ruin them. Again, she became illogically protective over her father's paintings. "Can I tag along with you tonight?"

"Thank you for asking!" Lucy blew her a kiss. "Do you mind giving me a hand behind the bar? Like in the old days when we shook and stirred at the Tipsy Cow?"

"It's been a long time since I made an actual cocktail. I may be a little rusty, but I'm good with opening bottles." Claire wanted to help her friend out but had to fess up. "Have you seen any of my dad's paintings at Sinjin's? I'm freaking out a little. I hope he's taken proper care of them."

"No. My mom only mentioned it to me," Lucy said, biting her lower lip. "No offense, but she isn't a fan of your dad's work."

"None taken." Her dad had a unique perspective. Some might not understand or appreciate his love of tiny details. Skewed by his harsh life, he tended to exaggerate with his use of bright colors. People either loved or hated his paintings of women in the twentieth century. But his portraits were always authentic to the subject's time in life, and he aptly depicted it on a canvas with limited space.

In the case of his *More Lace Please*, Claire had no idea about the woman portrayed in the painting. However, the black and lace dress in the portrait fit perfectly into her *Vectors* show with its steampunk theme.

"I think Mom's uber jealous," Lucy said. "Your mom came from France, and your dad was famous and rich. Sadly, they're goals she's been pursuing for a long time."

"True, he was and still is well-known. Wealthy? Completely false." Claire packed up her files and laptop to help Lucy. "But French? That's a tough one."

"She wears a beret. All the time." Lucy laughed derisively.

"Nothing wrong with Picasso's favorite hat."

Claire liked their plan for her to stay with Lucy in her apartment upstairs for the following week. Since there was an extra bedroom, spending time with her friend sounded like an easy escape from the troubled museum.

She sent a text to Mina.

I'm in Lake Bluff. Staying for the week. Sinjin Reid said he sold the sculpture. Larry's calling the world-famous sculptor a liar. A lot of questions. I want answers. Take good care. Claire

"Any chance I can raid your closet for tonight?"

"No prob. Or, if you want to go all *hipster*, you can borrow something from the shop."

Claire considered the velvet riding jacket but decided it would be too hot. "Any change of clothing sounds great. I need to give these overalls a rest. When are you heading over to Sinjin's?"

"He is persnickety but chill. My mom, on the other hand, is a tyrant. I had to block her messages," Lucy said. "So, whenever you're ready. No rush."

Rifling through a rack of women's vintage clothing, Claire decided on a puffy black skirt with a cummerbund waistband. Already she wished for a cool breeze on her bare legs. From a wall display, she pulled down a white eyelet tank top edged in lace with pearled bead buttons. She could've sworn the tiny buttons were authentic saltwater pearls. It was a nice improvement over her sweat-soaked T-shirt. "Fancying up for the night will be a treat."

Claire checked to see if Mina had responded to her text, but nothing. It wasn't unusual to get an answer from her true boss a day later.

They loaded boxes and crates filled with the makings for a selection of adult beverages into the flatbed of Lucy's red pickup truck and drove to Sinjin's house and gallery. Or estate? Maybe it should be called a mansion. What would Frank Lloyd Wright call it?

Claire wondered what Sinjin would do when she returned.

She had to admit, she was slightly jazzed to see him again. Her fingertips tingled, thinking of his shiny cropped hair the color of copper. And the tattoo on his arm—she wanted to get her eyes on it. Maybe decipher it…in an artistic, professional manner, of course.

By the main entrance, they pulled up behind a catering truck marked **Siebkens**. Men and women were coming and going, carrying trays, dish crates, and chairs through the house's mammoth Prairie-style doors. Claire blew out a hostage breath. *Great.* She'd chosen to wear a black skirt with a white top and blended right in with the rest of the wait staff.

A brassy blonde in a gauze sundress the color of processed cheese strode up to them. It had been years since Claire last met Julie Maxwell, and she looked nearly the same, until she was inches away. There were tinges of yellow on her cheeks that matched her hair color.

"Where have you been?" She crossed her arms over her chest, reminding Claire of a palace guard. "You two need to get your asses out on the balcony and set up the beverage station."

"Good to see you again." Claire reached out for a hug or even a handshake, but Julie ignored her and went back into the house.

"Got here as soon as I could," Lucy said to her mother's back and swore under her breath. "See what I mean? She's an obsessed woman around Sinjin."

"I like her orange beret." She ignored her inclination to mention Julie's unhealthy skin tone. "Let's get to work, roomie."

Claire adjusted the strap of her messenger bag and started to unload the boxes from the truck. She followed Lucy and the other catering staff inside Sinjin's house. Passing through the gallery, she ignored the artwork. On the balcony, she unloaded the boxes near the spot where she'd sipped a root beer only a couple of hours earlier. This time, she admired the trees surrounding the balcony. Fall and the change of colors fascinated her.

Inside, Julie repeated commands to the staff in a screechy voice. How could Sinjin work with such an annoying pitch in his ear? Although she'd endured the same thing with Larry. His high-squeaked orders always bounced around the museum's marble-lined halls.

After they unloaded their supplies and arranged them in Julie's artisan bar, Claire took a breather and eyed it up. The colors of the tulips were vivid. Shades of paint that took a lot of mixing. They were genuinely difficult pigments to reproduce. A sliver of envy pierced Claire.

She placed her messenger bag under the brilliant bar and slipped her phone into the front of the skirt's cummerbund. With Lucy's blessing, she set out to explore Sinjin's palatial designer home. Would he keep his collection of Raffens out in the open or under lock and key?

As she passed the kitchen, Fred and Ginger were barking. She paused before going through the foyer and down the main hallway. Around the corner was a sunken living room with standard man furniture: an overstuffed black leather sofa and matching love seats surrounding a stone fireplace with a mantel made of driftwood.

The halogen lights strung across the room's ceiling lit up the space. Made of wood planks, a catwalk stretched above, leading into a hidden loft area. The high walls displayed an assortment of paintings hung in the style of a French art salon. A portrait up in the corner, framed in black, stunned her. She stumbled backward, gazing up at the face of Monique Beaumont, her mother. She blinked furiously to make sure her eyes weren't playing tricks on her. But the white-blonde hair and bright red lips popped off the canvas, and her mom's gorgeous eyes stared back down at Claire.

"Damn, damn, damn," she mumbled and paced.

How the hell had Sinjin been able to acquire *this* portrait?

Shaking, she pulled her phone from her cummerbund and aimed the camera to magnify it. Was it an unauthorized print of *Fever*? She held her breath and centered the lens on the mole near her mother's red lips. It wasn't the right shape. Although she'd already known it, she still had to confirm it. She stepped closer to the wall and snapped a picture. This wasn't a print. In front of her was the original painting. Claire saw the paint on the mole and what an abysmal job she'd done with it.

Her father had insisted she'd brushed too many layers of the chocolate-brown pigment on the mole in the spring version of her mother. It came out too big and clunky. Then he'd gone on to demonstrate yet again his masterful technique of blending colors. The lipstick, a shade called French Red, brilliantly popped off the portrait.

Of the four paintings in the *Seasons* series, *Fever* was her least favorite. However, now was not the time for self-critiquing. This painting, along with two of the four other *Seasons*, should be hanging on a wall in the L. Finegold Gallery in New York. At least until hell froze over. What blizzard had she missed?

"Claire," Sinjin said. "You're here."

She bolted up straight and twisted around, nearly tripping over her own feet.

"Up here, Claire," he said from above on the catwalk.

How long had he been there?

She gazed up at him. Her heart pounded in an intense drumbeat. "Oh, hey. You scared me."

An epic understatement.

"You're a curator, painter, *and* a waitress?"

"What?" Then she remembered being dressed in waitress garb. "Yep. Waitress extraordinaire and helping Lucy. I took you up on your invitation and decided to come along with her."

"Ace. Good news." He stretched his arms up over his head and put on a white shirt. Still dressing for the opening, he leaned over the railing. "Don't move. I'll be right down."

"Uh-huh." She checked her chin for drool because a bare-chested Sinjin was worth drooling over. Then she gave herself a mental head slap, telling herself to focus!

There were four paintings of her mother. *Golden* was the fall version. It hung on her living room shelf at home. *Midnight* (winter) and *Sugar* (summer) must still be in the New York gallery? But why…

With her mother staring down on her, the questions multiplied too fast for her mind to comprehend.

"Glad to speak to you before the guests arrive." Sinjin came up to her, smiling and tucking in his shirt. His untied tie dangled over his chest. He retrieved a pair of cufflinks from his pants pocket, then struggled to clip the first one in place.

He seemed fidgety, which gave her a reprieve from her own case of nerves. She cradled his wrist and locked in the cufflink for him. "I love links. They remind me of my—"

"Boo?" he asked, sounding rather sweet.

"No. I. Don't. Have. A. Boyfriend," she joked, then stared at his disastrous tie. "Half Windsor or Pratt knot?"

"Are you calling me a prat?" He grinned.

"Windsor it is, then." Struggling to keep her hands steady, she focused on his tie, then straightened it out. A rush of calm spread through her as her fingers swept across his chest. "There. Nice tie."

"Are the lime and navy stripes too garish?"

She inhaled and caught the citrus scent of his aftershave. "I think it's perfect."

"Thank you for coming to this opening."

She stepped back for a hit of fresh air. "I should get back to the gallery. And the bar. I just wanted to pop around and say hello."

"Yeah, sure, but Claire, I'd love to know. Is David Raffen your father?"

To curtail the shaking, she clasped her hands together. Her father had died four years ago. Hearing his name shouldn't be life-shattering at this point. "Oh. Yes."

"I'm really an admirer of his work. Any chance we could, well, I have so many questions about him. Oh fuck, I sound like a real tosser."

"It's okay. He had that impact on me, too. Sure. I'd love to brag about him with you," she said, glancing toward the gallery. "I should get back. But I'm staying here for the week. With Lucy."

"I have a job to do, and thanks to you, I'm dressed and ready to suck up to everyone coming tonight. Please, take some time to talk to the guests. I'm certain you'll have much in common. It's an artsy crowd."

Before she stepped out of the room, he pointed at *Fever*. "Did you see it? I'm absolutely gobsmacked by this piece by your father. It has to be one of the favorites in my collection."

Slightly dazed, Claire was barely aware of the footsteps coming from behind her.

"There you are." Lucy tapped her arm.

Claire nodded.

"Hey, Sinjin," Lucy said before turning to Claire. "Can you help me with the wine? People are starting to come, and I want to get going on the smoothies. Especially yours, Sinjin."

"Better get on it." Claire clutched onto Lucy's hand and dragged her away.

"My mom is in a complete tizzy," Lucy said. "I'm sorry she was so rude to you earlier. I don't know what's gotten into her. She's convinced Sinjin is going to ask her to move in with him.

I love her, but she's completely off her rocker. He's been nothing but a cordial business dude to her all summer."

Once on the balcony and safe behind the bar, Claire dropped Lucy's hand. Although she tried, her worry had disconnected her friend's words. Sinjin Reid's favorite Raffen portrait wasn't by David Raffen but an original work by Claire Beaumont. What was going on?

Chapter 6

Sinjin stayed in the sitting room until Claire was out of sight. He tried to stretch it until she was out of his thoughts, but then he might have missed his own gala opening. All her fuss over his cufflinks and tie had rattled him. He'd botched up his brief chat about Raffen and acted like a proper idiot. Adjusting the cufflinks, he swore under his breath. Next time he faced Claire, he'd collect himself. Stay calm. He had to keep in mind that even though she was the daughter of David Raffen, she also worked for that wanker, Larry Chambers.

From the hall closet, he tugged his navy suit jacket off the hanger. He put it on and twisted his arms and shoulders, but it was no less restrictive. He'd been out of practice in wearing his official business uniform. T-shirts and shorts made life much more comfortable. He strode into the gallery and came up against Julie.

"The Madam has arrived," Julie sneered.

"Her name is Polly Easom Kohler." He'd never understand why Julie had to denigrate others in the art world. Polly had supported him through thick and thin. At times, she'd been dearer to him than his own mum. And since she had celebrated her seventieth birthday, her patronage was at the top of his mind. "She is loyal and influential."

"Sure about that?" Julie asked. "She has a lot of control over the who, what, and wheres of you and your work."

"You can have that opinion, but here's a tip…the pool of buyers, donors, and creators of art may feel vast, but it isn't. It's quite small. Best not to gossip." He wanted to keep this discussion civil. Julie had a habit of butting her nose into others' business. Truth be told, the end of her summer mentorship came at the perfect time. Her pettiness had worn on him, and after tonight, he would be finished with her malicious nonsense. "Your work is beautiful, Julie. Stay focused. Did you decide on a price for the bar?"

"Yes, sir. Five grand," she snapped, attempting to tug his elbow and lead him to the balcony. "Mrs. Easom Kohler is over there now. You should go greet Her Excellency."

Sinjin yanked his arm free from her grasp. "In a minute. You go ahead. I want to check the labels on the portraits and gather the price lists."

"Why?" She changed the angle of her beret. Tonight's color choice was orange. "Don't you trust me?"

"Not the issue." Sinjin ignored her neediness, a habit he'd learned from his dad, who'd had to deal with his mother's addiction. Sinjin had practiced it daily all summer with Julie. He'd never lost patience with her, even when she tried seducing him while he'd been welding a sculpture. She'd shoved her breasts into him, and he almost burned her with a blowtorch. Bloody hell. Her stunt had added on extra years to his thirty-eight. "Why don't you talk to Polly about your work. She may be interested in purchasing it. Five thousand dollars isn't too steep of a price for her."

"Whatever." With a defiant swagger, Julie strolled out to the balcony. At her exit, the stress creeping up his back plummeted down and disappeared. He thought about switching out the dress shoes for his sneakers, but instead, he went to one of the buffet tables. Loading a cracker with a pile of blue cheese, he shoved it in his mouth. Wisconsin's cheeses, even the proper Stiltons, were as delicious if not better than the English versions.

As guests arrived, his tensions and concerns dissipated. He hovered near the glass sliding doors, open to allow easy access between the gallery and the balcony. The sun had set, too early for his liking, but the cool breeze felt refreshing. It swept fallen foliage around, and folks unwittingly crunched on a beginning pallet of yellow and orange leaves under their feet.

Claire and Lucy talked to Polly and Julie. Claire's violet eyes caught him. He fiddled with his tie as a gesture of thanks. She winked and turned to the other women. Sinjin briefly considered if Polly would recognize Claire as the daughter of Raffen, then refocused on the business of the exhibit. Some heavy hitters were interested in purchasing these portraits, and if he sold all of them, he would have a hefty amount in the coffers for next summer's student retreat.

Sinjin greeted his old mate Quinn Laughton as he strolled around the gallery with his girlfriend, Sadie. The renovation work on the cabins would be in the capable hands of Quinn come next spring. When Sinjin had purchased the camp-ground, the walls and windows of the cabins were in such disrepair they were barely habitable. Quinn would make them right.

He then met up with two of his biggest sponsors as they admired Raffen's drawing of Claire. *Shite*. He'd been so discombobulated after meeting and recognizing her he'd forgotten to tag it as NFS.

Polly's son, Craig, and his friend Ryan, a onetime MLB player, were nearly pressing their noses against the protective glass. Those two could succumb to a bidding war for the drawing, but Sinjin kicked the idea out of his brain.

"Evening, mates," he said, interrupting their inspection. "This drawing isn't in the same stratum as the other artists tonight. It's done by the incomparable David Raffen."

"But is it really his work?" Craig set his chin in his palm and continued to stare at the drawing of Claire as a girl. "I don't have the same level of expertise as my mother, but how are we to know that this isn't one of the forgeries?"

"Sinjin knows his stuff," Ryan said, vouching for him. "Right?"

"Absolutely," he said, forgoing an exasperated *fuck*. "Yes. This is from a series of drawings done by Raffen in the nineties. One of the first purchases in my collection, and I'll continue to collect his work despite the smear campaign brought against him a few years ago. There's not a lick of bloody truth to that critic's obscene story." He cast an eye on Claire's young face in the drawing, pulled the stickers from his inside jacket pocket, and stuck a red dot on the label. "Sorry to say, gents. My mistake. This piece isn't for sale."

"Wait," Craig said. "I meant no disrespect. It's a hell of a drawing. My mother—"

"—can be a sore loser," Ryan said, "but not me. How much do you want for it, Sinjin?"

Unwittingly, he'd triggered the desire to want something unattainable. As tempting as it was, Sinjin wouldn't initiate a bidding war. The drawing of Claire had to stay in his collection. "Sorry, Ryan. You snooze, you lose," Sinjin said. "Go have a drink at the bar. It's on me. They're mixing up brilliant old-fashioneds."

As the two men laughed off their loss, they continued to survey the rest of the portraits in the gallery. Polly approached slowly, using the assistance of a cane he'd welded for her. A life-long tennis player, she'd had to replace one knee. He met and lightly hugged the grand dame of the plumbing industry. "How's the rehab going?"

"Painstaking, but worth it. I'll be able to play again by the end of the year."

"Are you almost done with the cane?" he asked.

"It's a work of art, so don't expect it back anytime soon. Where's Craig? Did he put an offer in on the Raffen?"

Sinjin grimaced. "Slight glitch, Polly. I took it off the market."

She aimed her cane at the balcony, where Claire, behind the tulip-covered bar, filled glasses to the brim with wine. "That woman. I'd recognize those eyes anywhere. She has to be Raffen's daughter. Where on earth did she appear from?"

"The Lafferty Museum. She's working with that prize arse Larry Chambers," he said, grabbing another cracker and popping it into his mouth. "She showed up this morning asking about *Coal or Steam*."

"Oh, oh. You think he's up to his old tricks?"

Sinjin didn't want to admit it, but since Claire had shown up on his doorstep, he'd been fighting this nagging feeling that Larry, and his ex-wife, were coming for *Coal or Steam*. He glanced at the shelf, now empty, where he'd displayed the piece after getting it back, only then forced to hide it again from Meg. If he hadn't acted fast, the day would have come when the piece was on the black market. "I believe so, but…"

"You think she's working for Larry."

His shrug was barely visible under his suit jacket.

She stared at Raffen's drawing of the young Claire. "Those purple eyes. The color of royalty and new beginnings. Easy to trust, but best to be wary."

Polly was right. He had to keep his wits about him. He despised the Lafferty, and Larry and Meg were beyond hate. But he couldn't be sure how or if Claire fit into their scheming. His mind had already been influenced by other parts of his body. He scanned the balcony and landed on Claire.

"Not sure if she's a stooge who's succumbed to Larry's charms or working on her own. I have no fucking idea."

"Do you want me to ring Mina Lafferty?"

"Are you volunteering to be my spy?"

She tapped her foot with her cane. "I'm moving slowly, bored as hell, and the US Open is finishing up. I might as well be of use to someone other than Julie. My heart goes out to the woman. I bought the bar from her. Do you think she knows her skin is an unappealing shade of chartreuse?"

"No, I... No." Sinjin took hold of Polly's hand. "And any calls you want to make would be wonderful."

Although hesitant to confess it, Sinjin was glad to be back in the art world with his good mates and confidants surrounding him. He hoped he could include Claire in this group of trusted confidants, but whenever the Lafferty came up, a sliver of doubt remained.

Chapter 7

Claire had uncorked so many bottles of wine that her thumb started to ache. Like a master sommelier of a three-ring circus, she poured glass after glass of wine. A couple of men hovered near her, looking like they wanted to ask her something, but she focused on the other guests to dissuade them from starting any kind of personal conversation.

Inside the gallery, Sinjin appeared and disappeared between the display panels. When visible, she caught him flirting with the many blue-haired ladies who had followed him about the gallery as he talked about the artwork. Occasionally the gals broke into laughter as if they were at a high school dance.

Lucy slipped behind the wine bar and shoved a silver platter filled with stuffed mushroom caps toward her. "Here. Go sit and eat."

Claire inhaled the earthy scent of sage from the mushroom stuffing, and her mouth watered. She'd last eaten that morning. "I can't."

Her conscience kept tugging on her. She felt sneaky, even though she hadn't done anything illicit. That painting should never have been moved out of Anita's gallery. None of the *Seasons* should have found their way into the art world.

"There's an original Claire Beaumont in Sinjin's living room," she whispered to Lucy.

"No way." Lucy set the tray of mushrooms down on the bench and pulled her away from those around within hearing range. When no one could hear them, she said, "Those four paintings of yours should be under lock and key in New York. Are you sure?"

"It's hanging in the living room. The woman with red lipstick in the painting is my mother. It's *Fever*."

"What are you going to do?" Lucy asked.

"Damn if I know." Claire's stomach ached. She'd told herself over and over that what she'd done, she did out of loyalty. But it was really an act of desperation, simply desperate measures to get through a horrible time. "You're the only one, Lucy. You know I did those paintings only because he was miserable. My dad could barely lift a paintbrush."

"Let's figure it out. Go to the worst-case scenario. What would happen if Sinjin discovered that his Raffen painting, *Fever*, is a forgery?"

"I'd have no recourse but to set the record straight about my dad. His reputation, already destroyed, would never make a comeback. Even with inserting *More Lace Please* into *Vectors* it's a slim chance. Very thin. My design of placing the celebrity of Sinjin's sculpture with an original Raffen to restore my dad's image is probably a pipe dream."

Lucy gave her a hug. "No one is the wiser about the *Seasons*. And maybe the universe is sending you a message. Telling you that it's your time to step out of your dad's shadow. You're a great painter, too."

Claire flexed her left hand. After trying to paint a damn cloud onto a damn sky, she'd dropped the brush this morning. The progress on her latest piece had come to a screeching halt.

"I appreciate your flattery, but it will get you nowhere. People have expectations. And rich artsy types like Sinjin have exceedingly high expectations when it comes to their valuable collections."

"Take one thing at a time. First, figure out where the other paintings in the series are," Lucy said. "Later, when we get home, you should call that gallery in New York."

Claire popped one of the mushrooms into her mouth.

Lucy added, "Go sniff around. I'll man the bar. No one's asked for a smoothie for over an hour. But be careful, my mom has been on a rampage lately. Try to stay out of her sight."

"Are you familiar with this place?"

"Sort of. My mom has talked about how many nooks and crannies there are in this house. She gets lost. Although she knows Sinjin's bedroom is upstairs in the loft."

"Bedroom sounds good. Artists always store paintings in closets. At least my dad did."

"It's quietening down," Lucy said. "I don't think this shindig is going to last much longer."

Claire took the platter, now empty of mushrooms, and set it in the kitchen. Fred and Ginger were asleep in their crates. She ventured into Sinjin's private residence, scoffing at *Fever* when she passed through the man cave. Once in the alcove, she hopped up a staircase, located the loft area, and steadily padded down a long, carpeted hallway.

Am I nuts?

At each door, she pressed her ear to the wood and listened for voices. Then she carefully turned the egg-shaped doorknob and cracked the door open to see if there was any kind of artwork. The hallway's row of mission-style sconces gave Claire enough illumination to distinguish shadows and outlines in each room. The first couple of rooms surprised her. They were empty; bare walls and cork flooring. She clicked the doors shut without an echo. The third and fourth were workout rooms. Ah ha. So Sinjin *did* sweat like everyone else. He wasn't just born with expansive shoulders.

Focus.

At the end of the hall, a floor-to-ceiling window looked out over Lake Michigan. The boat lights twinkled on the moonlit water. She relaxed a smidge since she'd heard nothing, and thankfully, no one in this isolated stretch of Sinjin's house. Opening the door on her left, she found his bedroom at last.

Inside the room, cool air clung to her bare arms and legs. A scent of lake water mixed with sand permeated her nose. Blindly, she rubbed the wall for a toggle and scraped her hand against a rough edge. After flicking on a light, droplets of blood covered her knuckles. She sucked the wound to contain her case of the jitters.

Why was she doing this again? Oh, right, to find the two *Seasons*. But what would she do if she came across them? She shouldn't be sneaking around a stranger's house, but Sinjin had expressed an intense interest in knowing more about her father. She concentrated. A sense of guilt slithered through her. One peek around, and she'd get the hell out of there.

A crystal chandelier hung from the ceiling above a four-poster king-size bed. The star-shaped crystals cast shadows on a flagstone wall as the light grew brighter. Seemed appropriate that a room in a Frank Lloyd Wright home had a fireplace in a bedroom. Above the mantel hung a painting by Helen Frankenthaler. The artist's bold watery strokes of color mesmerized Claire for a long second until she snapped back to the task at hand.

She spotted the closet, ventured into it, and whispered, "Eureka."

In the walk-in closet, shelves lined with dividers housed a multitude of paintings. Just like in their Chicago brownstone where her dad had stored canvases. He rarely thought about clothing.

She aimed her phone light to see the neatly stored pieces. All of the frames were gold-flecked wood or stained wood. Her dad had carefully curated his frame choices and always used black. The other *Seasons* were not in this space.

What a damn relief.

Grabbing the knob to exit, she heard the click of the bedroom door shut. She shoved her phone into her cummerbund and held her breath. Hidden in the dark closet with the door ajar, she spied through the crack expecting to see Sinjin. Instead, Julie tiptoed about the bedroom.

After a step, then a twirl, Julie caressed the bed with both palms open. Then she picked up a pillow and hugged it. Humming quietly, she lovingly stacked the pillow with the others on the head of the bed. Julie paused by the dresser and opened the top drawer. Searching briefly, she pocketed a bulky object. Socks? Suddenly, she turned toward the closet. Claire took a quick step back, relieved that the squeaky cork floor was covered with a thick braided throw rug. She stayed perfectly still, certain Julie would bust her.

But then, Sinjin's voice boomed in the bedroom.

"What the hell are you doing in here?" His British accent sounded harsh.

"Someone was occupying the bathroom. I came in here to find a clean towel. The lights were on."

"I'd appreciate it if you wouldn't wander around the house when I still have guests in the gallery."

Damn. Claire couldn't move. She prayed the two of them wouldn't hear her heart slamming against her rib cage.

"Right, no problem. I love your bedroom," Julie said. "Any chance I could get a tour when you don't have an audience downstairs? I've never seen this area of your house. It's beautiful."

"I don't sleep in here. It's a room for my father. Have you been drinking?" he asked, stepping near the dresser.

To face him, Julie turned with both hands behind her back. Claire caught the twinkle of a small and shiny object in her fingers. She must have stolen something else from the drawer. As Julie slipped her hand into the side pocket of her blousy dress, Claire recognized the object—a cufflink.

"No. I haven't had a drop of hooch." Julie caressed his cheek. "Tonight is important for you. Really, I needed towels for the guest bathroom and expected them to be in here." She walked past him and out of the bedroom. Sinjin glanced around the room, left, and shut the door.

Claire held her breath until her phone pinged. Exhaling, she silenced the message. Before making a break and getting the hell out of the closet, she waited to make sure Sinjin wouldn't come back in.

Pacing and hugging herself, she got choked up thinking about her father again. He was a gifted man, and one golf-ball size tumor—intricately woven in his brain—robbed him of his sight and then killed him.

After brushing the damn tears off her cheeks, she slipped back into the bedroom and halfheartedly opened the drawer to see what had made Julie—clearly obsessed with Sinjin—into a thief. It was mainly full of white T-shirts, and Claire gently tossed one aside. Underneath was a velvet box of beautiful antique cufflinks with one spot empty. She closed the drawer, and the doorknob clicked...

It sounded like an explosion in her head.

Damns tumbled in her mind like socks in a dryer. She dropped on all fours and crawled under the bed. The little air she'd managed to save in her lungs stayed.

She twisted her head to see who was coming back into the bedroom from deciphering the footwear—Julie's flip-flops or Sinjin's dress shoes. The dress shoes won. From her lowland vantage point, she spotted his socks. They were the red, white, and blue of a Union Jack.

He went into the closet, so she seized her chance and stealthily crawled backward from underneath the opposite side of the king-size bed.

The wool rug burned her bare knees. The tiny skirt she wore shimmied up around her waist. *Great.* A weird thumping sound came from the direction of the bedroom door. She paused before backing out further. *Busted and exposed.* Nothing could get more embarrassing. Until two furry creatures started rubbing against her legs. Fred and Ginger. They sniffed her ankles as her butt protruded from underneath the bed. They must have been in doxie-snout heaven while their cold noses snuffled her bare calves and thighs.

"Would you mind telling me what you're doing under there?" Sinjin dropped to all fours and lowered his face under the bed. Fred and Ginger licked his cheeks.

"Under here?" She flattened to the floor. "I'm inspecting for dust bunnies."

He shushed the excited dogs. "I have a cleaning lady. I'm certain she's hoovered under the bed."

Claire edged out and sat on the floor. The doxies jumped around and licked her rug-burned knees. Petting their silky fur calmed her down.

He stood and offered her his hand.

She grasped it and let him pull her upright. She stood erect to make sure he knew his height didn't intimidate her. But at her full height of five eight, she needed to stand on her toes to be eye-to-mouth with him.

She picked an imaginary piece of lint off her skirt. "Your cleaning lady did an inferior job."

"Why are you in here?"

The steel-edged tone in his voice made her shiver.

"Tell me. Why are you in *my* guest room and not down-stairs assisting Lucy?"

"I…" Inches away from Sinjin's face, she lost her focus.

Her secret mission disintegrated up in smoke. She clenched her hands—her palms were slick with sweat. "Need to find…"

She glanced up. His straight lips and flat stare froze her. He wanted, no, demanded some logical explanation as to why she had invaded his private domain. She didn't have a reason; she couldn't even find a word. She nibbled on the inside of her thumb.

He crossed his arms.

She stepped back to create more space between them but bumped into the end of the bed.

"What is it that you want, Claire? At my house and gallery. Were you sneaking around the studio, too?"

Had she lost her mind?

He glared at her with pure disgust, and a tiny ping chipped her self-preservation.

"I wanted to see if I could find *Coal or Steam*," she blurted out.

"You're conniving with the wanker? Is Larry paying you?" He paced in front of her.

"What are you talking about?" Utterly confused, she staggered backward and tried to escape. With her back pressed against the mahogany door, he stood inches away and over her.

"You're never going to get near my sculpture. Nor will the arse you work for. The Lafferty won't get it."

"Wait. I…" she sputtered. "What do you think…"

She couldn't finish. Sinjin opened the door, forcing her to stumble away from it.

"Please leave my house, Claire Raffen or Beaumont or whatever your name is."

"I'm so—" She straightened her shoulders, walked out the door, and turned to face him. She'd expected to see anger still emanating from him, but instead, he looked completely demoralized. Even sad. "Sorry. Good night, Sinjin."

She paused in the foyer to catch her breath. All the noises

around her were muffled by the blood rushing in her head. The kitchen door swung open, and the stainless-steel door cracked against the stone wall.

Julie stepped out. Threads of yellow hair had stuck to her sweaty forehead. While glowering at Claire, she wiped her hands on the cheese-colored dress. "Leaving?"

"I'm going outside for fresh air." She stared at Julie's dress. The ugliest piece of clothing she'd seen in ages. It was a potato sack with layers of orange fabric. Julie had stuffed her right fist into her right pocket, and it didn't budge. Claire could tell the socks and cufflinks were still in it.

"Tonight's been wonderful. I love your beret."

"Sure," Julie announced with a mouthful of doubt.

Claire checked around to make sure Sinjin hadn't made his way down from the loft. She wanted to say something to Julie but wasn't sure what, when the two men hovering around the bar earlier came over to her.

"There you are," one of them said, holding a hand out in front of her. "I'm Craig Kohler, and this is my buddy Ryan Braun. A baseball legend. We've been looking for you."

Julie strode back into the gallery, her flip-flops slapping the cork flooring loudly.

Claire grasped onto Craig's hand and shook it hard. "You aren't stalkers, are you?" she joked and then shook Ryan's hand.

"Not unless you consider fans of David Raffen stalkers," Ryan said with a handsome smile.

Claire knew nothing about baseball except how the world stopped when the Cubs won the series. She did, however, take this opportunity to get out of the damn house before Sinjin came around. "I was just going out. I can tell you a lot about David Raffen."

Outside with the two men, Claire took in a deep, cleansing breath of brisk fall air. She graciously answered as Craig and

Ryan asked her questions about her father. When Craig asked about a drawing of her, she was taken aback. "A drawing of me?"

"It's in the gallery. I'd say you're about twelve or so," Craig said. "I put an offer on it, but Sinjin's not biting. Staying in his collection."

Ryan stared at her. "It's definitely you. The eyes. They're a perfect match."

She blinked self-consciously. Her dad had painted a lot of portraits, but drawings of her? How had she missed it in the gallery? Too busy figuring out the forgery debacle.

After exchanging contacts with the two men, she sat on the hood of Lucy's truck and waited for her ride. At last, Claire had a chance to read the message from earlier. Mina had responded.

Stay in Lake Bluff. I'm meeting with Polly Easom. We'll touch base when I get there.

Claire lay back on the hood and gazed at the sky. So many stars, all of them shining and twinkling down on her, yet she closed her eyes. Today had been bad but not terrible. That day had been when she'd laid her father to rest and said her last goodbye to him.

Art & Form Review

In Memoriam-The Tragedy of David Raffen
By Arthur Silver

There is no better way to celebrate the death of an artist than the showing of a lifetime's work. With each piece at Finegold Gallery, the life of David Raffen was on display in a spectacular tribute to his portraiture career.

Every wall on all three levels of the Finegold brownstone displayed a Raffen portrait. Many of which had been in storage. Sadly, the paintings outnumbered the mourners.

The curiosity of the few paying homage to a brilliant twentieth-century portrait artist permeated the air in each room like a musty odiferous towel hung out to dry. The glory of what was once called *the talent and genius of David Raffen* had fallen on hard times. His tarnished reputation and questioned authenticity will surround and stagnate the artist long after his death.

It was a heady experience to again view the portraits—*Seasons.*

Except one of the four *Seasons*, *Golden*, was absent from the exhibit. After bumping elbows with Raffen at the Armory Show last year, his work in those four paintings continued to boggle my imagination. Although I was rebuked by a longtime colleague, I was saddened but not surprised when the Royal Society of Portrait Painters demoted David Raffen and removed his other works from the permanent exhibit in London. Apparently, rumors regarding Raffen and his work continue to circulate and flourish.

Anita Finegold has aged gracefully but required assistance from her great-niece, Lindsey Finegold. The setting of Raffen's memorial was unusual as those attending had to maneuver around a hospital bed situated on the main floor of the gallery. Will Finegold Gallery go on with the loss of David Raffen? He was Anita's sole client and, at one time, her bread and butter. After his heady decline left him without fans or followers, will she survive in the cutthroat business of contemporary art sales?

The loss of David Raffen will be felt dramatically in some circles, but only the closest of fanatics. Unfortunately, in the world of contemporary art, collectors, patrons, supporters, and enthusiasts have moved on from Raffen's life, but the rumors will continue to soar high and far, long past his death. **@ArtSilver**

Chapter 8

The barking dogs hopped around his mattress, demanding Sinjin get his arse up and let them outside. All night, he'd tossed and turned. The image of Claire—completely confused —floated in and out of his head. Had he gone bloody crackers? But she'd been snooping around his guest bedroom. Had he been too reactive? He didn't think he was nuts in asking her to leave, but maybe too rude. Groaning, he got up to take care of Fred and Ginger. Then, he'd find Claire to apologize.

Sinjin headed to Maxwell's. When he tried to park on Main Street, the road was blocked off for Lake Bluff's annual fall festival. The streets were open to people who came to stroll about, shop, eat, and partake in the equinox celebration. He'd been so absorbed with last night's opening he'd forgotten about today's festival. Ages ago, it had been an annual tradition to go with his father and two brothers.

After parking the truck, he maneuvered through the growing crowd on the street and strode into Maxwell's, where a few women were perusing the eclectic array of goods. He heard Lucy—or the whir of one of her blenders—concocting something at her juice bar.

Although he'd rehearsed an apology in his head repeatedly, it evaporated at the sight of Claire. Yesterday, he was operating on automatic. Yes, he'd noticed her, but today in a different environment, she wasn't the daughter of a famous painter or a subject of a fabulous drawing. Claire was flesh and blood and brilliantly gorgeous.

As soon as she spotted his approach, she crossed her arms over her chest. A defensive move. He deserved it. He slowed his pace and kept his mouth straight, hopefully showing her how sorry he'd been after his miserable performance last night. At the counter, he made sure to keep a safe distance. "I was a fucking wanker last night. I'm sorry. Will you give me a chance to explain?"

"Told you," Lucy chimed in, glancing at her watch, then at Claire. "I said by nine o'clock. It's five past. He's only a little late."

He gave both women a guilty grin. "Forgot about the festival. My bad." It soothed his nerves, knowing how predictable he'd become the past year. Since Meg had left his life in upheaval, he'd worked hard to achieve a steady routine. "Thanks for…everything. The exhibit was a smash, and I sold almost all the pieces."

"Why don't you and Claire get out of here and enjoy the festival," Lucy said. "I have to set up my apple cider sale on the sidewalk."

He stared at Claire with a hopeful expression. At least, he hoped it was hopeful. "I can show you the Kohler Preserve. If you're up for it."

Her nod seemed slow and calculating, but then she said yes. "The museum has been on my list of must-sees."

He hadn't considered asking Claire out on a date, but now that he'd done it, a hint of relief came over him. Connecting naturally with other people outside of his studio hadn't been part of his daily routine since Meg left last winter. And while mentoring Julie, he'd ignored his social skills and relied solely on his teaching skills to guide him along. "It's a good festival, this fall bash," he said as they strode through the store.

She stopped next to a clothing rack, forcing him to take a step backward. "All right?"

"I appreciate your apology, but I wasn't my normal self in your room last night. I don't usually go snooping around other people's private living areas. I'll say it again, I'm really sorry."

The color of her vibrant eyes flickered and then dimmed. Before his throat tightened, he spoke up. Probably too fast. "Can we...let's...start fresh?"

As if in slo-mo, she slipped her phone into her messenger bag. He flexed his fingers and scratched the back of his neck to appear calm. He was anything but.

She gave him a tenuous smile and said, "It's an art thing, I guess. *Vectors* has made me nuts with stress, so I really can't blame you for your reaction last night. I'm good with do-overs."

He silently exhaled.

Outside, many of the shops had already set up booths to sell their wares on the sidewalk. Folks milled around, and the morning had brought in a sizable crowd of tourists for the day-long festival. He shortened his steps to stay near Claire. When she paused at a vendor selling caramel apples, he cleared his throat. "Looks scrummy."

"Maybe after the museum, we can share one? Too hard to eat alone."

"I agree. I love caramel but hate how it's so sticky." He wiggled his hands and fingers to imitate two spiders.

She chuckled, and he relaxed. He wasn't nervous but definitely out of practice. Sinjin considered if he could take a type of refresher course on how to act on a date. Even though his shrink had suggested a couple of dating apps, he hadn't any interest in meeting another woman. His experience with Meg had damaged him. He'd made progress with his psych's help but continued to feel raw and couldn't risk exposure.

But Claire Beaumont—or was it Raffen?—had shaken him. Yet his nagging curiosity had nothing to do with her namesake or father. He had to know for sure that she wasn't working for Larry Chambers. But what if she did and had planned to nick the sculpture? He shoved the question out to stay in the present.

It was a short drive to the Kohler Preserve. A museum with a collection of indoor and outdoor sculptures that always fired up his creativity.

When they reached the museum with the timbers lining the façade of the entrance, Claire gasped. "This is beautiful."

With bigger-than-life sculptures made of metal, stone, or wood and the full installation of artist environments, it created a dramatic museum that Sinjin appreciated. The organization of elements, from the inside out, offered a rare and unique experience for viewers. The pieces had been installed within their working environment, and the restoration and typical behind-the-scenes work of a museum were on full view for the audience.

As they entered the expansive space, Claire's jaw dropped. Around them were vignettes and displays showing off a collection of self-taught and academically trained artists.

Sinjin hadn't thought about making this a date, but being in a museum with her seemed apropos.

On the first floor were a portion of the lake house and some wood sculptures by Mary Nohl, a Milwaukee artist. He pointed to a rowboat installed in a tree towering above them. "This had been previously located on the Nohl property. Story has it that it was a tribute to Nohl's husband and son, who had died in Lake Michigan."

Claire laughed. "The infamous tale of the witch. And not true. Mary Nohl never married and never had any children."

"Did you ever meet her?"

"No, she died long before I moved to Milwaukee. But Mina Lafferty has been part of this reconstruction of the Nohl house. Her mother was a colleague of Mary's."

Another reminder of the Lafferty. Between Polly and Mina, Sinjin had to overcome his aversion to the museum. He'd let his battered emotions order him around and confine him to a dungeon. His welding studio had become a jail cell. At the exhibit last night, except for Julie, all the guests and even the staff had shown him how gratifying it could be around generous people. With the show's success—all the works had sold, except the one of Claire—Sinjin knew his project to host young artists next summer was solid. And the Lafferty, he admitted, should be part of the equation.

"Are you and Mina close?" he asked, shoving his hands in his jeans pockets.

"She brought me on at the museum. My CV, with a business degree and an MFA in art history, made me knowledgeable, but my curatorial skills weren't as strong as the other applicants. But Mina knew that my restoration and curatorial assignment in Italy was cut short because of my father—" She paused. "—and his situation. When he became sick, I took care of him. Mina has a lot of faith in me."

Having divulged such private information to him, he had to address the elephant in the room. The question that had plagued him since Claire had arrived at his house in a vintage VW. "Are you working with Larry Chambers? Trying to get a hold of *Coal or Steam*?"

She shook her head emphatically. "No. Not at all. I mean, I really do want to see your sculpture, and I'd planned for it to be the highlight in *Vectors*. But Larry Chambers is a horrible person."

He couldn't agree more.

"The reason Mina hired me," she said, "wasn't because of

my artsy history but because of my business sense. The Lafferty is losing money. Since her cancer diagnosis, Mina has been so busy taking care of herself she couldn't figure out why. Although it's rooted around Larry. We're both sure that he's cooking the books. But just don't know how he's doing it."

With this not-so-surprising news, his aversion to Larry catapulted. The Lafferty was a brilliant museum in Milwaukee and should not go down because of the arse.

"Claire, I..." Relief spread through him. "I'm so happy to hear you say this. I don't know much, except Larry is getting help from my ex-wife, with whom he's had an affair. Meg is one of the museum's directors at large. They know that the value of *Coal or Steam* is well over a hundred grand and have been trying to get their hands on it for the past two years. They're like Boris and Natasha. It might behoove us to work together to ensure the Lafferty stays open."

⸻

AS WITNESS to way too much at Sinjin's house the night before, Claire hadn't been able to scrub the thoughts from her brain. Between *Fever* and Julie, she had flopped back and forth all night. It didn't help that when she tried to contact L. Finegold Gallery, it was closed due to a show in Basel, Switzerland.

Now, standing in front of her was a man who had shared with her a heartbreaking detail of his life. She wanted to wrap her arms around Sinjin, then wondered if she should tell him about Julie, his obsessed mentee. But she couldn't even bear the thought of telling her best friend that her mother wasn't quite *right*. Instead, she plopped down on a padded bench near one of Mary Nohl's wooden seven-foot-high creatures.

"Larry Chambers..." she said, watching Sinjin sit beside her. "Is sleeping with your ex?" She wanted to gag but instead shut her eyes and tried to picture her fastidious boss in a relationship with another human being. The man was wound so tight that Claire often mused if he had a belly button. "And her name is Meg Fisher. There are over twenty directors at large; I'm sure Mina has no idea about the affair. But full disclosure, I can't imagine Larry with another human being. Maybe an alien, however."

"Meg has a slight glow that radiates off her. A green tint. Must be her love of money."

"Makes sense, or should I say, C-E-N-T-S. I think Larry has been creating some of his own works of art by painting new numbers into the museum's accounts." Letting out a sigh, she glanced around the Preserve. A vast array of sculptures and paintings surrounded her. No matter what direction she looked, there was an installation of color and texture. Like looking through a kaleidoscope, she could shake her head and see a different painting. "Mina mentioned she would be coming to town. I wish I had more answers for her instead of so many questions."

"Does Larry know you've been working with Mina? Covertly?"

He crossed one leg over the other, and Claire appreciated the way his long, lean legs fit in his jeans, bobbing his one foot up and down.

"Larry is clueless. When we last spoke, he was irate. He called you a liar and insisted you were housing the sculpture."

"Then he's definitely still sleeping with Meg," he said, "as I've had a restraining order on her for the past year. She hasn't been around me or the house. In all likelihood, she assumes *Coal or Steam* is still on my mantel. And shared the location with Larry."

His openness compelled her to be honest. Within limits. "Last night, I said...I may have fibbed. A little." She waited, then watched as he slowly lifted a ginger-hued eyebrow. She forged on. "I wasn't trying to find *Coal or Steam*. I wanted to see your collection of Raffens. When Lucy told me you collected my father's pieces, I wanted to see which ones you owned."

"You were in the wrong closet," he stated. "The pieces in that room belong to George, my dad. It's his room when he stays with me. My collection of works by your father is housed in my cottage. Off-limits to everyone."

"Where is...never mind. None of my business." She knew the property around the house was large and wooded and near the lake. So, a private cottage could have been hidden in the area. "I admit I lied, but I was so damn curious. And then when your buddies—"

"Buddies?"

"Craig and Ryan? Aren't they your buds? Or should I say mates?"

"Right, yes. Go on."

"They mentioned the drawing of me. I hadn't seen it in the gallery. Those are rare. As you probably already know."

His trusting look gave her shivers. For an instant, she got the impression she could tell Sinjin anything. Even the whole truth, but then her survivalist instinct kicked the thought out of her mind. She'd come this far by controlling her fears and maintaining distance. Her boundaries were as consistent as her father's black picture frames. "Anyhoo. It's fantastic to know you're considering the viability of the Lafferty. Mina's family has been instrumental in building an environment to showcase the works of women and their causes."

"I think it's more about moving past my pettiness. Larry Chambers and Meg Fisher can go ride off into the sunset, but they'll have to do it without my sculpture. No reason for me to blame the Lafferty. Or Mina. You're right, it's a brilliant museum." He waved his hand toward the Mary Nohl house on exhibit in front of them. "I seemed to have forgotten that there are many women artists whose work needs TLC. A place to display."

On the verge of tears, she shook her head. "I get how invested you are in your project for next summer. But if I don't figure out how to plug up the drain of funds, the Lafferty will have to close."

"Messing around with the books? What a wanker. It's clear as day he wants the sculpture. But an embezzler? How he can look at himself in the mirror at the end of the day is beyond me."

"Talk about greed. Sucking the life out of everyone is quite an achievement. Is *Coal or Steam* really worth a lot? When it went back on the auction block, it sold for only fifty grand. Quite a trek down since the day in 2008 when it topped out a Jeff Koons sculpture and sold for one million."

"The art world thrives on salacious gossip and rumors. Larry and Meg could probably get around a million for it on the black market. But the last time I checked, it was appraised for around a hundred grand." He rubbed his temples. "What a wicked ride for a sculpture, and I've barely been able to keep up with it. It sold at Sotheby's for five hundred grand, shocking Koons fans. After the hubbub died down, Polly repurchased it from the disgruntled collector for fifty grand and returned it to me. When I discovered Meg and Larry's plan to pinch it, I hid it."

"Those two are so damn conniving. It's tragic. Really. I can't let the Lafferty go down because of them."

"Never thought I'd hear myself say this, but you're right." He paused, then let out a long breath. "The Lafferty is important. I've given Larry too much space—rent-free—in my head. I need to see the bigger," he said, making a square with his fingers, "picture. Ha. Get it?"

She laughed. Her thoughts whirled between the Lafferty, the Raffens, Mina, and then landed on Sinjin. "Money makes us crazy, hey?"

"Are you thinking it's the root of all evil?" he asked.

"I don't know about that, but I do know Larry is wicked," she said, "and it sounds like Meg is, too. They don't seem to understand the amount of pain they're inflicting on so many people around them because of their greed."

"Maybe it's up to us to stop them."

"Agree." Claire's sense of loneliness diminished.

Chapter 9

Sinjin lightly placed his hand on top of hers. "I'm sorry if I've overstepped and sound like a demanding twit. I don't expect you to drop all that you're doing and come fight Larry and my ex with me. It's enough on your plate to keep the Lafferty's doors open. And your own exhibit is important."

"You're right. My exhibit is significant and yet complicated. I'd been struggling to compile a collection of pieces that are solid representations of the role of women during the industrial age. The steampunk genre seems to encompass it." She sighed. "I've nailed it, but unfortunately, it hasn't gained much traction in the media. But when we included your sculpture, the hits on the website bumped up substantially. Interest spiked."

"Was it Larry's idea to include it?" he asked with a hint of regret.

Now his nemesis threatened to destroy another person's livelihood, not to mention cause the collapse of a dynamic museum. Sinjin couldn't turn a blind eye to Larry and Meg's original scheme to get his sculpture. He couldn't prove a thing because the two hadn't taken any obvious steps indicating they intended to steal his sculpture. He had heard rumors, and when he caught the two of them in bed together, he was certain.

Standing abruptly, Claire walked over to one of the bigger-than-life size wood statues. She turned back and held out her hand. "Let's go through this together. Easier for me to gather my thoughts when in the midst of beautiful works of art. And Mary Nohl's works are exciting. Such an incredible repertoire of pieces. Ceramics, paintings, sculptures."

He grabbed her hand, enjoying the feel of her palm in his as they strolled around the exhibit. Although it wasn't really an exhibit, since the entirety of Mary Nohl's yard, her sculptures and part of the actual house had been moved off her original property and installed within the museum. It was a spectacular example of how to protect and store cherished pieces of art.

"Had they not transferred the sculptures, the elements would have destroyed them since Nohl's house is right on the lake," he said. "Erratic temperatures, cold, humidity, and heat can all take a toll on the life of artwork."

Chuckling, she asked, "So can I assume the artwork in your guest room closet isn't valuable? Sorry, but I couldn't help but notice how the room felt damp and musty. Your house *is* situated beside the lake."

"True. Short-term arrangement. My dad will be taking them when he moves into a condo."

His thoughts wandered to the next time his dad would be coming to Lake Bluff. Should he bring the sculpture? One thing at a time.

"*Coal or Steam* is famous because it went for a higher price than one of Jeff Koons's balloon-style pieces. I think it may have been a fluke, but it worried Koons fans. How could a newcomer outbid the beloved Koons?"

"Never a fan of the guy. His sculptures are too simple and childlike," she added, "and way overpriced. Did you hear about how someone thought one of his pieces was an actual balloon? And broke it?"

"I heard. They should have put a Do Not Touch sign on it." The rough texture of one of the wood statues tempted him to touch it, but he resisted. "Um, *Coal or Steam* may be a good fit in an exhibit such as yours. I built it for my dad," he said, then paused. "The design of the sculpture is a tribute to Polly and her company. Immigrant families ran it, and the industry boomed at the turn of the century. I was being cheeky but showed off the brilliance of indoor plumbing from a bygone era. I'd been a big Rube fan back then."

"It's perfect for my exhibit, but I understand why it needs to stay wherever it is. There's no need to take any risks. Especially with Larry and Meg on the loose."

"The wanker has to be stopped," he announced. "I missed my first chance. I'm not going to give him another opportunity. Whatever his con is, he—they should be stopped. Especially now that the life of the Lafferty is at stake."

He let her lead him into the Mary Nohl room, and they stopped to watch the video displaying shots of her home as it stood in Milwaukee. Around them, much of her ceramic collection was in glass cases, and the walls were lined with her colorful paintings.

Claire stepped away from the video and gazed at a painting. Her profile—long black lashes, flushed cheek, and slightly pursed lips—clarified for him why her father had drawn her so often when she was younger.

"Quit gawking at me." She faced him. "You're doing that artsy thing. Always processing a subject."

He'd been caught red-handed. "It's a natural reaction from teaching so many drawing classes at the Art Institute. It's difficult to find subjects. You would have been a great model for Drawing 101."

"I know. Thanks to my dad." She tugged his hand, and

they left the space. Her furrowed eyebrows and creased forehead worried him. She let go of his hand and straightened to her full height. "I have something to tell you. But I'm unsure. It's none of my business, really."

He attempted to keep his chronic trust issues from rising to the surface. Calmly, he spoke. "I've learned a lot in the past two years. Some of it ridiculous, some of it not, but holding on to worry is the worst."

Her smile reminded him of the drawing. What a relief he'd taken it off the market last night. "Not to change the subject, but would a caramel apple help you out?"

"I'm all about caramels and apples. But this is about my best friend's mom, and I need to get it off my chest." She fidgeted. "It isn't any of my business, but last night, before you came into the bedroom, Julie, well, acted strangely. Very possessed. By your belongings. Specifically, your bedding. Then she stole something out of the drawers. My best guess, I think, is a pair of cufflinks?"

This news didn't take him by surprise but did concern him. He shoved his hands into his pockets. "*Shite*. I'm not sure what else I can do for Julie. As her mentor, I've kept our relationship completely professional. Julie is incredibly talented. She's expressed an interest in lengthening her mentorship, but..." It was a relief to tell Claire about his deep-buried worry. "But... her issues have kept me at arm's length. Our working relationship ended with the opening last night, and that may have spurred her. But stealing cufflinks?"

"Do you think I should give the details to Lucy? Although, she already has her hands full with her mother and knows all her pitfalls. This wouldn't be new news for her."

He sighed. "I've been straight up with Julie all summer, and Lucy knows how much I admire her mom. Let's take, I mean, I can keep tabs on the two of them. Not as if I'm moving out of town. And now..." He was about to say *you're here* but squashed it. "Since the mentorship is over, I won't have as much contact with her, which may be a good break."

"What a relief," she said. "Now, I'm starving and would love to eat. How about you?"

He nodded. As they drove back to Main Street, he thought about Julie. Truly strange and somewhat terrifying. The cufflinks weren't a complete mystery. She had forever complained about money, and the links were worth a few quid. But where he'd file it in his brain, he didn't know. Which was okay. He glanced at Claire and decided this moment with her was mega. His shrink would be proud of him.

———

EVERYTHING SINCE MEETING Sinjin had Claire's head spinning in a million directions. From playing waitress at a celebrated artist's opening to discovering *Fever* and viewing the Nohl exhibit, she was dizzy. Yet, his presence energized her frazzled nerves.

After they returned to the festivities on Main Street, she ordered two caramel apples—one covered with M&M's and the other covered with peanuts. The Victorian Shoppe, a candy store across from Maxwell's, had been tempting her since she'd arrived in town.

She held both treats out for Sinjin to choose from and anxiously waited to see his preference. The sweet apple with chocolatey M&M's or the savory one covered with a load of salty peanuts?

Sinjin picked the peanuts as she'd expected. Like her father, a true Brit.

"What?" he asked as they strolled over to the only empty picnic table on the street. "Did I disappoint you?"

A ludicrous idea. "Not in the least. It was a hunch. That's all. Brits enjoy their savories…meat pies and such. Which works best for me." She picked off one of the M&M's and popped it into her mouth. "So, you're not shocked about Julie obsessing over you?"

"Not now. I'm actually more concerned about trying to figure out how…" He struggled to cut the gooey and hard apple with a plastic knife. "To save the Lafferty."

All *she* thought about was how to save his poor apple. Before he mangled it, she dug her Swiss Army knife out of her bag and handed it over. "Try this. Might free up some time. You know…for saving the Lafferty."

"Ta." Sinjin took the knife and painstakingly cut the apple.

She bit into her own apple and watched as he organized the apple slices in a circle on the plate. He reminded her of *Monk*. She wondered if there were any wipes in her bag.

While Sinjin ate one slice of apple, speared onto the end of the knife, she took a big chomp of caramel-laden goodness and chewed slowly. She needed time to process all the happenings in the last forty-eight hours, and Sinjin. The caramel apple wouldn't be big enough.

When her phone pinged, she bit down hard on an M&M.

"It's Larry." She wiped her mouth free of apple and chocolate bits. "His daily call to check up on me. What do I say? Should I ignore him?"

"Relax. You're not in any trouble. You know Mina will have your back. Polly, too, when you see her. I'm here…too."

His words immediately made her feel calmer. "Thanks," she said, picking up the call. Instead of hiding away from Sinjin this time, she stared at him while speaking to Larry.

"Why aren't you back?" Larry sputtered. "In Milwaukee?"

Claire straightened her shoulders even though he couldn't see her. "I've decided to take the week off and explore Lake Bluff and Kohler. I visited the Preserve Museum, and it really inspired me. Given me new ideas for my show. I don't think I'll need to include Sinjin Reid's sculpture."

"That's idiotic," he screeched. "You're all beauty and no brains."

She set the phone down, tapped it on speaker, and closed her mouth. She wanted Sinjin to hear every foul word coming from Larry Chambers.

"Ms. Beaumont, your exhibit is a small show. Barely noteworthy. Not even mentioned in *Milwaukee Magazine* last month. Including *Coal or Steam* is essential. Were you able to see or discover its whereabouts? As I told you, he has the sculpture. My source is credible. Not gossip."

"Meg," she mouthed to Sinjin.

He gave her a thumbs-up.

"I haven't been near Sinjin Reid since yesterday. There wasn't another opportunity to meet with him or go to his house." Unsure why, but she relished how easily lying to Larry had become. "I'm visiting friends in the area."

"Well, I suggest you find a way to get back into his house. He's a pushover for pretty women, so use your beauty and go see him again. The Lafferty needs his donation. As you know, it will make or break this place."

There were so many levels of *inappropriate* with her boss's demands she didn't know how to respond. Larry had some nerve. Damn him. He wanted the sculpture come hell or high water. "What are you saying, Larry? Prostitute myself to get a sculpture for my employer? Pretty disgusting."

"Not in the least," he said in a higher pitch. "You misunderstand me. I'm merely making a suggestion. Sinjin Reid is celebrated in the art world and is accustomed to fans of all sorts making their way to him. It's a logical conclusion that with the way you look, he'd be interested in you. Use your strengths, Ms. Beaumont."

She wanted to find Larry and punch his smug face. A fire started to flicker in her stomach. For the sake of the Lafferty, she needed to expose Larry and stop all of his devious plans. She gazed at Sinjin, hoping for some kind of wisdom.

Sinjin mouthed, "Hold."

"Wait a minute, Larry," she said, "you're breaking up. I'm going to move to another spot."

She hit Mute and aimed her middle finger at the phone. "He's such a jerk."

"Hear him out, even though he's from another planet. A mutant. It's better to keep a tosser nearby. Definitely not a friend."

She unmuted the enemy. "What are you asking me to do exactly, Mr. Chambers?"

"I knew you'd see my reasoning," Larry said. "I'm not proposing anything illegal. We both know that's not what I'm about."

"Of course." She rolled her eyes.

"As long as you're staying in Lake Bluff, take time to get to know Sinjin Reid. I'm sure if you use your *strengths*, you two will become well acquainted. He'll eventually show you the sculpture. I have no doubt."

"And then what?" She self-consciously crossed her legs, suddenly feeling as if being forced into a walk of shame.

"Don't worry about the rest. I have the paperwork to prove he donated the sculpture, so I've already spoken to the police in Lake Bluff."

Her jaw dropped. Sinjin's eyes widened. They were the color of gunmetal, which seemed appropriate. "Have you expressed any of this to Mina Lafferty?" she asked.

"None of that is your concern, but no. She needs to concentrate on her treatment, poor woman."

Sticking her finger in her mouth, she pretended to gag. "Well, I'll do my best."

"Not only your best, Ms. Beaumont, because I won't accept failure. Text me at the end of the week with your update."

She ended the call and groaned. "Oh damn. This is insane. Did I hear him correctly? Larry wants me to play up my *strengths*, which in Larry-speak means *feminine wiles*. Basically, seduce you into telling me where the sculpture is?"

She expected Sinjin to be grimacing, but he was smiling and looking downright euphoric. "Have I missed something? I've been asked to...excuse the expression...suck you off. Which is despicable, and you're happy? Or are you actually expecting me——?"

"God. No!"

When he sat beside her, his jean-clad leg touched her bare thigh. She couldn't resist the warmth and made sure not to move.

"This is huge," he said. Remember, I told you about my love of Rube. Rube Goldberg? I'm a lover of twists and turns. Still am. Larry gave us an opportunity to catch him. With the sculpture."

"Didn't you hear him? If you unearth your sculpture, he'll have you arrested."

"Chambers is gormless. I've lived in Lake Bluff long enough to be on good terms with the police department. The top cop attended the opening last night. He would have mentioned it if Larry had really chatted with him."

She squirmed a little in her seat on the picnic bench. She hadn't broken any laws, but a fair amount of guilt resided in her conscience. Until *Vectors* opened and she figured out how the *Seasons* had escaped, she didn't want to get into trouble. "I'm not sure what you're thinking, but I don't really need to butt heads with any cops."

"I don't think, at least hope, it will come to that." Sinjin clutched her hand. "I have an idea. And with Polly and Mina in our corner, we can take down Larry and save the Lafferty."

Trusting Sinjin Reid after knowing him for less than two days concerned her. Was she giving out trust too hastily? She kept her eyes on her apple, now browned from where she'd bitten into it. "I'm not sure what you're thinking, but I'm comfortable working alone. Might be a holdover from gym class. Getting picked last for every team since middle school makes me prefer to go solo."

"I understand you and I just met, and this is a huge ask. Tell Larry whatever you want to about us. I've determined half-truths work as brilliantly as lies."

She better saw his tattoo beneath his shirt. The scrolls of ink formed gears woven into one another. "You really are a Rube superfan."

He glanced down at his arm. "Guilty."

Her thoughts wandered chaotically. How many other people had Larry Chambers slimed? Claire's dedication to Mina was only surpassed by her devotion to her dad. The vileness of Larry had to be stopped.

Since Sinjin had shown her some of his own deep slivers, she didn't feel he was a complete stranger. She could do what was needed, and if it meant giving up her exhibit, so be it. As long as the Lafferty stayed open, there would be other chances to alleviate her guilt and make it up to her father.

"I'm down for whatever your scheme is," she said and took another bite of her apple.

Chapter 10

Sinjin's idea would only work with Claire's help, and together, they could succeed in taking the bastard down. That she'd been picked last during gym class seemed wrong. Taking a whopping chance with him demonstrated she played well in the sandbox. Before launching into his plan, he wanted to talk about her father for no other reason than to find out more about him and her. He also needed to contain his rambling thoughts.

"Do you think you'll have a chance, possibly, to come by my house? Not the studio, but the cottage. I'd love to show you what's in my collection of Raffens."

"That's a damn good pickup line." She swiped a smudge of caramel from her plate and licked it off her finger.

He stared, riveted by the motion. Her lips mesmerized him.

"Not a pickup—" When she dabbed at her mouth with a paper napkin, he blinked. "You were surprised I own some of your father's earlier works. But when I taught drawing in Chicago at the Art Institute, his work examples were top-notch for my 101 students."

"You met him?"

"No, but he was a patron of the Chicago Art Institute."

"I'm grateful you collected my dad's early drawings. Really. But…" She propped her elbows on the table and interlocked her fingers. "I'm agreeing to work as a double agent and only know Larry's side. Please tell me what your plan is to get him."

"Okay. It came to me when we were in the Preserve. Larry needs to get caught red-handed."

"Doing what exactly? I mean, he's managed to remain invisible, getting away with stealing thousands of dollars from the Lafferty, and you said earlier he hasn't shown up and tried to take the sculpture. He's been only, supposedly, using your ex-wife. Lots of artsy rumors won't get Larry arrested."

It seemed a bit foolish. Simply because he'd watched every heist movie made, who was he to think he could get away with an elaborate con like in *Ocean's Eleven*. "Larry is at his wits' end. Probably knows this is his last chance, but he's seeking cover through the Lafferty. By using my sculpture as the bait, we lure him out of his safe zone."

She dropped her arms down on the picnic table. "I'm listening."

His imagination toyed with him. Sinjin's one brother Rob—the angel—sat on one shoulder while his other brother, Angus—the devil—danced on the other. In his head, he heard Rob's lecture on the sanctity of the law and Angus begging him for a role in the heist.

To clear his muddied thoughts, Sinjin bolted to his feet and paced.

"What if you move ahead with including my sculpture in your exhibit? If *Coal or Steam* makes an appearance, there's no doubt in my mind Larry will come after it. So, your show will have to move here. Into my gallery. We reinvent the exhibit however you want it." He recalculated. "I mean, your show doesn't *have* to move anywhere you don't want it to go. My idea is, though, Larry won't have any incentive if it stays at the

Lafferty. If we move it here, he and Meg will come hunting for it."

"Are you suggesting we steal my show from the Lafferty? I don't think any police department will give you a get-out-of-jail-free card."

He stopped pacing. "How about if we say we're borrowing the exhibit?"

"Damn, here I thought you were showing me Mary Nohl's art, and the whole time, you were concocting how to take Larry down while we were in the Preserve."

"Not the whole time. I do love the exhibits in the Preserve. Let's say the organization and transportation aspects of the displays clicked for me. The rub is, however, the only way to capture Larry or, as you say, 'take him down' is by getting him in our territory. And the timing is good. My dad will be coming…" Knowing how hard this truth was going to be, he forced it out. "He's coming here. With my sculpture. I sold it to him for ten dollars."

Claire dropped her head and hid her face under the drapes of hair. He couldn't decipher her reaction, and blood pounded in his ears. *Coal or Steam* was and always would be a jinx. Thinking of the way she'd nearly crumpled to the ground when he'd told her he had sold it made him sick to his stomach.

"Claire? I'm not showing you my best side. You see…I hope you'll understand why I misled you. Here you arrive, inquiring about the sculpture, and once again, my life is at its mercy. I spoke rashly to protect my—" He was about to say *sanity* but didn't think it would sound good. Too much, especially for a first date. "I had to be prudent. There's only been one upside to this work and way, way, too many downs."

"It's interesting to hear you say this." She tucked loose strands of black hair behind her right ear. Her face paled.

Had his cynicism and distrust stolen any chance he may have had with Claire?

"I'm not perfect either."

A heady sense of relief came over him.

"There's no way I could blame you for being judicious and careful. I understand self-preservation. Really."

At the moment, he could take on anything and succeed. Or anyone. Especially Larry Chambers. "It's not a foolproof plan. Getting your show to Lake Bluff and then adding in *Coal or Steam* is more of a rough sketch in my head. But what do you think?"

"I'm not sure. Maybe it could work? Since Mina asked me to keep an eye on Larry, he's revealed to me how truly strange people can be." She shook her head, looking amused. "He has a daily routine. It's carefully constructed…never out of the lines. And he's never taken a vacation. In fact, he's rarely left Milwaukee. He lives on Wahl Street, one of the most prestigious streets in the city. Every one of those old Tudor houses costs more than a million."

"That's a lot of dosh for a nonprofit director," he said. "If that's the case, maybe the chance to be one-on-one with my sculpture will be irresistible. We can make him an offer…" He paused, thought about his tried-and-true Vito Corleone accent, then tossed it. "We, if I can include you in this takeover plan, have to make him more desperate. From his voice on the phone, he already sounds fraught. We'll have to make the pot of gold so shiny he can't refuse our offer."

"And? Go on?" The color came flooding back into her cheeks. "I'm listening."

"Well…" He rubbed his chin, trying to think, but he couldn't focus. He was stuck. It didn't help that the crowd around them had slowly grown, and a blues band had started playing at the end of the block. "I'm spent. Can we move somewhere less populated?"

"How about a smoothie? I think we both need one of Lucy's magical concoctions."

———

THE SOLSTICE FALL festival reminded Claire of the farmers' market in Madison. They slowly made their way through the throngs of strolling and shopping festivalgoers. When they reached the shop, Claire expected to see Lucy selling apple cider in front, but she wasn't there. Instead, a line of people crawled out the front door onto the sidewalk.

Claire and Sinjin scooted past the line, getting a few choice words from those waiting, and entered the shop. It was a madhouse. A line of people wound all the way back to the smoothie bar. Milling around were prospective buyers with arms full of items, searching for someone to check them out. She scanned the crowd for Lucy or her mother and then jogged to Lulu's. She sighted Lucy sweating over six blenders for a full bar of patrons.

"What the hell is going on? And where is Julie? This is a huge festival, and her business is booming," Sinjin said, out of earshot of the customers.

Claire pushed off her irritation. She had no idea what was happening, but for Julie to leave Lucy alone in a store jam-packed with customers? Ridiculous. So, Claire went into action. She waved at Lucy and jogged to the front counter. She greeted the clients who were ready to pay and told them to come on over. Claire knew how to work the payment system from when she helped her dad at art fairs.

"Where do you want me?" Sinjin asked as he relieved a woman of an armload of clothes and set them on the counter. "Good choices," he said to the shopper.

Claire began to ring up the woman. "Check on Lucy. I've

never heard so many blenders droning at once. They might blow a fuse. Then fill in helping out with these buyers."

His walk off to the smoothie bar grabbed Claire's attention. His backside, especially below the hips, bobbed and swayed. *Nice ass.*

"Miss? Can you ring me up? It's getting hot in here, and I want to hear the band playing down the street."

She shook her head to get back to business. "So glad you took the time to shop in Maxwell's." The line in front of her had grown to five women, all wanting to buy items from Julie's store. Damn. Where was the owner?

After she finished ringing up the hefty sales, Claire asked the shoppers if they needed help. The line crawling out the front door had disappeared. Lucy and Sinjin must have succeeded in getting everyone their smoothies.

"This coffee table is gorgeous," a woman said, stroking the smooth copper top. "Are you the artist?"

"No. My friend's mom, she's the creator." *Who should be here.* With her limited knowledge of metals, Claire had a hard time coming up with the piece's attributes. "Hold on. Let me get an expert over. He can explain it to you much better than I can."

The clients in Lulu's were sipping on some drink or another. She waved at Lucy, who looked flushed and sweaty but gave her a thumbs-up. Sinjin broke free from the counter. "What's up? You all right? Things here are slowing down. But shite…Julie is AWOL. Never came in today, according to Lucy. And the part-timer decided to quit. Too much fun at the festival instead of working."

"Figures. About Julie," she said with a clenched jaw. "Can you answer questions about the furniture up front? I'm at a loss. Much better with the clothing deals."

"Sure." Sinjin made a beeline to the shopper in front of the coffee table.

Lucy came up and handed her a tall glass filled with a

pumpkin smoothie. "You two are lifesavers," she said. "Perfect timing."

"Had I known you'd be on your own, I would have come back from the museum earlier."

"Had *I* taken the time to think, I would have known my mother would be a no-show. Last night, she was a basket case. Sure as the blue sky, she's nursing a big ole hangover." Lucy nudged her with an elbow. "So...how's Mr. Hottie over there? Did you two have fun at the Preserve?"

Claire watched as Sinjin chatted up a couple about the metal table. He moved up, down, and all around the low round table, pointing out areas of interest for them.

"He is a honey," Lucy said. "Did you hear anything from New York? About *Seasons*?"

"Nothing yet. I need to make more calls but haven't had a chance. Part of me just wants to ignore it."

"We'll find the answers, girlfriend," she said, then bolted back to her juice bar.

Again, Claire assisted the folks shopping for clothes and knickknacks. When Sinjin asked her to ring up the couple who had decided to buy the coffee table, she silently squealed. What a huge deal. Thanks to Sinjin. The table sold for a thousand dollars. Not bad for rehabbed farm equipment. After the four of them had made all the arrangements for delivery and the couple left Maxwell's, Claire gave Sinjin a high five.

"You're a rock star," she said. "Smoothie maker and sales rep. Multitalented."

"I'm a man of many moves." He blushed. "In a business sense."

She briefly wondered about Sinjin's other *moves* but concentrated on the dilemma around them. Maxwell's was in complete disarray. The owner had abandoned it and left her daughter to fend for herself.

"This is a great store. So many eclectic items. When I first entered, steampunk vibes surrounded me." Claire pulled a velvet riding jacket off a rack and shoved it up to Sinjin's face. "This could be from an official dress code in 1895."

"Nice and British-feeling. Smooth and stiff." He pinched the sleeve, then shuddered. "Give me a cotton T-shirt, please."

She hung the jacket back up and hunted through a rack of T-shirts. "Here. It's a vintage Rolling Stones cotton tee. Can't go wrong with Mick Jagger's tongue."

He chuckled and set it on the counter. "Maybe this is where and how we present *Coal or Steam*. Make it shiny and more alluring to Larry."

Claire eyeballed the brick walls and the high, arched ceiling. It definitely was an old building. For the past hour, while helping her friend, she'd nearly forgotten about the Lafferty and the scoundrel Larry.

Crossing her arms over her chest, she inspected the layout of merchandise and the beautiful artisanal furniture made by Julie. She inhaled the scent of cinnamon pervading the air. "I get it. If this were to be the new home for *Vectors*, my exhibit would fit right in." Her excitement started running fast. "It feels so turn of the century. Maybe the building was built around the 1900s. It would be authentic." She pointed to the stained glass windows around the perimeter. "Those are original. But how will this motivate Larry to leave the Lafferty?"

"Because the sculpture will be here and not in my house or gallery. With less security and more open." He pointed to the front door. "The street is right there. He could come and go without anyone knowing if he wanted to."

"Damn, you are kind of scary with that twisty brain of yours." She jauntily helped some other customers. When they left, she seized the velvet jacket, found a tweed newsboy hat, and searched for a pipe and magnifying glass. Both were on a table display labeled Best Accoutrements for Mystery Parties.

"Now that I'm prepped, I don't mind if you want to call me Holmes."

"It's a good look on you." Sinjin took pictures of the pieces of furniture designed by Julie. "Do you think any of these would work in your exhibit?"

"Maybe. One or two." She circled around the shop and inspected the artsy tables and chairs. Again, she admired Julie's use of paint colors and mix of metals. They did have a steam-punk vibe. She didn't want to admit it, but the pieces in the store would be a fantastic addition to her show. "The space in the Lafferty has been arranged to accommodate twenty-nine pieces. Your sculpture was to be number thirty. None of the pieces are oversized. In fact, I avoided furniture like this because of my space restrictions. We would have to move all the clothing and the knickknacks out."

They both grabbed onto the sides of a round clothing rack and pushed it into the corner of the store. Immediately, the store felt spacious. The dressing rooms were made of metal dividers. If they removed the privacy curtains, each slot would fit a pedestal perfectly to display the show's smaller pieces. "Damn. This could be totally cool. But what if Julie doesn't agree? She is the owner of the place, and I get the feeling she doesn't like me very much."

"Oy, that woman isn't in any state to say no to such a grand opportunity. Especially since she sold her wine bar to Polly last night. This will now be my last, I promise, piece of advice to her as her mentor. It's a show. An exhibit with steampunk pieces and a piece or two of her own artistic endeavors. She can't say no. I'll make sure she doesn't."

This man demonstrated intent and focus. Qualities she adored as much as his ginger-colored hair. She had no doubt he could talk Julie into this plan. And Lucy needed the income for her smoothie business. The only holdup would be the actual holdup. How would they get her exhibit from the

Lafferty to Maxwell's? And worse, what if Larry wanted nothing to do with the plan?

Then Claire recalled all of the conversations when Larry had made it clear her show was irrelevant without *Coal or Steam* since it was the star attraction. With that in mind, she hoped all the craziness could save the Lafferty.

Chapter 11

Claire lounged on Lucy's couch for the majority of the next couple of days. She binge-watched *Leverage* to take a break and slow down her rapidly growing frustration. All her phone calls to Lindsey Finegold kept dropping into voicemail. The unknown whereabouts of *Midnight* and *Sugar* had kept her from sleeping, and why three of the four *Seasons* were let loose in the world baffled her.

The best news came when she learned Sinjin had worked his mentor magic on Julie, who was more than thrilled to have Maxwell's rehabbed into an art gallery. Apparently, she owned a barn where she could store all the extra merchandise that needed to be cleared from the space.

After turning off the TV, Claire pulled a sketchbook from her messenger bag and started doodling. Curling her feet under her butt, she got comfortable on the sofa. She let her hand wander and mindlessly drew scrolls, flowers, and loops on the paper. Her thoughts slowed, allowing her to think clearer.

Victorious Vectors had to see the light of day. She'd been painstakingly researching and pitching the artists for the past two years. All summer, she'd been traveling around the

Midwest, collecting the chosen pieces. It was a magnificent exhibit showcasing women, regardless of Larry's masculine toxicity.

Before she approached Larry with the idea of moving her exhibit, she had to make absolutely sure he couldn't say no. Even if Sinjin's sculpture would undoubtedly lure Larry in, she didn't want to take any chances. Plus, she had to stay true to her priority mission. *Vectors* needed to shout loud enough for her dad's archenemy Arthur Silver to show up. He needed to see *More Lace Please* and how David Raffen's work had been and always would be far superior to anything Silver had to offer.

Instead of twists and curls, Claire's drawings became lines and boxes. She combed her fingers through her hair and started a list.

1. Convince Larry she'd seduced Sinjin with her feminine charms.

She shook her head in disbelief. How messed up, really, was her boss? His misogyny was off the charts. What could she say to him? "Hey, Larry…just wanted to let you know I dressed up in a French maid costume and showed Sinjin my cleavage. And he said, *Oui, oui, mon cheri!* And then he added, *Voulez-vous coucher avec moi?*"

She wondered if her time watching *Leverage* had been over-the-top, but then again, the theme of *Vectors* was about time and levers. And energy and momentum. Women succeeding at fulfilling obligations, no matter how many rocks were thrown at them. She continued jotting her list down.

2. Take pics of her and Sinjin together. Prove to Larry that she was getting closer to
Coal or Steam.

People seemed to want what they couldn't have…in the

worst ways. Larry was already *fraught*, as Sinjin had noted. She had to push him right up to the edge.

3. Take more pictures. Inside Sinjin's house. Tell Larry it's not on the premises. More shots with no sculpture.

"I have to show Larry that the sculpture isn't anywhere near or around Sinjin's house to make him question himself or piss him off. I need to make him want it. Hard," she said into the empty living room.

Before even offering up a new locale, she wanted Larry to become more desperate. From her experience, desperation usually caused an avalanche of bad decisions.

When Larry's frantic with wanting it and off his game, BAM...I text him that Sinjin will only expose the sculpture if it's in *Vectors* and the exhibit is moved from the Lafferty to Lake Bluff.

Double BAM.

She reread her notes. This had to work. But then...she dropped back on the sofa. "If the exhibit is moved from the Lafferty, there will be a loss of monies to the museum. Damn."

She tossed the sketchbook on the coffee table and checked her ringing phone. The call she'd been waiting on: Lindsey Finegold, the great-niece of Anita Finegold. Her determination wavered, and she hesitated. How big of a nightmare was she about to face?

Anita Finegold was her mother's dearest friend. And because of their close relationship, Claire had allowed Anita to hang on to three of the four portraits in the *Seasons* series. Why did this unknown person stab her in the back?

"Claire Beaumont," she answered smoothly. "Thank you for returning my call."

Noise clattered in the background, and when Lindsey spoke, there were glitches. Claire tensed up. "Hello?"

The connection shifted, and for a second, she thought the call had died, but then Lindsey shouted, "It's Lindsey Finegold. Oh, fuck. If you're calling, I'm in a world of shit."

Claire didn't know whether to laugh or cry. "I just met Sinjin Reid, and he has *Fever* hanging in his living room. Yes. You're in deep doodoo. We both are. Those paintings shouldn't have left the gallery. I painted them. Did you tell him that? And where are the other two?"

"I'm in trouble. With you. But have you ever been desperate?" Lindsey asked, sounding apologetic.

Claire stopped to think.

"I mean really, really terrified?" Lindsey moaned. "The gallery. The upkeep. The costs. I could barely pay for the lights to stay on, and my aunt's hospital bills were exorbitant. The city was about to put a lien on the brownstone. A man walked in and offered to buy *Seasons*. I just fucking couldn't refuse the extravagant amount."

Another clatter echoed in the background. Claire shook her head, unsure of what to say. There were so many downsides to living in the art world; at times, she'd questioned her own sanity.

While she'd been living in Italy to learn about art restoration, Claire had been blissfully insulated from the nuts and bolts of making a living as an artist. Florence was the birthplace of Italian art, full of pieces that were treasured and revered and never to be sold or treated like chattel. Then her dad got sick. She returned to the States, and bills had to be paid.

"Tell me. Where are the other two? *Midnight* and *Sugar*."

"First, let me say that I never lied about the paintings. The buyers all assumed the authenticity of your father's work. No one ever questioned their validity. Another man bought *Midnight*. And a woman bought *Sugar*. I think."

"Who?" Her patience was slipping. "What are their names?"

"I don't know. I'm in Switzerland, at the Basel Art Fair, and my records are locked up in New York. I can tell you they were all bought two summers ago. And saved the gallery. I promise I'll get you the information when I return to New York next week."

"Good," Claire said, adding, "And you better schedule a trip to Milwaukee, Wisconsin, soon. We have a lot to discuss."

"Got it."

The call ended. Claire wanted to turn on the TV and crawl back into her safe zone with the pretend world in *Leverage* but stared at the list in her sketchbook. There were a lot of steps to work through with Sinjin.

He, too, must have made some desperate moves. She knew little about him but a lot about living with guilt and the pressure-cooking madness in the world of creative endeavors. And he'd misled her about the sculpture. What had he said...*prudent*? She pushed her doom and gloom out of the way and focused. The Lafferty was at risk, and she had to figure it out with Sinjin. Only he understood the machinations of greed, celebrity, and gossip in the art world as well as she did.

ON ARRIVING AT HIS HOUSE, he opened the door and let the two small dogs come out and greet her with licks and barks. Claire pretended not to notice Sinjin's expression of awe when she crouched down to pet Fred and Ginger. Most of her legs were bare since she wore her short waitress skirt again. This time though, she wasn't behind a bar opening bottles of wine.

When she passed him in the foyer, her bare arm grazed his chest. At first, she wanted to apologize, but when the heat from his pecs made contact with her skin, a crazy sizzle shot through her. She lost her footing and twisted her ankle. Before hitting the ground, Sinjin grabbed her gently and made sure she didn't do a face-plant on the floor.

The two dachshunds went quiet, then whined with worry.

"Hey," he said, holding on to her arm until she steadied herself. "I expected you to be in tweed, looking like Inspector Holmes."

"Well, it did cross my mind, but I've been thinking a lot the past few days. Maybe not thinking as much as watching a lot of TV. Damn, *Leverage* is a good show."

He balked.

"Oh, I forgot. You're a royal Brit. Too good for TV?"

Then he laughed so hard his abs vibrated. "Oh my god, I watched *The Italian Job* another time last night. My brother Angus is a fucking actor. And in some combination, every member of the Reid family has seen all episodes of *Law & Order*. When you meet Rob, I suss he'll coach you on the case highlights of his idol Jack McCoy."

"I should have known you weren't a *Masterpiece Theatre* kind of guy, but the Brits do have a reputation to uphold."

"We'll blow your mind when you see us together. None of us took well to being *subjects* of the queen...now king. We're satisfied with being citizens in the Midwest."

She liked his approach. Even though her father was born and raised in Norwich, England, he never talked about his childhood. Claire carefully surmised his life had blossomed after moving to Paris, meeting her mother, and moving to Chicago. "So today, I had a revelation. I need to make Larry beg. I can't take the risk of him saying no to whatever we propose about the new location." She pulled her notepad from her messenger bag. "Step one. We need to take a few pictures. Of us together. Canoodling."

"Snogging. Good idea." He led her into the gallery. It had been cleared out. Without the paintings from the opening filling the room with color and passion, it felt dismal.

"It's so empty today." However, she was relieved that she wouldn't come face-to-face with the drawing of her by her dad.

"Well, they all sold. I've been boxing and shipping them out. Why I haven't been around much." He wheeled a cushioned club chair up to her. "Have a seat. Tell me more about the *canoodling*."

She plopped down, crossed one foot over her knee, and massaged it. "We could send Larry a few photos to prove to him that I'm seeing more of you. Starting with some selfies—innocent, of course. Proper first draft. My biggest concern, though, is that if we move *Vectors* to Maxwell's, the Lafferty will lose the monies it would gain from the exhibit."

He pulled the chair's matching red ottoman over and sat in front of her. "I'd considered that. So, while packing up all the pieces that sold, I added in a note to tell the buyers about your show. I hope I'm not being too presumptuous. It seemed like a solid way to get folks interested in coming back to town."

"No, not in the least," she said, "but—"

"It's a start. Not enough, but thinking about showing *Vectors* here in Lake Bluff has me jazzed. Which hasn't happened in a long time." He scratched his jaw. "I may have contacts who will be appreciative of and useful for this bait and switch."

The sunlight pouring into the gallery warmed her.

"So. What positions were you thinking?" Sinjin gently cupped her foot, placed it on his thigh, and rubbed her sore ankle. "For our photos for Larry?"

As the heat of his palm pressed into the arch of her foot, she almost let a moan escape. "Thanks. So nice of you," she said in a raspy whisper, then cleared her throat. "Maybe we take a few different pictures. First with the two of us. Then a couple where you aren't directly in the frame. Making it appear as though I'm getting chummy with you but coming up empty on the sculpture."

He arched his eyebrow. Damn, he was so nice…and nice to

look at. She glanced above him, noticing the bare wall above the mantel. "Is that where you kept the sculpture?"

"Yes. With the lighting in here, the piece would shine. Nearly reflecting the lake."

She slipped her phone from her cummerbund and aimed it at the fireplace. She framed the photo to get the distinct cropped, ginger hair on the top of Sinjin's head. "Can you face the fireplace? I'll snap a pic of the mantel with the back of your head in it." She lowered herself and the camera to get a good angle of the now bare spot where the sculpture had been placed. "I need to shimmy down a bit. This will be a good one."

He then sat in front of her and laid her calf across his thigh. She kept one foot on the floor to avoid a straddling position. "This one looks, well...it could be the money shot, but let's not jump to conclusions."

"Hell, no. This isn't a money shot. We'll finesse every picture so there's no room for doubt. Larry needs to be completely duped."

Her hand trembled. She had to stay calm for the picture to come out clear and popped off several shots while Sinjin gently cradled her foot. As he massaged it, she relaxed and turned into putty. How frightening. Or exciting?

She showed him the pictures.

"These are pretty good. Let's go into the great room. Try for some *innocent* pictures."

Her legs felt rubbery. Damn, this sweet guy offered a whole lot of spice. Acting as if she and he were connecting wouldn't be too absurd, and for the sake of the Lafferty, she intended to do her due diligence. As they stepped into the man cave, she glanced up expecting to see *Fever* and was surprised. Or relieved? It had been removed from the wall above them.

"Where is she?"

He looked up. "*Fever*? It's with the others in the collection. I decided to reorganize this wall and place all my Raffens together."

She had to focus. Just because he moved it didn't mean he analyzed it. "Oh, it's just that…well…" Stuck for words, she hesitated. One mess at a time. "Do you think there's an area in here where you would place the sculpture?"

"Sure, but let's take a couple pics of us." He pointed to a corner with a lot of greenery. "As if I'm showing you my fern."

"Fern pictures. They say commitment like no other plant on Earth." She sidled next to him with the bombastic plant in the background. When he slid his arm around her waist, her skin vibrated under her blouse. A desperate need to remove the fabric barriers came over her. She clutched onto her phone. When her arm didn't reach high enough to capture the three of them—her, him, and Fern, he took the phone and pressed against her. She melted against his body. Smiling, Sinjin laughed and took a burst of selfies.

When they checked the photos, she blushed. Were they in the early and lofty phases of first love?

"Not bad. Larry will definitely be convinced that you and I are a proper couple from those shots." He removed the bombastic fern from a solid wood pedestal and set it on the coffee table. "Now, this would be the right size for *Coal or Steam*. It's too heavy to hang on walls, and Larry must know it weighs over fifty pounds with all the metal."

"Do you think we can use the pedestal in my show," she asked. "It's a piece of art in its own right."

"Great suggestion. It's a Stickley. Arts & Crafts design, meant to match the house. Mission style."

As soon as the words *mission style* left his mouth, she had an idea for the next shot, a solid money shot. "Interesting description." She tiptoed up to him, liking the feel of flirting. It had been a long time since anyone had tickled her fancy, even remotely. "This is only for show, but I'm more than happy to lie on the floor." She pointed to her knees. "I'm still nursing rug burns from the other night. Thank you very much."

Sinjin blushed. "Top. Okay. What's the picture of?"

She lay on the floor, glad to have her back on the pretty but rough Turkish kilim rug. Seeing the ceiling and the room from the ground up, she had to think. "Maybe, with you on top of me"—she ignored the fleeting sense of anticipation—"I can take a few pics of the corner of the room with the empty pedestal."

"Here," he said, straddling and then crouching over her. "Does this help? To get the angle right?"

With his arms on either side of her head, she faced a cotton layer hiding the hills and valleys of his muscular chest. Her fingers ached to reach under Sinjin's tee and massage every knoll.

"What do you think?" he asked with his head a good few inches above her.

"Incredible," she whispered.

"Do you have a good shot?"

Oh. Right. The photo. She scootched up and awkwardly aimed the camera over his shoulder. From what she could see, she could get half of the empty pedestal and his shoulder into the picture. "Bear with me," she said and lifted up his sleeve so some of his tattoo appeared in the picture. "This way, no one can say that this isn't you in the pic."

"Good thinking. Meg is quite familiar with my tattoo."

At the mention of his ex-wife, Claire's heightened sensitivity waned. She had to stay on top, or with it, for the sake of herself. For all she knew, Sinjin was showing interest in her to get back at his ex-wife.

She snapped another bunch of photos and slid out from underneath him. Standing up, she brushed off the lint from her skirt, legs, and blouse. He came beside her, and they looked at the pictures on her phone together, side by side. She couldn't move away. He'd been stirring her up for the past hour, and she wanted to boil over but couldn't. They were having a little fun, and no one around could tell her she was being naughty. The upside of Sinjin moving the portrait of her mother.

In the pictures, they looked as if they'd barely snogged before jumping right into the throes of coupling. Steps one and two finished.

"Which do you think is the money shot," he said.

"The last one. Your arm, the tattoo. Solid. No one can question that I was underneath you," she said, her voice sounding husky.

Growing warm, she fought the overwhelming urge to beg him to cool her off everywhere with his lips. She glanced down at his pants, seeing he was just as aroused.

She hadn't taken off a piece of clothing.

"If you'll excuse me, I need to take care of something," he said. "Help yourself to anything in the kitchen if you're hungry. It may be awhile."

She waited until he was gone. But instead of going into the kitchen, she stepped into a bathroom. At the sink, she splashed her face, and water dripped over her shirt. Her nipples puckered with need, and she shivered, thinking about Sinjin kissing and then playing with each one with his tongue.

Her hand slipped under her skirt, and closing her eyes, she saw his bare chest on top of her, muscular arms on either side, and his erection ready for her to welcome him in.

She slid her fingers inside, moving them slowly and then rapidly for a large dose of self-pleasuring so she wouldn't burst into flames and burn the whole damn house down.

Chapter 12

Despite the icy shower, Sinjin wasn't sure his desire for Claire wouldn't crop up again, so he slipped on a pair of heavy twill Dickies. He entered the kitchen, hating the painter pants but glad he'd slipped on his Birks. They were good for a stroll outside for some fresh air. Maybe a dog walk. Except Fred and Ginger were sleeping in their crates, and Claire wasn't around. Her voice echoed from the empty gallery. Before exiting the kitchen to find her, he sucked in some air. He needed to keep the randy bloke side of him on the QT.

Don't look below her eyebrows. Stare at her forehead.

Claire stood on the balcony with her phone at her ear. The furrow in her brow was disconcerting. He could see the goose bumps on her bare arms multiplying from the crisp fall air.

As he approached, she ended the conversation. "Thanks, I'll see you soon."

At the thought of her leaving, a wave of uneasiness engulfed him. "Heading out?" he asked with a forced bit of cheer. "I thought we could edit the pictures. Send the first one to Larry. Don't you think it would be best to be together in case he responds right away?"

"Actually, yes. I hope you don't mind, but I invited Mina Lafferty to come here."

"That's quite all right," he responded, letting the relief sink in. "Is she on her way now?"

"Leaving Milwaukee now. She'll be here in about an hour." Claire jogged back into the gallery. "I'm chilly."

"Let's go into the kitchen. It's warmer, and I have to feed the dogs. Did you tell Mina anything about our Scooby-Doo scheme?"

"Nothing. Too dicey." She crouched down and let the dogs out of their crates, petting them as they jumped about her knees. "I think I need to get some dogs. These two are so dang sweet."

He went into the pantry and came back with the makings for their dinner. As his fur babies were devouring their meal, he joined her at the Formica-topped table.

She tapped the boomerang pattern on the pink tabletop next to her phone. "What if Larry is or decides to be himself? An asshole."

"One step at a time. Open up the pictures."

He focused on the images and how comfortable they were posing next to one another. Even the fern looked especially green and healthy. He crossed his legs at the intimacy in the steamier shots. When she swiped back to an innocent picture, he announced, a bit too forcefully, for her to send it to Larry.

She straightened her shoulders. "Are you sure?"

"Oh, hell yeah." It had been a while since he'd wanted to face the world again, and it was time to get the ball rolling. "Really anxious to see Larry's response."

The dogs, eyeing their leashes at the back door, grabbed his attention. They all needed fresh air. "How about a hike around back. We can go down to the lake if you want. After you send the photo."

"Sure," she said, distracted with typing her text. "One

second… Here's what I'm saying. Let me know what you think."

Thinking was good for him. He stared at her forehead while she read the text.

"I've spent time in Lake Bluff and met up with Mr. Reid." She added, "That sounds more professional. To start with."

"Absolutely. Larry Chambers is good at cons, so he'll be able to sniff us out if we're not careful."

"Hold that thought." She continued tapping out the text while reading it out loud.

"He gave me a private tour of his estate. Had lunch yesterday. Here's a shot of us. Haven't seen the sculpture."

She made a dramatic flourish with her index finger and hit Send. "Done. Now, tell me, what do you know about Larry's conniving?"

From the coat hooks next to the back door, he grabbed the dogs' leashes and a sweatshirt. "Here. The breeze off the lake may get cold."

He suited up Fred and Ginger while she zipped up the hoodie. As they went out the back door, he sighed. Fall would always be his favorite season of the year. "Larry uses his charms and morphs them to fill the needs of older and very wealthy women. He made the mistake of thinking Polly was needy and vulnerable. How old is Mina?"

Claire, hopping and skipping around the bigger branches on the leafy path, stopped. "She's in her fifties, I think. I'm not good with reading faces, and the woman has phenomenal skin because she's an esthetician. Her mom and dad were both artists, but she's put her talent and her passion into creating healthy skin for people. When her parents handed over the keys to the Lafferty, she wasn't prepared to take over the museum. But they entrusted the whole enchilada to her five years ago."

"Larry swooped into Milwaukee about then. He probably

smelled Mina's weakness before he handed off his Chicago gallery to Meg." How clueless he'd been when he had exhibited his sculptures in a solo show at the exact gallery and met Meg. "I've never met Mina, so this will be an honor. The Lafferty has a good reputation. I'm assuming it's due to her stewardship."

She shook her head. "At first, Mina struggled, and then Larry took advantage of her. Even though the board had hired him, he negotiated a ten-year contract so no one could fire him. Not even Mina, the museum president."

"What a complete prat."

They continued along the leaf-strewn trail. He inhaled the scent of the Fraser firs along either side of them. The waves crashed along the rocky shore at the bottom of the ravine. They passed the chinked log cabins scheduled for renovation work by Quinn next spring. Originally part of a Girl Scout camp, there were old bunk beds and bathrooms in each one. With his old mate's help, the updated cabins would incorporate more comfort for the students arriving next summer. If the first retreat was a success, he'd add on more cabins and turn his private cottage into another gathering area.

"I think I've lost you," Claire said, jogging him back from his meandering thoughts.

"Sorry. My mind shifted to next summer. I'll try to focus on the job at hand. The man of the hour, Larry." He had a hard time spitting out the simplest of names.

"Tell me more about him." She paused. "As long as it's not too uncomfortable."

"I can only speak to what happened to Polly. Larry approached her, introduced by Meg. He asked about donating her collection of Georgia O'Keeffe florals to the Lafferty."

"As the director, it would be within his responsibilities to search out and acquire new pieces for the museum. The board, with Mina's approval, is always trying to expand the collection. Recently, we acquired a series of Japanese woodblocks."

"In that case, did Larry contact the creator?" he asked.

"Well, no. I did. With Mina's help."

"Here's my suspicion," he said, pausing to let the doxies sniff around a decaying log off the path. "Larry works on his own terms. He has a black-market source who is feeding him a wish list. Rare pieces that unscrupulous collectors want to get their claws on. I believe a petrol prince had wanted my sculpture. And a reclusive mega investor wanted one or more of Polly's paintings by O'Keeffe."

"Oh. My. God. Damn. Not only is Larry cooking the books, but he's also swindling little old ladies out of their savings. What an asshole. Worse than a charming Nigerian prince on the internet."

"Larry's mistake—" He stooped down to bag up Ginger's droppings. "—is that Polly and Mina have history. They met somewhere along the line and know one another. The circles in the art world are more like tiny bubbles."

"Oh, I know that." Claire stared at her phone. "Nothing yet from the beast. The Georgia O'Keeffe thing sounds weird. When Mina's parents dropped the Lafferty into her lap, they gave her a specific mission statement to work with. Women and diversity. Artists on the margins were to be given the highest priority. I'm pretty sure *Georgia* doesn't fit the bill because the Lafferty already has several of her paintings in the collection. The Japanese woodblock artists were all older women from small villages around Tokyo."

"Props to Mina. And her parents," he said. "I had no idea. On my end, I only know that Polly hid her O'Keeffe collection from Larry for safekeeping, and I stashed away *Coal or Steam*."

"What an awful human being," she said. "My skin is crawling at the thought of seeing him again. I can't believe I worked in the cubicle across from his office. I should have smelled something coming from behind his ostentatious carved wood double doors. Ew. Damn."

"Don't be so harsh on yourself. You're on Mina's side. This probably, instinctually, protected you."

When they reached his cottage, he dropped the doggie bag in the bin and kicked the foliage off the bottom of his Birks. He thumbed the security code on the keypad. "When *Coal or Steam* returns, this will be home. No more hiding." He opened the door and let Claire pass into his private living area without flinching. After he took off the dogs' leashes, he felt relief and some trust that had evaded him for quite some time.

WITH THE WRAPAROUND porch on the small house, his cottage belonged in the English countryside instead of a sausage-making town in Wisconsin. Claire kicked off her Vans. She didn't want to be rude and wear her shoes inside Sinjin's safe haven.

"You can keep your shoes on. My mum isn't here, and my dad won't be showing his mug around until next week."

Her cheeks tingled from the way he teased. His relaxed manner was mightily attractive. She kept her shoes off and gazed around the sitting room. Flowers decorated the fabric on each piece of furniture. There were more puffy pillows than on a shelf at TJ Maxx. "Are you sure your *mum* won't show up? I mean, no offense, but this isn't exactly what I would expect to see in a bachelor pad. Even if you're a Brit, this is a lot of flower power."

"Well, I had no choice. All of this furniture was left to me after she died. Eventually, I may use this house as a gathering space for the retreats, but all of that is in the future." He opened the fridge and came over with two bottles of beer.

"Take a seat. Sink in. I promise none of the flowered chairs will swallow you up."

"Don't mind if I do," she said, tucking her feet under her butt and relaxing. She sank into the thick cushion with a lavender design and chugged the ale. "Love a good IPA."

"Brewed at 3Sheeps in town." He dropped a dog bone onto each of the monogrammed plaid dog beds. Fred and Ginger curled up in their respective beds. "I have to show you something."

She held the bottle at her mouth. Frozen. What did he have to show her? The painting? *Fever*? Was he about to call her out on the portrait she'd painted of her mother? She finished her gulp of beer and willed her nerves to stay in check. "Oh? Really? Is it safe to assume it's of an artistic nature?"

"That's a good assumption. It's been on my mind a lot since you've arrived."

To prepare herself, she untucked her feet, planted them on the floor, and sat up straight. She steeled herself for Sinjin's presentation.

He disappeared into a room behind the kitchen and returned carrying a large square shape—a painting—draped in black velvet. She arched her back. *Damn.*

With a free hand, he grabbed an easel and strode toward her. She stretched out one leg, prepping to run, but where would she actually go? When he set the easel and painting down in front of her, her heart pounded.

He pulled off the cloth, and Claire faced a drawing of herself.

Pastels, chalk, and smudges of charcoal. Her father's rendition of her when she'd been only ten, maybe twelve years old. It wasn't that she recognized her image, more so how her dad's handiwork and supreme talent popped off the paper. Her throat went dry.

"I had placed it in the gallery the other night and initially wanted to sell it. Halfheartedly. Since Polly and her son were coming to the opening, I knew it would go for a good price. But—"

"I showed up on your doorstep?"

He tilted his head and scratched his cheek. "Well...yes."

She took a swig of beer to relieve her parched throat to talk, then stood to inspect the drawing. "He had such a knack for colors."

"The way I recognized you was his work on your eyes." Sinjin loped back to the secret room behind the kitchen, adding, "Would you mind? Grab a couple of those easels in the hallway."

She dragged her eyes away from her father's drawing to retrieve two more easels. Almost twenty metal and wooden easels lined the wall that led back to some kind of glass-type room. An atrium? Curious, she wanted to ask Sinjin. When she returned to the living room and set the weighty holders down with a sigh of relief, he had already propped four covered paintings against the couch. He strolled in with two more paintings.

Fever? Was she about to play a shell game that would expose her biggest nightmare of being caught red-handed? Taking in a few calming breaths, she saw that the pictures were too small. They weren't her father's typical larger-scale composition. Sinjin went back and forth two more times until he had a half-circle of easels propping six covered paintings. They surrounded her. Trapped her. To kill her death march of thoughts, she pulled her phone from her cummerbund. "I'm checking. To see about Mina. Or if the beast has responded."

"Whenever you're ready."

Her heart hammered in her chest. There were no messages to occupy her thoughts, and the only escape was to hurdle the easels around her—totally impossible—and run out into the woods. Except, she didn't want to run. She liked being around

Sinjin. They had a plan, a slightly nutty plan, but it was an opportunity to move away from the past and have a future of her own making.

"No news," she said, slipping her phone back.

He proceeded to reveal the first painting. She nervously twisted a strand of hair and put it behind her ear. The revealed image was a déjà vu. Another drawing of her, similar to the first but this one done all in charcoal. No color pastels.

He continued to uncover the other five pictures, stunning her. All images of her at varying ages, all under twelve years old, and her father had used a variety of mediums. Colored pencils, charcoal with pastels, two without pastels, and one an ink drawing. Each was a different spin on her image, and all together were dizzyingly beautiful.

She dropped down on the couch to take them in. Her eyes were on overload. What a feast of creativity, a side of her father she couldn't recall. She hadn't been more than a kid at St. Nicholas's Elementary.

Sinjin cleared his throat. "It's not that I'm stalking you. I promise."

She looked at the room where he'd retrieved the drawings. "What will I find if I go back there? Candles? An altar? With a poster of me dead center?"

"Not at all," he laughed, then added, "Maybe fingernail clippings, strewn about on the altar…I mean dresser."

She shook her head. The man had an amusing side, for sure. She squinted at one of the pastel drawings. "He had such a way with faces. This one must have been done when I was at least ten." She looked so carefully her nose nearly touched the glass. "I had tripped and cut open my lip. The scar is a smudge of carnation pink in this one."

Self-consciously, she rubbed her upper lip. "Damn Catholic school. Old and cold with stone stairs and halls. Even Jesus had sandals to soften his steps. Would a carpet here or there hurt?"

"I want to assure you, I had no intention of having this collection of you. Your father gave them to me to use in the drawing class while I taught at the Institute. I tried to compensate him, but he insisted they be considered a donation."

"Were they helpful...in the class?" She stared at the colored-pencil drawing. With no scar, she must have been five or six. "Funny, I don't remember much about my dad back then. I rarely saw him. He'd lock himself in his studio and only come out for dinner. He would say, *din-air* with a thick French accent, apparently an imitation of my mother. And then the two of us would sit down at eight o'clock." She chuckled. "While all my friends were done eating and doing homework or watching TV, we were sitting down to eat."

Seeing the stages of her childhood through her dad's eyes pulled her in, and she had to stare at each drawing. For a minute, she forgot where she was. The flood of memories came swirling into her mind, first slowly and then rapidly, threatening to turn into a hurricane.

As if on cue, Sinjin stood beside her and lightly clasped her shoulder. The skin-to-skin contact jolted her. The tumbling and falling into the well of her past came to a sudden halt. Sinjin's presence drew her back into the here and now. She hugged herself to contain the emotions bubbling up within. "They are beautiful. Each one. Although, it's hard. Dredging up long-buried moments, that..." Claire cleared her throat and sniffed up the threat of tears. "So much of our childhood gets lost. You know what I mean?"

He agreed, and she sensed with certainty he understood her because of the way he gazed at her. As if her many broken emotions were pieced together and coherent to him.

"My father was so brilliant, but also, he had an interiority that I had no clue about until, I suppose, I became an adult." When a tear dropped on her cheek, she swiped it away. Not needed. "Even then, he was a ghost before he actually died. I tried so hard."

Sinjin draped his arm around her shoulders and guided her into a warm and oh-so-persuasive hug. She obliged and leaned into his chest. His embrace felt like a respite on a tropical island. Lots of warmth and sun.

"And no mosquitoes," she mumbled into his shoulder, feeling delirious.

"Hmm? Not sure about the bloodthirsty pests." He folded her tighter against him. "You all right? I wanted this to be a joyful situation. I hope I haven't upset you?"

She rubbed her nose against his T-shirt. "I'm…good. This feels so nice."

When he brushed his fingers across her cheek, she shivered. She stood on the tips of her toes to reach his face. His lips. Although she came up a bit short, he cupped her cheek, leaned down, and kissed her. She wrapped her arms around his shoulders and melted against him.

An overload of sensations floated through her, fizzing and bubbling. She tasted the traces of the hoppy beer on his lips, pressed her cheek against his clean-shaven face, and inhaled the hint of citrus aftershave. A kiss like this had to be illegal.

When her phone pinged, she ignored it, but Sinjin's lips deserted hers. It seemed as if an asteroid had crash-landed. But it was worse. The beast had texted her.

Chapter 13

With her lips still puckered, Claire stared at the phone. She leaned her head against Sinjin's chest, unwilling to break away from his warmth. She read Larry's message out loud, maybe too loud, because she couldn't hear herself. Either her blood was roaring, or Sinjin's heart was booming noisily. She repeated the message, annunciating each syllable to let it sink into her brain—undoubtedly affected by Sinjin's kiss.

I don't buy it. Coal or Steam. Is in his house.

Sinjin dropped onto the flowered couch, shaking his head in complete irritation. She wanted to go back five minutes and continue the kiss. It had swayed her entire being. But this option had left the building. "All righty then. What next? Do we wait or send out the next photo? Too soon? Too late?"

"I say we need to get him hooked. Send out the photo. The one where I'm on top of you," he said. "I mean, hanging over you while you're snapping the pic. The one where my tattoo shows."

"The money shot. Okey dokey. What should I text?" She tugged her skirt down to hide the goose bumps multiplying on her bare thighs. His kiss, this man…they were all kicking up her heat level, closing in on spicy.

Again, as she composed the text, she read it for Sinjin to hear. He was hard to read since he kept staring intently at her forehead. She wondered if there was dirt or something on it.

"Thank you, Larry," she said while tapping it into the phone. "What I really want to write is a list of his demeaning comments. The many I've endured from him the past two years."

"How you've managed to work with the man, I give you credit. I'm already dreading the prospect of seeing the tosser. Once. After over an entire year." Rubbing the back of his neck, he turned away from her.

She knew there was more to his thoughts but didn't want to pry. "Fortunately, as a curator, my contact with Larry was mostly electronic and virtual. A lot of messages. Part of his scheme, I suspect. Keeping everyone tied to a short and invisible leash."

Closing her eyes, she thought through her next words, then started. "How's this—"

Easy to tempt Mr. Reid. While we toured the estate he anxiously showed me a lot. I flirted hard & to attract him I offered a closer look at my private tattoo. He then showed me his.

"I'm easy? Really? Where is *your* tattoo? Exactly?"

She glanced away from the phone. He'd blushed, and her heat level sped dangerously close to a ghost pepper.

"Never mind. It's not important." On her lower back, and it would stay well hidden. For now. "How does it sound? For Larry? Think he'll, as he said, *buy it*?"

"With that shot, absolutely." He began to slip the protective coverings over her dad's drawings. "I'm going to put these away. Mina will be arriving soon, and it may be nicer to meet her at the main house."

Nodding, she reread her text and cued up the picture. Blushing a little, she pressed Send. To help Sinjin, she retrieved one of the cloths hanging over the back of the chair and covered a Raffen drawing. She didn't want to get emotional again, so she did it fast to avoid giving her child-self any attention.

She followed the path to the secret room, where Sinjin came out and took the drawing from her without inviting her in. Claire became more than curious. Maybe there were candles, or voodoo dolls, or whatever...

"It's climate controlled. In case you were thinking about it," he said.

He let her pass by him to see the room where it all began thirty minutes ago. Metal gates resembling mesh fences hung off tracks located on the very high ceiling. Each piece was hooked in place. It reminded her of the door storage in an old kids movie. There could be a lot of scary things behind each piece of art.

"Have you visited the Wisconsin Museum of Art in West Bend?" He pressed an icon on his phone, and one large fence lowered to the carpeted floor. He secured the pieces onto it, tapped his phone, and the gate went back up and hitched into its ceiling track. "The storing system is fabulous. Where I got this idea from."

Claire had forgotten his question. "Where?"

"MOWA. Museum of Wisconsin Art."

"Oh, right. No. It's been on my list," she said, slightly ashamed of her lack of artistic exploration. But since the debacle of her father's ruined reputation, she'd been deeply averse to visiting galleries, museums, or art fairs. Avoiding any creative place or endeavor where her father might be mentioned or affiliated with had protected her. "One of these days."

"You'd love it," he said, grabbing the dogs' leashes.

She slipped out of the storage room. While Sinjin placed the easels in the hallway, her mind wandered back five years ago to the Armory Show in New York. As she took the last sips of her beer, Claire vividly recalled how she and her dad had cabbed it to the Javits Center. Of course, it was raining. And although her dad's legs were in good working condition, his eyesight had diminished to shadows. Thinking about the trip, to this day, still gave her a stomachache. She finished her beer and set the empty bottle on the kitchen counter.

"Do you want Fred or Ginger?" Sinjin proffered the two leashes.

She eyed both the dogs to see which would be her choice. When Ginger whined, she took hold of Fred's leash. "I have a feeling Ginger might get jealous."

He laughed. "I am her alpha."

"Really? You seem more of a beta type." She let Fred walk her out the front door. As Sinjin locked up the cottage, she played around with Fred's leash to get comfortable with the mini dog, who gazed up at her with sweet chocolate eyes. "I like you too, Fred."

Making their way back through the wooded path, the dogs allowed them to sink into a comfortable silence for their own thoughts. Even though Sinjin's kiss still tingled and lingered on her lips, she could concentrate on Fred, who seemed to want to sniff underneath every branch and leaf along the path.

"So, I'm a beta, hunh?"

"Classic beta. The artsy types usually are. And you're British. That's the only way they make them across the pond. Sensitive, royal and..." She stopped for Fred to sniff a decaying log and stared at a tree full of orange leaves. Sinjin was appealing and composed like the Brits but much more attractive with an unruffled edge. Again, the hot drummer vibe struck her. "Attractive. As long as you aren't a member of parliament."

Probably digesting her comments, Sinjin paused to let Ginger do some ground-floor exploration. She let Fred pull her along, and thoughts of New York drifted back into her head with the swarms of art aficionados at the Armory Show. The gallery owners, art collectors, art lovers, and critics had converged at the Javits.

During the four-day event, her father's energy had been suitable, considering all of the drugs he'd had to take to decrease the size of the tumor. Even though she'd tried desperately to talk him out of making the trip, David Raffen could not be swayed. The man knew it would be his last foray into the art world as his life was coming to a close. While at the show and as each day progressed, she'd forgotten her worries. Her dad was the happiest she'd seen him since the prognosis.

He laid on the charm and flirted with his eighty-year-old gallery rep, Anita. The dame of American contemporary artists. Her gallery on East Eighty-Seventh had represented Claire's father since the beginning of his career. And the two bonded like those who knew that life was best spent making moments that could not be forgotten.

Claire had been too nervous to really enjoy the show. At the beginning of the year, she'd left Italy and returned to Chicago to assist her dad, to help him get around, shop, cook, and clean. She should have shouted, "No damn way," when he'd asked her to paint for him.

But he'd been anxious to paint her mother. A series of portraits, one for each season, and he couldn't get himself to do it. Each time he lifted the brush, he teared up.

So Claire agreed to paint four portraits of her mother with the guidance of his shaking hand as his vision had failed. Anita Finegold assured them none would be sold when her father sent them to her gallery.

The unauthorized sale by Lindsey still bristled, and she had a hard time processing it. Making sure to be out of Sinjin's hearing range, she mumbled, "Fat chance."

In the makeshift brick gallery at the Javits, Claire's pieces, signed by her father, were displayed next to his originals. Nothing amiss in the lines or the form or the colors. No one could tell them apart. No one had questioned their authenticity.

Unfortunately, her dad had insisted on buying a glass of champagne for Anita. He ambled, with Claire's help, over to the cocktail lounge. Each table had been decorated with magnums of champagne, and every seat was occupied by the crowd of art lovers.

Suddenly, Fred barked, tugged the leash, and chased after a squirrel racing across the path, disrupting Claire's trip down memory lane. The dog pulled her up to the main house and driveway. Mina had arrived and was inspecting her namesake bus, Orange-Mina.

"Ace timing," Sinjin said when he caught up to her. "You've been so quiet."

"I'm thinking." She followed Fred. "About Larry."

Even though she hadn't really been thinking about Larry, she dismissed the fib.

"We'll take the wanker down," he said. "People like him always get their comeuppance."

Claire wondered if she would ultimately get her "comeuppance." If Art Silver hadn't witnessed her father mistake a ten-dollar bill for a hundred-dollar bill when paying for the glasses of champagne, Claire's life would have remained much simpler.

She tossed aside all her woes from that day five years ago. No going back. Nothing to fix. All she could do was try to make it up to her dad and ignore Art Silver's scathing critique, "A Decline Like No Other."

Maybe Claire should consider herself lucky. Before she, her

dad, or Anita could take a sip of champagne, the critic had slithered over to the booth and inspected the Raffen portraits on display. Anita had assured Art they were originals, but the critic didn't buy it. How could a man who couldn't distinguish between a ten and a hundred-dollar bill paint such detail?

Her father's secret was divulged, and the entire art world seemed to question the validity of every David Raffen portrait.

Claire puckered her lips and grimaced.

"Good to see you too," Mina said, breaking her from her dispirited reminiscing. "What's got you all tied up? I can see you're upset."

She shook her head and hugged her boss, the woman who had given her a chance to start over. Moving to Milwaukee, free from her father's life and death, had been lifesaving. Maybe this travesty with Larry, which had drowned her spirits, could be resolved.

"Now that you're here, I'm swell."

Sinjin came up and introduced himself. Then took hold of both the leashes and led all into the main house. "Mina, I'm glad to meet you. Make yourselves comfortable in the great room."

Seeing Mina reminded Claire she had another shot at making this miserable memory, like a clinging spiderweb, dissolve.

Once in the great room and away from Sinjin, she gently hugged Mina. With a deep truth punctuating every word, she said, "I'm so grateful you're here."

Claire admitted to herself that this fledgling thing with Sinjin could disintegrate when he learned about her painted past with four fakes. But with one redemption, getting her father's reputation back in good order, she could live with it. *Alone* had been guiding her for the past five years.

Art & Form Review

A Fond Farewell to Anita Finegold
By Arthur Silver

The New York gallery scene will never be the same following the death of Anita Finegold. A patron to contemporary artists, she retained and sold a treasure trove of paintings since the early seventies. She struck deals for the likes of Jeff Koons, Alex Katz, and fashion icon Vivienne Westwood. Finegold made negotiating on behalf of her clients an art form all on its own. She believed in the power of art and that it was the best language for humans to connect and communicate.

The works of her most revered client, David Raffen, are a mainstay in the brownstone gallery. Three of the four *Seasons* series, the last known works by Raffen before he died, still hang in the Finegold Gallery. Never have they been for sale or gone to auction.

It's rumored the paintings were the pieces closest to Ms. Finegold's heart. The woman portrayed in *Seasons* is the artist's deceased wife,

Monique Beaumont, a French beauty and, at one time, Anita Finegold's closest confidant.

Anita Finegold's brownstone may be worth more than the art on its walls, and questions abound about the gallery's future. Who will take over? Filling the great Anita's Stuart Weitzman loafers will be nearly impossible. Will her great-niece Lindsey Finegold know the ins and outs of running a prestigious New York art gallery? If Lindsay does take over, how will she keep the doors open? The doors in the world of contemporary art revolve fast and furiously. Before an order is filled, an *artiste du jour* can turn into cold leftovers wanted by no one.

Gallery owners who represent award-winning artists are like piano tuners; they hear the unheard and are able to grasp and garner the art world's attention, directing it to pieces all but invisible to the rest of the world. Even if Lindsey Finegold keeps the gallery doors open, will she have the ear to appreciate the symphony of a masterpiece in the making through the cacophonous din of the contemporary art world?

@Art Silver

Chapter 14

While they'd strolled through the woods, Sinjin had an opportunity to restrain his growing apprehension over this half-baked idea to catch Larry. Even if there were already plenty of sharks in the art world, ridding it of the fraudster Larry might make a dent. A big enough dent to regain the confidence of starving artists everywhere. Sinjin could once again see his livelihood as a gift and not a curse.

He hadn't expected a woman with hair the same color as the VW bus in his driveway, but somehow, Mina appeared exactly as he might have expected. The opposite of Larry Chambers. After a quick introduction, he'd rounded up the dogs and led the women into the house. To give them privacy, he settled the dogs in their crates and foraged around the kitchen for beverages to serve to his guests. Only one because after his kiss with Claire, he couldn't think of her as a guest.

He rummaged in the cabinets, opening and closing every cupboard. All his storage had been rearranged. He sighted a container of ground coffee in a drawer that once housed trivets. The collection of cast-iron trivets that he'd made was worth a bit of dosh and was missing. *Julie?*

Shaking off his unease, he retrieved the Keurig, made a cup of coffee and a cup of tea, placed them on a tray, and went into the great room to see what was going on.

The two women were head-to-head and staring down at Claire's phone. He cleared his throat. Looking at him, they blushed. They had been immersed in *those* pictures.

"What do you think?" He set the tray on the coffee table. Completely unsure of Mina Lafferty's knowledge about their plot, he didn't want to make any assumptions.

Mina glanced at him. "If I wasn't in a solid relationship, I'd be tempted. I even think my partner, Bianca, might be curious."

He eyed the room for a fire extinguisher to douse his utter embarrassment. "I…well…" he sputtered, then gave up. The two women giggled and exchanged sympathetic glances. Claire came over and patted him on the shoulder.

"It's okay. We've only been objectifying you for less than a minute."

"Thanks. Nice to know I'm a sixty-second stud."

Mina came up, grabbed his hand, and gave him a hearty shake. "It's an honor, really, to meet you. And a relief. I've been struggling with how to get you into the Lafferty's fold."

Her hair, with a mix of orange, pink, and red strands, glistened under the ceiling lights. There were shadows of fatigue under her eyes, but her handshake was strong. Mina Lafferty and her museum were towers of strength and had to survive. He'd stepped on board a mission, and there was no going back. He had to save the Lafferty and make sure Larry never ventured inside a museum again.

Claire took the cup of coffee off the tray and handed the tea to Mina.

As they sipped, he dove right into the gritty subject. "Have you and Larry talked at all? Has he given you updates about Claire's exhibit or my sculpture?"

Mina sat on the couch beside Claire and set her cup on the table. Claire sat with her feet tucked under her bum. She stared at Mina and drank her coffee as if in a trance or in the presence of a shaman.

"The man has sent me perfunctory messages about *Vectors*," Mina said. "All negative. He then sends me the daily attendance numbers as if to say, 'All is well. No need to worry your pretty little head about anything.' The board and directors hired him on as the executive director and assured me he was the best candidate. I voted *Ye* because all the others had raved about his qualifications."

Frowning, Mina stared at the braided carpet. "He was squeaky-clean on paper. His CV included his achievements at several small museums." She shook her head. "And I checked. Not one person had spoken a bad word about him."

"Probably fear of reprisal," he said. "There's a pecking order and survival instinct that breeds in artistic circles. No one wants to take the blame. Or fail." He glanced at Claire. "Hey, Velma! Have you mentioned anything about our *scheme*?"

"Nothing yet, Shaggy," she replied.

"What's going on, you two?" Mina leaned back on the leather couch and rubbed her face. "*Gawd*. My parents must be rolling over in their graves. I've been way more interested in the pH balance of my skin than the goings-on of the museum. In my defense, I tried to tell them before they passed away, but they were insistent. Assured me I would 'shine' in the founder's role."

"Well, they were right," Claire said, standing up and stretching. "You've been instrumental in bringing in fresh voices and giving marginalized people a spot in the sun. Every exhibit you've OK'd, all the artists, the staff, we adore you. And only maybe has your annual gift of a spa treatment influenced us."

"Bugger! What have I been missing?" Sinjin piped in. "A full day of manscaping?"

Claire sidled beside him, and he was tempted to take her hand but remained professional. "Here are our thoughts," he said, then coughed. "Larry wants to get a hold of my sculpture. And I want to help you, your museum, and the art world in general by getting Larry Chambers arrested when he attempts to steal it."

Mina fiddled with her earring, a small patinaed Hamsa hand. "The board, though, and the directors, they have no idea about his dishonesty." She stared at Claire. "And you're the smartest of smarts, Claire. Even *you haven't* been able to ascertain how he's been cooking the books."

"We have an idea," Claire said, kneeling in front of Mina and taking hold of her hands. "We need to get Larry out of his safe zone. Get him to come here by luring him with Sinjin's sculpture."

"I thought *Coal or Steam* had gone into a private collection, but when Larry insisted it was donated to our museum, I foolishly believed him." Mina looked up at Sinjin, her eyes shiny with tears.

"We've all been duped by the wanker. Our plan," he said, liking the sound of *our*, "is to move Claire's exhibit to Lake Bluff. At the moment, we're hoping he'll take the bait. Which is my offer to bring out *Coal or Steam*, only if it's presented on my turf."

Mina gazed at him. "You would do that? For the Lafferty?"

"It would be a privilege. I've been dealing with personal issues that have hindered my thinking. I've decided to grow the fuck up."

Both women let out exasperated sighs.

"Join the club," Mina said.

Claire lifted an eyebrow. "I'm still working on it. Definitely a work in progress. We all have tragedies that fall on our life paths. It's best to deal with them right away but tempting to bury them and keep moving forward."

"Were you a philosophy major too?" Sinjin asked.

Mina chuckled. "I told you she was smart."

Claire's phone pinged, and the three of them froze while staring at it. Sitting on the coffee table, it secretly announced Larry's rude presence. She picked it up and bounced it like a hot coal, then read the text aloud.

It's probably in the cottage. Try getting inside.

Here was the proof Sinjin needed. No one but his immediate family and Meg had ever been made aware of the cottage house. Larry and Meg were working together, a sad collaboration and waste of talent.

"How should I respond?" Claire asked, bobbing the phone in her palm.

"Let's make the deal with the devil. Tell him I'll show the piece as long as it's displayed here at my gallery."

"But what about Maxwell's?"

"It's the gallery, but let's see how he responds to my first olive branch. This will give us a few more clues about his state of mind."

Mina nudged Claire's shoulder. "Go, girl. We're here for you. And I want to know what role I'll be playing. I'm assuming I don't have to audition?"

They all relaxed, and Claire began to tap in a text. When she finished, she held up her phone for them to see.

You're right. Reid says it's here & he will only show it if the exhibit is in his gallery in Lake Bluff.

She pressed Send, and he jogged into the kitchen, returning with three beers. The liquor wasn't strong enough, but it was all he had, and this plan deserved a Miller break.

They were barely able to get a sip of beer down their parched throats before Larry responded.

AUDREY LYNDEN

Arrogant ass. His gallery space isn't big enough for *Victorious Vectors*. Are you at house?

"Damn, I shouldn't have made him think I was at your place. What do I say? Are you sure you want me to be Velma? I'm much better as Daphne."

"It's okay. Maybe call him. But tell him you've left the house."

She picked up the phone and called using a professional tone, but her voice quivered.

"I'm driving into town. I don't know what you want me to do, Mr. Chambers."

"Idiot. If you didn't actually see the sculpture, get the ass to show it to you." He bellowed loud enough for the dogs next door in the kitchen to hear. "As if I would bother moving your ruinous exhibit for him. For your sake, I hope his dick is as big as his ego."

Sinjin shook his head, disgusted. He felt pity for Claire and Mina, who also shook her head. Claire's jaw was locked solid.

With absolute certainty, he knew he had to lure the beast out of his slimy cave.

He carefully took the phone from Claire.

"This connection is bad, Larry. We're on the road. If you want to include *Coal or Steam* in the museum's inventory, it will have to be exhibited in Lake Bluff. My gallery is too small, but there's adequate space at a local artisan's gallery in town."

The bellowing disappeared.

Sinjin's hand had cramped up from holding on to the phone so tightly. It took every inch of him to remain composed since Larry had called Claire an idiot.

"Mr. Reid. Nice to speak to you. Are you sure it's large enough?" Larry's voice had turned from a roar to a whisper. "If so, this may be a suitable arrangement. Although, I'm not sure Mina Lafferty would agree."

Mina flung out an invisible fishing rod.

"I'll let you work that out."

"I'd be happy to work with you alone, making the arrangements for the transportation of Ms. Beaumont's exhibition from Milwaukee. As well—" Larry paused. "—there will have to be an arrangement made to secure the dollars *Vectors* would have brought into our museum. May not be much, but the Lafferty isn't exactly MOMA."

The thought of working *happily* and, worse, seeing the pompous jerk made him a bit queasy. But Sinjin knew he was reeling him in. "I'll be able to secure the lost funds from patrons."

Larry asked, "What schedule would you prefer for the exhibit? Once it's all taken care of, I'll let the board know of the venue change, as well as Ms. Lafferty, then announce it to the press."

"For the benefit of Ms. Beaumont, this show will be a success. We will be in Milwaukee tomorrow—"

"That's such short notice. Next week would be better." Larry sounded panicked.

"Monday. We'll pack and freight the pieces ourselves. It may take a couple of hours. Then we'll plan for the opening at the end of October as originally planned by Ms. Beaumont. I'll set up all my contacts and make sure they attend. And if you would like to bring Meg, be my guest."

From the other end of the line came a deadly silence. "As Meg Fisher is a board member, I'm sure she'll want to attend the opening. I'll let my assistants know that you'll be coming into the museum Monday. As it's closed to the public, I'm certain Ms. Beaumont will know her way around the freight elevators and conservation areas."

"Thank you. We'll contact you when we've completed setting the exhibit up in the new location."

He handed the phone back to Claire. "We're good to go, Velma. Or Daphne. Whichever."

Chapter 15

Once again in the hot van, Claire grumbled over every bump Orange-Mina hit on her way to pick up her partner in crime. What would Sinjin's meddling and her Daphne actually solve? True, second chances had been, at least for her, a glorious ray of sunshine. But moving this exhibit, with her stomach in knots, would it burn her? She squashed her dreary thoughts and concentrated on the beautiful fall foliage around her. Gold and orange leaves scattered the road along the drive through Peace Park and up the bluff.

Instead of being civil, she honked the horn and waited for Sinjin to get into the world's worst getaway car. Even though he had offered to drive or rent a U-Haul, she knew her exhibit wouldn't need much space to transport it. Her show was compact, with mostly 2-D paintings and a small selection of sculptures. She'd unpacked every piece and had lovingly designed the exhibit's layout. Now, Claire could probably reverse the process in half the time.

If any of this situation were normal, she would not have a high-pitch alarm zooming through her nerves. After all, she wasn't embarking on an illegal escapade. It was with Larry's say-so that she could move her exhibit to Lake Bluff, but having to pretend to keep Mina out of the picture kept rattling her.

Sinjin yanked open the door so hard she thought the old girl's right arm would fall off the hinges. "Good morning."

Glancing at her thermos filled with one of Lucy's juice concoctions, Claire groaned. "Tell me it's good when we're back here, with art, and safe and sound."

"What do you have to worry about? Larry gave us his blessing. Remember?"

"Sure, sure." She couldn't help but think that this operation would go haywire at some point.

"There's still an opportunity to change vehicles. My Bronco isn't a Batmobile but may be stealthier than Orange-Mina."

With absolute clarity, she shook her head. "Believe it or not, I'm prepared for this mission from road-tripping through Wisconsin all summer and collecting each piece for *Vectors*." All of the miles she'd trekked across the state to get her show off the ground were because of Larry. "Damn, he really hates me. Larry never once offered me the keys to the museum's official moving van."

The one-hour drive to Milwaukee was made in silence. It wasn't awkward or companionable. Twitchy was the only way Claire could describe it. While she wrung her hands on the steering wheel, Sinjin stoically made eyes with his tablet. His intense focus, she hoped, was on the business at hand—organizing another gallery opening.

Once, she glanced in his direction, and he tilted his tablet out of her view. As the driver of a very mercurial hippy van, she hadn't dared to let her eyes off the road for more than a second.

When they entered the Lafferty's underground parking, she backed the van inch by inch to butt the rear up against the loading dock. Only a few cars were parked in the lot. The damp fall air felt cool, but the back of her shirt was already soaked with sweat.

A boom and whir echoed in the dingy cement block lot. She twisted around and sighted the corrugated steel door slowly opening. A shadowed person was backlit by the bright fluorescent lights in the hallway leading to the freight elevator.

Mina.

Damn. Wearing a black cape, Mina played the part of a Deep Throat informant to a tee. Claire hopped out of the van, glanced from left to right to make sure no one else was in the garage, and then ran up the concrete steps. Before Claire could chastise Mina, her mentor embraced her with a soul-satisfying hug.

"I had to be here." She shook Claire's shoulders. "This is too much for you and Sinjin. I've tasked you with a lot of responsibility the past couple of years, and it's time I think bigger. And before you say it, I feel fine. All the treatments are working."

"This is risky," Claire said, shaking her head. "You. Here. In the building."

"I've been here since 4:00 a.m., and no one knows of my presence. We're in the clear. The tech team doesn't start for another hour, the janitorial service is still on the first floor working their way up, and Larry is buried in his office. He hasn't a clue I'm lurking around. But to make sure, last night I sent him a last-minute proposal," she said, adding finger quotes, "to keep him busy. Told him I had a benefactor interested in donating his Georgia O'Keeffe to us at his death. I asked Larry to work his magic and get it into the collection before the guy goes under the daisies."

Claire huffed. "Going for the octogenarians must be Larry's specialty."

"Let's get what we came for. Shall we?" Sinjin seemed irritated, but by this time, even his nerves must be brittle and ready to snap. Especially with the sudden appearance of Mina. He pointed to the double-wide elevator. "That's our ride, right?"

The three of them walked briskly to the elevator. Claire inserted her utility key, and the doors opened. Mina poked her head inside, looking back and forth. "We're good to go."

In the gigantic elevator, Claire leaned back against the wall covered with a gray, padded shipping blanket. When the elevator bumped to a stop on the third floor, she was jolted back from her floating state of mind. The early morning and lack of coffee had affected her.

They quietly moved through the darkened hall of the museum to a set of sliding glass doors. Crimson brocade drapes hung inside the doors of the gallery. A dolly and a flatbed cart were parked against the wall. Claire glanced at the security camera hoisted on the ceiling and aimed at the gallery entrance. The lens had been covered with black electrical tape.

"In case Larry breaks his habit of avoiding the security footage," Mina said.

Claire opened her messenger bag, retrieved the gallery key, and unlocked the door. With a shaking hand, she pushed open the doors and the drapes.

Sinjin wheeled in the cart, and Mina followed behind him with the dolly.

A red glow from the exit sign and an emergency spotlight illuminated the gallery. Having practically lived within these walls the last year, Claire could have moved the exhibit blindfolded.

The smell of fresh paint still lingered from the touch-ups she had painted around the brass nameplates next to each painting. A couple of stepladders were propped against the column support beams lining the center of the gallery. An exposed air duct on the ceiling rumbled. The humidity controller in the room buzzed alive and hummed.

The flatbed squeaked as Sinjin rolled it across the room. "I think we should lift the paintings first, then put them back in the crates."

Claire scanned the wooden shipping crates in the corner of the gallery. There were some discarded that would make nice beds. "We can layer the paintings vertically and separate them with the blankets for protection."

Sinjin hoisted the pine box onto the flatbed and lifted out the felt padding from the bottom. "This will have to do. We forgot the blankets in the bus."

"Right," Claire snapped. Her nerves were wreaking havoc with her brain. She had to focus on the big picture. Getting the exhibit out of the Lafferty and luring Larry into their trap. If the threat of the Lafferty closing its doors wasn't so tragic, this whole plan would be ludicrous.

Mina parked the dolly next to the flatbed. "I'll run and grab blankets from another gallery."

"Be careful," Claire hissed. "For all we know, Larry might be sneaking around."

Mina jogged across the parquet floor and into the hallway.

Claire watched Sinjin. Standing in the middle of the space, he gazed around the room. "This is one hell of an exhibit," he said, then strode up to the bronze and clay metronome sculpture. "How is this in the steampunk genre? It's a stone sculpture. Like something Mary Nohl might have created."

"It's about time. How it shifts," she said. Her views on time were prevalent in this exhibit, but now wasn't the *time* for discourse. "We can talk about it later. Right now, let's use it as a bookend on the cart. We need to make sure the needle isn't loose. It looks heavy, but there's resin in it. Easy to handle. Wait, second thought, let's wrap the needle with a blanket."

He lifted the sculpture onto the end of the flatbed. "Who is the artist?"

"A French or Belgian woman." She blanked on the

woman's name. Clutching her knees, she took in a breath to calm down and concentrate. "Her name is Ivy Marshall."

Sinjin went to retrieve a Tiffany-stained glass piece off its pedestal. He took hold of the fragile glass triptych and deftly wrapped it in a sheet of bubble wrap. "Take a break. Sit down. I'll work counterclockwise. Unhinge the paintings, wrap, and store them."

Mina dropped a pile of quilted blankets on the floor and then handed one to Claire. She sat, crossed her legs, and tightened the heavy blanket around her. She watched Sinjin and Mina work together, dismantling the paintings one by one around the room's perimeter. Mina handed each painting to Sinjin, who then wrapped and placed them into the crates.

"We need a name for this heist," she said.

"It is not a heist," Mina huffed. "We're simply moving an art exhibit."

"Sure. 'Simply' under the nose of the executive director." Claire tapped her forehead. "How about, *The Case of the Vanishing Metronome*."

"Oh, nice. Has a Nancy Drew vibe." Mina waggled her eyebrows.

"We're almost finished," Sinjin announced, sliding another wrapped portrait into the wooden box. "Think about how you want to place the pieces in Maxwell's. This exhibit is a fantastic building block for your curatorial resume. We're not Agatha Christies. Let's stay focused."

"You don't like mysteries?" Claire scoffed.

"What British bloke doesn't? Watched telly with my mum. *Vera* was her favorite. Let's talk about this when we're back in Lake Bluff, shall we?"

Looking at the bare walls, she had to admit that assembling her show over the past year had been an incredible opportunity to strut her knowledge. Even if she'd struggled as a painter on her own, she had sailed smoothly and shined while contacting artists and organizing this baby. She hadn't expected to, but she enjoyed the process. It wasn't a chore but a complete pleasure. Claire's only discontent had been trying to navigate Larry's demands and petty personality.

Mina wheeled the cart up to the last painting hanging on the wall, the original David Raffen titled *More Lace Please.* The woman in the portrait was dressed in a Victorian dress, but it wasn't a nineteenth-century replication as she'd thought. Claire had no idea who had posed for her dad, but definitely not her mom.

She'd spent a substantial chunk of time analyzing this portrait of an unknown woman dressed in black who appeared to be heading out to a funeral. But like the few of her father's pieces remaining in her possession, actually, she rarely *saw* them. She kept them neatly stacked against the wall in her apartment. Even though they were valuable, in her mind, they were family portraits. Like a photo album—still awkward but much bulkier.

Claire examined the color of the woman's eyes. The color was closer to her eye color than to her mother's. She snapped a photo and decided to research this woman. Was this a great-grandmother on the Raffen side of her family? The English side?

Sinjin stood beside her. "What's wrong?"

"I don't know who the woman is in the portrait."

He leaned in closer without touching his nose to the canvas. "Maybe a relative. Definitely pretty."

Claire became utterly confused. Was this a woman from her father's or her mother's side of the family? A familiar drumbeat pounded, a sound drawing her in and tempting her. She became anxious to head to her safe place, the Milwaukee library, to isolate and research. Since moving from Chicago, the library had been her sole power source.

"Do the honors, Claire. Take it down." Sinjin stepped

between her and the picture and set his hands on her shoulders. "We'll find out who she is. I promise." He kissed her cheek and glanced at the painting. "In a short time, it will be hanging again. No one coming to Maxwell's will be able to take their eyes off this beautiful woman."

He stepped aside, and she unhooked *More Lace Please* from the wall. With steady hands, she placed it with the other paintings.

"We are going. Now." Sinjin pushed the cart through the door.

Claire took one last glance at the bare sage-green walls, then followed them out of the gallery and to the elevator.

Mina, inside already, shifted her weight from one leg to another. Sinjin pushed the loaded cart in, pulled down a layer of the quilted wall, and placed it over the flatbed cart. Claire hesitated before stepping inside, frozen by crippling fear. Sinjin lunged out and pulled her into the elevator before the doors shut.

She fell into his arms. The adrenaline racing through her crashed, and her body quivered so viciously she could barely stand.

"We're two floors away from being done, and then we head back to Lake Bluff." He held her steady.

Pressing her face against his chest, she gulped in air smelling of apples and cinnamon, then peered up at him. "Why is this so hard?"

A strange expression shadowed his face. "Because you've been immersed in this exhibit for the past year, and now, pardon my English, we're moving your Stilton."

She laughed.

The elevator stopped. He loosened her arms from around his waist, freeing her from the cocoon of his dark warm jacket.

Mina glanced at them, then hurried out the door, pulling the dolly.

He held her hand and pushed the cart to the garage and van with the other. Mina went ahead and opened the back hatch.

The hard lines around Sinjin's beautiful lips and mouth told her something she'd overlooked. This man had lost something big. They both needed this exhibit to come to fruition but for innately different reasons.

Her phone rang from inside the front pocket of her overalls. Without looking, she knew it was Larry.

Chapter 16

"Talk to him," Sinjin said. "Go to his office. We'll pack up and drive away from the museum. Then we'll meet up later. Keep Larry occupied so we get Mina out of sight."

"Claire Beaumont," she answered the call.

"I assume you're in the museum. That atrocious orange bus is parked in the lot."

"Yes. I'll meet you in your office in ten."

She needed to have this face-off with Larry.

Pocketing her phone, she impulsively gave Sinjin a peck on his cheek. If he was surprised by her kiss, he didn't show it. Or did he? Jogging to the elevator, she really wanted to glance back at him but didn't. Had she imagined his cheeks reddening?

Once at the front entrance, the glass doors of the executive offices loomed over her with their big black lettering.

Lafferty Museum-Cardinal University
ESTABLISHED 1979
FOUNDERS
PAUL LAFFERTY
AND
MADGE WENTWORTH

She took a moment to admire the foyer's sculpture, a bronze nude by Mina's late mother, Madge Wentworth, then went inside the office. It was a typical cubicle farm with cubbies lining the space from end to end. The only separate office belonged to Larry. It offered a spectacular view of the lake that the rest of the worker bees could only see if his doors were open. Which was as rare as the lunar eclipse.

A bare-bones staff worked before ten on Mondays. Claire scanned the cubbies to see whose heads were bobbing up and down. No one but Donna, Larry's assistant, who was blessed with a free-standing desk, was at work. Claire stepped up to her as she ended a phone conversation, and they exchanged curt pleasantries. Unsure as to where Donna's loyalties lay, Claire had never made an effort to chitchat with her.

"Mr. Chambers will be returning momentarily. An emergency in the gift shop."

A gift shop emergency? Sounded like pure nonsense.

"Apparently," Donna said, "a part-timer mistook some ancient papyrus scrolls as recycled paper and threw them out."

Claire had a hard time keeping a straight face. Might be a tragic loss for the museum, but Larry deserved some tarnish on his reputation. What would the board think about this little nugget?

Instead of waiting around for him, she sat at her desk and collected all of the documents she'd accumulated for *Victorious Vectors*. Her paper consumption had become a seriously bad habit. Although she'd attempted to quit and bond with the cloud, the touch of paper gave her greater security.

She crouched down, opened the bottom drawer of the file cabinet, and grabbed the manila folders for each artist and the patrons who had donated to support the show. Claire had jotted down every quirk and nuance about each collector who had backed her exhibit. She and Sinjin needed every bit of info to help spin the new location. *Celebrating the last-minute move to a charming small town. Main Street meets steampunk and a time of high art.*

"Ms. Beaumont. There you are."

Larry leaned his shoulder against the nubby gray makeshift wall, propping his elbow on the divider. His yellow tie contrasted cleanly against his black suit and white dress shirt. His cuticles were translucent and moon-shaped—he must have had his regular manicure appointment recently.

He appeared to be his usual self, except the rims around his eyes were crimson. *Guilt-ridden and lacking sleep?* Because he had called her an *idiot*, she knew his true colors were red and demonic.

"Everything all right in the shop? And the lost papyrus?"

"Yes." Larry covered his yawn. "Let's step into my office."

Claire checked the time on the Alessi wall clock. The hands on the designer timepiece, made of chrome balls, struck at seven fifty-five. She nibbled at her thumb. Hopefully, Sinjin and Mina had finished loading the van and left the museum.

When she followed him into his office, the wood paneling and heavy drapes nearly suffocated her. The curtains blocked out the view of the lake. The man must have been allergic to the sun. "Larry, I want to apologize. I'm not sure what has happened to get to this point, but Mr. Reid assured me his sculpture will be included in my exhibit. As the curator, I promise this new location will be as successful as if it had opened in the museum."

"Did you actually see *Coal or Steam*? Or were you too *busy* with the artist?"

His "busy" definitely implied *sex*. The man must have had difficulty breathing with all the slime clinging to him. The lie left her lips smoothly. "Of course I've seen it. I actually asked to take a photo, but…well…you know artists. They can be very guarded and protective of their work."

"The unfortunate byproduct of swollen egos." Without offering her a seat, he sat in the Eames chair behind his desk. "You surprise me. Never seemed as if there was a lot going on behind those Liz Taylor eyes of yours. Now your sad little exhibit will be spectacular. Especially since, moving forward, you will be receiving specifications from me."

A dollop of this morning's pomegranate juice rose in her throat, and she coughed to clear out the bitter taste. "I understand. It must have been a surprise to learn Sinjin Reid didn't have the sculpture in his possession, but then he did. But this exhibit… Well, Mr. Reid told me his wife—I mean his ex-wife…" She paused to find some air in the stale office. "As I relayed to you, the sculptor had sold the piece before the divorce." She sounded professional, even though she wanted to tear Larry's throat out. She added emphatically, "This exhibit is pivotal for my resume."

His icy gaze slid over her, and then he flipped open a manila file sitting on his desk.

Directly in front of him, she pressed her legs against the desk and peered down at the file. Immediately, she recognized her own handwriting on the tab of one of her exhibit files. The file on her father's painting. Claire tapped her messenger bag, bulging with paperwork, recalling that she hadn't retrieved her notes on the portrait. Her nails bit into her palms, and she kept her fists locked against her hips. "If you needed information, you could have simply asked me for it. Did you really feel it necessary to remove my documents?"

"As the executive director, I don't need your permission to access museum property." He flipped the top sheet over and jabbed it with his glossy fingernail. "Ms. Beaumont, also known as Ms. Raffen, this tells me all I need to know. When you relocate your *Vector* exhibit, you will make sure to place the Reid sculpture front and center of the new location. The David Raffen will be placed in the back. The fact is the sculpture is what patrons want to see. Placing the dismal Raffen portrait first, coupled with his miserable reputation in the art world, might drive people away. And except for those two pieces, the rest of your exhibit is complete drivel. Do you understand?"

If it weren't for the way Sinjin had gazed at her exhibit less than thirty minutes earlier—totally appreciative of its brilliance from all her hard work—Claire may have been crushed by Larry's insults. Completely.

As he continued his tongue-lashing, she fought to steady her breathing. Insulting her father had been shattering, yet she wanted to remember every word to repeat it to Sinjin and Mina.

"You will send photos of the exhibit layout to me, at every stage, for my approval. Are we clear?"

Before she responded, he shut the folder and shoved it at her. "And if we're not, this may help. I'm willing to bet you will jump as high as I want because if you don't, I'll make sure you never have a job anywhere in the art world. And if you don't believe me, let me say this. There are four paintings out in the world that weren't painted by David Raffen but by you. And I don't think anyone, not even Mina Lafferty, will ever speak to you again when they find out."

With the dark and dreary room spinning around her, Claire gripped the strap of her messenger bag with two hands. There would be spots of blood on it by the time she left the beast's lair. But she wouldn't confess a thing.

"I'm not sure what you're talking about, Mr. Chambers. I am the daughter of David Raffen, but you know that from Mina. I'm sure she told you. My relation to Raffen has never been a secret. True, after his death, I wanted to define myself, so I don't mention our familial relationship too often. But I have always had my mother's surname." She knew she was babbling, but she had to at least get him off the forgery topic. "Rumors, as you know, are a dime a dozen in the art arena."

He nudged the folder toward her again, this time making contact with the bib of her overalls. "I'm well aware of the rumors. In fact, I've been known to start a few of my own. But I'm privy to a wealth of info, and what happened at the Armory Show—"

She snagged the folder out of his slippery hand and concentrated on shoving it in with the others.

"—Although Raffen is long dead and buried, his misstep, or maybe yours? Doesn't matter. The so-called rumor is alive and kicking. Better follow my directions, Ms. Beaumont, or history will kick your sweet ass to the curb."

"You are a horrible person, Larry Chambers," she shouted, making sure his assistant would hear her, then added, "and a narcissistic liar."

"Well, if I could fire you, I would, but unfortunately, I have Mina Lafferty to deal with. So do as you're told."

Storming out of the office and slamming the door was out of the question. The wood was too heavy, and all her energy had been depleted from maintaining her ramrod posture. With adrenaline rushing through her veins, she grasped the handle, strode out, and gently shut the door.

"Thanks." Donna smiled, then gave her a nod of approval and disappeared into a distant cubicle.

Now Claire was sure of the assistant's loyalties. And without a doubt, Claire knew she had to rid the Lafferty of Larry Chambers.

Beyond the glass door leading to the front entrance were a couple of security guards loitering around the Wentworth sculpture. One was on his phone, and the other spoke to a fashionably dressed woman carrying an expensive-looking handbag.

Claire speed-walked to the main entrance. From the top of the staircase, she saw a guard she didn't recognize leaning against the marble banister at the bottom of the steps. Growing nervous, she hugged her bag against her chest and whirled around to prevent the unknown guard from noticing her. With her back to him, she sidestepped down the stairs and jogged out of the building.

A cool fall breeze fell on her face, and she smelled the putrid scent of alewives coming off Lake Michigan after the warm weekend. Lost in her own head, she hoofed the few blocks across campus to reach her neighborhood.

Fall was her absolute favorite time of year. No one, not even the curmudgeon called Larry, could ruin her love for pumpkin lattes and hiking trails coated with plenty of crispy leaves to crunch over. Yet she looked up at the cloudless sky. When would the anvil drop on her head? Larry knew her darkest secret.

She unlocked the door to her apartment, trudged inside, and collapsed on her sofa. A safe refuge for now. All she wanted to do was forget about the pettiest man in the world but knew it wouldn't serve her best interests. She had to follow his orders. With a load of desperation threatening to take her down, she concentrated on *Vectors*. Its theme of steam, momentum, and time working as a trio of positive forces, like *The Three Graces*, portrayed a message of hope. As the curator, that could be on her side, right?

Her phone pinged with a message from Sinjin.

Where are you?

Appropriately, time had been lost to her. She returned his

text, assuring him she was fine—another lie—but a little discombobulated. The understatement of the century. She added her address and told him to come over. Since Sinjin drove a van full of priceless artwork, which seconds ago had become her sole lifeline, she watched out the window. If an empty parking spot became available out front for the van, she would believe her dad was watching out for her.

Booyah.

Glancing around her front room, she hastily moved the portrait of her mother from the bookshelf and stashed it in her bedroom closet. The fall version in the series of four, titled *Golden*.

Chapter 17

Before moving to Lake Bluff, Sinjin had lived in Chicago. When heading north to visit his dad in Kohler, he would regularly stop in Milwaukee and make time to pop into the Third Ward, the easygoing downtown area. Milwaukee was Chicago's smaller sibling but with much more charm.

He had made his way to a parking lot near a corner grocery store after dropping off Mina. While waiting to hear from Claire, he watched the shoppers stop and shop at the store's street carts full of fresh fall flowers and pumpkins. He considered walking over to buy Claire a bouquet of the purple asters because her meeting with the beast had to be the worst. But he wanted to stay right by the art. She would appreciate her exhibit complete and unharmed rather than a bunch of flowers.

A stream of unread texts from Julie lit up his phone.

Where the hell are you? I have plans. This is bullshit. Not waiting.

He blocked Julie and decided to ring his father. He'd hidden *Coal or Steam* in the trunk of his father's car to make sure it was safe and sound. Sinjin had kept a watch on it and his dad, with weekly updates. Since retiring, the man had a lot of time on his hands. Something he hadn't had while managing the corporate world in Kohler, Sinjin's incapacitated mum in Door County, and basically raising three teen boys alone back in the day. He'd become much tighter with George this past year because of the sculpture. Maybe the thing wasn't as big of a jinx as he'd thought.

George picked up the call with his usual British bluster. A mix of appreciative surprise, even though they had spoken five days earlier, and fatherly support tinged with bossiness. Sinjin was sure the roles of CEO and patriarch were difficult to shed after seventy-plus years. "How are you doing, Dad?"

"Cheers, but I'm due for a proper shave, and my barber is closed."

"It's Monday. Stag is always closed," Sinjin said, then sussed that the barbershop was located in Lake Bluff. "Where are you?"

"In Lake Bluff. Have you gone bonkers? You told me to come into town on Monday."

Sinjin had said next Monday but wasn't going to argue the point. "Oh, right. Sure. I'm in Milwaukee. There must have been a miscommunication."

"Milwaukee? Why the hell are you there? Don't tell me that you're cozying up with that evil ex of yours. Doesn't she live there?"

"No," he said, thinking about Meg's red BMW he'd seen in the parking garage. "All of that is in the past. Meg Fisher hasn't been near me since I obtained a restraining order. I'm here to assist some mates. We're designing another art exhibit. Which is why I called. Is the sculpture still in your Caddie?"

A car horn blared in the background. He hoped his father made use of the hands-free phone he'd given him. "Do you need to pull over, Dad? I really don't want you to get in a fender bender."

"Because of my health? Or the bloody sculpture?"

"You are seventy-five. I should be concerned…" Sinjin chuffed. "But *Coal or Steam* is worth a lot of quid." Oh, how he loved taking the piss out of his father.

"If that's how you feel, son…you can do this old bloke a favor. As long as you're galivanting around Milwaukee, go pick up your brother Gus at the airport tonight."

"What? You're contracting me to get Angus? I have a ton of shit to do today. Since when did you know that the FHW was coming home?" Sinjin was sure his father had knowingly kept Angus's arrival from him. His celebrity brother had a way of rankling Sinjin, and his dad knew it.

"Gus left a message. No need to name-call. Do you really think your brother deserves the moniker Fucking Hollywood Wanker?"

Yes.

Sinjin dropped his head back. The hard wood massage beads bit into his scalp. Because his dad didn't answer his first question, he tried another. "If I hadn't been, coincidently, in Milwaukee, what was Gus planning to do? Hike to Lake Bluff?"

"He rented a limo. But it has a bar. It's an ask, but the boy has to operate without hooch, and I think he can do it."

This was his dad's superpower—empathy. He'd used it with Sinjin when he struggled in school and then passed it on to him. How could he argue with his father's tolerance? "All right. On one condition."

"Speak up, and then I'll agree or disagree."

"Do you remember Lucy Maxwell? Or her mother, Julie. Maxwell's on Main Street?"

"I met Lucy at an Al-Anon meeting and know all about Julie's vices. Why?"

Sinjin forged onward. "The exhibit I'm working on will be opening at Julie's shop. I've worked with her all summer—she's a sculptor and artist, does beautiful work, but she's been having difficulties since we parted ways. Anyway, yesterday and today, she's been drunk texting me nonstop. I'm not sure what's going on."

"Ya didn't lead her on, did you?"

"Hell, no. She's older, and her drinking? It's terribly sad. I've learned a lot from you, whether you believe it or not. And her daughter Lucy is running around taking care of her. It's quite a mess when a daughter takes over as the mother to her own mum."

"I get it. What do you need? Any chance either of them can trim my mustache?"

Sinjin shook his head and chuffed. "If you're near Main, you'll see the shop name on the huge awning at the entrance. Lucy is taking care of my dogs for the day. And Julie...I'm not sure where she is, but if both are there, you can chat with them."

"I'd planned on heading to your house and taking a nap, but I'll go down the street for a chin wag. Plenty of time."

A thin layer of stress fell off Sinjin's shoulders. Julie's messages had been unnerving. Having his father keep an eye on her and the shop was a relief. "What time is Gus's flight coming in? And can you tell him I'll be in an orange VW minibus?"

"Sure. The flight from LA is scheduled to land at 8:20." He hesitated, then added, "Do you have his contact info, or did you block him?"

As much as he had wanted to cut ties, he'd never been able to block Gus out of his life. Unfortunately, his other brother, Rob, had done it. "I'll shoot him a text to confirm his arrival. Then expect us to be at Maxwell's if all goes well around ten tonight."

After swapping one stress for another, Sinjin said goodbye to his dad and texted Claire. He drove to her apartment on the other side of the campus. Maple trees lined her street and were in full autumn regalia. White wrought iron patios butted out of the red brick building, and ivy foliage parading the colors of gold and bronze covered the rest of the façade.

Before getting out of the van, he made sure all the pieces of *Vectors* were well hidden under the piles of shipping blankets. Sinjin locked each door, growing anxious to see Claire. It had been over an hour since she'd kissed his cheek, and he still felt the warmth on the exact spot where her lips had touched him.

He pressed the security button in the vestibule and shoved his hands through his hair to smooth it down, then dug out a breath mint from his bag and chomped on it. This awkwardness was— The grating buzz and loud lock release squashed his nerves, and he bolted inside.

Why was he taking the stairs two at a time? He reached her door, and before knocking, she opened it. Claire looked exhausted, and it wasn't even ten o'clock. He blamed Larry. "What the hell did he say?"

She showed Sinjin into her apartment, shaking her head. "I'm fine. Nothing I can't handle. A few insults aimed directly at my father's worth, and he tightened my leash. Every step I take in regard to displaying the exhibit needs his approval. Picture by picture."

"Ignore it." Following her into the living room, he gawped at the classic British chesterfield couch, the color of a green pepper. It faced a fireplace with shelves of books from floor to ceiling on either side of it. The crowning glory was the marble-topped sideboard table adjacent to the back of the couch with a vintage turntable. Under it, a collection of albums. Right away, he wanted to flip through the covers. As a teen, he'd listened to albums with his dad daily.

"Sorry, I spaced. Didn't mean to disappear on you. Larry

threw me off my game." She handed him a cup of coffee. "This is fresh. I love Lucy's juices, but I really needed caffeine."

"Ta. I hope you aren't in a rush to get back to Maxwell's." He hadn't expected to introduce her to his brother, but it couldn't be avoided. Angus Reid—TV superstar with legions of female fans—was coming home from LA for a visit. "I've been asked by my father to return to Lake Bluff with my brother. He's flying in tonight."

"That's fine. It gives me a chance to take care of a few things before we go back." She sat in an ornately brocaded Queen Anne chair and wrapped a quilt around her, then hugged her knees against her chest. "I really want to do some research. Try to start anyway, to find out who the woman in the portrait is. The pivotal piece of *cheese* that we're moving."

Her cocooning made him feel comfortable; he relaxed on the glamorous Hollywood-style davenport. "I understand." He went to set his mug on the side table and noticed it had a leather top. Glancing around, he spotted a coaster on the table with the turntable. He paused to admire the classic vintage record player, then brushed his fingers over the antique sofa. "Family heirloom?"

She took a sip of coffee. "I think I may have to be buried inside it. It was my grandfather's, handed down to my dad, and now I'm lucky enough to own the monstrosity. It's beautiful, but the size has made it a pain in the ass to move." She pointed at the balcony. "The thing is too wide for the staircase, so I hired a crane to get the sucker through the window and inside here."

He tapped the brass rivets on the end of the arm. "Did you ever consider adding it into *Vectors*? It belongs in a steampunk setting. Or time frame. Definitely has a *Titanic* feel to it."

"True, if my show sinks, it will be perfect." She shook her head, disgusted. "Larry's so abhorrent he basically called my dad a loser. If it weren't for that damn article, no one in the art world would have ever thought less of him. That pea-brain Arthur Silver writing about David Raffen. It was a rivalry like Mozart and Salieri." She took a sip of coffee. "Asshole."

He recalled the *Art & Form* article that had dismantled Raffen's reputation and then dismissed it. Avoiding critics had been his mantra from the time he'd taken his first welding class. "I'm a superfan, as you know, so my advice won't be objective. But that guy, I believe the magazine booted him out. And Larry? He wouldn't know the difference between a masterpiece and a paint-by-numbers kit."

Sinjin, without a doubt, had long ago determined that Larry's knowledge of the art world had been obtained from his relationship with Meg. As much as she'd become the sting in the ointment of Sinjin's life, she was highly intuitive and intelligent when it came to the nitpicky and volatile business of art. They were the attributes that, he had to confess, had forged his attraction for her. "By any chance, while you were in the Lafferty, did you come across an unknown or unfamiliar person?"

"Not at all." Standing, she wrapped the blanket around her shoulders and retrieved a folder from her bag on the dining room table. "I'm fixated on my dad's portrait. And even if Larry's insisting that the *Lace* painting should be shoved in a broom closet, I'm going to make sure that I have all its history on my side." She handed him the folder, then climbed the ladder to reach the top bookshelf. "I should have some kind of book around to get me started on research. But we really need to get to the library."

He opened the folder and halfheartedly paged through the copies of the Raffen painting. "Are you sure there wasn't a woman in the office? In an area near Larry?"

She pulled out a book and hopped off the ladder. "Donna.

His assistant." She paged through a tome of some sort, then stopped and stared at him. "*Damn.* Yes. An extremely well-dressed woman spoke to a guard as I left the building. Sorry, I rushed out of there and didn't—"

"It's okay. I had a gut feeling when a red BMW was parked in the garage. Meg's around town."

Setting a book on the table with brightly colored stripes on the hardcover, Claire sat on the sofa beside him. "What does it mean? Why is she here?"

"The two are working together. Larry needs her help, and he wants my sculpture placed in a spot that's easily accessible. This is going to be incredibly interesting over the next few weeks." He read the title of the book that Claire had set in front of him. "*How To Be An Artist?* Is this a hint?"

"What? Oh no. This author, he's a guy who was a good friend of my dad's. About the same age. I want to read it. Maybe reach out to him." She handed it to Sinjin. "Have it. It's a quick read."

The small book intimidated him. He sucked some air. "Is it on audio? I'm more comfortable hearing it." Avoiding books suited Sinjin, as dyslexia made reading a draining mental task. "I usually listen while working."

Without batting an eye, she grabbed her phone. "This guy is such a great writer, you need to hear what he has to say. As a token of appreciation, I'm gifting the audio version to you."

"Thank you." He was most thankful that she didn't flinch when he asked about the audio. He rubbed his hands together. Already he'd been granted two wishes, talent and success. He gazed at Claire and contemplated whether or not his third wish would be granted. Or was asking for love too much?

"When do you need to pick up your brother? What's his name again?"

"Angus. And his flight comes in at eight. If it's on time,

we'll be in Lake Bluff by ten. Plenty of time to unload the van. Lucy will be around because she's taking care of the dogs for me. And Julie. She's messaged me several times." Knowing that his father would be at Maxwell's kept him from showing his annoyance. "Ten o'clock seems to work for all."

Chapter 18

It wasn't until they were outside and walking to the library on Wisconsin Avenue that Claire recognized her Milwaukee apartment was strangely similar to her previous apartment in Chicago. It never hosted any male visitors.

She had often wondered if by repeatedly moving her deceased parents' collection of antique furniture and belongings, they had become like ghosts scaring away a chance for a normal love life or her ability to maintain a stable relationship with another creature. Her lack of pets and plants was evident. But damn, the way Sinjin had gazed at her father's turntable and album collection, even if they were inanimate objects, there might be a sliver of hope. After all, she'd maintained the music collection as if it were as fickle as a fern.

The fact that Sinjin had actually made his way inside her apartment, her sanctuary, was astounding. His proximity in her world rattled her, yet she couldn't decide if she was excited about it or petrified. However, each time they were near one another, her heart and head did a little dance number. Sometimes the Batusi but more often a steamy flamenco. But with Larry threatening to stomp on her heels, she had to stay as neutral as beige and as invisible as an introvert at a sweaty rave dance.

Before heading into the library, she had to placate her hunger, so they swung into the burger joint across the street. They ordered, and she asked the embarrassing question that had been on her mind since Sinjin had mentioned Angus Reid. "Is your brother the famous actor?"

He chewed on a bite of french fry so hard that his Adam's apple leaped about. "Unfortunately, yes. His celebrity status has turned him into a wanker. Always talking about himself."

She'd watched all of Angus Reid's TV shows but was mortified to admit it. She cut her burger into quarters to eat it presentably.

"My younger brother managed to turn a series of maca-roni-and-cheese adverts into a career on television. He's famous from playing a bloody Scottish vampire and now he's some kind of detective."

Before taking a bite, she added, "The sexy Scotsman who sucks the *blood* from fair-haired maidens conveniently stumbling across his moat and into his Edinburgh castle?" Claire blushed and recalled how she and Lucy had religiously watched the show every week. "I confess. Lucy and I were fans."

"Interesting. Learn something new every day. The *artiste* formerly known as Gus is as Scottish as you or I. Not a drop of broody kilt blood in him. He's getting too much attention from fans, driving us crazy. My youngest brother, Rob, completely avoids him."

As an only child and, in some ways, still living within the shadows of her long-gone parents, it sounded dismal and like a lost chance. She'd always wanted to know what having a sibling would have been like. "Well, I promise I won't gush over him when we meet tonight. But I'm not sure about Lucy. She had a major crush on the 'wanker.'"

When Sinjin offered to pay their bill, she protested and

insisted on paying her own half. Paying her own way made it simpler to stay beige around him. Easier to douse the red-hot flames licking at her toes.

After lunch, she made sure to keep an old pal/new buddy-like distance from him when they walked across the street to the library. Thankfully, once inside, Claire fell into her usual daze when she entered the foyer and gazed up at the Renaissance dome three floors above and the Italian marble columns. This library filled her with joy, even more than New York's library, with the collection of real Winnie-the-Pooh toys on display.

Sinjin cleared his throat, shoving her from the trance. Discovering that he'd had some kind of learning disability made so much sense. His artistic genius flowed from his heart to his hands. She often thought that her father, who'd had a short attention span, was challenged with some type of neuro-diversity.

It was good to know that reading and books weren't his jam, and thankfully, her devotion to the written word was tempered by her love of pictures and paintings. They strolled through the grand entrance, sky-gazing at the detailed rotunda and then pausing to take in the mosaic tiles at their feet.

"All right if I head up and take the stairs?"

"Go ahead, they're free. Like the library. Opening a story and a new world only takes a few flicks with your fingers. I'll be on the first floor looking—" She bit her tongue. Asshole Larry had put the idea in her head. She wanted to find all the articles Arthur Silver had written about her dad in *Art & Form*. "In the nonfiction section. I want to see if there are any new books about steampunk. And famous women in that era at the turn of the century. Before the depression."

"I'll meet up with you. I'm interested in the metals used in this building construction."

They separated. She felt adrift without him, but her time was finite. She jogged past the checkout stations and went into a carrel to access the search site Scout on the library's computer system. She popped in *Art & Form* and the dates around the dreaded incident at the Armory Show and the critic's name, Arthur Silver. She sent all the links to her email and left the carrel. She'd look later to see if Art and Larry had some kind of connection.

In the nonfiction section, several new steampunk books had been added. She had spent hours going through and completely exhausted all the original resources the past two years to research and learn about steampunk and the concept of time traveling. She combed through each new book to make sure she hadn't missed a bit of information that could be useful for *Vectors*.

Pulling up the pic on her phone that she'd taken of *More Lace Please*, she expanded it to get a better look. Seeing it constantly while setting up the show, she wasn't sure if anything would pop out at her now. But she stayed stuck on the title. There was a rhyme and a reason to each of the titles her dad had given to his works.

She willed herself to recognize the face of the woman in the portrait. It bore no resemblance to her or her mother. After seeing all the drawings Sinjin had in his cottage that her dad had done, she was totally relieved. She couldn't take seeing yet another version of herself through her dad's eyes when his vision was working perfectly.

She had a thought. Even though the date of the work was 1995, when her dad's vision was brilliant, Claire knew how he operated with the truth or, more accurately, played around with time. Had this painting actually been finished when his eyesight was nearly gone five years ago?

Rubbing her face, she stretched her neck to get the kinks

out. A pair of warm solid hands settled on her shoulders. "Hey."

The subtle scent of orange juice tickled her nose as Sinjin lightly massaged her shoulders.

"I'm not turning around. Don't want to break free from your grasp. Feels incredible. Don't stop."

"At least one of those sentences would be a solid porn title." His hands stopped. "From what I've been told. Not that I... Not a big fan of the genre."

"Shut the front door? Really? Hard to tell with those big strong hands of yours. Do you fix refrigerators too?"

"Find anything new about *More Lace Please?*" He ignored her, pulling up a chair to sit beside her in the carrel. With his nearness, all thoughts of staying beige were tossed out. "May I?"

"Go for it."

He took her phone and lightly pinched and fiddled with the screen in different directions, tilting his head to get a close look at it. "We can simply go back to your place and pull out the actual painting from the van?"

"It's just that I've looked at it so often it's embedded too deeply in my brain. I think I'm seeing what I want to see, not what's actually there."

"Ah, the old adage, paint what you see, not what you know."

Shrugging, she remembered how she had to paint what she saw when painting *Seasons*. There wasn't a choice. Having never actually laid eyes on her mom, the old photos had guided her.

"Hold on," he said, staring at the phone. "What is this lace around her neck?"

"A necklace. Actually a choker. It was a popular fashion accoutrement back in the 1800s."

As his long eyelashes nearly swept over her screen, he

added, "We have to look at the choker. This lace, I believe, is a design of cogs and wheels, like in a watch."

"The face. I've been so focused on the damn face I ignored the necklace." She retrieved the phone from his hand. A tingle of heat passed between them when their fingers grazed one another. She shivered. A beam of sunlight splayed over them from the glass ceiling. It reminded her of a rom-com scene. Blushing, she stared at the photo.

"Do you see it?"

She squinted and tilted her head. Widened her eyes, then squeezed them to nearly closed. Then it became glaringly obvious. A pattern on the white necklace with circles. They varied between thick and thin, but all with teeth jutting out and intersecting with each other. "Time. A clock gear. Damn. We need to go back to my place. Get it out of the van. I have to see the real thing."

Excited by Sinjin's intense scrutiny and brilliant observation, she knew the dull beige phase was in the past. She could only see fuchsia and wasn't sure how to feel about such an optimistic color.

Claire was out of breath by the time they arrived back on her street. She hadn't worn her best shoes for jogging. Doc Martens were made for stomping, not running. Her adrenaline managed to keep stride with Sinjin, but his long legs forced her to sprint to keep up with him. He reached Orange-Mina first and unlocked the back doors. With *More Lace Please* covered in a protective blanket, he hugged it against his chest as if it were his favorite schoolbook. She darted up the stairs and opened all the doors for him.

Inside her apartment, Claire scrambled around to find an unused easel. Unfortunately, she had to dash into her studio to retrieve one. Sinjin followed her down the hall, so she slammed her bedroom door shut. "The lighting is better in my studio," she said, "but do you think we should inspect the painting in the front room?"

"Are you testing me?" Clutching onto the edges of the midsize painting, he leaned against the doorframe and scanned her studio. "I mean…in here, I'll get to know a bit more about your creative side, but I'm dying to see what's in your father's record collection."

Knowing that Sinjin was taking in every detail of her studio, she grabbed an aluminum display easel, herded him away from the door, and shut it behind her. "The vault is sealed for the day. Besides, I think the albums and your recognition of the lace design might give us a clue. Something I had completely forgotten about. My dad loved Fleetwood Mac."

She led him away from her studio, and given that the man practically had x-ray vision, she hoped that she had closed her bedroom door fast enough. Even though she'd hidden *Golden* in the closet, Sinjin could pick up the scent of art like a damn bloodhound.

He gently unwrapped *MLP* and set it on the easel she had placed by her father's turntable. His record collection, another monstrous item she'd moved from their Chicago house, filled two long shelves under the bureau. Claire opened the drawer full of her dad's many antique magnifying glasses and handed one to Sinjin.

"Beautiful," he said, inspecting the brass handle.

Did she just announce that her dad was nearly blind before he died? "Yeah, he loved these as much as his brushes. I try not to use them too often because they're antiques."

Claire cast out her ridiculous notion. Magnifying glasses were standard equipment in every painter's toolbox. Using the magnifier, she looked at the painting through the thick glass. "I can't believe the design in this woman's lace escaped me."

Sinjin stood back with his arms across his chest. "I want to get a view from this distance first. You know I love your father's paintings, but this one I've never seen. Anywhere."

"It was a fluke, because of all the Raffens out in the world, I was only able to hold on to a few that weren't sought after."

She carefully fiddled with the angle of the magnifier and positioned it to enlarge the thin band of lace painted in white around the figure's neck. Twisting the magnifier, she saw what Sinjin had seen with his own eyes on the photograph.

Fine swirls of charcoal created a likeness of wheels and cogs, looking like what would be inside a Swiss watch. The intricate pattern repeated around the entire lace necklace. "You have one heck of a good eye. It must be your superpower."

"It's the way my brain processes configurations. My noggin..." He tapped his temple. "It's fantastic with recognizing patterns and shapes, but letters? They're a nuisance and made my school days rather hellish." He pointed to the albums. "May I?"

"Be my guest," she said, staring at the portrait. "This is a woman with a stylish necklace made of lace—that's perfect for my exhibit. But who is she?"

"When did he paint it? Do you know?" he asked without glancing away from the shelf of albums. Sitting on the floor with his long legs pretzeled, he pulled out album after album, gawping at each one before sliding it back into the vertical stack.

She'd placed this painting in her collection when her father gave it to her right after the Armory Show debacle. Claire had assumed that he'd painted it before, forgotten about it, and then passed it down to her because, by that time, he'd lost most of his vision. She'd made the assumption because otherwise, why would her father ask her to paint for her? The questions swirled in her head. "I don't fucking know," she blurted out and then apologized. Her frustration had bit her in the butt.

"It's okay. I can...we'll figure it out. But if you want to know what I think, it's right here." He held up the Fleetwood Mac album *Rumors* and handed it to her. "The subject is a dead ringer for Stevie Nicks. Her style. All the lace and stuff. The color of the hair is spot-on."

Claire examined the album cover.

"My fingers are itching to put an album on this turntable. May I?"

"Go ahead," she said. He had a point. The vibe of the painting correlated with the black and flowy clothing worn by Stevie Nicks on the album cover. Even the posture of the woman in the portrait looked similar as she bowed to something or someone out of the frame. It seemed ridiculous but made sense. In those last days, her father rarely went into his studio; instead, he'd opted to lounge on his big green couch and listen to music.

The soothing sound of an old sixties crooner filled the room. She decided this mystery woman would have to remain unknown. It wouldn't behoove her to get lost in the prickly garden once planted by her father. She gently covered the painting with the blanket.

"Still interested in seeing my studio?" she asked hesitantly. "I mean, if not, I get it. The collection of Raffen albums is pretty amazing."

Sinjin stopped looking at the Bobby Darin album in his hand. "Um. Absolutely. As long as it's okay with you. I mean. You are showing your studio first. Artists and kids both want to win the *I'll show you mine if you show me yours* game."

"If you'd prefer, we can play Spin the Bottle?"

"In the closet?" he asked flirtatiously.

She could easily kiss Sinjin, but they would not be going anywhere near her bedroom or her closet. His lips would turn to ice if he discovered the portrait of her mom. "Studio. Let's do it."

He snickered at her poor choice of words, and she playfully batted his shoulder. "Such a mind. Is it always in the gutter?"

"If you're talking about bowling, then yes."

She took hold of his hand, liking the warmth of it, and led him into the innermost part of her sanctuary—her studio.

Chapter 19

If the living room had been yelling David Raffen, the studio shouted out Claire. A howl to the moon of sorts. Because the interior of the room was perfectly akin to the various phases of painting. Without releasing Claire's hand, he made a quick study of each of the walls. Going clockwise, the first wall displayed sketches, and her easel faced the second wall where the south-facing window let in the afternoon's full light. To his right, crates and shelves stored brushes in tin cans, and her paint bottles were arranged by color from lightest to darkest. Her selection of pinks and reds was prevalent and quite cheeky.

He hesitantly released her hand and turned toward the wall behind them. Her semi-completed paintings were displayed. The sizes of the four canvases were varied and modest. The colors outdid the subjects, which were landscapes.

He smiled, thinking of the shade of blue that had been smudged on her jeans when she'd arrived at his house. He sensed that Claire was fidgeting and turned to face her. She nibbled on her thumb.

"Brilliant work," he said. "Your use of color is..." He

struggled to find an authentic description, then resorted to his own style of creativity. "Punchy."

"Punchy?" Hugging herself, she went to the window and lifted the shades completely. "Having only a southern view relegates me to no lake, but the shining tower of the Northwestern Insurance building is legitimately a beacon of light. It nicely punctures the skyline."

He looked out the window and agreed. The tall building with all its glass and gloss and silver appeared as though it cracked open the sky. He stepped back and considered her sketches. They were all vertical compositions, her terrains deep instead of wide. Then he went back to the incomplete pieces. In one, the shades of bright colors led his eyes to a magenta castle hidden in the back by the lush greens and foliage in the foreground.

Shaking his head, he ironed down the hair on the back of his scalp with one hand. "I'm at a loss. Your work..." He turned to gaze into her soul-shattering eyes. "No disrespect to your father, but your work is superior."

"Seriously? As if..."

"No, really," he said, recalculating. "Possibly 'superior' is completely too subjective." He flashed her a cheeky grin. "But it's your use of color. It warms the heart. Full of compassion. Where your father, his portraits are fantastic but more ominous."

"Oh my god. I think you're right—"

"Doesn't happen often," he quipped.

"Ominous. *More Lace Please*. The woman is probably Stevie Nicks. I'd thought he'd painted it before—"

Sinjin carefully filled in the blank and finished for her. "Before he lost his sight?"

She sat on a pink vinyl barstool behind her worktable and spun it around to face the window.

He knew it was a risk. But he couldn't deny that he'd been

privy to her father's ailments from the beginning, since before Sinjin had worked at the Art Institute. "I've known...well, it's a topic that came up semi-regularly long before he'd died. With my colleagues in academia, we discussed it."

The chair metal squeaked when she slowly turned toward him. Instead of stressed, the crinkles around her eyes had smoothed out, and she appeared calmer.

"Damn. It's truly been forever since I've been able to take in a deep breath." She sat up tall, shook out her shoulders, opened her mouth, and sucked in a long breath of air.

Sinjin smiled as her cheeks ballooned and her eyes bulged out. She then blew out the air with a lot of loud raspberries. "I never wanted to talk about my dad's challenges. It was so debilitating, and I was devastated for him. I guess I thought we were on our own."

He stepped over to the globe on an antique brass stand and gave it a light spin. "It's easy to do when you're lost in pain."

She came up from behind, wrapped her arms around his waist, and laid her head against his back. He clasped her hands and let her kindness sink into every single one of his bones, only turning because of his overwhelming desire to kiss her. Facing Claire, he cupped her cheeks and let her violet eyes capture him. He brushed his fingers along the smooth skin of her neck, and her hair tickled the back of his hand. Their lips touched, and a powerful sense of affinity came over him.

She slipped her hand under his shirt and caressed his back. As he deepened the kiss, Claire softly moaned. Gasps of air fanned their insatiable heat and kept it lit. His ringing phone doused it with a cold bucket of ice water. It had to be Angus. His famous bro had the worst sense of timing for an actor. *F-H-W*.

"Do you really have to answer it?" she sighed.

Still gathering his thoughts, he stared at her plump lips turned to a sweet shade of fuchsia. "Yes, but not because I want to. It's the Fucking Hollywood Wanker. His timing…I'm baffled that the man has made a career of acting. Since he was a kid, his timing has always been off. It's ludicrous that he actually hits his *mark*, as they say in TV land."

"We should get organized anyway. To be continued later," she said as he answered the call.

"Where the hell are you?" Angus bellowed so loud it filled the small room. Sinjin held the phone away from his pounding eardrum.

"I'm in Milwaukee, asshole." Sinjin checked his watch. "It's only four o'clock. Dad said eight."

"Got on an earlier flight. I'll be waiting at the bar. Perfect timing. Happy hour."

The line died, and Sinjin shook his head. "Oh, how I'd love to let the demanding diva sit and wait. But my dad…" He paused, then let it out. "Angus and his drinking, it's been worrying my father."

"Come on, let's pack up *More Lace Please* and head back to Lake Bluff," she said. "I'm going to pack a bag real quick. I'm sure Lucy is tired of lending me her clothes."

"Go ahead. I'll take care of the Stevie Nicks painting."

"It is Stevie Nicks. I bet she was so deeply etched in my dad's mind that all the details in the painting came from his heart, flowed through his brush, and landed on the canvas. He probably never really looked or actually saw his finesse."

"I'd put money on that theory," he added, "because when I'm working on a sculpture, it's impossible to know how the heat and the welding will land. I'm concerned with connecting the flame to the metal with a vision of the curve in my mind."

She escorted him out of the studio, and they playfully bumped shoulders as they headed down the hall and back into the front room. The last person he wanted to see was Angus, but at least he'd have more time alone with Claire when they returned to Lake Bluff.

. . .

YANKING his brother off a barstool wasn't the welcome that Sinjin had wanted to give Angus. But with Claire and Orange-Mina sitting in the fifteen-minute waiting zone at the airport arrivals, he had no choice.

"Fuck, man. That's a fresh gin and tonic," Angus complained as Sinjin, clutching his shoulder, pushed him ahead to keep him moving forward. Angus had had enough time for several stiff cocktails. Sinjin decided to keep this bit of information away from his dad.

He bought a couple of bottles of water and handed them both to his brother.

"You have an hour to sober up."

When the two men made it to the VW bus, Sinjin repositioned the art pieces in the van to accommodate another body directly behind the two front seats. As soon as Angus lay down, he mumbled something about the Mystery Machine and passed out.

"Claire." Sinjin hopped behind the wheel. "Meet the actor extraordinaire, Angus Reid."

"Damn, even stone-cold drunk and passed out, he's a looker," she said, gazing at the prone man beside her exhibit. "Do you think I should put one of the shipping blankets on to keep him warm?"

"No. Angus doesn't deserve your empathy or sympathy. *Vectors* needs the protection. Much more worthy."

He set up his phone to map the longest way back to Lake Bluff. "All right if we take the scenic route?"

"I'm not in any rush." She pulled out folders and a pad of legal paper from her bag. "I have some ideas I want to jot down. Thanks for driving."

"Anytime, Daphne."

Sinjin drove, following his usual route between Milwaukee

and Lake Bluff, by staying alongside Lake Michigan. They passed through small towns and local parks where the trees gleamed in bronze and gold foliage. In one park, the kids were crawling all over a bright red jungle gym. It reminded him of climbing across the monkey bars at Peace Park when his dad had first moved them to the States. The start of each new school year brought on a unique set of challenges. In order to cope with the annual stress, he'd climbed until his palms nearly blistered and grew dark outside. His dad, with a lot of patient cajoling, convinced him to come home for supper.

A groan came from behind his seat. "Drink the water, Angus."

Claire glanced at him with an understanding smile.

When he pulled the van in front of Maxwell's, he wasn't surprised that the shop was lit up like a lighthouse. Sinjin was prepared, thanks to all of Julie's aggravating text messages.

"Home sweet home?" Claire shoved all her papers back into her bag and hopped out of the van. "We really have to use the official Lafferty van next time."

"Agree." Sinjin checked on his brother, now snoring in the back of the van, and then looked up the quiet street. He spotted his dad's vintage Cadillac parked at the end of the short block. "It's here."

"What?" she asked, following his sight line.

"*Coal or Steam.*"

Chapter 20

Claire wrestled her gaze away from the train wreck lying in the back of Orange-Mina. She didn't get it. Where was *Coal or Steam*? A lack of sleep may have affected her. She grunted, "Huh?"

He pointed toward a monstrous white convertible with a glossy red interior parked down the street. Even with its top down, the thing was the size of a small cruise ship. "Is Captain Stubing around?"

"What? Oh. Right," he chuckled. "It's George Reid's pride and joy. A '76 Cadillac Eldorado, with a trunk big enough to house the crate holding the sculpture."

"The front end is bigger than the back. Wait a minute. Did you turn your masterpiece into some sort of an engine?"

"Not in the least. Even if I wanted to, the car is so old I'm sure I wouldn't be able to find the right pistons. Maybe I could..." He scratched his jaw. "If..."

"Cut it out, Mr. Rube Goldberg," she said. "Are you going to bring it into Maxwell's now?"

He shook his head. "It's going to stay put until the night of the opening. Plan the best space for it, and we can display it at the last minute." Sighing, he glanced at the van. "Can you give me a hand with my pissed-up brother?"

His plan was rock solid. It would prevent Larry from attempting any nefarious doings before opening night. But from somewhere small and immature, she wanted, and yes, yearned to see *Coal or Steam* and possibly touch it?

"Shouldn't you check on your sculpture?" Claire crawled into the van and pushed Angus Reid into a sitting position. The famous star forced out a spectacular belch. "You know, to make sure it's in one piece?"

Sinjin grabbed Angus's flopping arm and yanked him out. "One of these days, he's going to make a mistake where everyone who's anyone will notice." Sinjin hauled his brother's arm around his neck as an older man came jogging out of Maxwell's.

While lifting the celebrity's dead weight onto her shoulder, Claire stared at the Caddie.

"Blimey," George Reid said, taking Angus's arm off her shoulder. She shook off the ache and introduced herself to the elder Reid. He gave her a quick smile.

"Jolly good to meet you, Claire." He turned to Sinjin. "Where are we going with him?"

Claire followed the father and two sons as they awkwardly crossed the threshold into the shop. When the door threatened to slam their backsides, she again yanked her attention away from the hidden masterpiece and held it open for them.

The three of them passed the racks of clothing, and Lucy jogged up. "Oh my gosh, it's really him. George, you weren't pulling my leg."

"It's true. Angus is the Scottish Hottie." Claire shook her head in disappointment. "Sort of sad-looking right now though."

"Let's get him on the couch. It's a good spot for Angus...I mean Mr. Reid, to rest. And I have a scent I've been working on, which may ease his hangover. There's a lot of lavender in it." Lucy grabbed Angus's arm off Sinjin's shoulder. "Here, let me. I'm sure you and Claire want to start unloading the van."

Claire couldn't have asked for a better time for her good friend to go all starstruck on the inebriated actor/vampire/detective. It may have been the best time to ask Sinjin about seeing *Coal or Steam*, but she couldn't do it. She would come off sounding like a nosy nag or, worse, like Larry.

Lucy and George lugged the TV star back to the juice bar, and Sinjin followed. When they all disappeared, she tried ignoring her disappointment by busying herself with inspecting the new space for the exhibit.

Suddenly, Sinjin strode over, jingling a set of keys hanging on an ostentatious, glitzy key chain with the Cadillac insignia. "Come on. Let's go."

"Oh-my-god, oh-my-god. Really?"

"Really, really." He took her trembling hand and tugged her outside and down the street. Standing at the trunk of the Cadillac, she fretted and fidgeted, wondering if she would hate this much talked about piece of artwork. *Impossible*. But then again, taste, when it came to art, was purely subjective. Maybe she shouldn't be seeing this *hero* of sorts?

Hell no.

He popped the trunk, and even the wooden shipping box had a shine to it. Claire hugged herself—tight—to avoid the begging cuticle on her thumb. Her excitement over a metal sculpture was put on hold as her eyes couldn't seem to leave Sinjin's arms. He used a pry bar to open the crate, and his ornately colored tattoo flexed and expanded. Along with wanting to see a piece of sleek twisty metal, she craved him—twisting and turning—with her. Their few touches and select kisses were not enough. She wanted more from Sinjin.

Staring at his backside, she wondered if he was related to David Beckham. He lifted the top of the box off, set it against the curb, and turned. One corner of his sweet lips lifted. "Aren't you going to look at it?"

Busted. After gulping down her embarrassment, she gazed at the wooden box filled with packing peanuts.

Sinjin grinned. "Go ahead. Be my guest. Unearth the treasure."

Her fingers trembled as she scooped up the damn Styrofoam bits that clung to one another. Impatient, Claire plunged her hands into either end of the box and dug around for a cool touch of silver. Or gold? When her fingers made contact with a smooth, cool object buried in the bottom, she traced the curves of the objet d'art. When she lifted it, she was oddly surprised at its weight. Wasn't it merely a french horn?

When she pulled it free, she then understood. Yes, the base was of gold circular tubing that flared, much like an instrument in a band's brass section, but the trinkets of brass, and other semi-precious metals, were welded onto it in layers. A shiny garden of cogs and wheels blossomed and flowered over the edges of the *horn*. In the middle, after brushing away the sticky packing peanuts, she spotted the shiniest center within the piece. Gold toilet handles were arranged in a circle, like rays of sunlight.

Damn. What a feast for the eyes. And so many details she was desperate to ask about. Blushing, she gently set it back into the crate.

Sinjin paced with his hands shoved into his pockets. Like a naughty kid waiting to face the principal. Instead of words, she used actions. On her tiptoes, she wrapped her arms around his shoulders and laid her head on his chest to hear his thundering heartbeat. Her cheeks heated up. Hugging her against him securely, he dropped his chin on the top of her head. "Will it work? In *Vectors*?"

His genuine insecurity forced out one of her most unattractive snort-laughs.

"Damn. Absolutely."

As they held tightly on to one another, the noises of Main Street seeped in, and then the blast of an obnoxious car horn rudely interrupted them. A Jeep swerved, parked in front of the Cadillac, and Julie's brassy blonde head emerged from the driver's side. Huffing, she strode up and gave them a wild-eyed once-over.

"Where the fuck," she shouted at Sinjin, "have you been?"

Claire wasn't a violent sort, but her hand itched to slap this woman. Then Julie zoned in on her, and before she opened her mouth, Claire smelled something rancid. She grimaced at the abhorrent odor emanating from Julie and grabbed Sinjin's hand. Together, they stepped away from her to avoid the toxic fume. When she opened her mouth, Claire wanted to run away, but then Julie spotted the sculpture. Like the shiny ark in Indiana Jones, she gravitated toward it.

"This is…" Julie coughed. "It?"

With her hand, Claire covered her mouth and nose.

Sinjin moved the peanuts around *Coal or Steam*, replaced the shipping cover, and closed the trunk. "No need to be so hostile, Julie. I mentioned earlier when I returned your multiple messages I was going to be tardy." He glanced at his watch. "It's not even eight o'clock."

Claire took another step further away from the persistent noxious smell that seemed to be radiating off Julie. A health issue or byproduct of grain alcohol? God, had the woman drunk absinthe? Now she worried more than ever for her best friend.

"Hard to believe all the hoopla over it," Julie said, walking to her shop. "Whatever floats your boat, I guess."

"She's really sick, I think," Claire whispered, then gulped down a breath of clean air.

He hooked his elbow around hers, and they walked very slowly to stay clear of Julie and went back into Maxwell's.

"I've caught that odor around her once before. I'm not sure what's going on," Sinjin said. "But we have a ton of work ahead of us. Working with Julie is going to be unbearable if she doesn't fix it."

"I'll talk to Lucy about it. She is the scent queen." Inside the shop, Claire's nose was relieved that Julie had gone into Lulu's.

The two of them perused the new space for *Vectors*. The shop would be bigger than what she'd had in the Lafferty once all the clothing racks and knickknacks were moved out. With all the bright natural light, even her dad's dark version of Stevie Nicks would perk up.

If Claire were a religious sort, this new location could be considered a blessing in disguise. Instead, she skipped over the *blessing* and let her keenness for design take control. Creativity was easier to manipulate than prayers.

"George is feeding Angus a smoothie," Lucy said, joining them. "I can't believe your brother is actually Angus Reid, the Scottish Hottie and star of *Raven House*. I made a batch of Gecko Grass, a smoothie that's been proven to cure the worst hangovers. He's drinking it with George's help. He gets Angus to sip it, then Angus curses him out, burps, and plops back against the couch. Your brother is a complete man-spreader, Sinjin. You need to talk to him about that."

"Among other things," he said.

Julie came into the shop and rummaged around the cash register. "That mixture of yours tastes horrible. I can't believe it sells. And it doesn't cure any kind of hangover. Best bet is to imbibe the hair of the dog that bit you."

Claire strolled as far away as possible from Julie, and when Lucy came over to her, she squeezed her friend's hand with reassurance. What a burden it had to be, managing her mom, who smelled like Hades and was an antisocial drinker. Additionally, Lucy now had to entertain a TV star who burped like a baby. "I'll be here. Night and day for the next few weeks to set up the show," Claire said, "so anything you need, just give me a holler."

The sound of scurrying dogs distracted all of them. As Fred and Ginger jumped around Claire's and Lucy's heels, George came to them. He fiddled with one of his perfectly curled mustache tips. Though a patriarch, the man's age was a mystery, not one gray strand intermingled with his head full of ginger hair. Only when he smiled did a host of crow's-feet flow from eyes the same color as Sinjin's—a cool metal blue.

George shook Claire's hand. "Sorry for my rude entry. Lovely to make your acquaintance. I've heard so much about you."

"But we, Sinjin and I—"

"From Lucy. We have a lot in common." He glanced at Julie. "Lucy speaks often and highly of you. Says you're going to be a modern-day Mary Cassatt."

The dogs whined as Sinjin clasped their leashes. "I'll second that. Perfect comparison, Lucy."

Claire blushed at the flattery.

The cash register slammed so loudly they were all forced to give Julie their attention. "Will you need me to move the artwork into the shop?" She stuffed a wad of cash into her purse. "If you don't mind, I have a date. And Lucy's here."

"You're part of the show, too," her daughter protested. "Don't you think it's best to be involved with the decision-making process? With Claire and Sinjin?"

Claire desperately wanted Julie to leave the shop, so said nothing.

Julie scoffed. "Not my fault they came so late. Besides, Sinjin knows everything there is to know about my work and then some. He doesn't need me."

Claire's brain registered "want" instead of "need."

Sinjin, placating the dogs' demands, paused to stare at

Julie. "This is a fantastic opportunity for you. We came up short tonight, but there will be plenty of time for you to engage with *Vectors*. I'm certain Claire will need your assistance."

Claire cringed and almost gagged at the idea. The last thing she wanted was Julie's caustic opinion and toxic smell, even if she did own Maxwell's. "Absolutely. I can't do this all on my own." She glanced around the cluttered shop, realizing how much moving had to be done to fit all the pieces from the van inside. "By the way, which piece do you want included in the exhibit? Is it here now?"

Sinjin gave her a look of thanks.

"It's at the barn," Julie said, sounding less bitter while patting down her pockets. "Shit, I forgot my keys. I really need to meet up with a friend of mine. I suppose I can be here tomorrow." Julie rushed out the door.

Claire let out her breath.

"I have no idea what's going on with her." Lucy shook her head in despair.

George draped his arm over Lucy's shoulders. "It's a roller-coaster ride. But you're in good company now. You have support from all of us."

"I have to get the dogs outside, or I'll have another mess to pick up. Claire? Care to join me?"

They jogged out the door to keep up with the dogs. Claire was glad to have some fresh air to clear her head. It had been a long-ass day, and it was nowhere near to being over. As if reading her mind, Sinjin asked if she wanted to lock all the doors of the van and start fresh in the morning.

"Do you think it will be safe? Out in the open?" she asked as they strolled past George's Cadillac, crossed the street, and went into Peace Park. The dogs sniffed around benches in the green area. Several folks reclined on blankets reading, phone-scrolling, or basking in the last rays of sunshine. None of them seemed remotely interested in breaking into a hippie mobile to steal art.

"It will be for less than twelve hours. And if you want, I'll sleep in the van. To protect the show. Those buses were made to accommodate a good night of rest and blissful REM."

"And to make love, not war," she said, ignoring the embarrassing subtext. "Standing guard sounds perfect."

"I'll have my dad bring over an old boom box. Then, since I'll be right below your window, I can go all John Cusack on you and blast Peter Gabriel."

Chapter 21

Claire collapsed into bed and expected sleep to find her but ended up staring at the ceiling fan. Between the sound of the whooshing blades, she listened to every unfamiliar noise around her. Lucy washing up in the bathroom between their rooms. The rumbling snore of Angus Reid while he slept on the couch in the front room. Mostly, she strained to hear the first sweet notes of Lloyd Dobler's love song.

Again, she looked out her window to see the van safely parked below on the street. Sinjin had camped out in the VW as he'd promised, and a beam of light came from within the darkened vehicle. Without having heard one chord of *In Your Eyes*, she closed hers and fell asleep while fully expecting to wake up with the tune stuck in her head all the next day.

It was five in the morning when she woke, dressed, and went downstairs to Lulu's. The sun had yet to make an appearance, but Angus Reid shone and looked spectacularly handsome as he filled Sinjin's cup with coffee. The brothers, nearly head-to-head, shared matching profiles. To graciously announce her appearance, she coughed.

Their ginger heads both popped up and smiled at her. Sinjin waved. "Good morning. Ready?"

"She needs coffee first, big brother," Angus said with a hint of a Scottish brogue. She remembered clearly how hot he'd been on his vampire show. Starstruck, Claire took a second to contain her teenybop giddiness.

"Please, a cup of joe sounds perfect." She sat beside Sinjin at the counter. "I didn't get much sleep last night. I need a jolt of caffeine."

She sniffed around to make sure Julie hadn't arrived at this early of an hour. The only scent she caught was Sinjin's aroma of fresh citrus. Angus handed her a mug of coffee. "Thank you, Angus."

"Call me Gus. I insist," he said with a dazzling Hollywood smile. "Sorry for stumbling in like an arse yesterday. My manners are deplorable."

"Claire is not one of your screaming fan-zillas, bro." Sinjin rolled his eyes. "No need to act all suave and sweet. We might all go into hyperglycemic shock."

She touched her lips to the hot mug, hoping the steam would disguise the embarrassing truth of her fangirl status. "What's on the agenda today?"

"I'm fairly certain it will be only us rearranging the space in the front of the store. As we both know, Julie has a history of not showing up." Sinjin glared at his brother. "Any chance you're feeling up to giving us a hand?"

Gus bowed with a dramatic hand flourish. "I'm at your service," he said with an even thicker layer of a Scottish accent.

Claire could see why Sinjin's patience with this drama king would get old incredibly fast, but having an extra set of hands came in at the perfect time. Maybe this was one time he'd hit his mark? She recalled Sinjin's kiss and that his brother had an awful sense of timing.

Lucy came down the back staircase in the midst of a

heated discussion on the phone. Claire knew it was Julie on the other end. As soon as Lucy ended the call, she sighed. "She is so irritating."

Her comment caught Gus's attention. He intently watched Lucy approaching them. With his mouth slightly tilted, the family's actor appeared to be gobsmacked. The man's expression—complete awe—made Claire grin. She sensed that Cupid had come in for a smoothie and struck liquid gold with Gus and Lucy. Claire was sure that smoothies would be in a scene of their love montage.

"Morning, all," Lucy said, going behind the counter. When she came up to Gus, she paused. "How are you feeling today? I think you managed to swallow all of my Green Gecko."

"Oh. You made it...for me..." The famous actor seemed to be at a loss for words.

Sinjin chuffed. "Do you need a script?"

"I'm feeling fantastic. Fresh as a daisy. Thank you. So much." Gus spoke to Lucy as he scratched his temple with his middle finger toward Sinjin. "I'm here for the next month. I'd love to try every one of your smoothies."

Lucy poured a cup of coffee and blew over the rim of the mug. "Good to know. We haven't been officially introduced. I'm Lucy Maxwell. Owner of this juice bar, and with the way things are going, I may be taking over the rest of the shop."

Claire twirled around and hopped off the stool. "Since you're managing Lulu's today, we'll try to keep out of your way. Do you think your mom has a place to store all of the clothing and stock in the store? We'll have to move it out for the exhibit. Will she be okay? I'm sure changing the shop to a gallery will affect her business."

"Not in the least. She has a barn stuffed to the loft, where she sells vintage clothing. It's a nightmare. I can't go in there without sneezing, and it's not from the hay; it's from all the dust."

Claire was instantly curious about the barn and what other treasures it might hold.

"We can unload the art and then pack the van back up with Julie's inventory," Sinjin added. "She won't be missing any kind of opportunity, especially with her contributions to the exhibit. If she chooses to show. The recognition alone, will be tremendous for her."

Claire considered the sizes of all the pieces as the four of them made their way to Orange-Mina. Right away, she clutched onto her father's painting and brought it into the shop. She set it against the only area of brick wall that had been cleared of merchandise. As Sinjin and Gus began to bring the pieces in from the van, she and Lucy moved the racks of clothing from one side of the store to the other to free up more space.

It took the two men over an hour to carefully handle the pieces, emptying the van's contents, and gently place into Maxwell's. A wave of claustrophobia rushed through Claire. Too much clutter always made her feel overwhelmed, and Maxwell's was bulging with stuff. Way too much. Even the valuable works by brilliant artists had become confusing. She needed to contain the chaos around her before it stole away all her logic.

Pulling up the notes on her phone, she barked out demands to get the place organized. Lucy, who must have been pierced by a cupid's arrow, now flirted wholeheartedly with Gus. Sinjin, standing by a rack of vintage men's hats, tried on a bowler. Then he changed it up to a cowboy hat and pointed his fingers like pistols into the mirror.

"Hey, folks. I love all your help, but this amount of items…" She nervously waved her hands, palms out and fingers splayed. "Lucy, are there any cardboard boxes around so we can pack the clothes…" She stared at the ten-gallon hat covering Sinjin's head. "And the other accessories? Especially the hats."

"All right, I get it." Sinjin took off the hat, pressed it against his chest, and drawled, "Liddle lady."

"The title of this exhibit is *Victorious Vectors*. It includes an assortment of pieces that, in some way, honor time. And the process a creator commits to his or her art. There is at least one element in each piece which represents time and its alternating forms—weight, momentum, finite mass, or infinite wisdom." She gulped down her weighty words and laughed. "Right now, daylight is burning, so we need to get our asses moving. Besides, I might spontaneously combust with all this stuff around me."

"On it," Lucy said, running into Lulu's. Seconds later, she returned with boxes and the oversized blue bags that were IKEA's bread and butter. "I have a ton of these babies."

They emptied the clothing racks by folding each item over the hanger and stacking it in the bags. The men moved all items not needed for the exhibit into Orange-Mina. When the last blue bag was full and packed into the van, Claire sighed.

"I can take this load over to the barn," Lucy said, taking the keys from Sinjin.

Gus offered to drive along to help with unloading.

Claire and Sinjin exchanged glances as if to ask if they were thinking the same thing. *Something is happening here.* Before Claire or Sinjin could figure it out, the door slammed, and the two of them were in the van.

"Wow." She let out a breath and began to move the rest of Julie's eclectic inventory to one side of the space to clear her head.

"We should be able to get the rest of this in the next load when they come back," Sinjin said.

"If they come back? Or will they…" She bit her lower lip

and shook her head. "Roll in zee hay? After all, it is a barn, right?"

"Gus is an opportunist, but we both know Lucy has a good head on her shoulders. No hanky-panky will happen."

"You're right. The worst thing that can happen is she'll douse him with one of her love concoctions."

Speaking about matters of love with Sinjin made Claire skittish. All alone with him, she hoped she could muster the mental energy to stay calm. If it weren't for that damn song running in her head, she might have had a chance.

She unpacked the blanketed paintings and lined them against the wall.

"Where would you like me?"

The images that popped into her mind almost made her drop the painting.

"The, ah, blankets. Can you take them off the sculptures and find a place to store them?"

"As you wish," he said, standing so close his breath tickled her neck.

He crouched down and started unwrapping the sculpture directly next to her. She dragged her eyes off his thighs—every one of his muscles vibrated under his jeans. Claire sidestepped away, went to her father's portrait of Stevie Nicks, and removed the protecting blanket. Realizing there was nowhere to set it, she groaned. "Damn it."

"What's the matter?"

"I don't have any easels. Or pedestals. What am I supposed to do? Lay all the paintings on the wood floor?"

"Don't worry, I have plenty back at the cottage. I'll bring them over later, as well as the metal dividers I use to display in the gallery. It will be fine."

"Sure, as long as I don't freak out."

As he came closer, her heart pounded faster. Taking her hand, he pressed it between both of his. "I'm your man. I'll do whatever you ask. However hard you think this undertaking is, it's only a sliver of work compared to the spectacular success that's forthcoming."

She laid her palm on the back of his hand. "How do you know?"

His stubbled jaw grazed against her face as he whispered in her ear. "Because you're a *giver* and, even better, a spectacularly super-organized giver."

He dragged his lips across her cheek, then landed on her mouth. Closing her eyes, she leaned against him and enthusiastically returned the kiss. It was a wonderfully long, heavenly locking of lips. Then someone entered the shop. Their swoony connection vanished.

"You decided to start the party without me." Julie, wearing dark sunglasses inside and on a sunless morning, set an oversized and expensive-looking handbag on the counter with the cash register. Beside it was where Claire had placed the mannequin to be eventually dressed in steampunk garb. Julie dropped the shades to the tip of her nose and gave the mannequin an evil glance. "This old thing? How the hell is she going to fit into our exhibit."

With Maxwell's nearly empty of its contents, Claire—for only a second—sympathized with Julie, then immediately dismissed it. It wasn't *our exhibit* in any way, shape, or form. If Julie Maxwell wanted to be part of the show, she had to show up and work on its assembly. Smelly or not. But much better if not. Claire took in a whiff of air and only smelled a hint of coffee, which probably came from herself or Sinjin. Nothing rancid. She addressed Julie straight on.

"There is a rhyme and some reasoning to this exhibit. It's called *Victorious Vectors* and includes a lot of themes surrounding the concept of time. If you want to be part of every stage leading up to the opening, it would be best if you arrived earlier. Before noon might work best." Claire contracted her speech and kept the rest of her villainous thoughts to herself. "It's the best light to work with in here."

"Where is Lucy?" the wayward mother asked while she nosed about the uncovered works of art.

"At the barn. They're hauling loads of your store merchandise over there," Sinjin said. "We assumed you'd be able to keep up with sales since you sell goods online as well." He folded his arms across his chest and twisted around as he perused the semi-empty space. "There's still quite a bit of stock in here. Would you mind lending a hand?"

Claire sighted a vein bulging on his neck.

"Thinking about my future again, Sinjin?" She sneered. "It's a new world with this show. I'm pretty sure that I no longer need any of your *suggestions*."

Both laughing, Lucy and Gus came into the shop.

Julie stood taller, and Claire speculated. Was she going to salute her daughter? Even though Lucy didn't have an air of authority, she definitely had a mother's eye when she connected with her mom. Instead of saluting, Julie grabbed her handbag and threw it over her shoulder. "I'm going to put this in the office. I'll be back in a minute."

Lucy shook her head. "I'm sure she's hiding her bottle of wine in that Brahmin bag."

As Lucy went to follow her mom, Gus started moving more blue bags into the van. "Will this be our last run to the barn? You two might want to get over to the place. It's full of—" He paused. "Oh bugger, I don't have a clue how to describe it. There are racks of clothing from floor to loft. Vintage appliances. There's an old pink stove. Crazy stuff. Do you think Julie's been on that show...what's it called? When those two dudes go to farms and junkyards digging to find treasures among the trash?"

Claire recalled the show, but instead of remembering the name of it, she weighed up what kind of items might be in the barn that she could use for her exhibit. "I'm not sure about the TV show, but since Lucy has to take care of her mom, maybe you can stay here, and Sinjin and I can take the next load to the barn."

After filling the van, Claire retrieved the directions to this storage place. Surprisingly, Sinjin had never been there. On the road and alone with him as he drove, she tried and failed to contain the giddiness taking hold of her. He affected her, and whether it was lighthearted joy or hot excitement, it didn't matter. She wanted Sinjin.

Chapter 22

Sinjin had driven past this place so many times yet never noticed it. A monstrous red barn with an assortment of broken-down and rusty farm equipment on either side of the front entrance. They reminded him of soldiers guarding all of Julie's goods.

Inside, Claire craned her neck and turned slowly around, circling to take in the upper level. A hay loft with no hay but racks of clothing. He smelled musty hay strewn about the paths between vintage furniture and antiquated appliances. Sinjin spotted a turntable similar to the one Dad had owned while living in London. Was that a Goldring/Lenco model? Buried under a stack of books?

"Julie has to be a hoarder." Claire set one of the blue bags she'd carried from the van beside the bags that Gus and Lucy had previously transported from Maxwell's. "No wonder she acts so nutty. There's no way that one human being can absorb or live around this kind of chaos and clutter. In my opinion."

They unloaded Orange-Mina systematically. Arranging the bags in one long line helped Sinjin to exorcise the oppressive contents and avoid the claustrophobic environment around him. Claire followed his lead also. This routine must have made it easier for her to breathe around all the dust and clutter.

"I have a suspicion," he said, shifting around several boxes of wet and dank-smelling magazines to see the vintage turntable. "If I searched this place, I bet I'd find my dad's cufflinks."

"Damn. Anything else missing? This is terrible." Claire wandered over to a tall stack of books and scanned the titles. "These are from my Madison days. I'm sure Lucy has no idea that her mother hung on to them."

He reached the turntable and gasped. It matched his father's old record player. For an instant, he questioned if Julie had stolen from his father. Had the two of them crossed paths somewhere long ago? Shaking off the absurd notion, he dug it out from underneath a pile of textbooks. He sneezed, then released the turntable from its trappings. "I'm bringing this beauty back to the cottage."

"Don't you think you should tell Julie that you're taking it?" Claire asked, thumbing through a rack of old clothing. "I mean, if you do, then I'll feel inclined to dig a bit deeper into this catacomb of stuff. There must be incredible items to use for *Vectors* on opening night."

"Will she even know if anything's missing?" He tried and failed to absorb the enormous piles of hapless items. "How should I ask her? I mean, if she's suffering with hoarding, she may feel an attachment to every single piece of junk in this barn." Pausing, he stared at the turntable. "Excluding this sweetheart."

"Maybe negotiate and strike up a business deal. Julie hadn't seemed or expressed any distress earlier, and she knew Lucy and Gus were just here. Or, and I know this sounds horrible, but maybe make a trade of sorts. Let her know about the missing cufflinks?"

"And the trivets," he added.

She gave him a questioning look.

"My collection of artisan-made trivets. Welded and valuable. They're missing from my kitchen." He started a text to Julie. With one letter on the screen, he thought about what other trinkets she had taken from his house, the studio, or gallery. Thankfully, she'd never been near the cottage. She was a person with serious issues that he would never claim to know diddly about; her actions or her motives were chaotic and quite alarming. He tapped out his message.

Interesting barn. Can we use some items for Vectors?

Instead of staring at the phone and waiting for her response, he continued hunting around. He knew, even if she disagreed, he would suss out a way to get the turntable home with him. He shuffled around the clutter and bumped into a Victorian cabinet. A cloud of dust fell from its top, floated down, and dropped around him. He waved it away from his face, then sneezed.

"Bless you," Claire said from somewhere deep in the jungle of things.

"Thanks." He sighted a dimly lit corner with framed paintings leaning against a tall wood Victrola. The paintings were held in place by the crank on the outside of the cabinet. He set the turntable down on the dirt ground and carefully moved the three paintings free. "Fuck."

"What is it? Are you okay?" Claire shouted, trying to make her way to him. "Talk to me. Throw me a word or two. I feel like this ship is sinking. And by the smell of it, it's going down into a slime-filled lagoon."

When she came up to him, he set his hand on her shoulder. "Let me prep you. First, by saying that I had no idea this was in here."

He turned the painting to face her. It was a David Raffen.

The other painting he'd bought when he was with his dad. At the time he purchased *Fever*, his father bought *Midnight*. It had been an incredible trip to New York. A couple of summers ago, he and George had gone to take in the galleries and museums. They had visited with his New York representative and learned that Anita Finegold, the gallery owner who represented Raffen, had passed away. Sinjin and his dad had gone to the prestigious L. Finegold Gallery and purchased the two available *Seasons*— without balking at the high prices.

"It's the winter version of my mom," she said, as if in a trance. "How...where..." She staggered back a step, and her face had lost all its color.

"I'm sorry. Do you need to sit?"

She plopped down on an ottoman topped with embroidery.

"This painting belonged to my dad. I'm fairly certain he'd given it to Lucy. Julie must have gotten her hands on it and hid it in this old barn."

"I'm glad they're together. I never knew what happened to them. Do you know anything about *Sugar*? The last one?"

"One? Don't you mean two? Isn't there a fall?" he corrected.

"Oh, right. My math skills must be on vacation." Rubbing her cheeks, she stood and came up to the painting. "This is the frame. Black and scrolled. My dad's signature frame."

The sudden shift in her demeanor struck him as strange.

"My dad has been trying to help Lucy deal with her mom's quandary."

"Now I'm petrified to work with Julie. Do you think she'll steal from *Vectors*?"

He had to admit that *Midnight*, abandoned in a clutter of junk, made him edgy and irritated. What else had Julie nicked? Would she do something nefarious to Claire's exhibit? "Let me talk to him before we make any assumptions. Maybe he gave it to Julie to help her make ends meet. Money is always tight for her. For now, let's use these items as collateral for what we want to incorporate into your show."

She pointed at the turntable. "And your personal collection?"

He picked up the turntable, and Claire held on to the portrait by Raffen. They set them by the door and circled through the barn. The second time around, he barely smelled the moldy hay. She retrieved and held up several items of clothing. "For the opening, we can sell them to those who want to dress in steampunk garb."

"A few extra dollars, nice," he said, checking his phone. No response from Julie yet. "And some fun. I think I'm going to go search for a bowler hat."

As he dug through the hats they'd moved from Maxwell's, Claire disappeared into Julie's wonderland. He retrieved the hat, then decided that any of them in the bag would add to a solid steampunk costume. Out of breath, Claire jogged up to him. "You have got to see this." She grabbed his hand and pulled him to the ladder. Following behind her, he climbed into the loft. Front and center was a vintage wood bar with a brass railing and classic vinyl seats that swiveled. "It's beautiful."

"Not the bar." She went to a corner hidden by duck cloth drapes, pushed one curtain aside, and revealed Julie's studio. Or at least the beginnings of a studio. There were various neatly stored pieces of welding equipment. An easel with designs and a solid wood table in the center. It looked as though it belonged to another person, not the drinker and hoarder he'd learned was Julie.

"Such an enigma," Claire said, tilting her head from left to right. "This area belongs to an entirely different person than the Julie Maxwell I'm familiar with. And check this out…" She twisted a bulb and lit up a shaded area. "It's a chandelier."

He kneeled over the structure to look closer. It was a sculpture, but he couldn't see a chandelier. There weren't any lights, bulbs, or crystals. Not until he deciphered each outline of the piece. The whole was a spiral made up of four brass circles. The bottom circle was the largest, and there were small steel spirals welded onto its base, evenly spaced apart and rounding along to the top end. Beside it were other circles with various metal spirals broken off. There were twisted red candles in some of the miniature spirals. "This is lovely."

"Come on! This thing is incredible." Claire did a double take around the studio. "This is her safe zone. I bet Julie is stone-cold sober when she comes in here."

Nodding, Sinjin tapped around the metal chandelier for a secure place to lift and hold it. "It's coming back to Maxwell's with us. Do you think it fits with the show?"

"Oh damn. Yes. The drip, drip, drip of the wax. The melting away of time and light. It's beyond amazing." She clamped her mouth shut. "But what if Julie doesn't want this piece being displayed? I mean, it is hidden up here."

He grabbed a cotton cloth off the table and wrapped it around a damaged area. One of the candle holders was loose and needed welding. He gently picked up the circular mobile structure and lifted it. The circles separated, and he spotted more broken areas. Julie must have made this at the beginning of her mentorship with him. He saw typical novice welding errors. "I think I'm going to play the teacher/mentor card. It needs to be fixed, and she can do it. You saw that bar she made for my opening. She's made such progress since she created this. And it's fantastic. She can mend it. Finish it. And put it in the exhibit."

"Damn, you're a tough prof. Remind me not to take a class with you."

"Not quite. I'm passionate about art. And talent."

Claire snatched a few more rags and handed them to him. He finished protecting the piece, and together they lifted it out of the studio. When they came to the ladder, they stopped and dropped their jaws.

"What now?" she asked.

They set the piece down, and he glanced about. Sinjin spotted a set of double doors on the other side of the loft, where they brought in and dropped out hay bales. "Go down and outside and meet me below by the other side of those doors." He pointed to what he was talking about. "There should be a pulley. I'll rig it to get this down to you." His phone pinged. The response from Julie was clear.

Fuck no.

"Too late." He showed the text to Claire and laughed. "Now you'll really get to see my schoolteacher side. Julie's going to detention and redoing her homework."

"For a passing grade?" Claire joked. "What about the Raffen though? What if she stole it? That calls for expulsion, don't you think."

He shrugged. As Claire climbed down the ladder and went outside to the hay loft doors, he rang his dad, if only to get rid of one of the many questions lingering in his head.

"What's up?" his dad answered, sounding as if he was chewing.

"Sorry, are you eating dinner?"

"Not at all. Sampling the scrummy fudge at the Victorian Shoppe. What can I do for you?"

His dad's sweet tooth was insatiable. Sinjin would have to mention this to Claire. Her whole theory on the Brits and their sweet versus savory might need more experimentation. "It's about a painting. *Midnight*. You bought it when I bought *Fever*."

"Couldn't forget if I wanted to. A gob-smacking invest-ment, but worth it when I gave it to Lucy. Reminded me of her, and if she needed the dough, she could sell it. Since she's never received a dime from that delinquent mother of hers."

His father's generosity had no bounds. "Well, this is good

news. We're at Julie's barn and discovered it. There's a little damage on the frame, but nothing we can't fix. We'll be returning it to its rightful owner."

George groused about Julie but ended the call on an upbeat note. "People change. It takes time."

Feeling positive, Sinjin managed to push the heavy loft doors open. As he suspected, there was a pulley made from a hook and rope. He wrapped every cloth he could find around the chandelier and doubled up on the protection around the damaged bits. He tied all the base circles together with discarded cords. Then he carefully pushed it over to the loft opening, tipped it upright, and hooked it onto the pulley.

Slowly, he released the mechanism to get the chandelier to the ground where Claire waited for it.

She waved, then tipped up the ten-gallon hat on her head to shade her eyes. Stepping around in a square dance, she yelled, "I've got the moves. Do-si-do."

The chandelier swayed gently as it was lowered. Claire reached out and grabbed the biggest ring. After placing it on the ground, she gave him a thumbs-up.

It glimmered in the afternoon sunshine. No way was this work of art going to be stuffed in the corner of a hayloft.

He yanked up the pulley, shut the window, and climbed down the ladder. While he was brushing loose debris of hay and dust from his jeans, Claire came in and grabbed his hands.

"I don't do dancing." He stood still, not moving as she squeezed his hands, trying to pry his feet off the ground. Only when she dipped back, laughing, did he move. He had to make sure she didn't fall to the ground. Seeing her smile, he gave in and swung around with her. When they slowed, he pulled Claire tight against his chest. She clasped her arms around him and sighed. Her warm breath vibrated his T-shirt, tickling him.

"I've been dying to do this all afternoon," she whispered.

"What? Dance?"

AUDREY LYNDEN

She batted his arm. "No. Touching you. And feeling you."
She brushed her fingers over his tattoo. "Can we melt against
one another for a minute before leaving?"

An ache from down deep pleaded with him. He buried his
face into her neck and loved how strands of her hair played on
his cheek. "Are you sure? We are literally in a barn. Nothing
about it sets an atmosphere. You know?"

She popped open the button of his jeans.

The ache grew. Words stuck in his throat. Sinjin slipped his
hand under her T-shirt and dragged his fingers up and down
her back. When she sighed, he glided the tips of his fingers
under her bra and played with one nipple. He located her lips
and took hold of them with his own, then traced his finger
across the smooth skin between her breasts.

She unzipped his jeans and gently slid her hand downward.

They were melting together. Too fast.

Chapter 23

Claire wanted to explore every part of Sinjin so badly her fingers ached. His arms, his chest, his butt...and when his rough fingers grazed over her nipple, little fireworks exploded everywhere inside her. Especially between her thighs. She wanted to feel Sinjin's most delicious parts, and when her hand made contact with his erection, she succumbed to the sparks and began to tug his jeans down. Her lips never left his.

Until he spoke.

He gently fastened his hand over hers and dragged it out of his pants. Then he placed it against his pounding chest. Sinjin growled into her ear. "I want this. Too."

Catching her breath, she laid her head against him and listened to his heartbeat. As it slowed, a wave of calm returned her to her senses. What was she thinking? Nothing. She'd moved from cowardly to courageous, something she had never done with any man before. He made her feel brave.

"What a rush," she said, her voice strangled with too many feelings.

He combed calloused fingers through her hair. She tilted

her face toward his. He, too, was flushed and struggling to keep it together.

She tugged her bra back in place, then zipped and buttoned his jeans. "To be continued? Better time? Much better place?" She lifted an eyebrow, hoping for a yes, yes, yes answer.

He chuffed. "I need pillows."

"Comfort and cushions."

"I'm a mattress guy, too. Oh, hon, I have a lot of ideas, and as you know, I'm a man who works quite well with his hands. And worth the wait."

She blushed and relaxed, letting reality settle back on her shoulders. Then her damn mind went right to *Midnight*. The winter portrait of her mother. She clutched onto his shoulders, stood on her tiptoes, and gave him a big smooch on his cheek. "Let's get back to business."

Holding hands like old-school sweethearts, they strolled outside and to the back of the barn. After carefully lifting the chandelier into the van, they added some clothing items Claire was sure would fit beautifully on the mannequin in the shop. She'd unearthed lace slips and brocade jackets in good condition. Additionally, there were several vests and corsets that, once rehabbed with brass keys and pocket watches, might be perfect costumes for attendees at the opening.

Frowning, Sinjin inspected *Midnight*. "The frame is damaged. My father told me he'd given it to Lucy to help her out. And Julie damages it. I'm sure it's her fault. I bet Lucy has never seen it."

If Lucy had laid eyes on *Midnight*, she would have jumped over the moon to tell Claire about it. "Knowing Julie, there's a chance she stuffed it in this barn before Lucy even had a chance to thank your dad for it."

Claire analyzed the damage and fixated on the chips in the ornately carved wood frame. It had been painted black, and several bits were missing, exposing caramel-colored wood. "What a disaster, but I think I can repair the maple wood."

She let her words flow smoothly. Careful not to reveal her jitters. The frame and the painting had been painted by her, so she could absolutely fix it. Claire aimed her phone at the broken spots. "I'm going to take a picture of the frame so I can research the paint color. Get a match."

Nodding, he rewrapped it with a spare beach towel and maneuvered it into the van next to the chandelier. Sinjin placed the bags of clothes against the back of the painting so it wouldn't move.

What would happen if this painting were to be completely damaged…entirely destroyed?

She forced the terrible idea out of her mind, and her stomach started to ache. So much love for her family had been painted into these portraits. How could she even think such a horrible thought? Would her life be less cumbersome? Maybe. She glanced at Sinjin. Then at the forgery. She wasn't sure what to do. Maybe a full confession? She hadn't done one since second grade. Would now be a good time to catch up with the big guy above the clouds?

No. Not yet. After the *Vectors* opening. When *More Lace Please* was shown alongside *Coal or Steam*. Or in the general vicinity of it, per Larry's instructions. By then, Claire would have a clearer idea of what this thing was between her and Sinjin. Especially since her primal instincts were pushing her thoughts around. Once the exhibit opened and went out into the world for everyone to see, she'd have less on her mind.

Later worked nicely, and *procrastination* could enter the picture, as well.

When they returned to Maxwell's, Claire set the bags of steampunk clothing next to the mannequin. It was quiet. Too quiet. Where had everyone gone? Finally, familiar voices came from out front. She unfurled a roll of craft paper and covered the clothing she'd taken from the barn to avoid any confrontation with Julie about it.

Outside, she checked to see if she could get *Midnight* out and upstairs into Lucy's apartment before anyone else saw it. The fewer eyes on it, the better. And a small miracle occurred. Julie and Sinjin stood at the back of the van arguing about the chandelier as George and Gus tried to intervene with an occasional "Calm—" then, "Let's discuss this—" But the mentor and mentee weren't listening, and Lucy sat on the edge of the shop window. Her hands were covering her face, and she shook her head.

"This is so embarrassing," Lucy said when Claire scooched beside her. "My mother is a wreck."

"But her chandelier is a masterpiece. Sinjin is right. She needs to fix it and finish it."

Lucy wiped the tears off her cheeks.

Claire said, "I need your help, then we can do some armchair psych work on your mother. I have to get your painting out of the van with as little ruckus as possible. Can you join in and distract them? Please?"

"*My* painting? What are you talking about?"

Claire wanted to act now and talk later. She was getting too jumpy. "It's *Midnight*. From *Seasons*. The curse of my existence."

"Where did it come from?"

"George bought it for you," Claire said quietly.

Lucy gaped at her. "You're kidding. I didn't have a clue."

"It's okay. I just want to get it upstairs and into the bedroom."

Lucy left the windowsill and joined the argument. Claire slid open the side door of the van and carefully maneuvered *Midnight* out. She clutched the protective towel and went up the stairs and into Lucy's apartment. Inside, she set it against the couch, still covered with the bedding that Gus had slept on. Lucy came in and shut the door.

"They're in a full-on artsy negotiation. I don't think anyone spotted you coming up." Lucy stood beside her. "I have to see this painting. This is good? Right? We now know where the third *Season* is?"

"It helps. Lindsey from Finegold told me a man and a woman had bought the other two paintings. Which is confusing since it was Sinjin and his dad at the gallery." Claire removed the towel. "So a woman bought *Sugar*?" She wanted to hear from Lindsey, sooner rather than later, to clear up all the confusion and find out the location and owner of the summer version of her mother.

Claire folded the towel and moved the painting onto a high-backed chair to get a level view of it. "It was in your mom's barn. George gave it to you, not her."

"The barn gives me the willies. I hardly wanted to go in there today. It's like stepping into my mom's frenzied brain."

"I don't blame you—it's a mess. There's so much stuff in there I thought I'd go into shock." Claire added, "Thankfully, Sinjin's hot body kept me focused."

"The man has no clue as to how fit he is, so it's up to you, girlfriend. Keep him in the know about his sizzling animal magnetism."

"Ha, ha. I'll happily own up to turning all his dials on at once," she joked, then stared at *Midnight* to get her mind off Sinjin. She kept hearing him say, *I'm a man who works quite well with his hands.*

The winter sky in the background of her painting had a nice blue tinge. This shade had constantly challenged her hand and brush. She inspected the color of her mother's black fur cap. It, too, had a hint of blue speckled into it. She'd also dabbed some blue into the white of the snowflakes on the pill-box-style hat. "Not too shabby."

Lucy laughed. "I told you so. These portraits of your mom are incredible. One of these days, girl, you'll have to face the fact. You're a superstar artist. The world needs to know—"

"But not Sinjin." Claire cowered at the idea. "At least not now. I want time, just a smidge more. I like the feeling of how he trusts me." She nibbled her cuticle. "Back at the barn, I nearly spilled the damn beans. But couldn't do it. After the opening, I promise I'll come clean."

Lucy went to her kitchen, returned, and handed her a glass vial. "It's my latest scent. A first. I don't have a name for it yet. But it has some ingredients that are calming. Might even have an aphrodisiac effect on you and Sinjin. I don't know for sure, but I'd appreciate it if you'd be my guinea pig."

Claire inhaled the oil. "This is lovely. I'd be happy to wear it. As long as I don't have to analyze data or make flow charts for you."

"Not at all. This is my least scientific experiment to date. I'm testing my mixology skills to temper my intuition." Lucy glanced at her smartwatch. "We should get back to see what's happening with—"

"Gus?"

"I was going to say the chandelier, but I'll be checking out the Scottish Hottie's sweet ass, too."

"Both those Reid guys have nice *bums*. A perfect shape for squeezing." Claire laughed, growing warm. "While we were at the barn, I couldn't keep my hands off Sinjin. You're right. He is magnetic."

"I feel the same when I'm around Gus. Except he's probably not the best dude to go after right now. He's pretty self-absorbed. Drinks a lot of gin and tonic, and honestly, I'm not even sure he remembers my name."

"Maybe one of your love potions will help him," Claire said, covering *Midnight*.

"Possibly. Nice to know George is in my corner. I'm glad I

met him at the Al-Anon meetings. He's always saying how people change. And things work out."

They returned to the street where Sinjin and Julie's argument had turned into a discussion. George and Gus were inside Maxwell's.

"What's happening?" Claire asked. "If it's okay, I'm going to go inside and start measuring the space to map out a design."

"And I'm opening up Lulu's for the next couple of hours. This is my livelihood, Mom," Lucy added.

Julie ignored her daughter and glared at Claire.

"Go ahead. Be my guest. But make room for this thing." Julie pointed to the chandelier, then gave Sinjin an evil eye. "Apparently, I have to fix this piece of trash, or *he* won't let me be part of the exhibit."

"Yes, Julie. I'm an asshole." Sinjin adjusted the chandelier in the van and closed the doors. "I'm taking it to my studio. Tomorrow. One o'clock sharp. Be there."

After Sinjin gave Julie a stern, teacher expression, he waved. When his eyes locked with Claire's, she knew he was looking through to her soul. She scratched her neck without an itch, and her mind yielded to the way his fingers had caressed her breasts. Her whole body tingled.

He cleared his throat. She snapped back to her surroundings and kicked the vestiges of lust out of her mind. Pulling out her phone, she turned on the measuring app. "Let me get the size of the chandelier before you leave."

Julie scowled.

Claire kept away from Sinjin so his heat wouldn't turn her into a puddle and then measured the sculpture. After noting the sizes, she mustered what was left of her goodwill for Julie and spit it out before she chickened out. "You are talented. This is perfect for *Vectors*."

Chapter 24

Each of the damaged spiral light fixtures sat atop a block of wood cushioned with cloth. Sinjin glanced at the digital clock on his studio wall. Ten past one. He rummaged around his workbench and retrieved his stress ball. The neon orange squishy thing had seen better days. There were pockmarks all over it. Sinjin squeezed it and dug around the drawer for another one.

His frustration started when he and Claire had snogged and almost gotten naked in the barn yesterday and then leveled up with yet again having to deal with Julie. It wasn't an ideal situation. It was near horrific, actually.

Squeezing the tattered foam ball, Sinjin glanced at the chandelier. Once it was restored and shined, it would be the centerpiece of Claire's exhibit. It would probably turn the look of his *Coal or Steam* into a pile of scrap metal. Sinjin wasn't about to stand by and watch Julie Maxwell's talent go to waste.

When his studio door slid open, Julie strutted in and gave him the finger. "I'm here."

He was relieved that he'd lit several sticks of incense around the workshop. Even with the scent of nag champa floating in the air, he detected the sour smell that seemed to hover around Julie. "I think you'll be satisfied when this piece is finished."

She circled around it, scowling.

For a second, Sinjin thought she might kick it or damage it more in some despicable way. But her shoulders dropped a bit. A sign of relaxation in most people, but this was Julie, and she was dodgy. He'd learned to expect the unexpected. She rubbed her forearms as if she had caught a chill in his studio. Which was impossible because the room was gob-smacking stuffy and always too warm from welding.

"I'm steadying myself. My hands. For some reason, this sculpture has taken a toll on me. It makes me nervous."

"I understand very well." He retrieved his work gloves from the cart holding the electric welding machine and pushed the contraption over to her. "You know what to do, Julie. All your emotions are already visible in the sculpture. Stuff down the feelings, and think it through to the end."

Sinjin had never had such an obstinate student. He would much rather be with his dad and Gus back in the cottage where they were tinkering with the Goldring turntable he'd brought back from the barn. If anyone could get it working, it was his dad.

She dropped her oversized purse off her shoulder and pulled out a pair of safety goggles. He didn't react. Instead, he leaned back against his workbench and glanced down at his phone. "Can I ask where you made it originally? Or did you purchase your own equipment?"

Julie took off her sweater and, as usual, wore a revealing tank top underneath. She folded the sweater, set it on one of his utility cabinets, and then put on a pair of heat-resistant gloves. She sat on the floor next to a broken section on the chandelier and yanked on the welding hose to bring it closer to her. "At the technical college. I wanted to make a graduation gift for Lucy. But then I couldn't finish." She cackled. "Didn't matter anyhow. I never made it to the ceremony. I was pulled over on the way to Madison and given a DUI."

Sinjin didn't comment.

A small flame burst out of the hose when she started the machine with her gloved hand. Immediately, she connected the line of iridescent heat with the edge of one of the loose spirals and then attended to adhering a piece of brass to the base. As she crawled around the chandelier, her hand easily glided from one candleholder to the next.

He sent a message to Claire: **Piece may be done today.**

His thoughts drifted back to the barn while waiting for her to respond. When she had brushed her hand against his cock, he had wanted more. From her and for her, twisting and turning around and into each other. He hadn't wanted to turn off the passion, but it wasn't the right place. Claire deserved more than a quickie against a barn door. He chuckled. Maybe they could do that another time.

The machine went quiet. He looked up, and Julie hadn't finished, but she'd turned off the welder. "I need something to drink."

He narrowed his eyes. No way would he serve her a glass of chardonnay.

"Water?" she asked. "Please. It's hotter than hell in here."

He shot over to the minifridge and handed her a bottle of water. "How are you doing?"

She guzzled the water so fast it dripped off her chin. "It's pretty. But I want it to be prettier. Do you mind if we continue tomorrow? I could do it all today, but with each of the three candlesticks I finished, an edgier idea came to me. You know what I mean?"

Sinjin felt validated. Julie's artistry was taking shape. He stayed in his teacher role for continuity. Again, he forced himself to expect the unexpected with her. "Okay. Tomorrow. One o'clock. Sharp. If you're tardy, I'll have to—"

"Demote me?" she flirted.

Immediately, he regretted his choice of words. "Not in the least. Claire has a lot to do for this show. I'm making her life harder by having you here instead of helping her in your shop. The least we can do is give her a clear idea of when this chandelier will be placed with the rest of the show."

"Claire?" Julie played with her tight top, forcing her breasts to protrude further. "What a no-talent."

"I'll ignore that comment." He gulped down his rage. "By the end of the week, it's done."

She packed up her bag and he watched her carefully to make sure she didn't slip in anything extra. A wrench or brass plate to go along with the trivets and cufflinks. He escorted her out of the studio. There was a 99 percent chance she would nick one of the tiny pumpkins sitting on his garden fence and he could miss it.

She hopped into her Jeep and left. Finally, he relaxed.

His phone buzzed. A video call and not a text set him back on edge. He picked it up, and both Claire and Mina were on the screen. They looked distraught while speaking to one another.

"Hey. What's going on?"

They glanced at each other, not sure who should speak first.

"It's Larry," Mina said.

Claire jumped in and shouted, "Asshole!"

"What's he done now?" Sinjin's mouth went dry.

"Larry told Mina that the show isn't going to get any marketing or publicity. Nothing. According to Larry, anyone who was originally coming to the opening at the museum isn't interested anymore. Or doesn't care. So, he's not going to bother promoting it."

"He's merely being his shitty self," Sinjin said. "And Mina, what did he tell you about the new location?"

Claire added, "He made sure to control the narrative by keeping info from you."

"Larry's claiming that you took the exhibit without his approval, so believes it's in the best interest of the Lafferty to downplay it." Mina fiddled with her orange wig. "If I contradict Larry, then he'll know something is going on between us. And if I contact any of the donors or anyone previously invited, it will inevitably come back to me. I don't know how to be clandestine. I feel like I'm between a rock and a hard place."

"It's okay, Mina. This is all because Larry wants to peruse the new location and steal *Coal or Steam* without interference." Sinjin purposefully neglected to mention Meg, who would likely be Larry's date as she was on the museum board. "This is good news, ladies. I can take over and jump on the publicity train. Hey, I know people. Lots of them. And Mina, I'm making sure that there will be big donors showering the Lafferty with the dollars lost by moving *Vectors* to Lake Bluff."

"Thank you, Sinjin. What should I do now?" Mina asked.

"Nothing. Check your email for your invite, and keep us posted on Larry's actions. Send us details at the end of each day."

"Sounds good," Mina said.

In the small square where Claire's face had been, he now saw the mannequin in Maxwell's. It was dressed in a black corset, a black leather vest, a black bowler hat, and fishnet stockings held up with black garters. It also had knee-high black lace-up boots with stiletto heels.

"She scares me," he said, pretending to bite his nails. "Badass."

"There's a leather chastity belt I want to incorporate." Claire adjusted the camera to show him the back of the doll and pointed to its bum. "This *badass* will be ready and waiting for Larry."

He had an idea. "She needs another pair of eyes. Let's get a security camera on her."

"And a name," Mina said, now off camera. "What should we call her?"

"Liza," Sinjin said, "For Liza Minelli. It reminds me of the movie *Cabaret*. There's plenty of room to hook a small surveillance camera on both sides of her." As he strode back into the house, his connection was getting hinky. "I'll bring them to the shop. Claire, have you had a chance to repair the frame on *Midnight?*"

"No. It's stored safely in Lucy's apartment."

"I've got some tools that may help in the repairs. I'll drop them off as well."

They said their goodbyes, and Sinjin went into the studio. He pulled up all his contacts—digital and paper—and began listing out every person he'd met, done business with, friends or foes, and anyone he'd ever sold to or bought from in the art world. His contacts were vast; the list stretched on and from around the globe.

Larry is such a fool. As if Sinjin hadn't thought of this plan already.

When L. Finegold Gallery, where he'd purchased the Raffen portraits, appeared, he deliberated, then punched in the New York number first.

Art & Form
TWO YEARS AGO

The Magic is Gone
Review By – Arthur Silver

Attending a gallery opening can be a magical experience. One can compare it to the birth of a child. Especially in New York City. Works of genius are plucked from nowhere and shown to virgin eyes. Bold cultural interpretations and brave social commentaries are on display for the art world. Yet, after attending the opening of L. Finegold Gallery, I discovered that the quintessential shine once found at Anita Finegold's gallery has dulled. Even though the doors have stayed open, the glamour has disappeared.

Lindsey Finegold re-opening her great-aunt Anita's fine art gallery had been no small feat. The old brownstone had little income and a lot of bills. Most of us at *Art & Form* placed the gallery on the extinction list when Anita died. With few artists on the Finegold roster and the biggest star, David Raffen, a long-gone painter with a questionable reputation, the gallery had little chance of surviving.

Although the opening show was well attended, most were from the high art echelons of Chicago, as the star of the exhibit Zoe Kittleson is from the Windy City. New Yorkers were intrigued by her work but showed little interest in staying late until Jerry Saltz arrived. When Mr. Saltz is in the house, the creatives pay attention.

Unusual for the rehabbed gallery? Only one of the four *Seasons* painted by David Raffen. The label next to *Sugar* showed off a bright orange dot—SOLD. Many in the art world had long considered the *Seasons* series as if they were Anita Finegold's four children. Where is *Sugar* going? Who has kidnapped the other three?

However, the biggest question is one I've wrangled with for years. If David Raffen hadn't been able to distinguish between a ten and a hundred-dollar bill, how did he manage the exquisite brushstrokes on a woman's lips he hadn't seen since her long-ago death? Too many questions, not enough answers, and maybe best to keep them buried. Fat chance. This is the business of contemporary art. Rumors never die.

Best of luck to Lindsey Finegold and her opening of the L. Finegold Gallery. Maybe there's a glimmer of hope for her grand revival. After all, everyone loves a good magic trick.
@Art Silver

Chapter 25

She hadn't been thinking of *Cabaret* when she put the clothing on the mannequin, but Sinjin was spot-on. Its look and the story's history fit in well with the other pieces in *Vectors* because of the German setting and pre-WWII time period. Claire googled pictures of Liza Minelli and added fake eyelashes to her shopping list.

Walking around the mostly emptied shop, she remeasured her masking tape outlines sticking to the floor. In the center was a large circle to designate the location of Julie's chandelier. The hook dangled off the ceiling post above her. She considered what piece would be placed below the hanging candelabra and became stymied, so moved on.

Where should the Raffen go? She spun around toward the rear wall and shook off her latest bout of irritation with Larry. His conniving seemed unending. Without waiting for any of his so-called approvals, she'd sent him pictures once a day with updates and the status of the exhibit and then promptly ignored his stupid suggestions. His refusal to promote the show was a ridiculous stunt. Sinjin had more friends in the art world than Larry. Even if he was dangling her secret over her head, she'd already planned to tell Sinjin the truth after the opening.

She retrieved her father's painting that she now thought of as the Stevie because of Sinjin's astute observation when they were in Milwaukee. She set it on the 1950s metal shelf that had been used as a store display. The rickety shelves had to be one of Julie's pet projects because there were so many of them stuffed in the basement storage. With this treasure trove of shelves, Claire didn't need to use Sinjin's copper display walls.

Much of this past week's hours had been spent spray-painting the shelves silver, gold, and bronze and attaching copper rivets into the holes on the armatures. The upcycling made her job feel easy. There were old bikes in the shop's basement, so she'd stripped away the chains and gears and used Gorilla Glue to stick them onto her found metal shelves.

A thought crossed her mind to ask Sinjin to weld them together, but she cast it out. He'd been working painfully to get the chandelier ready for the opening. His time occupying Julie had made Claire's time much easier inside Maxwell's. Only once had the raunchy-smelling woman dropped by to see how things were going. Claire had covered her nose and listened as Julie spewed one complaint after another. Even Lucy was frustrated. She'd been trying to concoct a smoothie for Julie to drink to override her pervasive sour-cabbage scent.

Poor Sinjin. Working in the studio with her, he'd run out of incense and had resorted to candles from Lucy.

Claire twisted her hair into a ponytail and pushed it under the bandanna wrapped around her head. She'd gotten paint in her hair one too many times. The last pedestal she wanted to design was challenging. What was the best way to show off *Coal or Steam*? Nothing too flashy. Sinjin's masterpiece couldn't be displayed near anything that would conflict with its beauty.

She went downstairs to the old building's cellar and flicked on the ceiling bulb. Each time she'd entered, she had to squash the temptation to reorganize the disarray of storage items. It wasn't as bad as the barn, but close enough. Scratching her arm where there wasn't an itch, she hunted around for something that would complement and enhance the crown jewel of her exhibit.

The clutter was less stifling than the barn, but Claire was determined. She had a clear vision of the sculpture in her head, and Sinjin had given her the measurements. What she needed to think about was the artist. His breezy but guarded manner had surprised her when they'd met.

As Claire searched for a stand, she smiled, thinking about how embarrassed Sinjin was when he admitted to being a superfan of David Raffen's. And when he was so captivated by her dad's turntable and albums. Yet, their artistic natures were far apart. She wondered what her dad would think of *Coal or Steam*?

"Good gawd," Sinjin said, coming down the stairs. "What is this? A bargain basement?"

She almost jumped out of her Doc Martens, which was next to impossible. "What are you doing here?"

"Julie finished the piece earlier than expected. I thought you'd appreciate my..." With splayed fingers, he waved his hands. "Jazz hands at your service."

"It's music to my ears, but won't Julie want to participate in hanging it?"

"Sure. She's visiting with her daughter. I hope Lucy is serving her a Gecko Grass."

Claire had appreciated her one-on-one time with Lucy while designing *Vectors*. They'd talked a lot about what, and even how, to help her mom. They hadn't come up with any solutions though. They both hoped Julie's chandelier would infuse her with a sense of renewal.

She shuffled around the basement one last time, defeated. "There's nothing here to use for your sculpture."

"You've been upcycling all week. The shop/gallery is coming along brilliantly. For *Coal or Steam*, how about using the plant pedestal? Do you remember the one in my great room?"

Her cheeks tingled, thinking about when they tumbled about on the floor as a photo op for evil Larry. "Good idea. It's sturdy and high enough. And it's emblematic of a time that coordinates with *Vectors*. Nice call, babe."

It came out. *Babe*. What the hell. "I mean Sinjin."

"It has a good ring to it." He grinned. "Let's get out of this dungeon."

Upstairs, they found Julie, and the three of them carefully lifted the piece out of Sinjin's truck. They maneuvered it through the door and into the shop without causing a scratch. With Claire in control, they placed it within her circle of masking tape on the floor. The chandelier shone. Every candle-stick holder gleamed, and within each, an orange-and-red-striped faux candle stick had been inserted into the swirled metal holder. The effect was magical.

"Your work is ace," she said to Julie.

"Agree." Sinjin stood right next to Claire, and she enjoyed how he'd become her comfy backup.

Julie stared at it, showing zero emotion. "If you two think that after all my work, I'm going to let you show it here on the floor, you're nuts."

It took a full second for Claire to understand what Julie was talking about. Then Sinjin nudged her shoulder and pointed to the hook dangling from the ceiling. With force, Claire did not roll her eyes. "No. Julie. It will be hung up there." She pointed skyward and watched Julie to make sure she grasped onto her error. "It will be lit up and sparkle over us at the opening."

Her hands closed into fists at Julie's frown. The woman had

no clue what a wreck she was or how her pain affected everyone. Most of all, her own damn daughter. But Claire downed her shot of frustration. "Your piece may even outshine Sinjin's."

Sinjin gave her a look that expressed, *good call.*

With her eyes narrowed, Julie glared at Claire and Sinjin standing side by side. "You two don't fool me. With all of your stuck-up, artsy, holier-than-thou bullshit. I don't need your pity." She stomped over to the ladder and opened it. "I can hang it myself."

Claire rehinged her jaw and grabbed another ladder and her tool belt. "Not going to happen." No way would she engage or give credence to Julie's vile view of her and Sinjin. And there was no way in hell she'd let Julie deconstruct all her beautiful work.

"The three of us will hang it. So. Dammit all. You can just deal with it, Julie." She'd gained an enormous amount of patience from dealing with her suffering, ill, and at times a curmudgeon of a father.

It took over an hour to sling the chandelier in place on the roped hook to dangle stately and gracefully from above. The striped candle sticks were lit with faux LED flames. She had to convince Julie to turn them on, and then they sparkled and illuminated the entire shop.

Claire could have sworn she'd seen Julie smile, but then it turned back down to her frown. Lucy came in, hugged her mom, and showered her with compliments. Claire had a gut feeling that the chandelier could outshine *Coal or Steam.*

The pedestal. The mission-style pedestal was the last item on Claire's to-do list because it wouldn't be set in place until the week of the opening. Butterflies batted around in her stomach. An exhibit opening. Her first. Her curatorial debut. *Is this really happening?*

Julie left in an ill-tempered huff, and Claire and Sinjin went back into Lulu's to go over the guest list. It was as long as

Santa's naughty list. She'd scanned the first page, and on it were names that the art world revered. Jerry Saltz, an art critic and author of *How to Be an Artist*, which was the book that she'd recommended to Sinjin. "Ha. Ha. So you know Saltz? You could have told me."

"Why ruin the moment. I can't wait to tell him how you went all fangirl over him."

She concentrated on the rest of the list to shy away from Sinjin's loving expression. The man was not good for her bland emotional diet, but maybe it was time to incorporate a new flavor.

Scanning the list, she read the formidable names: a buyer from Christie's Auction House in Chicago, several reps from two of the biggest galleries in New York—the Pace and Gagosian—editors and critics from *Art & Form*, and last on the list, the new owner of Anita Finegold's old gallery, Lindsey.

The butterflies in her stomach dove like kamikazes while reading, *L. Finegold Gallery – Proprietor, Lindsey Finegold*. She tried to convince herself that this was good. They had to talk. They were going to talk. She knew it. The situation over *Seasons* would get sorted out.

Somehow.

It occurred to her that she'd completely forgotten about the articles she'd dug up on Arthur Silver at the Milwaukee library. "By any chance, did you run across the reviewer Silver when in contact with *Art & Form?*"

"He's gone."

"Where has he moved, and who is his new target?" She really considered dropping him a personal invitation to *Vectors*. God, it would be great to make Arthur Silver eat a big huge slice of humble pie. "If he's still in New York, I bet I can convince the jerk to stop by the show."

"Not likely, as he's dead and buried. The editor of *Art &*

Form told me he'd had a heart attack." He sipped his smoothie. "Sorry, babe."

"Damn him for dying on me."

The good news was that rumors in the art world usually died faster than mayflies and possibly now Art Silver. Maybe the debacle over her father lived and breathed solely inside her own head. The art world had plenty of other artists to skewer in the past few years. She released her hold on the bottom of the barstool. Funny, she hadn't remembered clutching onto it so tight.

"I'm impressed. This is outstanding. How can I ever thank you, Sinjin," she said, squelching her nerves. At least another *babe* hadn't slipped out of *her* mouth.

"I should be thanking you. I haven't felt so much support in a long time. Everyone I spoke to assured me that they would get here for the show. Even the New Yorkers who barely know where I exist. We are in flyover country." He took her hand. "If you hadn't come here looking for *Coal or Steam*, I'd probably still be cowering in my studio, resenting the world. There's a lot going on in the art world that I've missed, and now, thanks to you, I want to play catch-up. Gotta say though, it would be a much better time if you would join me. Maybe a trip to New York?"

She paused to think it over. Her nerves were bound to make her say something stupid, or reckless, or cheesy. She couldn't decide. But a trip to NYC with Sinjin would be better than…sex? No, no. Couldn't be. A complete catastrophe? A possibility. She knew for sure that they would never board a plane together after he learned about *Seasons*. Claire's thumb gravitated up to her mouth. Sinjin gently pressed it down into her lap.

"A lot is going on at this moment in time, or should I say, in the time of *Victorious Vectors*. Don't think about my invitation. If you tuck it into the back of your brain though, I'd appreciate it."

"Will do." She got up from the stool, collapsed against his chest, and hugged him. "In the meantime, do you wanna find the movie *Cabaret* and watch it with me? I feel like my mannequin needs some more zhuzhing before we can christen her *Liza*."

Chapter 26

Claire had fixed the frame on *Midnight* perfectly. She'd carefully replaced the chipped wood with slivers she'd shaved off the back of the frame. After gluing the layers, it looked like new. She'd also been lucky to find the exact shade of black her dad had used on all his frames. Still so popular, Blicks' stock was nearly sold out online.

She gazed at *Midnight* and released a low whistle. This painting of her mom was called *Midnight* for the shade of blue —the winter sky—in the background. How she'd mixed up the pigment, she'd never remember. It was positively a one-hit wonder. She covered the painting with bubble wrap for the trip to Sinjin's cottage. Lucy had insisted that for now, *Midnight* should be near *Fever*.

Delivering it to Sinjin, she willed her nerves to keep from jittering. He'd simply invited her to dinner and a movie, *Cabaret*. It wasn't a date but a celebration since she'd finished installing the exhibit. *Almost finished* because the star sculpture wouldn't be making its entrance until Saturday. With the opening of *Vectors* a week away, she was terrified.

Arriving at the property, she passed George's Caddie and

Lucy's truck parked by the main house. She hoped Lucy might be having fun with Gus but knew it was probably a visit with George. Recently, he'd been popping into Maxwell's and sharing chocolate treats with Lucy while discussing healthier living options for Julie.

Before ringing the doorbell, Claire considered how tonight would be the perfect opportunity to come clean. Tell Sinjin about everything that had happened with her dad and why she'd painted four canvases for David Raffen. But this nip of courage wasn't biting deep enough. She would avoid the pain a little longer.

Sinjin jogged out of the cottage, and the old door slammed shut. There was a cold breeze off the lake. October was here, and sweater-weather season had officially kicked off. She was glad she'd slipped on her pumpkin-colored sweater and tights to go with her skirt—a plaid of fall's golden hues—and her cherished Doc Martens.

"Let me get this for you." Sinjin took hold of *Midnight* and kissed her on the cheek. "I'm glad you were able to mend it. It's a big ask with the opening right around the corner."

As she followed him inside, his little peck on her cheek still tingled. She hooked her bag on the coat stand and inhaled the delicious scent of sweet oranges. In the background, Stevie Nicks sang her duet with Tom Petty.

Since she'd been here last, Sinjin had added the old turntable they'd brought back from the barn. "It works?"

"Yeah. Thanks to my father and brother." He pumped up the packaged painting. "Do you mind if I store this with *Fever*? So good of Lucy."

"Be my guest." Hiding the painting away suited her perfectly. Leafing through the first few pages of a *National Geographic* magazine on the coffee table, she lightly rubbed her cheek and tried to focus.

On the cover was the vintage prismatic color wheel. She

flipped through to find the story about the system of color developed by Moses Harris in 1776 but abruptly closed the magazine when Sinjin came back into the living room.

"You can have it. I have stacks of Nat Geos. My father has been giving them to me since I was a kid. I'm mixing up brandy old-fashioneds. Would you fancy one? Or are you interested in anything else?" His polite demeanor and scrumptious look made Claire's throat dry. A drink could be dangerous with the way Sinjin was dressed. From the bottom where his gray suede loafers with no socks grazed the hem of his sweet-fitting Levi's, and topping it off, a charcoal-and-white button-down pinstripe shirt. The combination of cool blue and metal colors heated her up. "Yes, please."

"Cocktail? Mocktail?" he said with a slight curve of his extremely kissable mouth.

Cock? Mock? "I'll have an old-fashioned." She followed him to the open kitchen and leaned against the stainless-steel-topped island.

"Would you say this is a date?" She slid her fingers over the cool metal surface. "And if so, would it be the first, second, or third?"

They'd spent a considerable amount of time together in less than a month, and she'd become comfortable, almost content around him. The unusual feeling unsettled her.

"I think…" He muddled cherries in the bottom of a high-ball glass. "Our trip to the Preserve Museum constitutes our first date. However," he said, dropping a spoonful of liquid sugar into the glasses and then dribbling in bitters. "There was a date-like feeling when you initially came to the gallery and fixed my cufflinks."

He stirred in the brandy and soda, added a slice of orange to the rim, and handed the glass to her. "Take a sip. More booze or more soda?"

The sweet brandy tingled her tongue. "It's divine." She

took another sip and made the decision. "I'm calling it. This is our third date. The museum was our first. Our second was in the barn. And here's to our third," she said, tipping her glass to his. "Cheers."

"Agreed. I have something to show you." He led her over to the turntable, where another song by Stevie played, this time something about the rain.

"What album is this?"

"It's *Bella Donna* from my collection. I put it on to give it a fresh listen. This is a strange question, but did your father like to play word games?"

She tried but couldn't think of any time David Raffen had ever played a game. When she was in elementary school, her dad's idea of playing games always involved paints. She had learned hands-on from him while playing with a lot of finger paints. Word games weren't quite their jam. "Not a lot of game playing in our house. He was a single dad, so he doted on me and spoiled me rotten with love." Without meaning to, she sounded a tad melancholy.

"I didn't mean to make you sad." He pulled out several albums and handed them to her. "After we spoke about your father's painting, I considered the title *More Lace Please* and his record collection. Could *More Lace Please* be an acronym for More LP or More Long Playing? Or maybe, More Time Please? It might fit if he painted it later in life rather than earlier in his career as you originally thought."

She dredged a cherry from her drink and popped it in her mouth. He had a reasonable theory. She'd taken so much direction from her dad in the days before he passed; a lot of those last days were a blur. It wasn't in her to admit that he didn't want to die and that he wanted more time on this earth. But then again, while he was in the hospice, the morphine turned most of his thoughts chaotic, and his words began to slur together. Their daily chats devolved into peaceful hand-holding and gazing out the window.

"I'm only thinking this because of *Coal or Steam*." He touched her knee, jolting her back from the past. "The name of the sculpture is really Kohler for the town and Steam for all the steam in a spa. Also in Kohler. A play on words. I was such a sucker and still am for the spa in Kohler, and don't forget my love of a good loo."

A rush of happy endorphins filled her. "Makes total sense. His fondness for Stevie Nicks could have been considered borderline obsessive. I just wasn't sure if it was her music or because she resembled my mother. And he was cheated out in some ways. Mostly time. He was sixty-two years young when he died."

"But you were able to spend every one of those years with him."

"I was. I'll never regret putting my life on hold for him." She tasted the sweetness from the cherries on her tongue, and the brandy softened her earlier trepidations.

After setting her glass on the table, Claire wove her fingers between his and brushed her lips against his cheek. She inhaled the sweet orange he'd just eaten and kissed him. Sinjin devoured her lips.

Then he stopped. "Do you want to eat? I mean, I did make a lovely lasagna for us."

She gave him an exasperated look of apology. "You went to so much trouble, I'm sorry, but…"

Laughing, he pulled her off the sofa. "Just mucking about. I made a reservation at Il Ritrovo in…" He checked his watch as they stumbled over one another to get into the bedroom. "A couple hours."

"Think they'll hold it?" She pulled his shirt out from the waist of his jeans. "That's not long from now."

He turned her around and gently pushed her onto the end

of the bed. It was a nice cushiony fall. Then she remembered she was wearing her Doc Martens. Ten minutes to get on and twenty minutes to get off. Or was it the other way around? And the tights? Damn. She really hadn't dressed with a bedroom romp in mind. "Wait. I have to untie—"

"Let me have the honors." He kneeled in front of her and started to unlace her boots.

When he rid her of the work boots, he feathered his fingers up the length of her legs and over the tights. His hands slid under her skirt and over the cumbersome waistbands until his fingers landed on the edge of her skin.

"I've struck gold." He tickled her hip bone. "Can you feel this?"

She giggled. "I didn't plan well. I should have left my chastity belt at home for the evening."

Dropping her head onto the bed, she took in a deep breath and relaxed. Sinjin's flowery bedding wasn't quite what she would have imagined. But when he peeled down her tights, she lost track of the garden of roses surrounding her.

Claire scooted on her elbows to the head of the bed. He cupped her butt and slid her the rest of the way, stood at the end of the bed, and started to remove his shirt.

She bolted upright. "Let me."

As she unbuttoned each button, she pressed her lips against the cotton of his T-shirt, moving from one well-muscled shoulder to the other. She tugged off his pinstriped shirt and let it drop to the ground. Slipping her fingers under his T-shirt, she brushed her hands along every ridge of his abdomen. Her fingers tingled, and he moaned.

Sinjin combed his hands through her hair, brought her face close to his, and kissed her temple. Dragging his lips down her cheek, he murmured, "All right?"

The heat seemed to thicken her thoughts, and she couldn't reply, squeaking out a sound and nodding.

"Is that a yummy sound?" he whispered, gently pushing her back down on the bed. "Much better than the barn, yeah?"

She splayed her arms on the bed, exposing herself to his touch.

With the chance to indulge her urge to touch every wheel and cog tattooed on his well-built arm, her eyes and fingers absorbed Sinjin. Instead of colliding, the image on his arm and the muscles underneath made her feel encompassed by a compassionate soul.

He gently separated her thighs, and she sat up to strip off her T-shirt, almost kneeing him in the gut. "Oh, sorry. I wanted—"

"To take over my job?" He straddled her, lifting her tee up, over, and off. With one finger, he stroked the skin between her breasts and then popped open her front-closing bra. "Easy. If you don't mind, I want to show off my handiwork."

She lay back, and the swath of flowered comforters cushioned her. Sinjin's fingers worked magic, delicately pulling and tugging on her nipples. When he circled each peak with his tongue, she moaned.

The heat between her legs sparked into a fire. She ached to feel him inside her. To fill her and make every part of her body sing in delight. Claire finished what she'd started at the barn and tugged Sinjin's Levi's off his hips in triumph. Next, she released his lovely hard-on from his black briefs.

"Are you in a rush," he murmured in her ear, nipping at her earlobe.

"When you do that, yes." Sighing, she let her hand do some talking. She stroked Sinjin and tickled the sensitive skin beneath the crown of his cock. He returned the favor by teasing her breasts with his chest hair.

Sinjin moaned. "I think. In the…" He reached over to the

side of the bed. The table clattered as he opened the drawer. "Bingo. Wait. I better suss these out."

She drifted in bliss. Every nerve ending buzzed and hummed while she lay beneath him.

"Sorry, babe. These are no good." He groaned. "We can hold off. I'm safe and haven't been with anyone since before… but I don't want you feeling like you've climbed in the sack with a chancy rake." His fingers slipped inside her. "My hands and mouth, however—"

She gasped, and he stroked her deeper.

"This may work," he whispered, sliding his tongue across her navel, "until new condoms."

The magic of his hand worked wonders, but Claire throbbed for more of him.

Her skin melded against his with a thin layer of sweat tinged with a heady scent of cherries and oranges. And maybe brandy? Their cocktail was a much stronger elixir than she could have anticipated. "Not to worry. I'm fanatic about taking my pills and prepared for a chance with a British rake."

Kissing Sinjin, she wrapped her thighs around his waist. He propped his solid arms on either side of her head, and she stared into his magnetic eyes. She wanted more friction, so took hold of his face and rubbed her thumbs across his stubble.

He leaned down and kissed her, pushing at her entrance until he sank inside. Absolute joy overcame all her senses. She clutched onto his shoulders as he dove into her deeply, his cock and her inner walls playing an erotic game of tug-o'-war until her breath came and left in spurts. She clung tightly and squeezed her thighs around him, arching her back with each of his thrusts. It was an impassioned game no one would lose; simply a matter of who would come first. She wanted him to have the honors but wasn't sure she could hold on long enough.

Cupping her ass and thrusting into her, he launched her

backward onto the bed with half groans and half moans. She laughed chaotically as her entire body shook while orgasming. She had to take hold of his shoulders to contain the delight as she came. He lapped up a bead of sweat on her cheek and swiveled his hips, his chest vibrating with his release. She pulled him against her. Still inside her, they stayed looped and tangled around each other. The sound of their heavy breaths lulled them into a doze.

A powerful sense of trust overtook Claire. She kissed his ear and let the curled tips of his damp ginger hair tickle her lips. Words of *love* floated in her head, but she batted them out. It wasn't like that. Couldn't be like that. Before sleep took over, she lifted the rose-covered quilt over them and spooned tightly against him.

Chapter 27

The pounding on the cottage door was so violent Sinjin thought he was dreaming. He rolled over and kissed Claire on the cheek. "Duty calls. Probably Gus or George. Stay in bed. I'll get your coffee."

With a huge goofy smile on his face, he pulled on his sweats and a tee. Last night had been incredible, and even if he'd been satisfied from beginning to end, he wanted to start all over again.

More rude knocking from the front door.

"Hold your horses. I'll be right there," he shouted and checked into the bathroom. His mouth tasted as if weighted with garlic.

Shite. He'd brushed and rinsed his teeth three times after he and Claire had returned from the Italian restaurant. He should have avoided the bruschetta at Il Ritrovo, but it was too delicious. Besides, Claire had eaten as much of it as he had. They'd definitely worked up an appetite in the bedroom last night.

He washed out his mouth with more Scope and then swallowed it. "Blech."

"You okay?" Claire croaked from under the pile of quilts.

"Sure," he said, ignoring his burning throat. *Jackass. This better be important, Dad. Or Gus.*

He jogged across the sitting room and opened the door to let his dad inside. Except instead of George or even Gus, it was Julie. Fuck. He stumbled back in shock. What the hell was she doing? How did she know about the cottage?

"Your dad told me I could find you here," she said as if reading his mind and pushing past him. He casually glanced behind him at the bedroom door and was relieved he'd remembered to shut it.

Julie paced in front of the couch.

The coffee maker in the kitchen drew his attention, begging him to start a fresh pot for himself and Claire. Begging. But if he made it, Julie would ask for a cup. He crossed his arms over his chest. "It's not a great time. What's going on?"

She scanned the living room. "Where is she?"

He wanted to lie or fib but then recalled that Orange-Mina was parked right outside.

"Claire is not a topic of discussion."

"Oh yes, she is," Julie said. "Her show. The installation is a complete disaster." She raised her voice, adding a vengeful sting to each of her complaints about *Vectors*. Sinjin feigned interest until realizing his jaw had locked up. What the hell was Julie's problem? He and Claire had given her the chance of a lifetime, and all she did was grumble about the location of her chandelier? When Julie sat on the couch, he kindly told her that now wasn't a good time and that this was a conversation to have at Maxwell's.

"Go get her out of bed," she retorted.

He opened the front door, glared at her, and pointed outside. "Please leave, Julie."

Several seconds passed. His frustration grew as he calculated ways of getting Julie out of his cottage. When it became abysmally clear that she wasn't going to move, he declared, "You've been stealing from my home. My cufflinks? The trivets? If you leave now, we call an ace an ace."

Julie turned bright red. "You are a narcissistic asshole."

He could have easily agreed with her, but she'd still be sitting on his couch. "The cufflinks are my father's, a gift from my mum. They're very sentimental. The trivets are worth several thousand dollars. If you return the cufflinks and pay me for the trivets, we'll call it even."

Probably because a dollar amount entered into the discussion, Julie stood up. She swung her big handbag back onto her shoulder. "I'll be at Maxwell's every day, keeping an eye on the show. Tell your girlfriend to come see me. We'll need to adjust several of the pieces."

Sinjin wouldn't fall into Julie's trap. He had no intentions of debating with her. Claire was the curator of *Vectors*, and her word was final in every respect.

Julie slammed open the screen door. "The cufflinks and trivets will be returned to you by the end of the week."

He didn't close the door until she'd climbed into her Jeep. It was a relief to have Julie out of his home. During the days they'd spent in his studio to repair the chandelier, she'd been unusually friendly. He began to worry she'd mistaken his work with her for something completely different. Maybe she did, or not, but her crashing in this morning set him on edge.

The bedroom door cracked open, and Claire peeked around it. "Is it safe to come out?"

"Yes." He strode into the kitchen to get the java brewing. "How much did you hear?"

"The whole thing," Claire said, adjusting a blanket around her bare shoulders and sitting at the island.

He would have rather strolled back into the bedroom for another round, but the mood was ruined.

"I don't know what all her gripes were about," he said, inhaling the scent of coffee being brewed. "I was half-asleep."

"She said something about the space and that it was too sparse, like people wouldn't know that there was any kind of exhibit happening inside Maxwell's."

He poured them each a cup of coffee and set a creamer and sugar bowl out for her. He'd zoned out when Julie had spoken, but this rang a bell. "So, do we need to add more pieces? I'm not making any suggestions, but possibly Julie has a point we should listen to. For the sake of any show, it's good to consider the harshest of critics. At least try to see it from another perspective."

"I completely agree with you, and as much as I don't want to, I see where Julie's coming from. It's a steampunk exhibit turned into a minimalist show. I place the blame squarely on Larry's stupidity. He's kiboshed all of my arrangements. Every time I send him a photo of the presentation, he sends back a list of changes. He's a tyrant. It's his way or the highway. This past week, I've rearranged pieces hourly. Hell, he'll probably ask me to completely rearrange the opening."

"Can you ignore him?"

"I don't want to piss Larry off."

Since hanging Julie's chandelier, Sinjin had only been to Maxwell's to deliver the pedestal for his sculpture. They had placed it by the door, and at that point, Claire hadn't completed much with the installation. He had to confess that he'd been too busy enjoying the afternoon with her, attaching the security cameras on the front and back of Liza the mannequin. There were probably false eyelashes stuck on his T-shirt from the other day.

"I like how you blackmailed Julie to get her to leave," she said.

"It's not my finest moment." He contemplated *Vectors*. "When Larry arrives at the opening, he will have zero choice in the matter of the installation. It's not as if he'll walk in to where all the bigwigs in the art world have gathered and make demands." He took a swig of coffee. "I think you're safe to do whatever you want. It's your curatorial debut, not Larry's. If you think it will help, I can speak to the bastard myself. Give him another earful."

"No," she shouted, then smiled sweetly. "That won't be needed. I'm sorry for the outburst, but he's exhausting me. Part of me just wants this night to be over with, which is so contradictory to the theme of time in *Vectors*. It's a shout-out to relishing each moment in our lives, because time moves so damn fast."

He slipped his hand under the blanket and onto her shoulder. "Then ignore Larry. Block him on your phone. Do your thing, 'babe.'"

She dropped her head against his chest and laughed. "I promise. Only 'babe.' No 'boos' will escape my lips."

"I'm fine with any term of endearment," he added, "Sweetie pie."

"Now you're tempting me again, except this time with food." She embraced him around the waist, and the blanket fell off her shoulders.

She wore nothing.

The whole time they'd been sitting at the kitchen counter chatting like an old couple, she'd been completely nude.

"I'm dressed for business. Casual birthday suit for our one-on-one." She took his hand and led him into the bedroom. "You don't have anything scheduled on your day planner right now? Do you?"

They tumbled onto the bed, and he kicked off the blankets. His lips couldn't find hers fast enough. "I'm all yours, honey buns."

Chapter 28

She was right. Claire had called it an exhibition of minimalist artists, and that's exactly what it looked like. The opening was days away, and Claire had pared the show down to the barest of basics. The chandelier was beautiful, but the other pieces were dulled by their positioning. The lack of wall accents diminished the paintings instead of highlighting them. The Raffen painting could have easily been on a frat house wall next to a picture of dogs playing poker like it was any old portrait. *Liza*, though, looked lovely. Sinjin speculated on whether or not she would be sold to an insistent buyer. His mates Craig or Ryan might buy her up.

He'd heard the excitement for the show in everyone's voices when he'd spun it while in the role of public relations genius. Unfortunately, Larry had made his mark and stomped all over Claire's talent. It needed to be upcycled back into her show. Fuck Larry.

Determined to keep his dismal thoughts off his face, Sinjin methodically examined each piece. He felt Claire scrutinizing his every move, and he wanted to speak carefully. When he made a full circle around the perimeter of Maxwell's, he stood beside *Liza* and checked the cameras.

"It sucks." Claire sighed, defeated. "Larry hated the displays I'd created, so I hauled them downstairs." She clutched onto the back of a vintage couch—a chesterfield smaller than the one in her apartment and ruby red instead of pepper green.

He wanted to ask her about it but focused on the matter at hand. The show needed to be revamped. "It's my fault, not yours."

She groaned and shook her head. "Not in the least."

"If my hatred of Boris and Natasha hadn't been so poisonous, I wouldn't have gotten you into this situation."

She hugged him. "We wouldn't have found each other if you hadn't."

"You're right." Embracing her, he let that truth seep into him and then stood back to get into action. "Okay. What I suggest, if you allow me, is to add in more display items. I'll get them from the barn. And you, if you can handle it, bring up all of the items that you put in the basement. Can you do it without me?"

She pumped up her fist à la Rosie the Riveter and looked grateful. "I've got some guns, but if it's too heavy, Lucy can help me out."

"This time, not a word to Larry. You do you. Ignore the wanker. Everyone coming Saturday night is anxious to see a steampunk exhibit with a shout-out to women's issues. An exhibit created by Claire Beaumont."

His encouragement seemed to do the trick. She spun on the heel of her Doc Marten and marched to the basement. "See you later, alligator."

Alone with *Liza*, he contemplated his next move. Larry had stripped away Claire's confidence, and he needed to know about it, but Sinjin would head to the barn first.

His dad and Gus met him as he'd asked, but when they went inside, Gus sneezed ferociously and begged out of any lifting. So Sinjin and his dad retrieved an antique Victrola with a hand crank and bagged up every old hat they came across. There was a box stuffed with incredible hammered copper ceiling plates that he grabbed and stuffed into his Bronco. As they were about to leave, Sinjin spotted an antique typewriter and knew right away that Claire would love it.

He thanked his dad and chided his brother, then drove into town with the stash of wonders for Claire in the back of his truck. Through the glass front door of Maxwell's, he spotted her topping *Liza* with different hats. He looked behind him, wondering if any of the hats he'd grabbed from the barn would be appropriate. It was almost suppertime, so he made a reservation for them at the Immigrant Room in Kohler. He was about to get out of the car and unload when a nagging feeling returned. Larry.

How the idiot had the balls to make so many outlandish demands on Claire bothered Sinjin. All for Larry to gain easy access to steal *Coal or Steam*. Oh, how he wanted to give Larry a dose of his own medicine, push him around a bit to see how it felt. But this wasn't his gig. This was Claire's pride and hard work. He couldn't step in and ignore her like he had some kind of proprietary right. That was getting into rogue and wanker territory. The Lafferty's contact number was displayed on his dashboard. Claire stepped close to the front door's window. She deserved so much better for a boss than Larry Chambers, a manipulating and conniving grifter. On second thought, he needed to be out of her sightline to think. A dose of fresh air couldn't hurt.

At Peace Park, he walked down to the beach and kicked around rocks and sand. The warm days of fall had started to wane, but there were plenty of folks milling about on the pier by the yacht club. After expending some pent-up energy, Sinjin gave in to his primal instinct to protect, tapped in the Lafferty, and requested Larry Chambers.

He watched a couple of ducks traverse the foamy ripples in the water as it swelled near him on the beach. His moment of calm shattered when Larry picked up the call using his Cyndi Lauper pitch. Even the ducks floated away.

"Chambers? Sinjin Reid here."

A beat of silence was followed by a tap-tap-tap. It baffled Sinjin. Was there someone else listening in on the call? He really needed to stop watching movies with spies, heists, and bad guys. Nothing wrong with rom-coms.

Larry snorted obnoxiously. "Mr. Reid. What can I do for you? She's been working hard on *Vectors*, correct?

"If *she* is Claire, then absolutely. But you already know this because of how difficult you've made the exhibit for her. You and all your pedantic demands. Regardless of your inane directions, *Vectors* will be a success. I'm making sure of it."

"It's an inconsequential show, yet I can see why you'd go to so much trouble. Your piece is the only one worth seeing. But in the grand scheme of things, your career is dwindling, and this show isn't going to jump-start it."

It had nothing to do with his career. Larry was trying to bait him. Sinjin kicked about one of the larger stones near his foot. "As my sculpture is only one of the many *star* pieces in the show, the curator will install each one according to her design. Any way she chooses."

There was a muffled scoff. "I haven't asked Claire to proceed in any other way. My only intention is to guide her into being objective when it comes to the Raffen painting. She can be emotional when it comes to her father's work."

Sinjin picked up a rock and threw it into the lake. "Don't make this about Claire Beaumont. She is a brilliant professional."

"And quite a painter, as well," Larry said. "Her work is resplendent and imitates her father's."

Sinjin only half agreed. From the work he'd seen in Claire's studio and her use of color combinations, in many ways, her talent surpassed her father's. "The display for *More Lace Please* will be rearranged how Claire had originally designed it. Understand?"

"Yes." Larry's curt response echoed, and he sounded as if he spoke from inside a metal chamber.

Sinjin remembered when Claire had thought of the guy as an alien without a belly button. At the memory, he chuckled until the little green man started to talk again.

"But. While Claire Beaumont is *repositioning*, you should watch her every move. There are four *Seasons* in a year. You have two. I have one. Who do you think has the fourth?"

"What the hell are you talking about? The Raffen portraits? I'm not surprised that Claire would have one of the four. I am shocked that you claim to own a Raffen. Must have cost quite a bit of dosh."

Sinjin made sure to keep his thoughts clear of his feelings. When he had spoken to the NY gallery where Raffen was represented, Lindsey, the new owner, made mention of a recent interest in the *Seasons* paintings, and she'd thought it was unusual. Since Sinjin now had the spring and winter portraits in his hands, he had called to find out about the summer and fall paintings in the series and assumed that Claire had the other two in her own private collection. How Larry had come in contact with either *Sugar* or *Golden* was perplexing. And the why was a complete conundrum.

"I never took you for a Raffen fan," Sinjin said. "Didn't you only go for the highest-value pieces according to the auctioneers at Christie's? *Seasons* and the salacious gossip surrounding them are ancient history."

"But are they rumors?" Larry snorted. "You and I both know every art scandal starts with a morsel of truth."

Sinjin dashed the idea out of his head. It was pure fantasy to think that Claire had painted *Seasons*. He'd seen her work, and it differed vastly from her father's. Although a sculptor, he had taught drawing long enough to have a good eye and could distinguish, fairly competently, the difference between individual artists' brushstrokes. "I think we are done talking, Larry."

"Certainly. As I always say, best to watch your back. Desperation makes us act in unsavory ways. Claire Beaumont's no stranger to need, and she's running a show with high-ticket items. Especially your sculpture. I'll see you, Mr. Reid, at the opening."

After speaking to the devil incarnate, Sinjin stomped along the shoreline, kicking at the stones threatening to engulf his hiking boots.

Jackass.

Larry could not be trusted. He and Meg were deceitful, and both wanted to abscond with his sculpture. What Larry said made little sense. Sinjin knew Larry was a conniving wanker trying to throw him off the scent. Like a dog though, Sinjin had to keep sniffing for the bone. He was tempted to return to the cottage and inspect *Fever* and *Midnight* with a magnifying glass.

He shook off the thought. Had he gone mad?

Sinjin jogged to his Bronco and drove back to Maxwell's.

Not Claire. It couldn't be her work on four paintings signed by David Raffen. Impossible.

When he opened the back hatch of his truck, she came out of Maxwell's, hugged him, and squeezed his bum. He returned the affection with a kiss on her temple, but an undistinguishable question kept badgering him in the back of his brain.

"What did you find at the barn?" She crawled into the

truck and lifted off the sheets of plastic he'd wrapped over the items he'd brought for her.

"Not a lot, I'm afraid.' It might be best if you made a trip yourself."

"Are you okay? Why so formal?" She squinted at him. "Watching *Masterpiece Theatre* again?"

"A bit hungry." The color of her eyes, like the blues in her painting, dashed away his misgivings.

She squealed when the old typewriter came into view and then yelped when she uncovered the Victrola. "These are incredible. Perfection. Fantastical!"

Feeling as though he was back on his own two feet, he decided Larry Chambers had no clue what the fuck he was talking about. "Glad you like my choices. Think you can use them for displays? Or costumes?"

She opened the bag of hats and donned a bowler. Then she played around with the crank on the Victrola and punched at a couple of the keys on the vintage typewriter. "I bet I could find a new ribbon to get this baby working again. If so, I can set it in the doorway and have people type their names on a piece of paper. It will be a steampunk guestbook."

"Brilliant idea. But weren't you going to have *Coal or Steam* by the door? Near *Liza* to keep a safe watch on it?"

"Since I've abandoned Larry's manifesto, I've been playing around and doing some brainstorming." She touched the Victrola. "I wonder if I could put this on the pedestal. And set your sculpture next to it? No. What am I thinking? Your piece is a solo act."

"*Coal or Steam* is heavy and needs a solid support underneath it. And it should be where Larry asked you to put it. Don't you think?"

He wasn't comfortable questioning her about a french horn and mannequin like a KGB spy. He backed off. "This is your show. Do what you think is best. If need be, we can make sure the sculpture is fine anywhere in the space."

"I would never put your masterpiece in any sort of danger. That's why moving it deeper inside the shop will give us leverage over Larry if he tries to steal it. I mean," she said, butt-scooting out of the van, "if the man actually thinks he can enter a crowded gallery and walk out with your sculpture, he must be nuts."

Sinjin agreed completely. Larry was delusional, and all of his tall tales were tall tales. Full stop. But he wanted to know one more thing. "I wanted to let you know. I reached out to L. Finegold Gallery and confirmed that Lindsey will be coming to the opening. Any chance you could include *Fever* and *Midnight* in the exhibit? I mean, they are rich pieces and such a beautiful representation of your mother. They would fit nicely into your theme of strong women."

She opened her mouth and then closed it. "That's an interesting idea." Her thumb's cuticle caught her undivided attention. "Can I think about it? I mean, those paintings of my mother are beautiful. But my father, he wasn't. When they were painted, he wasn't, well…quite all there. You know what I mean?" She concentrated on her thumb.

"I see." He had to suss out all of her backpedaling. "I asked the gallery about the other two in the series. Any idea who owns them?"

Her face, already devoid of color, slackened. Her lips quivered. "Oh. I'm not sure. Really."

She was lying to him. Not a fib or a little white lie but a bald-faced whopper. Then it hit him. In the barn when they'd discovered *Midnight*. She'd asked about the other *one*? Not the logical assumption about the other *two* paintings left in the series. Whether she was referring to her own painting or the one in Larry's evil lair made no difference. A thin layer of deceit on Claire became visible to him. Sinjin struggled to stay composed. "Let me help you get these things inside the shop. I have to get going. I remembered Dad and Gus wanted to meet up tonight. All right if we take a rain check on dinner?"

"Oh. Sure," she said, her voice cracking. "Whatever you want. You sound upset. I mean, if you want your sculpture near the door, it will be placed where you want it. It is, after all, your masterpiece."

"No. You have a point." Seizing the typewriter, Sinjin carried it in and dropped it on the counter. Then he manhandled the Victrola and shelved it beside the typewriter. He caught her eyeing him suspiciously and fought off the urge to demand more answers about *Seasons*. His emotions kept twisting his logic. "If it's in the middle of the action, it will be harder for Larry to steal it."

Threads of Claire's black hair crept out from the bowler hat and streamed down her shoulders. A look of innocence or a cunning disguise?

She removed her hat and crushed it against her chest. "It's not that I don't want any more of my dad's paintings in the exhibit. It's…it's because there may be too many. And it might appear as if I'm biased. Favoring David Raffen."

Another lie. And worse, it was exactly what Chambers had conjured up. That she couldn't be objective about her father's —question mark—paintings. Such a load of rubbish. Big lies were falling on top of him, threatening to crush him.

"Are all four of *Seasons* forgeries?"

"Let me tell you what—"

"You. You painted them."

"Please," she pleaded, "let me explain."

"You really had me and everybody in the art world fooled." He couldn't control his scorn. "Quite an accomplishment."

"You have to listen—"

"To you? A fraud and liar. No, thanks." Her eyes turned into purple shards of glass. "There's no explanation or excuse to justify this level of dishonesty. None. Worse, Larry—the lousiest excuse for a human being—was fucking right about you. Played me like a fool again."

She glowered, a volatile rage radiating off her. "Not everyone has an agenda. Not everyone is a Larry. Or a Meg. Just because she screwed you over doesn't mean all women are out to get you—the high-and-mighty Sinjin Reid."

Fucking Meg. He willed his blood to stop boiling and failed.

Claire shook her head, looking disgusted. "You're a liar too. You think you're all supportive and giving, but it's all in your big fat ego-driven head. All about Sinjin Reid. Ever hear of paradigm shifts, or better yet, understanding?"

Any coherent thoughts were strangled by his frustration. He kicked the door open and bolted out of the fucking place.

Chapter 29

With one finger, she punched down the F key. Then U. The keyboard on the old typewriter shuddered. So angry, hurt, and frustrated, but not wanting to damage the antique, she poked the C and the K.

What had she been thinking? That she could pull a fast one over on one of her dad's most steadfast admirers? A better name for the "art world" could be the "wolf pack."

Claire clasped onto the edges of the mission-style pedestal and inch by inch shoved it back to its proper place by the front door and near *Liza*. A sliver of wood from a rough edge pierced the ball of her hand. She yelped, and Lucy charged in from the juice bar.

"What's wrong?" She glanced around. "Where's Sinjin? Wasn't he just here? I didn't want to bug the two of you."

"Gone. For good, probably." Claire sucked on the sliver and then tried to wedge it out with her thumb. "He knows about the forgeries. And he wouldn't let me explain. Then…it was so damn frustrating. I couldn't get a word in. I threw Meg in his face."

"Men." Lucy grabbed her hand, dragged her back to the

sink, and held it under cold running water. "Such babies. This may help. Stay put. I'll get the tweezers."

Claire stared at the icy water splashing over the palm of her hand, trying to numb her feelings in the same manner. It wasn't working. The moment Sinjin had brought up *Seasons*, she'd panicked. It took all of her strength to keep the storm inside her hidden from him. "He called me a fraud. Which is true in ways. But what hurt more was when he called me a liar. I tried to tell him the truth but failed. Miserably."

Lucy turned off the water and clasped her hand. "Close your eyes. This might pinch."

She did as she was told. More than grateful to have Lucy nearby as her hand was injured and her heart was shattering.

The tweezers bit into her. The metal chomped through layers of skin, seeking its wooden treat. She closed her eyes and held her breath to endure the discomfort that she truly deserved.

"Voilà." Lucy cheered and let go of her hand. She held up the tiny sliver of wood that had caused so much pain.

"Damn. That stung. I fully expected you to be the one taking care of my old lady whiskers at the Sunny Up Ranch or wherever we end up together when we're ninety. Not anymore, sister." Claire was about to suck on the broken skin again, but Lucy clutched her wrist, dabbed the wound with a smelly cotton ball, and put a Band-Aid on it. "Such a mom thing to do," Claire said.

"What can I say. I'm good at mothering, thanks to Julie."

"That's so wrong. I'm hoping that this show and her chandelier will knock some sense into her. She might see, when others *Oohh* and *Aahh* over her work, how talented she is."

"Let's get back to the other fire that needs to be doused. What happened with Sinjin? How did it come up?"

She shook her head and recounted the conversation. Considering her nervous energy had stolen any semblance of reason, Claire remembered the gist of the convo. "It started when he suggested I incorporate two of the *Seasons* into the show. Yours and his."

"I think that's a great idea," Lucy said. "Get them out in the open. Show the world your work." She captured her with an X-ray glare. "You didn't do anything illegal. The paintings were never supposed to leave Anita's gallery. You and your dad painted them together and put that in writing. Unfortunately, Anita died, and her great-niece didn't have an inkling when she took over her great-aunt's gallery."

"I kept *Golden*. Sinjin and his dad bought two. But Lindsay told me a woman bought one. Must have been Meg working at the behest of the evil overlord Larry. That's how he got his hands on *Sugar*. He's been threatening me. Holding this night-mare over my head. I'm sure he got to Sinjin somehow. Prob-ably told him something completely diabolical," she sighed. "Damn. I painted them for my dad with his help simply because he couldn't see. He signed them to make them an asset for Anita, and she wanted them because she and my mom were good friends."

"Again, you did nothing wrong. It's never been proven that you forged the work. And the only one who profited off the sale was Anita's gallery. Which kept it open after she died. One way to look at it is that you saved her legacy."

"All good points, except I never had a chance to tell Sinjin any of it." Claire was lucky to have such a good friend who remembered every one of her sordid stories. "Sharp memory."

"You can thank Rosemary."

"Rosemary who?" Claire asked.

"The essential oil, goof. It's good for concentration." Lucy tapped her temple. "It helps me stay focused."

"I think I need help from Rosemary, too." Claire touched her hands together prayer-style and brought them to her lips. She closed her eyes to think. "What should I do?"

"About *Seasons*?" Lucy asked.

"Sinjin!"

"You need to ignore the bad-tempered Brit. Stay focused on your exhibit and consider displaying *Seasons*. It's time for you to brag."

Hanging them out for the world to see would be a huge risk. New critics from *Art & Form* were attending. They were bound to know the history, the gossip, and all the rumors that spread after that day at the Armory Show, thanks to Art Silver. Even though dead, his scathing indictment of David Raffen still reverberated in the art world. The jealousy of her father's archrival wasn't only about painting. It was deeply rooted in the love they both had for the same woman, Monique Beaumont. An ancient love triangle that Claire was fortunate to have missed.

"Sinjin might have me carted off and thrown in jail." She nibbled her finger.

"Impossible. You haven't broken any laws." Lucy took hold of her shoulders. "I'm here for you. We're all here for you. With all of us in your corner, you'll be safe. If worse comes to worst, I'll arrange for you to go undercover and into witness protection. What would you like for your new name? Madge? Or Mildred?"

"You know how to make me smile, girl." A ray of sunshine gleamed through the transoms around the shop. Like a halo, the light aimed at the Stevie portrait. "A message from above?"

"No. That's what happens when Stevie Nicks is in the house. She doesn't let anyone drag her heart around," Lucy said, using air quotes. "And neither should you. Get back to *Vectors*."

"I will. And I'll reconfigure the space to allow for *Midnight*. Is that cool? After all, you're the owner of it."

"Please. My mom must have lifted it and shoved it in the barn before I laid eyes on it. George has been such a friend since we met in Al-Anon. I suppose at the next meeting I should bring up her addiction to stealing."

"If it helps, I'm not giving up on Julie. She's a creative, and I understand firsthand how their struggles can be debilitating."

Claire wandered around, thinking about where to put *Midnight* and considered how she could retrieve it and *Fever* from Sinjin. It seemed impossible. At this point, they both needed to cool down. His anger had been awful, her frustration childish. If only he would have let her speak. Unfortunately, when she finally had a chance to say something, she'd lost it. She cringed, thinking of how she'd called him a liar and brought up Meg.

"Do you think I should go get *Golden*?" She asked Lucy to get out of her dreadhead. "It's in my closet in Milwaukee."

"I'm not sure. What about the fourth one?"

"*Sugar*. Meg or Larry must have gotten their hands on it."

Together, they finished pushing the heavy pedestal back by the front entrance. "This is where Sinjin wants it, so he gets what he wants."

"Title of your sex tape?" Lucy joked.

"Getting laid won't be happening anytime soon."

"Go get the paintings from Sinjin," Lucy added, "but not today. Still too raw. Maybe tomorrow. If you show up at his doorstep, he can't turn you away."

"The British boy with a girl just standing in front of him? Isn't that a movie?"

"When in doubt, always remember your best rom-com etiquette," Lucy said.

Claire's gloomy disposition was alleviated by diving into *Vectors* for the rest of the evening. With Lucy's help, the entire space reverted back to how it had started. But every time she closed her eyes, all she could see was Sinjin's face contorted with anger and pain. Some of it was meant for her, but not all of it. Which made her even more sad.

Chapter 30

"Sit the hell down," George yelled. "You're giving me an aching neck."

Pacing in front of the Raffen portraits, Sinjin ignored his father. With each step, he tapped the magnifying glass against his thigh. "How come I can't see it?"

His brother Gus took a sip from his gin and tonic. "Exactly what are you gunning for?"

"Proof. Tangible proof that the four *Seasons* were painted by Claire Beaumont."

Sinjin had sprinted into the cottage and inspected the two *Seasons* after he'd left Claire. He couldn't and wouldn't believe she'd painted four portraits of her mother and passed them off as her father's work. How bloody ludicrous. But Larry's words were embedded in his head like a bad jingle, so when Claire confessed, he'd gone off the deep end.

Was her nature really so deceitful?

The bleak lighting in the cottage frustrated him. Sinjin brought the two paintings into the gallery and invited his father and brother to help him understand. Maybe they could see what he'd missed. While he spent an hour adjusting the lighting, the two of them barely showed interest in his quest for the truth. Instead, they prodded him with questions about Claire. Her exhibit, her life, her work, and then they showered her with compliments.

"I need another painting by Raffen," he said to his audience, who looked completely bored, "to review the brushwork."

George asked, "Don't you have a collection in the cottage?"

"Those are drawings. I've collected his works that weren't mainstream." Sinjin thought about the drawing of Claire. When he'd struggled to get the lighting perfect and then recognized the color of her eyes in the drawing. "Maybe I should test a sample of the paint. Especially the color of the eyes."

Groaning, Gus strode up to him and dropped his arm over his shoulders. "Are you jonesing for an excuse to stay clear of Claire?" He aimed his cocktail glass toward the canvas without spilling a drop. "If she admitted to painting this beautiful woman—"

"Her mother." Sinjin gently guided his brother and the liquid in his hand a step away from the painting. "She was French."

"I stand corrected," Gus said. "This beautiful French woman. It's pretty obvious that Claire is as talented as her father. Maybe she and her parents have had a rocky road. Much like ours, bro." Gus glanced at George. "No offense."

George stood and joined the two of them. "None taken."

"I'm no expert, but looking at these two portraits by Claire, I think she has more talent in her pinky than you do," Gus said.

Hubris came to mind. Not to mention a lengthy list of ethical and moral breaches. Sinjin wouldn't go into it with Gus. Especially since he'd guzzled down his second cocktail.

Although Gus had a solid point. Every family was riddled with dysfunction, health issues, and mental health challenges. His mother's alcoholism almost tore them apart, but the one thing that kept them from splitting into shards was a sense of loyalty.

Sinjin knew Claire was loyal to her father. She'd moved a fucking huge chesterfield couch into her apartment. Using a crane. If that wasn't loyalty, he wasn't sure what else could be. A fucking crane. An old turntable. All those albums.

Standing in front of the Raffen portraits, the trio of Reid men gazed at *Midnight* and *Fever*. After a long minute or two, Sinjin shoved the magnifying glass into his back pocket and broke the silence. "What the hell is wrong with me?"

"Is that a rhetorical question?" Gus added, "Because I can come up with many answers if you want me to."

Sinjin dropped his head and shook it. A feeling of dread invaded him. Once again, he'd let Larry and Meg's machinations burn a hole into his life. There were reasons and explanations. Claire had tried. But instead of sticking around to find out, he'd booked out of Maxwell's. "Not going to ogle these paintings anymore."

"Good idea," his dad said. "Want a bit of fatherly advice?"

Gus snorted. "Go ahead, Dad. Give what you've got to *The Beav*."

"Sure," Sinjin said, punching his brother's arm.

Gus growled and waved a fist at him.

George gently pushed them apart, and Sinjin apologized. "I'm treading in rough territory. Since Meg, I'm not sure what to think. Or feel. For fuck's sake."

"You were burned," George said, "badly. My wisdom isn't as wise as I think it is. The rub, though, is that when I see you and Claire together, it clicks. You two are stark mad for one another. It's clear as day."

"I agree with Pa." Gus slapped his back hard. "I haven't

seen you two together much, but you are definitely happier than I've ever seen you."

"How would you know? The last time we were together, we were at the courthouse. When Meg and I swapped rings." Sinjin took the paintings off the easels and set them by the door to return to the cottage.

"My point exactly." Gus set his glass on the floor and carried the easels into the corner with others. "That day, I witnessed a bloody miserable man marry a woman who looked bored out of her mind. Why the hell did you do it?"

The embarrassment of the truth flooded his cheeks. He debated ignoring Gus's question, but then his father's gimlet stare made up his mind. "Who said the truth will set you free?"

"Out with it," Gus ordered.

"Meg told me she was pregnant," Sinjin said, feeling a weight lift off his shoulders. Even though he had questioned the validity of Meg's claim, she'd never shown him the pregnancy test. "I wanted to do the right thing."

"There were plenty of choices at the time," his dad said. "But I wouldn't beat yourself up over picking the path that— since the days of cavemen—has infiltrated stone tablets, our storybooks, movies, and music. Over and over again, they tell us marriage and babies make everything happy."

"Foolish. I was duped by the oldest trick in the book."

His dad framed him by clutching his shoulders. "Look. They're grifters. Meg and Larry."

"And need to be stopped," Gus added. "And you, with the help of the amazing Claire, are on the way to trapping and stopping the buggers once and for all."

Sinjin shook off the embarrassment that had been plaguing him since the day he agreed to marry Meg. He let his family's words resonate in his mind.

With his hands full, Sinjin hiked back to his cottage and

placed the two paintings in his storage. His mind continued to reel, so he flipped through his albums and put on an old Steely Dan record. The songs soothed his mood as he tried to plan how to make it through his trust issues with Claire, but worse, he'd been a complete asshole. Name-calling?

When his phone chimed, he hedged. His plan hadn't been fully formed, and he couldn't trust himself yet, so he declined Claire's call. He was icing her out, but he'd been burned, and Sinjin needed time to smooth over the dents that had formed on his armor.

He went to his studio, turned off his phone, and fired up his welding equipment. Sinjin stayed there and forged spoons. Melting the silver, molding the scoop, and styling the handle with twists and turns of metal. The process worked well, and by the next morning, he felt calmer and more rational. He'd figured out one essential thing. As much as he needed air to survive, he needed Claire and her brilliance to live.

Still in his clothes from yesterday, he left his studio. Instead of being a normal human and showering, he had to find his dad and Gus. It occurred to him, during his spoon-making and emo-purging, that Claire's idea to move the pedestal for the sculpture away from the front door was pivotal. Larry and Meg were absolute grifters. His dad was spot-on. To actually catch them stealing a sculpture in the middle of an opening, Sinjin had to trap them.

"Claire had a fantastic idea, and I crushed it like a rotten egg," he announced, storming into the kitchen. "We need to arrange my sculpture in the center of the room, under Julie's chandelier. Make it harder for Larry to nick it."

His father and brother were sitting at the kitchen counter. They both looked at him, surprised. "Good afternoon to you, too," his dad said. "Have you slept at all?"

Afternoon? Sinjin glanced at the oven clock. It was one

already? "Guess not. Shite. Sorry men. Must have lost track of time."

"An all-nighter," Gus gave him a fist bump. "Nice. Feeling fresh as a picked dandelion." He sniffed. "Sort of smell like one, too."

Sinjin ignored Gus. He wanted to plow ahead with his stream of thoughts, but then the dogs barked. He rambled on while feeding Ginger and Fred. "*Coal or Steam* should be placed in the center of the room."

"Won't the two pieces clash?" Gus asked.

Taken by his brother's astute and rather artistic observation, Sinjin chided him. "Taking a master class on art?"

The dogs gobbled up the kibble.

"No, smart-ass," Gus said. "But I work on stage sets, and I'm in tune with how they're designed for maximum viewing pleasure."

Sinjin poured himself a cup of coffee and shoved it into the microwave. "I can see to the positioning of the pieces, but Larry said something yesterday that has me rattled. He talked about desperation and referenced Claire, but what if he's transferring? I'm concerned about the security at the opening. I really have no idea how volatile Larry is. He was right about Claire. Could he be talking about himself, too? Desperation leads to turns sharper than Rube Goldberg's."

The microwave beeped. Sinjin grabbed his cup out and shuddered at the digitized "END" on the screen.

"Whoa," George said. "Do you think Larry may bring some kind of weapon?"

"Or Meg?" Gus added. "A gun?"

Sinjin shook his head. "I've been trying to suss it out."

"The best plan is to expect the unexpected. Call the cop shop," George said, scrolling through his phone. "My contact in Lake Bluff is Charlene something."

"Perfect," Sinjin said. "A woman. I think Claire will appreciate it. Given the theme of her show."

"Speaking of Claire," Gus said, pulling leashes off the backdoor hook. "What are you planning to do about that? Any moments of clarity while you were...what were you doing all night?"

"Melting spoons." Welding was not only a creative outlet but also a fantastic diversion from his most difficult mental conundrums. Nothing like the loud noise of a hydraulic press to soothe the soul. "First thing first, security."

"Here it is," George said, "Charlene Renz. Not sure if she'll be around the night of the opening, but she'll get the security set up for you. In fact, call her now. I'm surprised you don't have a guard there at Maxwell's at this moment."

"You're right. Male ego, I guess." He recalled Claire saying something about his big fat ego. "I've been thinking solely about *Coal or Steam* sitting in your trunk. But now, with the other pieces, I'll get on it." Sinjin added Charlene to his contacts.

Before Gus left to take the dogs for a walk, Sinjin asked, "Do you think Rob will wanna come up? With his babe? What's her name? The supermodel?"

"Her name is Francesca Marcheti. Do you really need to poke that bear?" Gus whined, then Fred and Ginger whined.

"Yes, you two need to get it together," Sinjin said. "What happened in Door County is old news. You're grown-ass men."

"Call Rob," his dad said, ambling out of the kitchen. "I'm taking a ride into town. I have a sweet tooth."

"Does the Victorian Shoppe have anything left?" Sinjin asked, tapping the cop's number into his phone.

Gus laughed as he walked out the backdoor. "A grown-ass man eating more candy than Willy Wonka."

Sinjin made his obligatory calls and sighed when the security for the exhibit was set up and would start tomorrow. When he'd spoken to his youngest brother, Rob, he grunted, then hemmed and hawed over his frustration with Angus and their besmirched past in Door County. Ultimately, he agreed to come to *Vectors* with Fran. Sinjin was about to ring Claire when her call came in first.

Chapter 31

Sinjin hadn't bothered to make an appearance at Maxwell's, and Claire felt not only miserable but incredibly foolish since she'd called him two times. The first call he sent to voicemail. Give him time, she thought. Maybe he would shed his hardhearted shell and transform back into a kind person.

When she called the second time, he answered with a curt hello. She tried to get in a word, maybe two words, but he launched into a lengthy explanation about how he'd hired security for the exhibit. When the call ended abruptly, she was finally able to talk and said, "Hi, there."

Two words, too late.

When a Lake Bluff policewoman named Charlene came into Maxwell's today and introduced herself, Claire called Sinjin for the third time. Number three must have been a charm because Sinjin was on his way over to check on the exhibit. At least, that was her assumption. All he really did was grunt and say something that sounded like, "In an hour." Or maybe it could have been "In her ear." Who knew? But after three days, she wasn't sure if she gave a damn.

Claire gathered her pencil and clipboard and approached

the cop strolling around *Vectors*. To have a person with a gun walking around the art seemed strange. None of the guards at the museum had firearms; at least, she didn't think so. She'd been so immersed in *Vectors* she hadn't really thought about it. Yet, because of the recent trend of vandals charging into museums and destroying historical art pieces, Claire wondered if the Lafferty had changed its policy. She jotted down a note to ask Mina about it.

"I'm honored to work for you," Charlene said. "I think this exhibit is really interesting. I'm familiar with steampunk. A lot of these items are valuable. If anything happens at the opening, I'll be prepared." She tapped her gun in its holster.

Claire gave her a nervous smile, then explained several of the paintings and sculptures that were on display. She also described the history of steampunk and how every piece in the exhibit was an example of a time or an era when women made a stand or instigated a change. They stepped up to the empty pedestal where Sinjin's sculpture would be placed, and Claire offered one other detail to Charlene. "Sinjin will be delivering his sculpture *Coal or Steam* on the morning of the opening."

"Already confirmed that with Mr. Reid," Charlene said.

Of course. Claire wondered what else Sinjin had spoken to Charlene about. Glancing around the room, she spotted the empty spaces on the wall she had prepared for *Fever* and *Midnight*. She had no idea where, when, or if the two paintings would be integrated into the show or if she would be arrested for painting them.

She'd made a valiant effort to talk to Sinjin about them on call number two.

Claire reminded herself that she'd done nothing illegal.

She'd wanted to discuss the portraits of her mother. Instead, she dutifully jotted down notes to keep up with all of Sinjin's asks and never had a chance. Or maybe never *took* a chance? But it was probably easier to avoid after he'd called her a liar.

"This chandelier is so unique. Did you make it?" Charlene asked.

Claire escaped from her own head. "No, but Julie, the owner of Maxwell's, did. She's incredibly talented."

Standing under the chandelier, they stared up at it. The curvy details of Julie's welding work on each candlestick were spectacular. The shadows from the metal circles spun slowly around on the ceiling, adding in a little something extra that made the sculpture even more special. Having Sinjin's piece directly below it, Claire hoped, wouldn't spoil the unique effects of the chandelier.

"This is where *Coal or Steam* will be displayed," she said to Charlene. "I'm not sure how much Sinjin told you, but we suspect that there will be a man and a woman coming to the opening who will want to steal the sculpture."

"We've developed an action plan if Larry Chambers and Meg Fisher decide to steal it." Charlene gazed at the Belgian artist's ticking metronome, and added, "Would it be all right if the other guard and I dressed appropriate to the theme of the show? A British bobby costume might be fun, and we'll be less conspicuous."

"Be my guest. Add in a monocle, and you'll fit right in." Claire laughed too hard. Like she was guilty. *Of nothing.* "We'll have a basket of hats for the opening. I'll make sure there's a bobby style included."

Julie charged in, and already on edge, Claire jumped. To cover it up, she introduced Charlene to Julie, who didn't look quite right. However, the sour odor that had been following Julie around had gotten lost. Claire sniffed just to double-check. Nope. The smell wasn't hovering in the air.

When Charlene left Maxwell's, she and Julie were all alone. Claire grew tense and fidgeted. The air in the room became stagnant, as if time were at a standstill. Julie kept gazing up at the chandelier and down at the pedestal. Her face went up, then down, and up again. Claire wanted to ask but couldn't do it. They couldn't converse without it elevating Claire's cortisone levels. The woman was creative, talented, completely obtuse, and pigheaded.

"This isn't going to happen," Julie announced with a bit of spit escaping her lips. "When his sculpture sits below mine, it will reflect shadows on the ceiling that will disrupt the shadows of my piece. The shadows are part of the viewer's experience."

Julie had a valid point. Unfortunately, Claire was jammed between two rulers: Larry and Sinjin. One she hated, and the other hated her. "I can't do anything about it. Sinjin requested this position. I'm sorry, Julie."

"He's not what you think," she said.

Claire casually reached behind her head and combed her fingers through the bottom layer of her hair. At least this way, Julie wouldn't see them trembling. Nothing about the start of this conversation made Claire inclined to talk. "It might be best to end this discussion before it starts."

"Sinjin's been a sweetheart all week. While you've been sweating and slogging through the layers of dust to create your vision, we've been together on an entirely different level with our art."

Oh, dear god. She had no interest in knowing whatever was happening with Julie. She'd turned into a monster, thanks to Sinjin. "Creative types, I understand. We're an eclectic group. Out-of-the-box thinkers tend to stick together." Unsure of what else to say, Claire glanced at Lulu's. "Lucy's upstairs, but there's bound to be some Gecko Grass around."

"You think I'm hungover? Not in the least." She clutched her unusually large handbag, setting off a racket of glass-against-glass rattles. "It's been such an inspirational week I haven't needed a drink."

"Mrs. Maxwell." Claire hoped that addressing her friend's mother formally would create much-needed space. "It's not any of my business. You and Sinjin are spectacularly talented, and I'm thrilled to have works by both of you in this exhibit."

Julie sighed. She seemed to soften from the compliment. Claire wondered if her lengthy sigh signaled relaxed, or was Julie defeated? Sad? Resigned to follow whatever bottle of booze she'd stuffed in her purse?

In her limited experience with alcohol abuse, Claire wasn't certain if Julie was sober or drunk. There were no outward indications. No smells, no slurring. But from all the pain that Julie had caused her best friend, Claire would put money on drunk instead of sober.

A loud engine roared down Main Street. She glanced out the window, hoping to see Sinjin, but it was George Reid. At the sight and sound of the big white Cadillac with its top down, she felt a pinch of relief. George had been making a daily pit stop at the chocolate store across the street and then coming into Maxwell's to visit Lucy.

Claire was not thrilled to be alone with this chaotic woman.

Julie swung her glass-filled bag off her shoulder and set it on the mission-style pedestal. "I'll be planting another piece I designed right here."

She then pulled out what looked like a three-tiered metal plate stand.

For hors d'oeuvres?

"I made a wine bar for Sinjin's show. Remember? This is a mini stand for cocktail plates, and I think right here is the best spot for it. The circles will imitate the shadows from the chandelier."

Claire clamped her mouth shut. This woman had been a pain in the ass, and there was no way in hell that she would let Julie make ridiculous demands with a freaking plate holder from Marshall's. Her patience evaporated. "Not going to happen. We don't need an appetizer display within the exhibit. How about in Lulu's. That's where all the food and beverages will be served."

Julie's eyes seemed to bulge out of their sockets as she looked around wildly. Then she grabbed the thing and threw it to the floor. It broke into multiple pieces. Dropping to the floor, she retrieved the scattering of metal hunks and piled them into her bag.

Claire crouched down. "Let me help."

"Get away from me. All Sinjin does is talk about you. I'm sick of it. I never wanted to be part of this shitty show." She flung her bag over her shoulder and traipsed out the door.

Should she run upstairs to get Lucy? Claire decided against it. Maybe this time, she could help out her best friend and return all the favors.

Claire would tend to Julie's latest tantrum.

Julie and George were across the street, talking. From the looks of it, they were getting along. At least Claire didn't see any flying wine bottles or waving hands.

Growing up without a mom hadn't been easy or hard for Claire. She didn't know the difference. Her father had simply been a spectacular guide whenever she came up against drama at school. Maybe a mom would have been a whole lot more comfortable to talk to when it came to the usual *girl* stuff, but her dad managed to make it through those times by calling Anita and having Claire talk to her.

To deal with an adult tantrum, Claire tapped into her inner Anita voice and walked across the street. A tough New Yorker, Anita didn't put up with shenanigans and could negotiate top dollars for a painting, even if it had been painted on a slice of bread. And this was before Banksy.

"Julie. Hi, George. You two all good?" Claire fortified her posture by hugging herself. "What kind of chocolates did you get today, George?"

He held up a waxy white bag along with his jingling Cadillac key chain. "The best English toffee in Wisconsin. Lucy will be thrilled."

"What are you? Some kind of candy man?" Julie grumbled. "She doesn't need all that sugar."

Claire had to hold her tongue. A last-ditch effort to play mother of the year? What a load of bull.

George indulged the worst mother ever. "It's one more tool for our work in progress. We're strategizing on a project. With her lavender and my sweet tooth, we're planning to rehab Lulu's."

The word "rehab" called out to Claire. She stood up straighter. Had Julie understood all of George's double entendres? Probably not. Even Claire had to think hard about it, and she'd been in Maxwell's more often than Julie. Although she wasn't privy to most of George and Lucy's convos while working on the exhibit, she'd picked up hints here and there that the two were concocting a rehab plan for Julie.

Through gritted teeth, Claire tried to sound civil. "There's a lot of happiness with the opening. Don't think about how your piece could be overshadowed by Sinjin's. There's plenty of glory to go around."

Julie's face was blank. Holding no expression, she stared at the back end of George's Cadillac. Where inside the trunk, *Coal or Steam* was safely hidden.

George gracefully hopped off the curb to lean against his convertible. He twisted the end of his mustache and gave Julie a quirky smile. She blinked, then shook her head. Her cheeks swelled, and her face turned red and blotchy.

Claire checked left to right to see if Charlene was still nearby or if anyone was around to help. Julie was going to explode any second, and she had no clue how to prevent it.

"All summer, while working under your son's tutelage," she said to George, "I'd been fascinated by his work. Sinjin's a genius with metal. But his people skills are sickening. He tormented me, constantly telling me how brilliant I am, but they are all lies."

Julie clutched onto the handles of her purse and yanked it off her shoulder. As she swung it back and forth in front of her, the load of broken metal and wine bottles crashed about loudly. Her arm strained at the weight of the bag. She hollered, lifted it, and then swung it at George.

He jumped away, dropping the keys and the bag of chocolate. He stepped back to garner more space between him and the vicious-looking woman carrying a designer wrecking ball. "Julie. Take it easy. No one wants to hurt you."

Staying behind Julie and out of her sightline, Claire grabbed her phone and hit 9-1-1. When she spoke, Julie pivoted and swung the bag. The phone tumbled out of Claire's hand as she jumped to avoid getting hit. She failed.

Flames of pain shot through her thigh. She lost her balance and fell back, her head hitting the sidewalk with a clunk. Through blurred vision, she saw George stumbling over to her.

In slow motion, Julie pushed George, grabbed his keys off the ground, and hopped behind the wheel of the Caddie, then squealed away.

Was this really happening, or was she watching TV?

Another ridiculous thought crossed Claire's mind. Where was the bag?

She sat up to check on George and tried to move her leg. A sharp pain radiated through her thigh, making her nauseous. Claire grunted and gagged down the bitter vomit. She squinted at the contents of Julie's bag scattered around on the ground. White wine dripped out of broken bottles. Spears of metal pieces jutted through the fabric of the bag. Remnants of the plate rack had escaped the bag and— Were those trivets?

The gross feel of sticky blood made her take a glimpse of

her leg. Something gold and shiny stuck out of a tear in her tights. She squeezed her eyes shut. "This isn't good. Anybody?"

For hours, no one responded. Or was it minutes? She fell back on the sidewalk.

"Here," a man said, sitting behind her and propping her upright. His chest radiated warmth.

"Glad you made it to the party," she said. Was she as delirious as she sounded?

Then another guy clamped down on her ankles. She blinked and saw a stretcher beside her on the ground. Damn.

"Ma'am, keep your head up and eyes open," the EMT behind her said, then counted, "One, two, three." The two men shifted her onto the stretcher and cradled her neck and head in padding.

Her eyelids were so heavy. When her lids started drooping, the EMT chastised her. "Stay awake. Open up your eyes. You fell hard onto the sidewalk."

Inside the ambulance, he pinched her eye open, and a flood of light dropped in. She wanted to block out the scorching sunlight, but the man wouldn't let her. "Yuck. What about my leg? It really hurts." Although it had now gone numb. "Am I going to be able to walk?"

The EMT didn't answer, only tucked a blanket around her.

Both men clutched onto the safety bars as the ambulance moved. She felt much better now that she wasn't lying on a cold slab of concrete. "I am sort of delirious, I guess. Sorry if I…"

"The older gentleman will be meeting you at the emergency room. Is he your father?"

She tried to nod but couldn't. "No. But." She didn't know what to say. "We're family. Please let him come into my room."

"When was your last tetanus shot?" the guy who had shined the horrible light in her eye asked.

"I have no idea. Did I ever get one? Why?" Her tongue stuck to the roof of her mouth.

Everything about this situation sucked.

"You'll need stitches. And the rod that lanced your leg is rusty."

Again, she tried to see her leg. Her view, however, stayed fixed on the ceiling of the ambulance. Which may have been for the best. Seeing her own blood, she would surely fight to the death with this dude to close her eyes. One tear slid out the corner of her left eye and down her cheek. "Damn."

The light guy took hold of her hand and squeezed it. "It's okay. You have a concussion and will probably be feeling a massive headache come on any minute."

"But—"

"Yes, you will walk again," he said with a chuckle.

"An EMT with a sense of humor. I like it." She snorted, making sure to keep her eyes wide open.

Chapter 32

Even with the Lake Bluff area code, the call was probably spam. Sinjin stared at the number, trying to recognize it. Was it Claire calling him from a different number? It had been two days since he'd seen her, and for half a second, he thought maybe it was her. The last three times she'd rang him, he all but ignored her.

But Claire wasn't the needy type. And using a different phone ranked high above needy and into obsessive. Julie was obsessive.

He banished his delinquent thinking and answered the fucking call.

An unfamiliar woman's voice entered his ear and sounded deadly serious. "Is this Sinjin Reid?"

Sinjin froze, standing on the front porch of the cottage. "Yes. Who is this?"

"This is Charlene Renz from the Lake Bluff PD. We spoke a few days ago about security."

"Sure, sure," he said, relaxing a little. "Everything all right?"

"I have an unusual situation, sir, and I'm uncertain about how to handle it."

His Spidey senses started to tingle. "Tell me. Did you recognize Larry Chambers from the pictures I sent to you? Is he in town?"

"Nothing like that. It's a woman I met in Maxwell's this morning."

"Claire? Is she okay?" He tapped his foot in a rapid beat.

"No. I mean yes, I think so. I'm referring to a Julie Maxwell. I've arrested her and taken her to the lockup in Lake Bluff. I caught her speeding on the highway in a white Cadillac. She told me she had an important delivery for you. But, sir, she acted in an inebriated manner, so I gave her a breathalyzer, and she failed."

While trying to comprehend what was happening with Julie, another call beeped in. This time, the caller ID announced St. Mary's Hospital. "Shite."

"Excuse me, sir? Would you like to come and bail out Ms. Maxwell?"

"I've got another call. Hold on." Every neck muscle tightened as he switched between calls.

"Sinjin!" his dad shouted into the phone. "Get your arse down to St. Mary's. That bird Julie went loony. Claire's here, getting stitches."

His mind went numb. Claire was hurt?

"Be there in five." He switched back to the cop. "Hell no. Julie can stay behind bars."

He rushed to the Bronco and held on to the door until he caught his breath. Stitches? How many? Was Claire unconscious? The questions racing through his mind didn't help. He got in the truck, concentrated on the road, and, even without speeding, made it to the hospital in less than ten minutes. When he strode into the emergency room, George flagged him down from behind a curtain at the end of the hall.

This was good. Claire hadn't been admitted.

When he saw her, he released a long breath and let out all the air that had been stored up until this moment. She was sitting up in the bed, covered to the shoulders with a beige blanket. She seemed alert, and he thought he caught a sparkle in her eyes. Relieved, he almost missed her leg. Exposed from under the bedding, her outer thigh was red and bandaged. He wanted to say something pithy or wise but couldn't think of anything. He went up to the bed and dropped down to hug her. Holding her tightly against his chest, he whispered, "I'm sorry. I should have been with you today."

"You're right. Dammit. You left me to fend for myself alone, Dr. Frankenstein."

"What?" Confused, he gauged her facial expression and came up with livid. "I don't know what you're talking about."

"Julie! She's a monster, and you created her." She pointed to her leg. "She came after me with her bag of horrors and sliced my leg open. With an extremely sharp metal stick. Ten fucking stitches and a tetanus shot."

Holy shit. What the fuck did he do? Julie had gone mad. His whole world seemed to shift. How could he have been such an idiot?

"I tried like hell to appease her," Claire went on, "but she was so belligerent. Telling me that she hated being in the show. That your sculpture would reduce hers to junk." She moved her leg and groaned. "Then she charged across the street and confronted George. To give Lucy a break, I decided to try and defuse the situation myself."

Believing he was helping everyone and doing the art world a favor by introducing Julie Maxwell as his protégé, his ego had grown so big on his shoulders he was surprised he could still walk. Even though the monster was behind bars, what Julie had done to Claire was unforgivable. Sinjin had to find a way to make it up to her, but it wouldn't be easy. He'd been a miserable arse over the whole *Seasons* debacle.

Despondence flowed out of him. He glanced at his dad sitting in the chair, mesmerized by his phone. When George sensed he was being watched, he glanced up and gave a disapproving shake of the head.

"When will you be released?" Sinjin took hold of Claire's hand. He squeezed it, trying to communicate his unspoken hopes. Could she forgive him for being such a pompous jerk? But there really was no good reason and no excuse for his behavior. He held on to her hand and let his heart ache, believing that somehow, he could right his so many wrongs. "After they give the okay for you to go home, I'll be here for you."

"By the end of the day. Then I'll need to have someone watch me for the next twenty-four hours. To make sure I'm sleeping normally, they'll have to wake me up each time I fall asleep."

A ray of hope found him.

She added, "George said he'd hang out with me for the next day or two."

Sinjin stared at his father. He attempted an evil eye, but his misery took hold of him. He only managed a hangdog look.

George laughed. "Such a sucker."

"What? He's the candy man, and I'm craving the English toffee from the Victorian Shoppe. Sorry, inside joke," she said, sounding exhausted.

When she smiled, the gray cloud hovering over him decided to leave him alone. "So, you have a concussion. A bruised brain?"

When he tried to move away, she squeezed his hand. "Don't go."

"I'll be your night watchman, babe. Do you want to stay at the cottage or the apartment?"

"Lucy's apartment. That way, you can take over as curator, and I can stay clear of Julie. Please? I don't want to be near that woman ever again. Ever. Without you. Or George. Or Lucy. Even Gus would make me feel safe. I can't be in there alone. She terrifies me."

"As we speak, Julie is behind bars," he said.

"Thank god. I hope they took away that damn bag of hers. It must be holding a hundred pounds of metal in it. Julie tried to hit George first and then went after me. I fell and hit my head on the sidewalk; she ran off with the car. And your sculpture."

"Where the hell is my Cadillac?" George asked. "Is your sculpture still in the trunk?"

Sinjin had no idea. But if Julie had destroyed *Coal or Steam*, he'd holler so loud all of Lake Bluff would hear it. The thing was and forever would be a jinx. "The cop from Lake Bluff didn't give me any information, Dad. Maybe you and Gus can head over to the police department. I'm not leaving Claire's sight."

George came to the side of the bed and kissed Claire's forehead. "It's been a right good time with you today, young lady. Next time, let's skip all the bloody drama. Hey?"

The color flooded into Claire's cheeks. "Thanks for being my dad for the day, George. Oh, and since you're Lucy's pseudo-dad, can you please go check on her?"

George patted her hand.

After his father left, Sinjin sat on the edge of her bed and stared at her hand. It fit comfortably within his own. His guilt stifled every one of his thoughts and feelings. He rallied the courage to come clean. "Whatever happened with those paintings, I don't care. And I'm sorry for calling you such abominable things."

"You should be," she said straight up and to the sharpest of points. "You didn't give me one freaking chance to speak." She sat up in the bed, moved her leg, and winced. "Forcing me into a state of fight or flight." She tried to loosen the blanket trapped under her hip. With a sigh of exasperation, she gave up and fell back onto the pillows.

"I've been a wreck. Really. Feeling terrible," he blathered. "You have no idea how many spoons I welded."

"Spoons?"

"It's a coping mechanism."

"I have *Golden*. It's in Milwaukee. Anita insisted I keep it since it's my favorite season of the year, fall."

"Good to know...I mean about the season. And the painting."

Her lips curved slightly. Perhaps a smile? Too soon to think anything. Good or bad.

"Anyway," he said, clearing his throat. "*Midnight* and *Fever*. Both paintings should be displayed in the show. Your name, as the artist, should go on the description plate. Only if you want."

"I have a lot to tell you, but *Sugar* is with Larry...it's horrible." She released a discouraged sigh, dropped her head back, and closed her eyes. "I really don't want him to have it."

"I understand, but they're merely paintings. Paint on a canvas and boxed in with a frame. Two dimensions. Flat and lifeless. I shouldn't have been—"

"A judgmental asshole?"

"Correct. And a fucking wanker." He put his hand to his heart. "But I'm also learning, at least trying to be a better listener."

"I don't think that's in your male DNA." She yawned loudly. "I'm glad you're here."

They remained silent, and she dozed off. He listened to her quiet breathing and the occasional beeps from the monitor attached to her chest. He laid his head on the bed but stayed alert in case anything bothered her.

"I was cruel," she whispered without opening her eyes. "And heartless. To throw the tragedy of your ex in your face."

He stared at her leg, realizing his pain was nothing compared to hers. "It's on me. Sometimes, I'm caught off guard, and my past bites me in the arse."

"You're wrong, you know."

"A common occurrence lately," he said.

"I disagree with what you said about the paintings. Sure, they're just paint and just canvases, but they are also story-telling and history. Your sculpture and my paintings…they speak volumes when words fail us." The violet color of her eyes intensified, and she reached out to pull him into a hug. "I want a hit of your citrusy aftershave. It might help my concussion."

Burying his face into her neck, he kissed her, feeling a new sense of trust.

Chapter 33

Claire lifted her knee for the nurse to change the bandages. When Sinjin moved away from the bed to allow the caregiver access, she wanted to scream, *No!* Thank goodness her reactions were slow with all the anesthetics inside her.

"How do you feel?" The nurse checked her blood pressure. "How's the head?"

"The Tylenol is working. Only a dull throb." She moved her leg a smidge, and it smarted. "But the stitches feel tight, and they're pinching."

"Use the cream I'm sending home with you and try not to go up or down stairs. I put in an order for crutches in case you need them. Not that you'll be moving around a lot the next twenty-four hours."

"Change of plans," Claire said to Sinjin. "If your offer of the cottage is still good, I might take you up on it, babe."

"Absolutely." He hopped out of the chair. "Only three or four steps to go up the front porch. Much easier than Lucy's apartment. I can be your *crutch.*"

It seemed as if the rest of the day passed with Claire gazing at the gray ceiling tiles, turning to see Sinjin, and then snoozing. It repeated: tiles, Sinjin, snooze.

The hospital let her out to face the real world again in the early evening. She went out the pneumatic doors with Sinjin holding her on her stitched-up side and her new crutch on the other. It was more challenging than when she'd come in on the stretcher but much more fun.

She couldn't help it and kept bumping into him. Each time she hopped and stepped to get to his truck, a case of embarrassing girlish giggles took hold of her.

He was a good-natured sport with her from the time she sat in the truck until she sat on the end of his flowery bed. He left her alone to change from her clothes into one of his T-shirts. Inhaling the fabric, she groaned. Sinjin's scent intoxicated her. Or was she just horny as hell? Too sore to decide, she slipped on the T-shirt and carefully dropped into bed. Her leg ached, and she was exhausted. But too exhausted?

Sinjin came back into the bedroom, and she curled her finger in what she hoped was a sexy way to make him come into bed and lie down with her. Then she moved her leg and yelped. So much for seductions.

"No sex, babe. You need to get some sleep," he said, covering her with a layer of blankets. "Later. I promise. Besides, with all the drugs you've ingested, you won't remember a thing. I can't have that. Not good for my ego."

"I'm much more horny than tired. I'm fine with you taking advantage of me."

"How about we lie side by side in bed. I'll take the top of the covers, and you take the bottom."

"Really? I suppose you're going to suggest we watch something erotic to torture me more?"

"*Leverage?*" He gave her a cute smile.

She carefully dropped her head back on the pillow. Behind

her eyes, there was an annoying throb, so she shut them. "I shouldn't watch TV. Movies. Play video games."

"You play video games?" he asked. "Which ones?"

"Once. Pac-Man. Maybe. My dad hated those games. Said they would turn my brain to mush. Little did he know it was another *artiste* who would do that."

"I hope you mean me, not Julie."

"I meant Julie. She's the one who knocked me down," she murmured, laying her head against his chest. He cradled his arm around her and gathered her close to him. She felt safe.

"*You* are making me and my *heart* all mushy." She jabbed a finger under his tee and into the valley of one of his finely formed abs. "You're bewitching me."

He laughed, nodding at several of Lucy's *Love* candles burning on the dresser. "I seriously think that Lucy's candles are working."

"You might be right." She straightened up to think seriously. At least try. Even if the day's trip to the hospital had rattled her, she needed to get the truth out. "Anita and my father signed a document or had a verbal agreement. I'm not sure. Essentially, none of the *Seasons* were to be sold. To anyone. Ever."

"But Anita's great-niece, Lindsey, didn't know?" he guessed.

She nodded against the soft fabric of his T-shirt. "In Lindsey's defense, after Anita died, the gallery was about to be permanently shut down. She may have broken a promise, but she saved Anita's legacy."

"True. Why did you do the paintings? It's hard for me to believe that you painted the four of them. Because your father's brushwork is incredibly tiny. His micro strokes are hard to duplicate."

"Wasn't he a true master with his brushes?" She wistfully recalled all the hours they'd spent together. "I never played video games because I was too busy with my father teaching me how to use a brush. You know how some kids practice piano every day? Well, I had painting practice. Gawd. It was awful."

"It worked. You're a brilliant painter."

"Maybe, but I adore curating. I love it more than painting. I don't think I've ever said this out loud. Especially when my dad was around. He desperately hoped I'd be some kind of wunderkind and paint the next *Mona Lisa* by the time I turned eighteen."

"Being a wunderkind is so fucking overrated," he groused. "Take it from an expert."

Her body melted against his. "I painted *Seasons* to make him happy. To show him how everything he taught me had come to fruition. He didn't have much time left on this earth. His vision was slowly being robbed from him each day. If not, minute by minute."

A couple of tears formed. She wiped them away and continued.

"He was so over the moon when we took *Seasons* to the Armory Show, and everyone raved about the paintings. He knew that his legacy would live on. He'd taught me everything, and his genius protégé had painted four perfect portraits of his beautiful wife.

"When that Art Silver, who I refer to as Salieri, noticed how my father couldn't see, he knew it was his one chance to take his lifelong rival down. But it wasn't just about painting. Dad told me that Art Silver had a serious thing for my mom. The three of them were living in New York and hanging with the who's who of the art world. And Dad was concerned about the hospital bills; he wanted to sell them. Also, he wanted to show up Silver. But Anita and I talked him out of it."

Sinjin added in more of the old details that the art world had circulated five years ago. "Silver was a petty and vindictive person. Instead of blatantly accusing a dying man of being a liar, he saw *Seasons* and used the magazine to skewer your father's long-held reputation by questioning his ability, his talent, and his life. And then the rumor mills took over."

"And when the Royal Society removed his portrait of Princess Anne from their gallery in London, it nearly killed him." Her eyes grew heavy with fatigue and sadness. "Get back to me in ten. Do you mind? Damn, what am I going to tell Mina? She will boot me out of the Lafferty as soon as she finds out."

"Oh. Gossip is fast in the art world. I'm sure Mina already knows. And you've been helping with the books at the museum. She has no reason to kick you out."

"The fucking books. I never figured out how Larry got his hands on those numbers." She yawned. It was useless. Sleep kept tugging, and now it yanked at her to get some rest. "Good night, boo."

━━

HIS ARM FELL asleep under the weight of Claire's head. With his free hand, Sinjin set the phone alarm to go off in twenty minutes. He wouldn't move from the spot and was certain he would stay awake all night after downing several ounces of Red Bull.

Learning Claire's story, he sussed how big of a jerk he'd been and decided to make it up to her every day from now until whenever she'd let him.

He texted Mina so when Claire woke up, he could put her fears to rest about the Lafferty.

When will you arrive in Lake Bluff? Assume you know about *Seasons*?

Mina immediately returned his message, confirming what he'd expected. She'd known all about Claire's paintings even before she came to work at the Lafferty. With a couple more texts, they figured out a way to retrieve *Golden* from Claire's apartment. Then Mina would bring it with her on the day of the opening.

Sinjin had devised a twisty way for Mina to get into Claire's apartment: Dress up as a bereaved relative and ask the landlord to unlock Claire's door to retrieve her rosary since she was the pastor at the funeral.

He was disappointed when Mina laughed. "I have an extra key. No need to wear any black. I'll see you at the opening."

His alarm went off. He jogged Claire out of her sleep. She fluttered her eyes open and snorted. She'd done it three times already, so this had to be her normal way of waking. With each time, he was more relieved.

"What time is it?"

"Four a.m."

"Can I go for a whole hour the next time?"

He skimmed the doc's instructions. It cleared longer chunks of sleep after twelve hours. They'd been lying in bed since four yesterday afternoon. She was good as gold. "Yes. Go back to sleep, and dream all you want. You're out of the woods."

"Sweet." She snuggled down under the covers.

"Before the sandman finds you, know that Mina's in your corner. And has always been."

With a smile, she fell back asleep again. He listened until she started to snore, then slowly crept off the bed. It was early, but there was so much to get done. With the opening a few days away, he had to figure out how to get hold of *Sugar*. It might have been more enjoyable to devise a plan with Claire, but maybe surprising her would be a nice way of setting her mind at ease. After all she'd been through with her father, Sinjin knew that no one at this opening would dump on Claire, and he would make sure of it.

He showered, then asked his dad to come to the cottage to

give him an update. Over breakfast, they discussed everything that had happened in the last twenty-four hours. The day had to be one of the longest on record.

The Cadillac was in the shop for minor repairs, and his dad and Gus had moved *Coal or Steam* into Maxwell's, where Charlene was guarding it. And there wasn't a scratch on the sculpture. Apparently, Julie hadn't even had a chance to open the trunk. All in all, things were moving in a good direction.

Until George told him more about Julie.

"She's going to be incarcerated for a few days—"

"How many?" Sinjin asked, more worried about Lucy than Julie.

"I don't know," George said, then added, "Lucy and I have been researching facilities in the area that work with addiction. There are several centers for her to check into."

"Why the time behind bars?" Sinjin asked. "Can't Lucy bail her out?"

"Lucy doesn't want to. She feels terrible. Her mother attacking her best friend? And as the victim, it will be Claire's decision whether or not to press charges."

A pit sunk to the bottom of his horribly empty stomach. "Claire is terrified of Julie."

"The Lake Bluff PD isn't rushing to process Julie. She's an unusual case since she grew up in this tight-knit community. They're treating her with kid gloves.

"Lucy will work it out, I'm sure. She's miserable because of Claire's injuries and has no sympathy for her mother." His father sounded defeated. "I'm glad to be here for Lucy."

Sinjin relaxed. If anyone could be counted on to do the right thing, it would be Claire. With him, his dad, Lucy, and even Gus surrounding her, there would be plenty of hope for Julie.

Chapter 34

Her unwanted cane made it difficult to pace in front of the bench at the police department. She'd sat for ten minutes while waiting for Charlene to finish talking to Julie in an office behind the dais where uniformed officers worked.

It hadn't been how she'd envisioned *Vectors'* opening day. With a show dedicated to the affirmative force and energy of women, this moment couldn't be any less optimistic. Claire was about to send her best friend's mother to jail.

"How long do you think she'll be incarcerated for?" she asked Sinjin. "Julie really needs to get help. Mental health challenges are usually at the core of addictions."

Sinjin stopped pacing.

She tapped her cane, glad she'd ditched the crutch. Although she was able to walk fine, her stitched leg ached if she stood for too long. Claire wanted to save all her strength for the opening. Starting this afternoon, she would be on her feet for hours. "Well?"

"I'm not sure," he said, sitting beside her. "Are you sure you want to talk to Julie? I mean, according to Charlene, you really don't have to say a word to her. Only need to sign a form and make a statement to the cops."

"Don't freak out. I'm not scared. More anxious. I want to help Lucy as much as possible since she's refusing to talk to her mother. And then move forward for my sake and Julie's."

Sinjin had insisted that she'd been terrified on the day of Julie's attack. So frightened that she had him promise to keep Julie away from her. Claire didn't remember her fear at all because of the concussion. Now she felt only sadness. What a terrible tragedy for two wonderful people. "I'm going to tell Julie that she needs to get help. To talk to a therapist or whatever counseling is available to her. And this is the only way to do it. Period. Nothing more."

The office door opened, and Charlene waved her in. Sinjin gave her a quick hug. "Good luck."

She handed him her cane, strode into the office, and sat at the table across from Julie. She seemed despondent, but her eyes were white instead of yellow. Being behind bars probably made it hard to drink. Probably why Claire didn't detect any noxious odors either. She focused on signing the forms Charlene placed in front of her and set down the pen when finished.

Julie, staring off as though in another realm, suddenly eyeballed her. "Where's Lucy?"

"I'm here for your daughter. She needs time to process what's happened. I've decided to file a complaint against you. To help you get treatment. I hope this is one of those moments when you discover a new resolve and you're able to change."

Julie's face seemed to shrivel. Her lips were dry, and crust nestled in both corners. Her tongue ferociously licked and flicked around her mouth. "I knew the moment Sinjin told me about you showing up from Milwaukee I'd lose him. I didn't think I'd lose Lucy though. My own daughter." She shook her head, distraught. "After everything I've done for her."

Claire spoke slowly to control her anger. "You're in

complete denial, Julie. All you've *done*—" She stood, lifted her skirt, and exposed the bruised, reddened flesh around the bandaged, aching gash on her thigh. "All you've done is cause pain. Oh, this baby will get better, and there will be a little scar. But you've hurt people, especially Lucy, much worse than this. I'm not sure if her heart will ever heal. I hope you realize all the hurt and pain that you've caused your own daughter."

Lowering the layers of lace on her skirt, she thanked Charlene and left the stifling room. She exited the police station with Sinjin at her side and her cane in hand.

"Are you all good?" he asked.

"One hundred percent," she said, taking hold of his hand and squeezing.

They walked the five-block distance to Maxwell's, discussing their half-baked, no, quarter-baked, plan to obtain *Sugar*.

Lucy handed Claire her clipboard as soon as they walked into the shop. "How did it go?"

"Fine," she said. "I didn't let her say too much. When she asked about you, I told her that I was your proxy and it was time for her to grow up. Not those words exactly, but we'll get her through this."

Sinjin stepped over to where three of the four *Seasons* portraits had been hung.

"Are you sure you don't hate me?" Lucy twisted the tie on her apron. "Hell, if this had happened to me, I'm not sure I'd be so nice about it."

"No way. Not sure if it's good or bad in the world of mothering, but tough love comes easily for me."

"Tonight's going to be huge. Congratulations. I'm mixing up another batch of my Tesla Tea," she said, then returned to Lulu's.

The security guard came up and explained how *Liza*'s cameras would transmit the video to his device, and he would report to her and Sinjin every hour during the opening. He checked his low-tech watch. "In one hour, *Vectors* will commence."

Claire shuddered. Finally, this day had arrived. She gave the guard a thumbs-up, then perused the onetime shop that now housed an art exhibit.

She'd created most of the lighting effects by twisting cords around the ceiling beams and letting the attached Edison bulbs dangle from above. There were no dark spots anywhere. Each painting was spotlit by a lamp made of pipes fitted with retro bulbs and placed nearby.

"Are you sure we should leave an empty space for *Sugar?*" Sinjin asked. "I mean, this scheme we cooked up is pretty flimsy. Banking on Larry's assistant to kidnap it?"

"True. I may have been a little out of it when I called her, but Donna will follow through. Especially since we both hate Larry. A lot."

While Claire was recovering in the cottage, she'd grown antsy. She kept thinking about the Lafferty's books and *Sugar* between her bouts of rest. She'd decided to call the only person Larry hadn't crushed yet. His assistant didn't have any specifics about Larry's secret bookkeeping, but she did confess her hatred of the director. Claire was disappointed until Donna launched into all of her complaints about her boss and the demeaning chores she'd done for him. When Donna mentioned delivering the jerk's dry cleaning, Claire's ears perked up. She suspected *Sugar* was in his house on Wahl Street. Donna confirmed that when she delivered the shirts the next day.

"I suppose…" Sinjin pulled out his pocket watch chained to a belt loop and popped it open. "We'll find out in an hour if Donna nicked the painting without getting caught. I *prophesize.* Like it? Such a steampunk word. Hey?"

"We'll need to cross all our fingers and toes," Claire said, feeling inspired by Donna's courage. "How does *Golden* look next to the other two *Seasons*?"

"Fabulous, doll."

"I missed Mina earlier. I can't wait to see how she looks. She's dressing up like Inara Serra."

"Wow."

"Clearly, you were a fan of Inara? Or *Firefly*?"

"Uh-huh." He scratched his jaw. "My bros and I, the three of us really enjoyed *Firefly*. Really. Inara was okay."

Claire punched his arm. "*Okay*, my ass. She was the hottest character in the show. And Bianca, Mina's partner, will be dressed up like Malcolm."

George and Gus came into the gallery.

Gus held Fred and Ginger in each arm, showing off the miniature bowler hats strapped onto each dog's head. Both cuties seemed less than thrilled to be dressed up and out of their crates. "Like them?"

"Make sure to keep their leashes on," Sinjin said, leading Gus and the dogs to the juice bar.

George pulled Claire aside. "How did everything go this morning?"

"It's done. I guess I learned some motherly instincts from Anita, a true New Yorker, and they kicked in. Julie needs to get her shit together."

"That's the truth." George played with his monocle. "And Lucy can't be the one to do it. Many thanks to you." He glanced around the exhibit, holding his monocle. "Spectacular."

Before the guests arrived, Claire double-checked the displays. The antique typewriter at the entrance had been oiled and inked, ready for folks to type in their names. She'd decided to place the Victrola near *More Lace Please* and then added Sinjin's turntable with a Stevie Nicks album on it. She used rolls of lace to separate the vignette from the other displays.

Her dad's painting gleamed in the light. She could make out every one of his tiny brushstrokes. It still amazed her that he'd painted it when he was nearly blind.

Charlene, carrying a baton and wearing a British bobby's hat, played with the strap under her chin. "This may not stay on all night. Anyway, I completed my first survey around the outside of the building. It's all secure."

"Thanks. And thanks for your kindness this morning. With Julie."

"No problem. I'm thinkin' this will knock some sense into her. The whole squad's been concerned about her for a while."

With a quick check of the three *Seasons*, she returned to Sinjin, who was fiddling with one of the armatures on *Coal or Steam*. The star of the exhibit took center stage and deserved a standing ovation. It gleamed under the lights and shone brighter than bright. Should she be wearing sunglasses? Every crevasse and curve of the brass, copper, and gold glimmered.

Sinjin pulled out a buffing cloth from the back pocket of his work pants and rubbed each of the gold toilet handles in the center of the sculpture.

"Double flushing?" She joked. "Isn't that bad for the environment?"

"Very funny." He concentrated on shining his masterpiece so hard she had a full minute to admire how his tattoo rippled and bulged on his arm. Wearing a black tank with leather suspenders, both arms were bare and…

She licked her lips and watched, mesmerized by every movement Sinjin made. When he snapped the cloth, she nearly jumped out of the many layers of lace in her skirt. "Damn."

"Shouldn't you be greeting guests instead of fixating on me?"

"Is that a serious question? Because the truth is—"

The door banged open behind her, and Donna came rushing up to them. "Dang, I couldn't do it."

"Slow down." Claire hooked her arm with Donna's and admired her costume. A pirate shirt paired with a Victorian bustled skirt. "It's okay. We know you were going out on a limb for us."

"It's good. We'll get *Sugar* eventually," Sinjin said.

Lucy came up to them, holding a tray. "Have a drink. It's Spirited Cider. It might relax you. All of you have a shot."

They all grabbed a shot glass, and Donna started to explain what happened with *Sugar*, but Lucy's gasp cut her off.

"The candles." She looked at the chandelier. "I forgot to put them into the holders." Lucy jogged back into the juice bar and returned with a box and a step stool. She untied the rope anchored on a wood beam and lowered the chandelier.

"Is she the Phantom?" Donna said with her mouth hanging open.

Claire and Sinjin laughed, and Lucy inserted swirled red sticks into each candle holder. After she pulled the chandelier back into its original position, she used a small remote to click on the LED lights inserted into the faux flames on top of each candle.

They *Aaaahhhhhhed* together, held their shot glasses up to the chandelier, cheered, and downed the spirits. The sweet cider infused with whiskey tickled Claire's throat. "Damn, that's delicious."

"I'll get another round." Lucy skipped joyfully back into Lulu's.

"Before I get bombed," Donna said, "let me tell you what went down with the beast. I delivered his dry cleaning this morning. He was wearing a pair of silk pajamas when he opened the door, and get this—" She held up a finger. "—a brocade lounging robe. He claimed he was sick—'deathly ill'—grabbed the hangers out of my hand, and slammed the door in my face."

"Fuck." Sinjin groaned. "Larry will be a no-show tonight."

"On the bright side," Claire said to Sinjin. "We can relax and enjoy the rest of the night. Not be watching over our shoulders and stressing about Larry."

Donna shook her head. "Sorry about *Sugar*, guys. Is it all right if I head back to the bar? I need a few more of these." She held up the empty shot glass.

They stood alone for a second, and she could feel the wheels in Sinjin's mind vibrating. She caressed his arm along the contours of his muscles and the Rube tattoo. "Hey, I bet the beast isn't really sick. Knowing Larry, he's conniving another plan. But tonight's security is top-notch. We'll be able to catch him. However he does it."

"I'm not so sure of that." Sinjin glared at an attractive woman strolling in with a parasol over her head. "Meg Fisher is in the house."

She tipped her bowler to hide her eyes so she could stare at the woman. She was the one talking to a guard that day at the Lafferty. Was Meg here for Larry? Or Sinjin?

Chapter 35

Sinjin questioned if Meg had hidden a weapon of some sort inside the handle or in the flowery lacy folds of the umbrella. *Ridiculous*. Or not? The brolly was John Steed's weapon of choice. Sinjin greeted his ex, who was no Emma Peel, with an outstretched arm, ready to give her a formal handshake. He killed the impulse to clutch and shake too hard.

"Meg. Surprised to see you. You're a steampunk admirer?"

She shook his hand with her own, clad in a leather driving glove. "It's a fascinating genre. I'm sure there are many things you don't know about me."

Talk about dropping a truth bomb right out of the gate. He crossed his arms over his chest and shivered. He should have added the tweed jacket to his costume, but it itched too much. "Are you here at Larry's request?"

Nothing like matching one truth bomb with another.

"I haven't seen Larry at all the past year." She turned to type her name onto the guest list.

Her first lie, and Sinjin was pleased that he showed zero reaction. She'd been at the Lafferty the day they'd moved the exhibit. Her red BMW was parked in the garage. Even Claire had seen her.

"What have you been up to lately?" he managed to ask casually. "I hope you aren't here for Fred and Ginger."

"Never occurred to me to take back those two mangy mutts. Worst barkers ever. I should've had their vocal cords cut."

Sinjin reeled in horror. Meg wasn't exactly likable, but he didn't think she was cruel. Until now. "Well, stay out of Lulu's, please."

"I'm sure I'll be able to cover this exhibit in less than a half hour. I'm here to do a review for *Art & Form*. I've been free-lancing since business is slow in the gallery. I should have moved to New York instead of Chicago. Big mistake on my part. The Midwest doesn't understand high art or culture unless it's in their yogurt."

Sinjin pressed his hands, now fists, against his legs. Meg wasn't the brightest bulb in the box, but he'd seen goodness in her when they'd met at her gallery. It may have evaporated, but most likely, it had all been an act.

Furiously and swiftly, a sense of relief swept through him. Thank god she'd slept with Larry and revealed their deceit. Thank Buddha there was no baby. Thank Krishna he hadn't collapsed and disappeared into a pit of despair. And thank the blue sky all around him that Claire had come knocking on his front door.

He took Meg's hand and led her to *Coal or Steam*. "Why don't you start with the least important piece in this exhibit. Mine." He pointed at the three *Seasons*. "Those are the spectacular elements of this show, as well as the Raffen."

She pushed his hand away. "I can find my way around a gallery perfectly well all by myself. There's no need for you to escort me. Besides, I'm sure your bias will show because of

Claire Beaumont and her work." She directed her gaze toward *Seasons*.

Confident that any insinuations about the *Seasons* paintings would be put to rest with this exhibit, he ignored Meg's slander. She was here on a reconnaissance mission for Larry, and without a doubt, as soon as Meg exited Maxwell's, she would be talking to the wanker.

"All right, understandable. I do have my favorites. But let me show you one piece I think would be of interest to your readers. It's called *Afternoon Delight* by a Chicago artist. Her name is—" He scanned the nameplate beside the flat TV, where the artist's collage played across the screen. "Zoe Kittleson."

"Oh, yes. She exhibited in New York. At L. Finegold."

How spot-on he'd been about his ex. The woman had visited the gallery where *Sugar* was and probably bought it at Larry's request.

They watched the screen as images of sections of Georges Seurat's masterpiece, *A Sunday Afternoon on the Island of La Grande Jatte*, receded and diminished, and then new portions advanced and slid off the screen. It was a remarkable perspective, how new-tech videography could combine with a classic painting and deepen the impressionistic view. Even Meg appeared to be fascinated by the piece.

"Enjoy the show." Sinjin strolled over to Charlene. "Watch her like a hawk. She's here instead of Larry. Tell me when she leaves."

"Sure thing." Charlene immediately texted the other security guard.

The air in Maxwell's heated up as the gallery became crowded. He talked to Claire, and they decided to have George watch the door and allow each guest twenty minutes to view the exhibit.

"How did it go with your ex?" Claire asked.

"She's a mole. Said she's writing a review for *Art & Form*."

"That's interesting. I think I'm canceling my subscription."

"Do it," he said.

With George taking care of crowd control, the gallery cooled down. Sinjin chatted with his mates, Craig and Ryan. Both, as he'd expected, were eager to buy *Liza*. When Mina and her partner arrived, they looked as if they'd walked off the set of *Firefly*. Their costumes were exact matches to the characters Inara Serra and Malcolm Reynolds.

Polly tapped his shoulder blade, and he jerked away from Claire. He'd been whispering nothing into her ear, wanting to kiss her surreptitiously.

"Is Larry here?" Polly asked, leaning hard on the cane he had welded for her.

"He's a no-show," he said. "I'm sorry."

"Don't be. I've been busy spying with Mina exactly as you had asked of me. Remember?"

Claire stared at the left side of his face as it turned red and hot.

"I...it's been a month. I guess I forgot," he muttered as if he'd been busted by a principal. "I hope I didn't send you on a wild goose chase."

Polly shook her head, glanced at the crowd, and stopped, then waved Mina over. A burst of raucous laughter interrupted the piped-in Steely Dan melodies. After, the three women exchanged quick hellos.

"I am, with Mina's approval, acquiring the Lafferty." Polly didn't bother burying the lede. "As soon as the deal is signed, I'm firing Larry."

Claire jumped up, hugged Mina, and twirled her around. Stunned, Sinjin took Polly's hand and tried his best to bow, or curtsy, or whatever dance step they did in the steampunk era. He looked foolish but ignored it. This was a moment of joy.

"Thank you. Again, you give back, and the art world is better and more brilliant."

"What about all of Larry's fraud?" Claire asked. "He's tricky. I never figured out how he skimmed off the Lafferty's financials."

"When I say I'm going to spy, I spy. I used my O'Keeffe painting as bait. I told him I was an old man on his deathbed." Polly side-eyed Mina. "With a nudge from Mina, he fell for it. When he paid me what I asked for instead of the insurance value, I knew I had him. Since he'd been acquiring valuable paintings from those poor souls who had already passed away, no one bothered to note the difference between the prices."

Clearly disgusted, Polly tsked. "Larry resold pieces to other museums and patrons, skimming the difference and stuffing it in his pockets. He'd been doing this for quite a while, using museums as a front for insurance fraud. I contacted his previous employer, and they had let him go for questionable transactions."

Mina shook her head, defeated. "I should have double-checked Larry's credentials instead of allowing the board to hire him. Thanks for giving me a second chance."

"It's a new day," Polly said. "Let's celebrate. But..." She pointed her cane at Sinjin. "Larry's in a lot of hot water. He still thinks he can get *Coal or Steam* and sell it on the black market."

"Security is tight tonight," he said, "with everyone. Especially Meg."

"Good." Polly vigorously tapped her cane on the floor. One time.

The dogs charged into the gallery, weaving about all the ankles around them. They madly barked when they came upon Meg taking photos of his sculpture. She was about to kick Fred and Ginger away when Gus scooped them up to safety.

Sorry, bro," Gus said, "FYI, Rob and Fran are here. They

came in through the back on the down low. Fran is famous. So jealous." Gus went back to Lucy. His brother had spent all night in the juice bar.

Sinjin faced Meg. "I think you've been inside more than twenty minutes. And there's no photo-taking allowed in the gallery. Time to go."

"Okay, okay. Don't get your knickers in a twist," she said, stuffing her phone in her purse. "I still have to review *Seasons*."

"Too late," Sinjin said, escorting Meg to his father, who hooked his elbow around hers and tugged her out of Maxwell's. Sinjin sighed once Meg was out of his sight. The toxic cloud that had been following him around for ages had finally evaporated.

He was about to find his brother Rob when Claire yelled, "Woot!"

The famous art critic from New York had arrived. Jerry Saltz.

Chapter 36

Her heart was beating so loud the crowd noise diminished as Claire approached Jerry Saltz. She wiped her hand on her skirt and held it out, even though he was crouched down, inspecting *Fever*, and completely unaware that she stood behind him. "Good evening, Mr. Saltz."

He turned and shook her hand vigorously. "Are you Ms. Beaumont? The woman who painted these portraits?"

"Yes. But..." Her Midwestern nasally twang sounded embarrassingly high talking to a New Yorker. She lowered her voice. "Although I painted them, tonight is my curatorial debut. I'm thrilled that you took the time to see the incredible show. I have no problem bragging because of the talent in this room tonight. Thank you."

"You're a talented painter in your own right." He pointed to the copper ceiling plaque placed next to the painting. She'd used it to mount the piece descriptions. "Says here that *Sugar* is on loan? Who has it? Anita was a good friend of mine. She nor her niece would have sold or given these paintings to just anyone."

"I think Lindsey was in a dire situation when she sold

Sugar," she said, vaguely aware that she was opening up to a man she'd known for less than ten seconds. "I mean, I don't want to sound gossipy."

He guffawed, then looked her in the eye. "Gossip is inherent to the business of art, unfortunately. And I'm here not only for this exhibit but to see these paintings. I wrote about *Seasons* in my last book."

Her stomach ached. "I had no idea. But let me explain—"

He gently tapped her elbow. "Don't be alarmed. I never believed any of the claptrap that was floating around about *Seasons.* Anita told me as soon as I first saw them that you had painted them for your father and mother."

She blew out a big sigh.

"And Arthur Silver from *Art & Form* had no business being a critic. Demoting David Raffen to a neophyte smacked of pure jealousy. He had it in for your dad. Shameful. It wasn't long before *A&F* moved past his malarky. That magazine needs to see more authenticity and reclaim some of its integrity."

Getting validation from Mr. Saltz almost stopped her heart. Thankfully, she had a good ticker.

"I've been planning this exhibit for a long-ass time." She stepped over to Stevie. "Do you see what we figured out about *More Lace Please*?"

"It's a dead ringer for Stevie Nicks and one of his best."

They continued chatting while the party swirled around them. A conversation all about David Raffen. And as she'd suspected, *MLP* had been painted right before her dad had died.

"His brushstrokes," Mr. Saltz said, "were easy after sixty-plus years, and he only had to paint with shades of black with white. It really wasn't such a stretch for David to create this piece so eloquently. I'm sure her music inspired him, and her beauty was clear as crystal in his mind."

Mr. Saltz had been a lifelong friend to her father. Claire

spoke to him as if speaking with her dad—about how life and art were interchangeable.

He scrutinized her painting *Fever*. "Any Raffen fan could have seen from a mile away that your father did not paint this. The mole is way off."

She laughed. "Right? It's been a pain in my butt forever. After my painstaking lessons with Dad, the mole was the only feature of my mother that I couldn't master. I think he ended up doing it himself on the other three."

He inspected *Golden* and *Midnight*. "You're right. In these two paintings, the mole is perfect. If anyone wants to call these paintings forgeries, they're full of it. With these moles, it proves that Raffen had his hand in the creation and had the right to sign them. Even with *Fever*. All of *Seasons* are your work but created with David Raffen's inspiration."

"Sweet," she said as pent-up fretfulness whooshed and disappeared. "*Sugar*. I tried to get it out of Larry's hands for tonight, but it didn't work."

"I'm fairly certain that Lindsey knows who Larry Chambers is and wouldn't have sold it to him. Is there anyone else who would have been to Anita's gallery?"

"Meg Fisher," she said, checking around to see if Meg and her wretched umbrella were still in Maxwell's. "Sinjin Reid's ex-wife. Larry and Meg are like Boris and Natasha. That's why we have extra security here."

"Excuse me," Sinjin said, "I don't want to interrupt you two. But I couldn't help overhearing. Meg bought it. Or stole it? I don't know what she did for Larry. But she told me she'd been in Lindsey's gallery."

Claire yanked her attention away from the men to look at the supermodel Fran Marcheti standing next to Sinjin. Claire couldn't look away from Fran. It took a lot of courage to go from a swimsuit model to a breast cancer survivor and back again.

"This is my brother Rob and his friend Fran," Sinjin said, introducing Claire and Jerry Saltz.

"Hello," she squeaked, shaking their hands and letting it rest a second too long with Fran. Sinjin's brother Rob was his opposite. Wearing khakis and a button-down shirt, the youngest of the three brothers might have been the one who had accumulated all the *serious* genes in the Reid family.

Claire spoke briefly to the two before they strolled over to Sinjin's sculpture.

"So, you're a Raffen fan?" Mr. Saltz said to Sinjin. "Tell me, which one of the four *Seasons* have you had in your collection?"

Sinjin proudly pointed to *Fever*.

Claire and Mr. Saltz exchanged a giggle. She bonded with the critic in a meta-like fashion since both knew such intimate details about her father's works.

"Can't be a superfan if you didn't see the mole," Mr. Saltz said, patting Sinjin's back. "But I'll be generous and call you a Raffen admirer."

Sinjin's cheeks turned red. "Thanks, Mr. Saltz."

She and Sinjin seized a quiet moment later that night as the opening was winding down. For two hours, there had been a line outside of Maxwell's. George had to shorten viewing times to ten minutes to manage everyone who wanted to see *Vectors*.

Around midnight, Claire and Sinjin stole away into the restroom.

"How are you feeling?" Sinjin said, then kissed her.

She answered him with her kiss, a desperately wanton smooch that she wanted to last as long as possible. Even if they were standing next to a toilet. "Incredibly hot."

"We can get some fresh air if you want," he murmured.

"Not that kind." She nipped his earlobe. "Tonight's been perfect."

"We'll have to get back out there shortly," he whispered, "or I won't be presentable. Even these work pants and tool belt won't disguise a raging hard-on."

"Let's get out there and do goodbyes. It's time to shut down this exhibit for the night. Then we can go upstairs and do a little role-playing? I'll be your Inara to your Malcolm?"

"Let's do it," he said, taking her hand and leading her back to the show.

She was relieved to see that fewer than ten people were left in the exhibit, and they were mostly family. As much as she wanted to get upstairs to remove the layers of itchy lace that made her skirt and strip off Sinjin's pants, she resigned herself to finishing the night with a congratulatory drink. Claire would never have been able to pull this night off without all the help of those around her. Even Mr. Saltz had stayed to the bitter end.

Sinjin left her side to lock the front door, then turned off the music. Lucy and Gus brought out a bottle of champagne and a tray of glasses.

As Lucy poured and passed out glasses, Claire's excitement and exhaustion rolled over her. She leaned against Sinjin to keep upright.

George held Fred and Ginger. The two dachshunds were as quiet as a couple of mice for the first time. Holding Fran's hand, Rob stared at his brother Gus with an evil eye, making Claire curious. Mina and Bianca sandwiched Polly. The three women reminded Claire of *The Three Graces*, and she felt their beauty, mirth, and abundance. Jerry, no longer Mr. Saltz, held up his glass. "Here's to those around us but no longer with us. David, Anita, and Claire's mother, Monique."

"Here, here," Sinjin said, "And to Claire Beaumont, a true believer in second chances."

She guzzled the champagne to cool down and calm her nerves. "This is good bubbly. Wow. Um. Being here, with you all. I can't say how honored I am to have you believe in me. Thank you. And to every artist or woman who's had to brave the naysayers and climb over the disbelievers, then come out the other side. Maybe broke, but with a monumental sense of direction and refusing to turn back."

The end-of-the-night celebrations lasted until the morning, with a lot of bad voices singing along to Fleetwood Mac songs. Claire and Sinjin fell into bed, barely able to talk. They were both so exhausted. Inara and Malcolm would have to make out another time.

Chapter 37

It had been a long-ass time since Sinjin had woken up to the bickering of his brothers. For a moment of sleepy-filled confusion, memories flooded him of their house in Door County, where the three of them had spent their teen years with Mum.

He rolled over and kissed Claire's bare shoulder. Sprawled face-first on the bed, she murmured something into the pillow. Seeing the goose bumps on her arms, he covered her up with a quilt. Before leaving the bedroom to see what was going on in the living room of Lucy's apartment, which had been ground zero for both his younger brothers, he quietly rustled through his backpack for comfortable clothes. No way in hell would he put those steampunk pants on again.

Wearing a tee and jogging shorts, he stepped out of the bedroom and gently shut the door. Lucy and Fran huddled in the kitchen with Mr. Coffee while his two brothers squared off at the counter. Gus and Rob glowered at each other with straight-lined lips shut tight.

"Morning, blokes." He put a brotherly hand on each of their backs. "I see we're at it again." Then added, "Is this how we want our lovely host Lucy and good friend Fran to see us?"

The two women turned their back on Mr. Coffee and smiled at him. He'd arrived in time to break up the latest squabble between his brothers. There had been so many of them when they were younger; Sinjin was relieved to be out of the house and on his own right after high school. He was four years older than Gus, and there were only sixteen months between Gus and Rob. The house in Door County had a constant stream of repairmen coming in to fix drywall holes (from wrestling) or clogged plumbing from grooming during the long-hair stage.

This morning, however, Sinjin knew that the two men were glowering at one another over a tried-and-true divider, a girl. Sinjin stretched his arm out between them and graciously accepted a cup of coffee from Lucy. He took a sip, not too hot, and deliberated on dumping it in his brother's lap, but he didn't know which one and did not want to be rude toward Lucy. She'd been an accommodating host and downright generous.

Instead, Sinjin held the mug of coffee over Gus's head. When all four pairs of eyes landed on him, he said, "The next man who says the name Maddie will get a latte hair washing."

His brothers sneered at him. "You can't be serious," Rob said, then Gus mimicked, "You can't be serious. Such a teacher's pet."

"At least I'm not a Fucking Hollywood Wanker," Rob said. "FHW."

Sinjin moved his arm over Rob's head. "Name-calling? Aren't you a little old for that? Or did they teach you that in law school?"

The women chuckled.

"You two," Sinjin said, moving the mug of not-so-hot coffee between the two men. "It's been years, and the girl in question has moved on. I suggest you both do the same." He lifted his eyebrow at Lucy and Fran standing on the other side of the island. A feeling flashed through him that Lucy and Gus would somehow meet up again, not sure where or when, but with Lucy's candles and Gus's fumes, he suspected something would explode. With Rob, he couldn't guess. Sinjin's intuitiveness wasn't that good with the baby of the family.

Gus took hold of the mug, set it down, and shook Rob's hand. "All's good."

"I suppose," Rob mumbled.

Sinjin wanted to go back to bed with Claire but remembered. "Has anyone checked on the dogs this morning?" He glanced at the clock. "I mean afternoon."

Lucy shook her head. "No. They haven't made a peep. I figured they were just as exhausted as we were after yesterday. Sleeping it off in their beds, not their crates. They were so good with all the goings-on and crowds of people. I can check on them if you want. It's time to face the cleanup anyway."

"Oh no, Lucy. You're not in charge of taking on the day-after-the-party chores. It's your day off, and with the shop and Lulu's closed, Claire and I can take care of it. I'm sure once Claire gets up, she will want to review the exhibit before it opens tonight."

"Are there more people coming again?" Lucy asked. "I mean, there were a ton of people here already."

"Several of the no-shows, I think." Sinjin shook off his disappointment. Claire's effort was a nice idea, and he wouldn't burst her bubble, but it was done. Opening the show for another few hours would not entice Larry. He glanced at the cup of coffee and considered the situation between his two brothers and *the girl*. He, like those two, needed to move on. Get over it. Hell, with Claire, he'd made good choices, and it was fucking time to give that blowhard Larry a swift kick out of his head.

"I'll go downstairs and check on Fred and Ginger," Lucy said.

Gus added, "I'll go with."

"We're going to head over to see Dad at your place and then back to Chicago," Rob said.

Fran came up and gave him a hug. "Tell Claire her show is spectacular."

"Will do," Sinjin said, excited to crawl back under the covers with Claire.

Once inside the darkened bedroom and relieved to have successfully put the latest family drama to rest, he slipped under the sheet and caressed Claire's back. It was smooth as silver but so much warmer.

She turned around, and her eyes fluttered open like they were violet flower petals. He felt protected and whole again. He wanted this moment to be on repeat every day.

"Hey," she growled. "You owe me a scene from *Firefly*."

"I'm sure you're not into redressing with the lace skirts and velvet corset." He caressed her bare bum. "And I'm not going near those wool pants ever again."

"Ugh. Good point." She turned and propped her head on her elbow. "Everything okay out there?"

"Yep." He smoothed a wayward strand of hair off her face and placed it back with the other messy bits. "Everyday brotherly bickering. Not sure how my mum put up with it, but she did, somehow." *Booze.* He skipped saying it.

Claire's hand glided over his stomach and slid under his shorts. He swallowed hard and groaned. "Nice."

"There's really no need to open the exhibit tonight," he said before losing any last vestiges of reason as her hand brushed over his cock. "It's a…"

He forgot what he was about to say and let his eyelids drop and close.

"This is where we are now," she whispered, lightly taking hold of his dick and stroking.

She straddled his thighs while continuing to caress him.

When he attempted to hold her waist or massage her ass, she shushed him. "I'm in the driver's seat, babe."

As her strokes sped up, he lifted his hips and arched his back. His head dug a deep groove into the pillow behind him. He grew harder with every one of her touches. Some were feathery light, and others were rough and bossy.

He gasped when she flicked her tongue all around his cock. Frantic, he clutched her bum. She rubbed her breasts against his chest, and he glided inside her.

She released a lovely sigh of pleasure.

They rocked in every direction, the bed starting its own sing-along for their ride. He sighed, then whispered, "Your leg? Is it okay?"

She kissed his neck, murmured, "Uh-huh," and nipped his earlobe.

He concentrated on Claire's little coos and gasps, wanting her to come first.

They twisted around one another, and he was on top. At her mischievous grin, he lunged deeper inside her. Where his mind stopped, his body took over. The bed seemed to be singing an opera all around them.

He nuzzled into her neck and kissed it like gasping for air. When she growled, he felt her come around him. Sinjin playfully nibbled her nipples, and she shouted.

"Sinjin!"

He responded with a chaotic series of pushes and pulls until he exploded inside her. He floated down and on top of her. Deliriously satisfied, he kissed Claire.

"The music—it stopped," she whispered.

"Give me five. I'll start it again. Maybe a new song," he said, lying beside her and sliding his fingers between her thighs. He tickled her softest skin.

Claire's legs opened, and he kissed her shoulder.

From the bedside table, his phone rattled with an annoying call.

Like the noisy bed, he ignored it and kissed Claire's breast. He couldn't wait to get to the other one.

The fucking phone rang again.

"You better get it. No one calls twice anymore unless it's important."

He dropped onto the bed. "To be continued."

"Damn right." She sat up and lounged against the headboard. "I'm thirsty, anyway. For water. Or coffee. Good time for a hydration break, bud."

He fixed his eyes on her ass and couldn't breathe as she tugged on a pair of sweats and a tank top. The phone beeped and knocked him back to consciousness. He grabbed the demonic device.

Liza's sending messages. On my way to Maxwell's.

Sinjin blinked to make sure he'd read the message correctly.

Liza who? What? Shite. The lover's fog lifted, and he sussed out it was the security guard talking about the mannequin. He kicked off the sheets tangled around his ankles, tripped out of bed and dressed.

He called out to Claire in the other room. "Is Lucy here?"

"No," Claire said as he jogged into the kitchen. "What's going on?"

"Hell if I know. But we need to get downstairs ASAP."

They grabbed their phones and padded down the stairwell that led to Main Street and paused in the compact foyer.

Claire held his hand. "Where's Lucy?"

"I don't know." He glanced out the entry window. A few cars were on the road, and a family strolled across the street and headed into the candy store.

A blast of fresh fall air hit him in the face as they left the apartment foyer and took the few steps to the front door of Maxwell's. "She said she was going to check on the dogs." He cupped his eyes to get a better look into the darkened store. A pinhead-size red light from *Liza*'s cleavage caught his attention. "Shite."

He yanked on the door handle. It didn't budge. It was locked up tight.

"Here comes Lucy," Claire said, pulling his elbow and nudging him to peer down the street.

Fred and Ginger charged in front of Lucy, who struggled to keep up with the mini dogs as they ran full force in front of her. She gave up and let the leashes go. The two dogs ran up, panting, barking, and then started licking him. Then they did the same to Claire.

Lucy met up with them, patting her chest to catch her breath. "They were so groggy earlier when I went to check on them in Lulu's. I decided to take them for a walk. We went down to Peace Park for some fresh air by the lake."

Sinjin grabbed the dogs' leashes and stood. He furtively glanced around for anything suspicious. "They were groggy? Did they bark when you woke them up?"

Staring down at the dogs, Lucy said, "Not at all. In fact, this is the first time they've made a noise. All they did at the beach was sniff around the slew of gross dead fish. My nose will never recover."

He checked to see if the guard had contacted him again. Nothing. "Do you have a key? I need to get into the exhibit."

Sinjin ignored how Claire was hugging herself and pacing. He had to focus.

"That door's bolted from the inside. We need to go around to the back entrance," Lucy said.

"Come on. Let's go." He picked up the two dogs, started jogging to the end of the block, and then turned toward the alley behind Maxwell's. The women ran alongside without questions, and the dogs didn't make a sound. Sinjin had a suspicion that Meg had gotten to them last night.

Lucy struggled to put the key into the lock at the back door.

All his nerves chaotically zipped through him. *Sensory overload, here I come.*

"Oh damn," Claire called out, staring toward the opposite end of the alley, where a white van was parked. "That's the official Lafferty van."

He squinted to shade the sun from his eyes and read the logo. "No, that doesn't…" He squinted, then looked through the camera focus on his phone. "Son of a bitch. It's a dry-cleaning van."

"What is happening?" Claire asked.

"That's weird." Lucy pushed the door open. "I could have sworn I locked the door on the way out. Maybe I wasn't paying attention. The dogs sort of freaked me out. Worried me."

"You two stay here and wait for the security guard. He's on his way." Sinjin handed the dogs over to Claire, whose face was scrunched. Trying to keep from crying? "What's the matter?"

"It's my fault. Whatever is going on. I shouldn't have gotten Donna and the damn dry cleaning involved."

"Let's not go down a rabbit hole. Besides, Larry and Meg are the Beasts. No one else." He kissed her and quietly went into the back of Maxwell's. Glass bricks placed around the top of the brick walls allowed the afternoon sun into the juice bar and gave him enough light to walk to the front without making a sound. Except for his pounding heart, he couldn't hear a thing. With his deep affinity for a good album on a turntable, he detected the subtle sound of a needle scratching a few record grooves. Then came a low sigh.

He saw the remote control for the chandelier and grabbed it. He waited for another noise or sound to allow him to decipher who was in the exhibit. Had Donna tricked them? He shook his head. This was all Boris and Natasha. Meg's ridiculous parasol hadn't hidden any of the times she'd snapped multiple pictures last night.

Behind him, Claire and Lucy were outside with their faces stuck to the back door's glass, and there wasn't any sign of the security guard.

He clicked the remote, and the chandelier slowly illuminated the darkened gallery. Should he be wearing a Phantom mask? Feet shuffled across the wood floor.

Sinjin strode into the gallery, turned, and faced Larry. He held on to a rope attached to a large red bag. But it was most assuredly stuffed with three paintings instead of toys because Larry was not the Big Guy in Red. "Ho, ho, ho. Is *Sugar* with your dry cleaning?"

At the very least, the man had the common sense to set the bag down gently.

Sinjin had expected that when he made direct contact with Larry, a concise and derogatory speech would come to him. After all, he had been plaguing his thoughts for the past two years. But no speech formed in his mind. Not even a belittling remark. A couple of feet away from him stood a legendary loser and a grifter.

"This isn't what it appears," Larry said. "I'm doing this for Claire Beaumont."

"Larry, you are a gormless twit." Sinjin scanned the gallery for *Coal or Steam*. From what he could tell, it hadn't been fiddled with or moved. It shined brighter than it had last night. "Were you planning on coming back for my sculpture?"

Larry's eyes shifted to the front entrance. Searching for an escape hatch?

"No. I believe that a series of paintings should be kept together." Again, he glanced at the front door. "It's my duty as the Lafferty director to contain the legacy of these pieces by David Raffen."

Sinjin couldn't bear to listen to any more of Larry's high-and-mighty lies. "Well, I *believe* that stealing is against the law. And the police are on their way to show you the *light*." Sinjin went up to *Liza* and pulled the security camera out of her leather vest.

Finally, he was gifted a beautiful reaction from Larry. His mouth dropped open, his eyes bulged, and silently, he mouthed, *What the fuck.*

Larry took a shot at jogging to the front door, and Sinjin was faced with Sophie's choice: save the paintings from crashing to the floor or stop Larry. He picked the paintings and grabbed the bag. The double bolts on the inside of Maxwell's front door worked in Sinjin's favor. Larry wasn't going anywhere. He dropped back against the door and banged his head against the glass.

"I'm going out on a limb here, Larry. Are you expecting Meg to drive around in the van? Hoping she's getting anxious? Or nervous? Coming to check on your whereabouts?"

Seeing Larry squirm, hedge, and nervously scratch his elbows gave Sinjin a sick sense of superiority, but he wouldn't let it go to his head. Or maybe he would, then start over tomorrow. One day of gloating wasn't a lot to ask after how the con artist, with Meg's assistance, had abhorrently treated him, Claire, Mina, and the Lafferty.

There was a commotion behind him.

"Did Meg drug my dogs?" he blurted out before the cavalry arrived.

"Last night." Larry held up his hands, and Charlene came into the room with a gun pointing at the would-be thief.

Sinjin sighed when Claire wrapped her arms around his shoulders. "The other guard is arresting Meg. She was supposed to be their getaway driver."

"And a drug dealer. Meg slipped something to Fred and Ginger to make this all happen. She's worse than Natasha."

"I actually think that's possible, but it's a point we can discuss at another time." Claire took the bag of her portraits from him. The rope seemed to have been soldered onto his hand. "It's okay. They're safe now from Boris and Natasha. But I don't get it. These are painted by me, and I'm not famous like you."

"I disagree. You're a star too. But as for the four *Seasons*, Larry's black-market friends would never know the difference. They would have paid him more for four paintings by *David Raffen*—" He paused. "—than one sculpture by Sinjin Reid."

Chapter 38

Her mother's straw hat in *Sugar* still bothered Claire. She should have used a tinier stroke or a different brush style. The gold brim and blonde hair clashed. She stepped away from the portrait. She would nitpick until the end of time, but Claire had nailed the summer vibe in this *Season*.

The blue shade of the sky as it touched the blue of the pool water in the portrait's background was balanced and calming. Wearing a black-and-white checked cover-up, her mom lounged on a beach chair, reading a magazine. It was propped on her belly since Monique Beaumont was eight months pregnant with Claire.

When Claire had painted *Sugar*, she'd used her dad's old vacation photos. The first photo where she was actually with her mom. Of all the paintings in the series of *Seasons*, it was the one where she felt as if she'd remembered the moment or viscerally experienced the memory. It was a strange but lovely connection to have with her mom.

"The four *Seasons* are in the house. The band's back together." Sinjin nuzzled the back of her neck and wrapped his arms around her waist. "*Sugar*'s my favorite."

"Big words from only a Raffen 'admirer,'" she teased.

He stood beside her and crossed his arms over his chest. "Hey though. I may not have spotted the Beaumont mole, but I caught a real mole this morning. Two. Larry and Meg will not be going near a museum or any fine art, translated as expensive art, for a long, long time."

"And thanks to you, I can keep doing my thing at the Lafferty without having to answer to the beast."

Claire had squealed earlier when Mina relayed the fantastic news.

Polly had organized an emergency board meeting at the Lafferty. She announced she was the new administrator, and Larry Chambers was history. Mina Lafferty's role would be in marketing, and Claire Beaumont was promoted to curatorial director. She was thrilled at the prospect of overseeing all of the exhibits in the museum.

"I'm thinking about a new show. What about—"

"Woah. Enjoy *Vectors*. It will be staying put until the end of November. Then, when we move it back to the Lafferty, you can decide on your next steps, Director Beaumont."

"You're right, you're right. I should be planning the closing event. " She claimed her clipboard from the counter and winked at *Liza*. "She's the woman who saved the day. Or should I say, your camera saved my ass."

Sinjin flipped through a pile of albums. "Stevie Nicks, Nancy Sinatra, or Peggy Lee?"

"My dad's records? How did you get a hold of them?"

"Mina brought them along with *Golden*."

"Let's go with Lee. It's only appropriate we play Ms. Piggy's most famous song. *Fever*."

He turned on the record player, and the sultry voice of Peggy Lee filled the gallery. Claire swept and swayed with a broom before they opened Maxwell's for a couple of hours.

She had no idea how to thank Jerry Saltz. He would be

coming for a private showing with a few other gallery owners and a Royal Society of Portrait Painters director. Not only did the organization want to reinstate her father's portrait of Princess Anne, but they also wanted to apologize to Claire in person for their failure. They admitted their negligence regarding the rumors defiling Raffen's reputation. And the Royal Society of Portrait Painters wanted to purchase *More Lace Please*.

"Do you think Stevie will find a move to London agreeable?" She danced around Sinjin as he polished his sculpture.

He set down his cloth. "By George, yes. Absolutely brilliant. Stevie Nicks could save the king," he gushed in a thick British accent, then added, "Bloody hell. That's *starkers*." He dropped his chin and gave her a serious look. "Truthfully, I think *More Lace Please* deserves to be placed with the other royal portraits. It's about time those chip-chip-cheerios figured it out."

"And you? What have you figured out?" She pointed to *Coal or Steam*. "Where are you going to put her once *Vectors* closes? It's not that we wouldn't love it at the Lafferty, but you're not obligated to follow through with any false promises told by Larry and Meg."

"Not even thinking about those two swindlers." He brushed his fingers over one of the sculpture's brass plates. "I think, though, that there's a lot to learn with this piece. I spent many hours designing and creating it. It will be a perfect example for the artists coming to the retreat next summer."

"Can I book a spot?"

"Maybe. But no special treatment. I can't play favorites."

"Are you sure," she said, caressing his arm and fluttering her lashes. "I can be very persuasive with my googly eyes."

"I'll think about it." He slipped his hand under her minikilt and squeezed her ass.

"Good news," she murmured, then forced herself to stay

focused. "I'm looking forward to meeting Lindsey Finegold. She's another soul sister, like Lucy."

"My dear old dad is always right. Everything works out." He took the broom away from her and held her hands. "I'm cutting in."

"Sorry, Mr. Broom." Laughing, she let Sinjin twirl her around his sculpture, then they stopped and held onto each other. "Is it too early in the day for pillow talk?"

He lifted one eyebrow seductively. "Here. Now?"

She playfully slapped his shoulder and ignored her jitters. "No. Not...I have to admit something. I'm all feely. Full of butterflies, rainbows, and puppies—mini dachshunds—are everywhere when I'm with you. Is it too light outside to whisper sweet nothings in your ear?" She tried to stop but couldn't. "I really like you."

"You like me? What a coincidence! I like...pizza. And I really like...beer. It's fantastic we are both serial *likers*. I have to say that I'm not a big fan of butterflies though. Too much like moths. They can fly into your ear and be irritating and messy."

"You're such a smart apple." Her cheeks burned.

"What? I'm telling you the truth." He combed his fingers through her hair and kissed her ear. Then he whispered, "I like you a lot too. But really, I'm feeling the love, babe. I love you."

With her heart pounding, she wrapped her arms around Sinjin. "I'll always have your back, 'babe.' I love you, too."

As if on cue, Fred and Ginger charged into the gallery, barking like mad and dancing around their feet. They each picked up a dog, found the leashes, and took a walk. When they headed into Peace Park, Claire knew that everything would be all right.

Art & Form
ONE YEAR LATER

A Grand Afternoon by Lake Michigan
By Zoe Kittleson

The opening of Claire Beaumont's exhibit at the Lafferty Museum
surpassed all my expectations. It's aptly titled, *Elements Unleashed*.
The exhibit stars her partner, Sinjin Reid. The well-known sculptor
came out of semi-retirement. After hosting a summer retreat for
budding young artists, he plunged into his work and created four
metal sculptures to honor each season of the year.

Fair warning, this review will not be impartial. My career and artistic
success have been shaped by these two creatives, Sinjin and Claire.
They were instrumental in getting my passion for Georges Seurat out
into the art world when I exhibited in Beaumont's debut show *Victorious Vectors*. Since then, I've grabbed every chance to see her curatorial talent in action. Claire Beaumont's latest show did not
disappoint.

Sinjin Reid's four sculptures are magnificent, but don't overshadow
the other pieces in the exhibit. The students, while at the retreat,

created a mix of drawings, paintings, and sculptures interpreting how our four seasons have changed in the 21st century. To any casual observer, the message of the exhibit will move them: it's time to face climate change.

Even Monsieur Seurat saw the truth in the 1800s when he painted *A Sunday on La Grande Jatte — 1884*. He painted his environment. His images were beautiful landscapes that included elusive elements of burgeoning industrialization. If we don't look out and take care of our world, we won't have anywhere to picnic.

However, the messages from these two creatives weren't all doom and gloom. Their passion for our world shines brightly in this collection of work. Our future is in good hands. The evening's positive vibes lasted all night. Capping off the evening, Sinjin professed his love and proposed marriage to his partner in *crime*, Claire. While all eyes were on the couple, Claire accepted the ring that Sinjin had forged out of platinum and then slid a matching band onto his hand. This engagement combined two equal partners while opting to stay true to their love of the elements. This reviewer is looking forward to all of the couple's future collaborations.

Overlooking the glorious view of Lake Michigan, *Elements Unleashed* will be on display at the Lafferty Museum until the end of the year. Don't miss it. Your heart will thank you.

@Artist&ParkProtector—Zoe Kittleson

Keep Reading!

Cheers!

HERE'S MORE ABOUT GUS REID AND LUCY MAXWELL

Hey lovely readers!

Thanks for taking time from your day to meet Claire and Sinjin. I hope you enjoyed these two creatives as much as I loved writing them. The second book in the Brit Brothers series is **To Sense a Passion**. It's coming out in February of 2024 and here's a sneak peek just for you.

Cheers!

Audrey Lynden

To Sense A Passion
BRIT BROTHERS SERIES #2

by
Audrey Lynden

"It's such a happiness when good people get together."
— Jane Austen, *Emma*

~To Sense a Passion~

CHAPTER ONE

While waiting for her mother to be frisked, Lucy Maxwell drummed her fingers on the edge of the cardboard cutout on the table. The purple and green Christmas tree covered the dingy beige linoleum. She took a deep breath. The prison cantina smelled of butter. A shockingly out-of-place scent, appropriate for the holiday, and much better than the security entrance.

Earlier, when she'd surrendered her phone, hair bands from her braids, and a piece of jewelry (her poison ring), into the basket before passing through the metal detector, her gag reflex got its usual workout. How could such a small space smell so rancid and so consistently? She suspected it had more to do with the ragged and ruined emotions of the families coming through during visiting hours. They were filled with hopes, frayed nerves, and desperate not to get turned away by the guards.

Last summer, Lucy had learned her lesson the hard way. On the first trip to see her mother while incarcerated, she'd worn an underwire bra and the metal detector screeched. Lucy was escorted off the premises by an officer, the size of a bulldozer. At the time she'd thought it was absurd, but if she had been honest with herself, it was an absolute relief to leave the House of Corrections. What a horrible house that her mother had to call home for the past year.

Since then, Lucy always wore the same outfit for visitations: black leggings, a red sweatshirt, and all-cotton unmentionables —no wires hiding anywhere. While stepping through the security corridor, she pinched her nose shut.

On several occasions, she'd been tempted to sneak a vial of one of her essential oils past security, but she'd always chickened out. Instead, she kept a collection of scents stashed in her truck. Really though, what could the guard do if a vial of her *Soul-U-Tion* broke and filled the tiny corridor with the aroma of oranges and cinnamon?

At the table next to her, a young girl sat straight-backed, wearing a turtleneck and trendy jeans with asymmetric rips and holes. The girls' Ugg's made a swishing noise as she swung her legs back and forth while sitting beside her father. Lucy assumed they were waiting for her mother. What a treat it was to be together with your mom and dad for Christmas. Even inside a prison, it was a feeling that Lucy hadn't experienced since her dad had disappeared when she was ten.

The chatter in the room quieted when the door, made of steel and wire-insulated glass, buzzed open and the next inmates strode into the dining room in a single file line. Their beige jumpsuits matched the color of the walls and tables. Lucy recognized her mother because of her hair—matted, dull, and the color of dirty water. The knotty strings covered her bony shoulders. Julie's sunny highlights of gold and blonde had disappeared long ago.

A swell of emotions passed through Lucy. How had a beautiful and successful artist found herself behind bars? As a sculptor, Julie Maxwell wielded the flame of a blow torch like a magician, creating incredible metal sculptures. Now the only metal she looked at greeted her every morning when she woke up in a cage.

"Merry Christmas." She hugged her mom gently and was careful not to exceed the time limitation for bodily contact. "You look great."

"Don't lie, Lucy." Her mother's movements, usually calculated from welding, were slower. Sitting on the bench was a laborious task as she adjusted her knees under the table. "Why do you have to wear the same red and ratty sweatshirt every time you're here?"

The irritation in her mom's question reminded Lucy of the expectation level in her mother that couldn't be achieved. Ever. She'd been successful in the art world, but not known well enough. She'd sold her pieces consistently, but never to the highest bidder. The money in her savings account was never enough. So, when she'd collaborated with the world-famous sculptor, Sinjin Reid, she had to have what he had—fame and fortune. Unfortunately for Julie, the only way to get it was to try and steal one of his most valuable sculptures. Her attempt had failed miserably.

"You love this sweatshirt. It's full of Christmas cheer." Lucy mustered all the optimism she could in her tone. "We're together. And they brought the ping-pong table in from the yard. Wanna play a game after dinner?"

"At least we'll be eating food made for human consumption. My cellmate, if she can be trusted, told me someone donated real turkeys for today and a baker is here from the outside to make cookies."

"My nose detected butter, so I think your roomie is telling the truth. Otherwise, what would have been served? What did you have last Christmas?"

Julie inspected her fingernails. "A year. I can't believe I've been in this hell hole for an entire trip around the sun. I don't deserve this shit."

Yes, you do.

Lucy thought about Claire. Her closest friend was a talented painter and museum curator who would be sharing a romantic holiday dinner back home in Lake Bluff with her fiancé, Sinjin. Except Lucy was still worried. Even though the two lovebirds were together, in all likelihood Claire continued to nurse the injury that Julie had inflicted on her. A little over a year ago, when her mom had stolen Sinjin's car, she'd also attacked Claire. Pushing her to the ground and hitting her with a bag full of wine bottles. It landed Claire in the hospital to nurse a concussion and a deep cut on her leg that needed a lot of stitching up. Yes, Julie Maxwell deserved to be at the House of Corrections for three years.

Julie let out a ragged sigh. "I sat in my cell last Christmas. There was no need to come out to eat. Especially since none of my family bothered to show up."

"Understandable," Lucy said, free of any guilt. As her mother's only family in the state of Wisconsin and probably in the world, she tried like hell to maintain a distant, really distant, cousin-Eddie-like relationship. The healthiest option for Lucy. Her life had been turned upside down that single day —the attack—and she was still struggling to turn it right side up.

A woman dressed in a black skirt and crisp white blouse stepped between tables. Gray curls broke free of her habit's headdress as she placed a plate of cookies on each table and spoke briefly to the surrounding inmates and their families. Lucy liked the woman's smile and oddly, her sturdy orthopedic shoes.

"Sister Jan. She's a Sunday regular." Her mother stared at the modern nun. "How are things going on the outside?"

"Good. Really good. I'm almost sold out of my *Lust* stock and—"

"Stock?" She scowled. "James. My case. What's the latest?"

Lucy pinched her thigh to contain her exasperation. Would there ever be a day when her mother thought of anyone else but herself? "Same. Your lawyer is doing his job."

"Wouldn't it be wonerful if my sentence got reduced to half? I could get back to my work by summer."

So subtle Lucy almost missed it, but it broke beyond the surface. *Wonerful.* The slip of a slur. She stared down at the purple Christmas tree. How did an alcoholic in jail get her hands on booze? Was it cherries soaked in rubbing alcohol?

"Cheerio mates. Would you like some cookies? Or as they say in jolly ole England, biscuits?" The Sister's accent sounded awkward. "Happy Christmas, Julie. Who is this?"

Lucy's heart melted into her snow boots. Her mother hadn't once mentioned her daughter to this emissary of kindness and wanna-be Mary Poppins?

"I'm Lucy. Her daughter." From the paper plate, Lucy grabbed a sugar cookie shaped like Santa and bit off the head. "Her only family. Are you British?"

"Oh, no, no, *love.*" She smiled sweetly. "Only changing my message up for folks. And I thought, your mother…Julie…had ties to England. She's talked a lot of St. John."

Her mom giggled.

Holy fuck. Even if she were to get out early, Julie Maxwell had a lifetime of learning ahead of her, and a lot of necessary sobriety to get past Sinjin—St. John—Reid.

Lucy took in a deep cleansing breath and caught the vestiges of olive oil on this odd duck, Sister Jan. What a soothing scent. She'd used it to make her oils every day, but now it felt entirely different when on a woman with religious faith. "We're from Lake Bluff. Do you know where the Kohler corporation is located, in Wisconsin?"

"Known for bathrooms. Or loos?" Sister Jan chuckled, sat next to Julie, and gave her a beaded rosary. "Yes. I'm familiar."

"The Reid family…the father and three sons, are well

known in the area. George Reid retired now, held the CEO position of the company. He moved his family from England when they were kids. We were friends or acquaintances with Sinjin, Angus, and Rob." Lucy added, "Now though, I live in the cute town of Baileys Harbor. Up north."

Thanks to George, she'd been able to start over since her mother with all her legal drama had made it impossible to live and thrive normally in Lake Bluff.

"Oh, I love Door County," Sister Jan said. "All those small, picturesque towns up and down the peninsula. It's like the Cape Cod of the Midwest."

"Lucy worked for Sinjin," her mother said. "But he's, my protégée."

Protégée? Now who's lying? Julie acted more like one of Sinjin's groupies.

"I'm an aromatherapist. And since Sinjin is working with flames as a sculptor, I created a balm for his minor burns." Lucy explained. "He's a great guy."

"Not as great as the other one." Her mother snickered. "Angus. He's a famous actor. Have you ever watched *Raven House*, Sister Jan?"

"Why. Yes." She clutched onto her rosary and blushed. "I confess, it's an engaging television show. The mysteries are full of twists and turns. I never would've known the actor was British. His accent isn't *detectable* as an American detective."

Lucy pulled another cookie off the plate, this time an angel, and gobbled down the frosted wing. "Mom, do you watch the show in the community room?"

"Every week. We all fan girl over Angus Reid." Her mother nibbled on a cookie shaped like a Christmas tree. "Have you seen any of the Reid boys?"

"Not at all." Never sure if knowing the Reid family was a blessing or a curse. However, since moving to a new town, thanks to George, she felt compelled to put *him* in the boon column. "I've been super busy. Wicks & Balms will be opening in the new year."

"What's that?" Her mother rubbed her temple, leaving a smudge of green frosting stuck onto her gray roots. "Aren't you tending to my business?"

Lucy shuddered. How many times had she told her mother the details? Over the phone and during visits. Everything about prison came at a cost that needed to be covered. Lucy sold most of her mother's sculptures, all but a beautiful chandelier. The house where she'd grown up in Kohler, sold right away. Most of the money went to her mother's lawyer. Since Julie pled not guilty, having not remembered the tragic event, her mother's lawyer doled out one bill after another for court fees. And the Reid "boys" didn't want anything to do with Lucy or her mother.

"Mom, there have been a lot of changes in the past year and a half. I spoke to your lawyer. He's not sure about having your sentence reduced. After all, you did hurt my friend Claire."

"It was an accident." She crossed her arms over her chest. "Why won't anyone believe me? I had no fucking idea that a woman was behind me. I thought she was coming after me. That's why I hopped in the car and drove off."

"Even if your memory is fuzzy…the judge had all the facts, and they are crystal clear." Sister Jan sighed. "You injured another person and nearly ripped them apart from their soul. And a dependency on alcohol isn't an excuse. We work with a lot of women like you. Again, I ask, join the AA meetings I run on Tuesday nights."

Lucy stared at Sister Jan. What a relief, the nun understood. Lucy wasn't particularly religious, but since always dealing with all of her mother's self-inflicted mishaps, she was spent. She would take all the help she could get. "Thanks."

"Do we need to hire a new lawyer?" Julie's dull blue eyes

widened. "I'm sure I can get Sinjin to pay for it. Or what about the famous guy? You were close to him, weren't you?"

"Changing lawyers won't help but changing your plead to guilty will!" Lucy paused to navigate her mother's chaotic line of questioning. "Sinjin isn't a bank. And the famous one? You mean Angus. We met a couple of times, but he's an A-list celebrity and lives in LA. Why would you think I was close to him?"

"I remember the way you two looked at each other. At the gallery opening."

Lucy wanted to gag. Julie Maxwell couldn't recall assaulting another human being, but she recalled the tiny interactions between her and Angus Reid.

"Totally absurd!" Lucy cringed.

Had there been a spark, or two, passing between her and Angus Reid?

Angus had been charming and funny, but he was an actor. And she was simply doing her job. As the local mixologist, she'd assisted Sinjin regularly on various occasions.

She remembered making small talk with—*Gus*—as his brother had called him. Mostly while facilitating and helping with Claire's art exhibit, *Victorious Vectors* last fall. Unfortunately, Gus had loved his gin and tonics too much, so she'd filed the memory and closed the drawer.

Another inmate dropped a divided tray in front of them. The smell of something unnatural accosted Lucy. It looked like a roll-up made of gray meat. Maybe her mom's cellmate couldn't be trusted because this wasn't anything close to real turkey. At least the cookies were authentic.

Sister Jan stood up. "Merry Christmas ladies. Have a happy New Year. I'll pray for both of you. That you'll be free Julie, and you two will be celebrating together again next year, but on the outside." She pointed to the cardboard tree cutout. "And with an actual tree with ornaments."

"Ho, ho, ho, Sister." Lucy blew her a kiss. "Merry Christmas."

Her mother plopped her head into her palms. "This is so unfair. I *dint* mean for any of this to happen."

"We can't change the past, Mom." With her fork, she played with the food on her tray. "At least the cranberry sauce is real. From a can. How we love it."

Her mother chuckled. "It's perfect."

"Did you know Wisconsin produces more than half of the cranberries in the US?" To survive eating a single meal with her mother, Lucy resorted to Wisconsin trivia. "The bogs. I went last harvest season. The zillions of ruby red balls floating in the water are beautiful."

When her mother didn't respond, Lucy focused on the plate of odious food in front of her and took a small piece of the slice of jellied cranberry. She chewed slowly, thankful that it tasted normal.

"You know I'm right," her mother said, between bites. "Sparks glimmered between you and Angus Reid. It's the gift."

"The *gift*?" Lucy dropped her fork and it nearly bounced off the suspect meat roll-up. "You are hilarious. Are you talking about a box? Wrapped and sitting under some Christmas tree?"

"Lucy, you know it's intangible. Not any corners and impossible to wrap."

She sniffed the plastic cup of soda sitting next to her mother's plate. "Have you been drinking some kind of woo-woo juice?"

"Ha, ha. Laugh all you want. You know what I'm talking about. It's a spark of intuition. Like a breeze floating across your face on a humid summer day. Or a snowflake that lands on your nose and melts. As silly as it seems, you can't ignore it. I've always been able to sense when couples were destined to be together."

"You don't have some kind of karma, new-age, Zen-like ability to match up couples for goodness' sake," Lucy said. "There is no such thing as a *gift*. One time, during some hippie convention…two people you met happened to fall in love? Or at one of your bartending gigs?" Lucy recalled how many bartending jobs her mother had lost from drinking on the job. "You're not Emma Woodhouse. I'm guessing there were a lot of cocktails being doled out to the folks who bellied up to the bar and thought you were some kind of love doctor."

"Since when have you become so pessimistic? The *gift* is the one trait that I've passed along to you. We're forever bonded. You know it's true. You connected Sinjin and Claire."

"It's called science. My essential oil, *Lust*, was designed with pheromones. The scent is factually known to chemically induce or encourage physical attraction. There's no such thing as a DNA sequence for matchmaking."

"I've developed the *Anja* or third-eye Chakra. It gives me the ability to see the big picture. Connect to my intuition. And I know the truth. You and Angus."

"I appreciate your insight, but my heart is all good. For me, creating kismet is nothing more than business. And you. You're a lot to take care of. I've survived because of science, lots of beakers, and no extra eyes." She gulped down a fork full of beige-colored meat. Along with her mother's whacky intuition or *gift*, the flicker between her and Gus was pure nonsense.

Acknowledgments

As there are layers of color on celebrated paintings, there are a lot of people who add depth to a story and help make a book into a masterpiece. Writing is a lonely endeavor and a frustrating task. Support from friends, relatives and other writers is like air. It keeps my love for words alive.

My steadfast critique partner Carla Luna Cullen has kept me focused on finishing every chapter and cheered me on to get to THE END. Our camaraderie has been going on for over the past decade and it's been full of writing adventures. She taught me how to develop my word craft, the importance of 80's hit songs and what spices are the absolute best for my tacos. I'm looking forward to the next ten years.

Jennifer Rupp writes Scottish romances as Jennifer Trethewey. She is a fabulous historical author who roots for me and my contemporary stories. While she prefers to sip on a French 75, I'll enjoy a brandy old fashioned, Wisconsin style. With Jennifer's eye for details, I'm confident my books have heart and authenticity.

If it weren't for my friends at Red Oak Writing I may have never learned (with some suffering) how important it is to read your words out loud. Not only do you hear your thoughts as they are opened up in a familiar voice, but other readers divulge their interpretations of your words as they are new to them. I won't lie, it's excruciating and an exercise not for the faint of heart. But writers who brave it are better off in the world of storytelling. So thank you to Kim Suhr and all the other writers who I've faced and read to during our round table sessions. I'm proud to know and write with all of you!

One of my beta readers, Joanna Moynihan, made one comment that gave me an AHA! moment. Her single mighty suggestion gave *The Artful Bargain* another fun twist.

My sisters, Jill and Kathy never gave up on me. They listened to my frustrations, sometimes daily, and shed tears along with me. Love you to the moon and back.

I have been incredibly lucky to have circles of close friends in life who have taught me the meaning of compassion and loyalty. They also make me laugh a lot. I don't have to worry about my sometimes-embarrassing raucous laugh that my mom passed on to me. We all know that laughter is the key to happiness!

Having found author Bianca Marais and her terrific podcast, made me stay focused on the task at hand…finishing the damn book! Her stamina and persistence is addictive. It was a shot of hope that kept me going through the darker times. Her one tweet was the medicine I needed to get my stories out into the world.

The foundation of my life has been built by my family— my parents, aunts, uncles, siblings, cousins, nieces, nephews and all the others. Thanks to all of you, I'm fortunate to have a solid hold on this earth. To my three sons, Spencer, John, and Barry: you have made life sweet, smart, and hilarious.

About the Author

Audrey Lynden writes contemporary romances and sets them in her beautiful home state of Wisconsin. There are always fun happenings, interesting histories and quirky traditions that happen in the many charming towns around the state. They happily find their way into her stories.

She's a mom to three incredible sons and has a Hollywood crush on her husband. Once told he looked like Chris Noth *and* George Clooney, he's never let her forget it.

As a onetime journalist, she's inclined to keep up with news, but dives deep into celebrity gossip for fun. She's an avid cheerleader for the Milwaukee Public Library, the Literacy Services of Wisconsin, and the Milwaukee Art Museum.

For sneak peeks, giveaways, and book recommendations, sign up for Audrey Lynden's newsletter:

www.audreylynden.com

Printed in the USA
CPSIA information can be obtained
at www.ICGtesting.com
LVHW040831201023
761202LV00002B/48

9 780997 340013